TRANSFORMATION

Girard glanced at his sister who stood very still, her face paled, yet knowing something he did not. Hesitantly, he reached and let his fingers close around the suggestively complex hilt of this unique weapon. Silken textures, undefined—yet it molded perfectly to fit his grasp. And he felt at once the strange chill that seeped from the sword to penetrate his skin. Nay. No common weapon this, he knew as he stared at it . . .

THE DARK SWORD'S LOVER

More praise for Gail Van Asten's THE BLIND KNIGHT:

"Her writing is smooth, her characters well-drawn, the plot interesting."

—Sharan Newman, author of
THE GUINEVERE TRILOGY

"Van Asten uses and builds on the Arthurian legend rather than simply copying or rehashing it . . . Well written!"

—OtherRealms

"A first-rate combination of historical and mythical fantasy . . . Recommended for active fantasy collections!"

—Roland Green, Booklist

Ace Books by Gail Van Asten

**THE BLIND KNIGHT
CHARLEMAGNE'S CHAMPION
THE DARK SWORD'S LOVER**

The DARK SWORD'S LOVER

GAIL VAN ASTEN

ACE BOOKS, NEW YORK

This book is an Ace original edition,
and has never been previously published.

THE DARK SWORD'S LOVER

An Ace Book / published by arrangement with
the author

PRINTING HISTORY
Ace edition / November 1990

ISBN: 0-441-13849-7

Ace Books are published by The Berkley Publishing Group,
200 Madison Avenue, New York, New York 10016.
The name ''ACE'' and the ''A'' logo
are trademarks belonging to Charter Communications, Inc.

PRINTED IN THE UNITED STATES OF AMERICA

10 9 8 7 6 5 4 3 2 1

The past can never be restored.
Cling to the things that gave it life,
And even memory will play tricks
In the end . . .

—Gail Van Asten
1989

INTERIM

779–792 A.D.

In a high mountain gorge, deep in the western Pyrenees, where a ghastly battle had occurred, the impartial seasons passed as they always had. Stark and arid terrain continued to feel the bombardment of an intricate interplay of elements. Floods washed the gorge in spring. Snow and bitter cold froze even the great boulders thereabouts in winter. And in the summer, the hot sun scorched the rubble-strewn ground and made mirages across that brutal valley where bushes continued to grow, and clumps of hardy grasses.

The dead of that terrible battle, stripped of flesh by scavengers, eroded to become bleached bones naked even of marrow. Once-bright cloth frayed to shreds of grey material, then disintegrated to yield to the tug of the hard winds that blew through the valley, and disappeared. Armor and weapons rusted away, gradually becoming no more than the dull sienna hue of iron given back to the earth from which it had sprung.

And the white bones, once clustered in the patterns that told of the fierce men and hot-tempered warhorses that had fought there, scattered amid the rocks and hard rubble of the valley floor, became brittle, and fragmented to mere splinters.

The years passed in irretrievable sequence. And the evidence of the bloody, treachery-wrought Battle of Roncesvalles vanished as though the struggle had never occurred.

Except, in the minds of men.

One song of wonderful intricacy and absolute truth, once sung before a king for the resolution of justice, was not forgot. It could not have been, for it wove spells of significance that went far beyond the accounting of a solitary battle. Imbedded within the fabric of the verses were truths of courage and honor embodied forever in the persons of the men who had died, and, by their deaths, had become something most profound.

Heroes . . .

Knights, and lords of high estate—of singular duty and purpose—they had become definitions of all the meanings of honor.

And of the shrouded, crippled jongleur, from whose throat that song had first issued, no memory remained. More completely than a ghost, he vanished.

But the Song moved on to be sung again and again in the castles and manors across western Christendom, passing from soul to soul like knowledge that must never become lost.

Deep within the impartial granite of a forgotten gorge near the westernmost tip of Brittany, another participant in that tragic Battle of Roncesvalles endured.

Chained tempest . . . The essence of War bound into a weapon forged to great power, to have dominion over time—and life— the Dark Sword, Durandal, was imprisoned by no more than the unforgiving force of a single thought.

In another far place, in the heart of Aix La Chapelle, where a chapel had been built to house a king's prayers and solitary meditations, were a pair of white marble tombs. Side by side, their perfectly aligned proximity was but an echo of the bonds of love that had once bound the two men entombed therein.

Here, too, time wandered by in a silent, irrevocable progression. Only the most delicately insidious changes marked its passage. Dust settled from the air to nestle in the chiseled grooves and crevices of those wonderfully carven marble effigies. And smoke from the sconces kept perpetually lit about the tombs of these particular dead of Roncesvalles diffused into the air, and undertook another alchemy upon that pliant stone.

Features once graven to perfect resemblance lost their smoothness, eroded and blurred to become mere generalities of human faces.

And the King, who came in solitude to brood upon these

images, and upon secrets tightly imprisoned within his soul, saw these first ravages of time and knew another kind of knowledge.

Past events slipped relentlessly away, beyond regrets—or hope—to become the silent, formless sod upon which trod the feet of the present moment.

Only the Song remained to make echoes on the mind.

Part 1

ONE

792 A.D.

The wind howled around the stark, high keep. Rain poured out of the darkness to splatter against the wooden shutters of the single narrow window. One, open, thudded rhythmically against the stone.

Standing beside it, uncaring of either damp or chill, Lord Amaury De Hauteville frowned as he stared out into the night.

Bitter, the weather. Like his life . . .

Behind him, anchored to the top of a broad oak table by two guttering candles, his map fluttered a little in response to the wet, gusting drafts that thrust into the chamber.

He did not have to look at it. He knew intimately every line and detail, every place name and boundary inscribed upon it. Little more than an outline of the reaches of western Christendom, it included as well the names and borders of every fief held of the King. It had become one of his most prized possessions since he had acquired it upon the death of his cousin, discovering it among the personal effects of the disgraced and butchered Lord Ganelon De Maganze some thirteen years before. Countless hours spent brooding over its contours had brought him to perceive its deepest value. For him, it had become a geography of power. The skeleton of a vision.

Bordeaux . . .

There was a hard rapping on the chamber door. Lord Amaury spun around alertly.

"Enter!" he barked. The door opened to reveal the person of his steward.

"My lord . . ."

"Well?"

"The monk is arrived, my lord," the servant announced.

Lord Amaury's eyebrows rose briefly in surprise, then his face relaxed. "Is he so?" he murmured, then nodded. "I will attend him then. Do thou seek thy rest."

The steward nodded. "Very good, my lord," he responded and, a moment later, disappeared.

Lord Amaury moved to the table, removed the map of fine lambskin, folded it carefully, and slipped it into the wallet at his belt. Then, snuffing one of the candles, he seized the other and strode briskly from the chamber. His soft boots made very little sound as he passed along a short corridor, then headed down long, steep, circular flights of steps that led from his high tower chamber to other parts of the keep. Carefully shielding the candle flame with one cupped palm, Lord Amaury emerged at last through the portal at the very bottom of the stairs into the branching point of a pair of dark corridors in the depths of his keep, well below the great hall.

"My lord?" a melodious voice greeted him, and a cowled figure in a monk's coarsely simple attire emerged from the shadows.

Lord Amaury smiled. "Thou are well named, Brother Oborion!" he remarked with dry familiarity. "For, truly, it is wonderful, the manner by which thou do appear!"

The monk chuckled and made a moue with one shoulder. "Thou do me too much credit, Lord Amaury," he said mildly, large, clever brown eyes gleaming in a heavily lined face only partially concealed by the hood of his robe. "There is too much to accomplish to waste more than the most essential time in traveling!"

Lord Amaury nodded and began walking along the narrower, left-hand corridor that led away from the alcoves and rooms along the other where grains and wines and salted meats were stored.

"Still, I had not thought to see thee for another pair of days," he commented. Again, Brother Oborion shrugged. Lord Amaury did not see the gesture. Instead, upon reaching the heavy oak door at the end of the corridor, he found a key at his belt, inserted it into the lock, and thrust through the door into the chamber beyond. Waiting briefly for the monk to enter, he closed the door again, then went about lighting several of the numerous candles set about the chamber that was his most privately kept place. "There is wine, my friend," he said gently. "Do thou refresh thyself."

Brother Oborion inhaled deeply. "Aye. I will, my lord!" he declared, moving around a large, manuscript-laden table to the corner of a second where a flagon and a pair of cups were placed within easy reach of the chair beside it. He sat down.

Lord Amaury looked at him eagerly. "Thou have procured for me?" he asked.

The monk inclined his head, shifting back gracefully to extract a tightly wrapped bundle from beneath the folds of his robe where it had made the entirely false impression of a paunch. "I have, my lord." He held out the packet. "The skins are difficult to obtain, but I have been fortunate enough to acquire one more than I had hoped."

Lord Amaury's face brightened at once, making him seem suddenly a much younger man. He strode forward to reach for the bundle. "Let me see," he breathed eagerly, setting it down upon the table to loose the cords that bound it.

Pouring himself some of the proffered wine, the old monk watched as Lord Amaury opened the wrappings of the packet, then, with an almost sensual care, spread out the three fine, pale skins it contained. He bent closer to examine each one in turn.

"These are perfect!" he exclaimed. "Flawless! I see no blemish of any sort!" He straightened and faced the monk. "It is well done in thee, Oborion, to contrive such as these!"

Delicately, the monk sipped wine. "They died of lung fever, these boys," he said quietly.

Lord Amaury nodded. "That accounts for their perfection, then," he said, his tone revealing his satisfaction. "No pox marks to blemish . . . And there will be sufficient here to finish the Aristotle!"

"Just so, my lord," Brother Oborion murmured, relaxing farther into his seat.

Lord Amaury smiled as he unclasped his cloak and set it across the back of another chair. "Such genius must be suitably housed, and there is no finer parchment to be got from any other beast!" he said softly, glancing at the exquisitely inscribed sheets spread across the first table amid an array of ink pots and goose quills.

The old monk sipped again, his wily gaze bland as he studied the other man, well aware that he, himself, had instigated the passionately scholarly Lord Amaury's untroubled preference for parchment got of immature human skin for the making of his works. It had become an interesting and singular perversity in a man given to unusually civilized demeanor and pursuits, even intellect, in these . . . aye, most curious times.

"It is a peculiar immortality to give these children who would otherwise rot away entirely," he remarked. "But. Not, I consider, unworthy!" Lord Amaury shot him an appreciative look, preoccupied firstly with rolling up the sleeves of his undertunic, then, in taking the skins to the racks set into the wall at the back of the chamber, there to stretch them out for the final curing that would render them into parchment so fine and smooth and uniform, it was beyond compare.

Beyond, as well, any recognition . . .

It was a point of partial appeasement to the rage that festered deep within him, Lord Amaury knew, to make this use of the hides of highborn younglings sent for schooling to the great monastery at Tours nearly two hundred miles to the north and west of his own fiefs.

His scholarly works and craftsmanship . . . so admired at Court. His name, his blood, once among the proudest in the land, accursed and reviled since his cousin's death.

"Impossible, my lord!" he heard Brother Oborion remark. "I will dispute with thee! Men may learn from divine . . . sources, but they may never aspire to the attributes of true divinity!"

Lord Amaury smiled as he finished stretching the first skin and began the second, welcoming the debate. "Assuredly, they may," he countered. "For it is those very faculties of reason and learning that endow men with a divine potential apart from any other beast in nature. What other creature is given the wit and ability to contrive such that Nature herself must yield before his will?"

"Aaah, my lord!" Brother Oborion straightened, his wily eyes gleaming. "Consider, rather, the ingenuity and tolerance of Nature as it may include her human children!" The stretching of the second skin complete, Lord Amaury turned to face the other. The monk thrust back his cowl to reveal grizzled, unkempt hair and a face that was, except for the brutally weathered and lined skin that covered it, remarkable for its youthful symmetry. "Consider this," he went on. "Men may plant the seed in the earth, but it is Nature's rule that brings forth the plant to ripen and fruition.''

Lord Amaury frowned a little, the image conjuring a recollection of their first encounter when he had discovered Brother Oborion carefully planting flowers by the cloister walls of St. Martin's at Tours a number of years before. Curiosity had generated this very singular friendship for him. ''But man is given to rule supreme in the world,'' he undertook. ''The highest of creatures, by God's own word, it is man that hath dominion . . .''

''Mere manipulations!'' Brother Oborion cut in, his gnarled lips curving in a wry smile as he held out one remarkably supple hand and flexed the fingers with emphatic significance. ''Superficial! Do not forget that it is Nature that wrought the seed in the first case. And what does man contrive that is not readily given of Nature, or returned to the same? Consider the ruins of ages past, my lord. Mere ghosts to prove . . . Yet, even by the most precocious alchemy, man may not undertake the undiluted use of the elements of fire and water, earth and air, that are the very instruments of Nature herself . . . And,'' he added, ''of whatever beings that are endowed with truly divine composition!'' Lord Amaury frowned, his fingers occupied with stretching the last of the three skins. ''Man is got of Nature.'' Brother Oborion nodded toward the three pallid hides. ''Even as these boys . . . and must return to the same. Thou know as well as I, save for this other use thou make of their skins, those boys are naught but food for maggots now, and will, as with any other beast, become no more, in time, than mere earth!''

Lord Amaury's frown deepened at the single word that jarred most of all.

''Time!'' he muttered with baleful frustration. ''Therein lies . . . all manner of predicament!'' Brother Oborion continued to watch him. After seven years of somewhat sporadic acquaintance, his knowledge of Lord Amaury's mind was intimate and absolute. He waited as Lord Amaury finished with the skins and turned to face him again, moving across the chamber to stand before his current work, there to trace fingertips delicately across the carefully wrought sheets that awaited completion and binding. ''And what, I must wonder,'' he asked with sudden violence, ''is the composition of divine being, Brother Oborion? Be it air, or fire? Of a certainty, it is not earth, or water. And why this peculiar dichotomy between mortal flesh and immortal soul? The former is most assuredly got of earth, while the latter . . . ? Beyond disputation, it is composed of insubstantial things such as air. Yet only in the brief span of a man's allotted years are the two brought together. For the rest, I do not know. I do not know . . .''

"Only faith provides an answer, my lord," the monk said quietly, well aware of the un-Christian direction of their discussion.

Lord Amaury eyed him balefully. "For all their divine immortality, even the ancient Gods are vanished to become no more than myth!" he pointed out, thinking of questions provoked by his reading of the Roman poet Ovid. "It suggests an even more ingenious supremacy of Nature, Brother Oborion, than thou have declared."

This time the monk nodded. "I understand, my lord," he said gently. "And man, constrained by his very mortality, can only accomplish in fragments what may be given entire to . . . a more enduring creature such as, perhaps, the ancient divinities."

"Dust to dust!" Lord Amaury muttered, glancing down at his work. "And from dust, such fragments as these! In the end, there is only the moment."

Silence hovered between them. Brother Oborion rose to his feet and drew his cowl back over his head.

"I must leave, my lord," he said softly.

Lord Amaury looked up in surprise. "Now, my friend? Surely, thou may rest in comfort and await the morrow?"

The monk smiled and shook his head. "Nay, my lord. I must return before my absence is too much remarked upon." He moved, briefly touching the work on the table. "Nor, I think, shall thou rest this night!" he added.

Lord Amaury smiled. "Nay, Oborion, I will not!"

"God preserve thy endeavor, my lord. I am thy servant in all things . . ." the monk said softly, disappearing through the door with a graceful silence that belied his years.

Lord Amaury stared after him for a moment. He must have Brother Oborion with him, he decided, when he returned to Court this time. He found a chair and sat down before the sheets of flawlessly inscribed manuscript on the table. Aristotle. Pure genius . . . and, hereto, unknown to Christendom.

Aye. Here—here in this chamber, secreted away from the eyes of the world and the Church, were the most brilliant accomplish-

ments of his life. Here, with passionate care and exquisite craftsmanship, he had brought together and copied, translated, tattered fragments of forgotten knowledge from the nooks and
crannies of Christendom—from, as with the Aristotle, heathen
places to the south.

He glanced across the chamber toward the skins he would
shortly scrape and work for final curing, and frowned.

The moment, he thought.

Head of the House of Maganze since his cousin's bloody demise, he was now in his thirty-seventh year. Unwed. Childless.
Without heir, save for Ganelon's young son, Baudoin, who was
nearing manhood.

Youth had eluded him, Lord Amaury knew. Had slipped away
into a bitter and unfulfilling past. The studious boy he had been,
devoted to the making of books, could never have been prepared
for all he had been forced to endure for the past near decade and
a half. Kept at Court as a tutor, and as a scholar to aid Abbot
Alcuin of St. Martin's, and for his knowledge of Latin and Greek
and Arabic, even the wealth and resources of the fiefs of Maganze that he ruled had not brought him respect. Instead, he had
inherited all the brutal consequences of Lord Ganelon's appalling treachery.

Not even time and dutiful service had tempered the relentless
antipathy that even his resemblance to his late cousin evoked.

He was tolerated. Nothing more. His achievements knew none
of the overt glory that was given to soldiering men. Instead, kept
alive by a ballad that had come to be called the Song of Roland,
the repute of dishonor and suspicion overhung his name like the
ghastly miasma of an infectious pestilence. The Battle of Roncesvalles had not been forgot to become no more than one additional confrontation in the numberless encounters of
Charlemagne's perpetual wars with the heathen that abounded
on all sides of Christendom. As a result, any villainy attributed
to the House of Maganze was rendered ever worse by contrast.

Forever unforgiven.

Time . . . ? His fingers delicately caressed the fine supple
sheets of parchment before him. What he wrought here would
last beyond the life of any one man . . . or prince.

Prince? Lord Amaury stiffened briefly as, for no apparent
reason, the image of Charlemagne's elder son came into his
mind. Curious. He'd seen very little of Prince Charlot during
the past two years, his tutoring duties with the elder royal youth

complete. Yet . . . ? Lord Amaury's expression softened slowly as his mind reached out to grasp at an idea. An idea that he must understand and consolidate fully before his departure to return to Court a sennight hence.

The rain continued to fall out of opaque black skies, muffling other sounds as the monk departed Amaury De Hauteville's stark and unpretentious castle high in the mountainous country of Auvergne. It obliterated any tracks in the accumulating mud as he trod with light-footed ease down the path that led from the castle toward the village in the small valley below.

Unperturbed by the autumnal chill, or the rain that saturated his barely visible, coarsely woven, indeterminate grey robe, the monk paused and turned to stare back toward the castle, his pupils dilating to accommodate the penetrating darkness. He smiled to himself, perfectly able to see every small rivulet of rainwater that trickled down between the stones of Lord Amaury's tall, bare keep.

Delicate pricklings of the spur had brought Lord Amaury well up into the bridle. Touches so fastidiously applied as to render them imperceptible. What better way to train such a man to compliance than to strip him of faith by feeding his discontents and nourishing the full scope of his intelligence? Like a good warhorse, the instrument of the man had been brought unknowingly to consider his master's will synonymous with his own.

The monk shifted abruptly as, like a spasm, an itching sensation crawled across his flesh. He reached up reflexively to scratch at the skin of his face, then caught the movement and stopped it. Nay, he thought. This sheathing of an old man's brittle hide was not sturdy enough to endure such. He sighed with resignation, and resolved that, next time, he would undertake a more youthful appearance.

He turned away, and, after a few more steps, abandoned the main path to veer north and west toward Tours, becoming a faint shadow of enduring piety as he trudged through the night.

TWO

It was always the same. The tomb of Count Roland of Brittany, never the other beside it. Why? Prince Charlot wondered for the thousandth time since he had discovered his father's solitary, nocturnal habit. Concealed in the darkness behind a pillar, he watched Charlemagne stand very still, keeping private vigil beside the tombs in the final bay on the opposite side of the chapel, the light from the sconces there making a warm, shifting nimbus of his silver hair.

Why this secretive, even obsessive preoccupation with that particular dead lord? Granted, the glory of Roland and Oliver was unique, but they were dead men, and had sufficient immortality through the legends and Song that had sprung up to commemorate their names.

Prince Charlot frowned as he recalled information got from Lord Geoffrey De Baviere this summer past while on campaign against the ever turbulent Saxons along the northeast frontier, information Lord Geoffrey had got from his sire, Duke Naimes, who had known the two. Lord Oliver had been revered by all for attributes that were, evidently, not at all embellished by subsequent tales. But the Count Roland . . . ? Bastard got, and by all accounts witch bred as well, he had been of brutal disposition and crass demeanor, his singular genius being confined to the battlefield.

Prince Charlot's frown deepened with resentment. His father

revealed by these vigils a devotion never bestowed upon his sons. Charlemagne had more care for the dead.

Suddenly the King made the Sign of the Cross over his breast, and turned in a swirl of blue and maroon robes to stride with a vigor undiminished by his advancing years, across the choir, toward the chapel door. Moving with practised, facile stealth, Prince Charlot headed along the darkened aisle to intercept his sire.

"What do thou here, at this hour, Charlot?" Charlemagne demanded harshly, his blue eyes frigid as he stopped to face the young Prince emerging from the shadows. Charlot stopped, belligerent courage making his young face sullen.

"Curiosity, Sire!" he retorted, then fell silent, feeling the palpable remoteness of the King's critical assessment as Charlemagne scanned him from toe to face. The Prince stiffened, he had endured that look more times than he cared to recall.

"Even a king must remember the dead who served him!" Charlemagne said with frigid quiet. Then, in the tone of one disinterestedly observing the antics of a fly on the rump of another's horse, "Thou are grown, boy! Thy service against the Saxons appears to have wrought some benefit!" Prince Charlot's teeth clenched, but the King brushed past him and disappeared through the chapel door.

Alone, the Prince stared after his father, his frame rigid, his hands clenching into fists at his sides.

Grown! Aye. He knew it. In his fifteenth year, he had reached a height nearing his father's considerable stature. Childhood, in all its aspects, was behind him. He shot a baleful look at the chapel door, turned, and walked back across the deserted, circular choir, past the altar—deliberately neglecting proper obeisance—to the pair of tombs on the other side. Reaching them, he glanced briefly at the sconces always kept lit, then moved between them to stare down at the marble effigy of Count Roland.

Who is worshipped here? he wondered. God . . . ? Or these dead men? His eyes traveled up to the recumbent marble figure, the stone, once purest white, was now yellowed to an ivory hue. He took in the rendered armor and the pose that embraced both a helm and the legendary sword Durandal with its eagle-winged hilt, and moved closer to let his gaze rest on a face that the artisan had doubtless idealized for the perfection of its features.

Stone man that slumbered in an illusion of peace . . . This

dormant likeness showed none of the ferocity that comprised so much of the dead Count's repute. Instead, it showed youth, and a most perfect beauty. Almost gently, Prince Charlot drew the dagger from the sheath at his waist. Then, his lips formed into a bitter line, he turned the point and began to chip away at the unmoving stone face.

The marble yielded in diminutive fragments, the details of a commemorative identity becoming blunted by the unhappy malice of the Prince's jealous temper.

The Prince eventually abandoned his destructive efforts and, resheathing his dagger, left the chapel. Alone in the night, he passed across the great inner bailey of Aix La Chapelle, pausing once to listen to the faint, rustled munching sounds that came from the stables. Quiet night. Everything slumbered. He moved on past guards who knew him, up a broad flight of steps, and into the main portion of the great keep. Again, the Prince hesitated. Then, instead of making his way to his own chambers, he turned and walked across the great hall.

Embers from the hearth fire glowed in the darkness. The high granite pillars that supported the great vaulted ceiling were dimly revealed by the flickering light from occasional torches on the walls. Empty now—except for a brace of wolfhounds dozing by the dying fire. And, on the other side, Charlemagne's throne nestled in the shadows, beckoning in the silence.

Deliberately, the Prince stepped up onto the dais, up onto the smaller, raised platform that held the throne itself. There, he stopped to look at the great ornately carved and inlaid gold chair.

It was the throne to an empire . . . And only Charlemagne himself ever sat there. It was certain death for any other to even attempt it. His jaw set, Prince Charlot turned deliberately and gracefully sat down upon the scarlet-cushioned seat. He reached to curve his palms and fingers over the carved dragons that comprised the arms of the throne, and, tightening his grip, stared out across the deserted great hall.

This, he thought, was the perspective to which he was entitled.

There had been twin thrones here once. Long ago, when his father had inherited the crown in conjunction with his brother Carloman. But Carloman had died, and his young sons had long since vanished . . . There was little enough information to be got on the subject, but Charlot knew his father's capacity for ruthlessness . . .

And Charlemagne had not yet declared him heir.

It must not be divided, he thought fiercely. To share with his younger brother Louis was unthinkable. Louis, who was better suited to the priesthood than to rule. Aye. Better the newer tradition of primogeniture . . . Yet Charlemagne's silence on the matter of the succession was absolute.

"I am the heir!" he whispered with virulent force. "I am strong enough to hold it."

Silence answered. And shadows.

"And I will have it!" he added softly, thrusting to his feet, then stepping down from the dais to stride briskly away, out of the great hall. Impatience echoed in the fading rhythm of his muted footsteps. Soon . . . Soon, they whispered. Old kings must give way to young.

Long journey . . . Lord Amaury brought his weary horse to a halt in the inner bailey of Aix. Some sixth sense made him glance up before dismounting to see the figure of the man who had been watching his arrival shift from the shadows at the back of the balcony above the main portal of the keep to emerge into the full evening light. Lord Amaury's eyes widened in surprise as he recognized Prince Charlot.

Tawny-haired and stern-featured, there were no traces of the boy he had known apparent in this young Prince. His eyes locked with a penetrating blue gaze similar to Charlemagne's, and he bowed from the waist in proper obeisance. The Prince nodded acknowledgment, his look assessing, and turned away to disappear from view. Lord Amaury dismounted, handed the reins of his animal to the groomsman who had stepped forward, and turned back to see Brother Oborion slide awkwardly down from the mule that had been his mount.

"Aaaah!" the other murmured. "Now I understand the excellent wisdom of Our Lord who saw fit to endow men with long legs and broad feet!"

Lord Amaury grinned, glancing at the mule that stood, head hanging and ears back with an expression of martyred resignation. "Thy beast has a point of view, I'll warrant, that is not in disagreement!" he commented. "Some point concerning the impact of backsides!"

The old man shot him a dry look and rubbed that part of his

anatomy. "Our discourse on the subject has been most intimate, my lord!" he intoned solemnly.

Still grinning, Lord Amaury shook his head as he issued orders for the care of his animals and the disposing of the packs that burdened the third beast. Then, indicating the keep with one hand, he turned back to the aged monk. "Come, Brother Oborion. Comfort awaits us in my quarters. And I, for one, wish to be rid of this excessive mud!"

The old man nodded and hobbled stiffly after him as Lord Amaury strode briskly through the portal, past guards who knew him, and headed toward the south wing.

I am a shadow here, Lord Amaury thought, his smile fading quickly as he stopped a passing servant who would otherwise have ignored him, and curtly ordered meat and wine to be brought to his chambers.

Up flights of steps, along corridors, he led the way through the mazelike intricacy of Aix until, deep in the south wing, he reached the door to the chambers allotted to him since his first arrival at court all those years before. Unguarded, unlocked . . . He thrust through the door and walked briskly through them, scanning everything, making sure that nothing had been disturbed in either his private chamber, or the large room that served his duties as both scholar and royal tutor. He sighed at last, and turned to set his helm on a table. The old monk had found a chair and sat wearily, his head bent as he studied the muddy, sandaled feet that emerged below the equally grimy skirts of his robe.

"If this is my condition," he murmured, "pity the beast that bore me!"

Lord Amaury's features relaxed. "Servants will attend us shortly, Brother Oborion," he offered, realizing that in persuading Bishop Alcuin to give him the service of this monk he had, for the first time, brought an ally to Court with him.

The monk looked up. " 'Tis of little import, my lord. Mud too is God's creation!" Lord Amaury laughed just as the commandeered servant entered the antechamber with a large tray well burdened with food and wine.

Prince Charlot's brows gathered into a thoughtful frown as he turned from the balcony and made his way in a leisurely fashion back to the great hall. He had spent the past weeks carefully scrutinizing and assessing every soul at Court, and he had not thought of Lord Amaury De Hauteville at all. Now, seeing that lord upon his return but a few moments before, he had felt the startling sense of being alerted to some potent, contradictory, yet hereto inconspicuous force.

Strange . . . for all he could recollect of Lord Amaury was that individual's quietly docile, scholarly, and unambitious demeanor.

Unambitious? That was the first contradiction, Prince Charlot thought as he stood by one of the supporting pillars to scan the noble assembly of the Court still gathered for the evening's feasting. What lord of De Hauteville's rank even made a pretense of being content with his station? The Prince's lips curled with the cynical knowledge of a lifetime spent as Charlemagne's firstborn amid the ever-fermenting brew of the Court.

Despite the camaraderie that had sprung up between them this summer past, he knew Lord Geoffrey De Baviere sought the office of King's Champion now that Lord Thierry had retired to his fiefs in Brittany. Friendships? Princes had no friends, Charlot thought sourly. Allies, perhaps. Servants. Foes, of course. But never friendships such as were shared among other men, or glorified by the bards in the example of Roland and Oliver.

Prince Charlot's mouth tightened as he turned away to seek the solitude of his own chambers. He was vastly changed, he knew, from the boy who had struggled against all manner of frailties, overcoming the long succession of illnesses that had plagued him since infancy, to finally discover a vigorous good health. Louis, his brother, who seemed in his twelfth year a reed, a twig to snap in the slightest breeze, had never been so tested. Nor had Louis ever endured the perpetual censure of their father's remote, even contemptuous stare . . .

Other changes were needful now, Prince Charlot thought with a surge of virulently concealed fury. Power. Aye, some power by which he could loose his father's resolute grip on the realm and insure the birthright that was the reason for his own existence. He needed instruments to serve as means . . . Aye. He would probe the ambiguities that surrounded his former tutor. Head of the once powerful, still intact House of Maganze, Lord Amaury suggested useful possibilities. De Hauteville too, the Prince understood, had spent a lifetime under the censure of the King.

• • •

''Surely, my brother would be more productively occupied in the practise field, attempting to acquire some rudimentary skill at arms!'' Startled from his review of Prince Louis' current efforts in the curricula of the Trivium, Lord Amaury looked up to see a tall figure lounging by the antechamber door. Young Prince Louis frowned and bent farther over his parchment.

Recognizing Prince Charlot, Lord Amaury stood promptly and bowed. ''Highness?''

The Prince acknowledged Lord Amaury's obeisance with a brief nod and a probing look unpleasantly reminiscent of Charlemagne, then strolled silently into the middle of the chamber. ''My lord!'' he said softly, his eyes scanning books and parchment sheets, chalks, quills, and slates. ''It has been a long time since I spent my days here.''

''So it has, Highness,'' Lord Amaury acknowledged equably. He had forgotten, he realized, this Prince's capacity for stealth, and now, staring at the tall, powerful young man the Prince was becoming, he found the knowledge disturbing. Charlot bent a little and touched his brother's shoulder.

''Go, twig!'' he ordered quietly. ''Find a sword and try to break it!''

Prince Louis jerked away from his brother's hand. ''But . . . ?'' he protested. ''I am not finished.''

''Go!'' Charlot said with icy soft menace. The boy did not argue, but set down his quill, jerked away from the bench on which he had been seated, and fled. Prince Charlot stared after him with dislike, then turned back to Lord Amaury.

''Highness?'' De Hauteville inquired.

Prince Charlot smiled. ''Time away from such studies as these have brought me to wonder, my lord, what facets of the jewel of princely wisdom have been neglected in my own education.''

Lord Amaury glanced down at the well-littered surface of the table before him. ''I have but provided those skills, Highness, that enable thee to seek such knowledge as thou choose to have,'' he countered warily.

The Prince moved closer, appreciation flickering across an expression that had become hard-faced and searching. ''So I recognize, my lord,'' he said. ''But my experience of thy tuition has brought me to recognize, as others may not, an intelligence that must, by the very nature of its honing upon the anvil of such intellectual exercise, be more ingeniously capable by far than the office to which it is applied!''

Lord Amaury stiffened, unprepared for this new, penetrating boldness in the Prince he had always known as a sullen, quietly secretive, unhealthy, if manageable, individual. He found a slight smile.

"There is a vast difference, Highness, between a hypothetical exercising of the wits and their application to the convolutions of practicable circumstance!" he offered cautiously.

Prince Charlot inclined his head, his eyes still studying the older man. "I understand, my lord," he said softly. "But it is the truest value of that very nimbleness of mind got through the same that I seek to comprehend."

Couched in the dialect of debate, this was an invitation, Lord Amaury recognized. He shrugged. "Possibilities are always more numerous for the agile, Highness," he said reasonably. "Choices, therefore, are both more complex and plentiful."

Again, the Prince nodded. "Just so, my lord. It is a direction that must be examined, then. Each possibility points to a different consequence and circumstance, and the ramifications must be understood!" His gaze hardened, and Lord Amaury felt a surge of cautious admiration.

"Astutely phrased, Highness!"

The Prince smiled. "How else, my lord, may power be managed?" he inquired gently.

"How else, indeed, Highness!" Lord Amaury responded smoothly, bowing fractionally to indicate his acceptance.

"We must talk again, my lord," Prince Charlot said briskly then, and, turning away, strode from the chamber. Lord Amaury stared after him, a thoughtful frown gathering on his face as his fingers moved to touch where his map lay folded away inside the wallet at his waist.

The moment . . . ?

So simple to prepare . . . When Prince Charlot entered his chamber three days later in a vigorous swirl of rich green and gold, Lord Amaury smoothly swept aside the documents he had spread over his unfolded map, then looked up as the Prince closed the door behind him, to seem as one startled from deep preoccupation. He rose abruptly to his feet and bowed.

"Highness!" he breathed, but the Prince's hard eyes fixed on the figure of the monk, hunched over a transcription in a corner of the room.

"Who is this, my lord?" he demanded, striding forward.

"Brother Oborion, Highness." Lord Amaury made a disconcerted movement with one hand, as though he wished to cover
the map. "From St. Martin's. He is an intrepid scholar with
whom I have enjoyed much profitable discourse over the years.
His service has been given to me by the Lord Abbot—to our
mutual benefit and satisfaction."

Prince Charlot did not comment, but turned his gaze from the
old man and moved closer still, his obvious restlessness the only
indication of an uncertainty got of his very real youth. Lord
Amaury continued to stand with the map before him, waiting
until the Prince discovered it.

"What is this, my lord?" Prince Charlot asked with a sudden
frown, seating himself on the bench on the other side of the
large table.

"A map, Highness," Lord Amaury stated the obvious, accepting the permission to seat himself offered in the impatient
flicking of one royal hand.

"So I perceive!" Prince Charlot muttered acidly, bending forward to examine the document more closely. Lord Amaury did
not reply, but sat quietly waiting. Aye, he thought. Far better that
it come from the Prince, that which lay before them both . . .
"A curious document for one given to the study of the writings
of dead men?" the Prince said softly, looking up at last to lock
his gaze with Lord Amaury's.

De Hauteville inclined his head. "Perhaps, Highness. But my
responsibilities extend far beyond the duties that occupy me at
Court. I am Lord of Maganze, Highness," he pointed out.

Prince Charlot reached to turn the map around. "I am aware
of that, my lord!" he muttered, his gaze lingering over the area
of the map that defined the extensive fiefs of Hauteville and
Maganze. "But Maganze is held in stewardship until thy heir is
of age, as I recollect?" he probed further, looking up.

Lord Amaury inclined his head. "In two years, Highness,"
he said tonelessly, "young Lord Baudoin will attain his majority,
and I will give the rule of his fiefs into his hands."

The Prince frowned. "Lord Baudoin has not been to Court
as is customary for highborn youths?"

Lord Amaury allowed himself a bitter sigh. "Nay, Highness. I thought it best to keep him among his own. Our name
is tainted . . ."

Well aware of the deceased Lord Ganelon's probably exaggerated treachery, Prince Charlot nodded, his mind quickly calculating and balancing possibilities.

"And so, my lord," he said slowly, watching the other, "it has fallen on thy shoulders?" Lord Amaury's tightened features and brief, evasive glance across the chamber provided all the information he needed. "It seems unjust, my lord," Charlot murmured. "I cannot think thou are content?" Lord Amaury did not reply. "Well, my lord?" the Prince demanded in a harder tone.

Lord Amaury exhaled, his mouth still taut. "I am not ashamed of my lineage, nor of the glory that, while now forgot, endowed the name of the House of Maganze!" he said at last. The Prince thrust away from the table and stood to pace restlessly in a manner reflective of his sire. Lord Amaury stood as well and waited. The Prince stopped suddenly and faced him, a determined frown removing all traces of youthfulness from his sternly cast features.

"Then, my lord . . ." he said with slow and regal deliberation, "we must see that glory restored!"

Lord Amaury allowed his features to soften into something intense and hopeful. "Such is my most fervent desire . . . my liege!" he rasped forcefully.

The Prince continued to study him. "Great kings are never well served by ordinary men!" he said deliberately and, as Lord Amaury bowed, swung away to depart the chamber.

De Hauteville exhaled slowly as the door closed, then moved to reseat himself behind the table, there to trace his fingertips across the map, across the contours of his own fiefs, and those of the rich, vast demesne of Bordeaux . . .

It was accomplished, he knew. The alliance had been made. Now, at last, he had a foundation upon which to construct his dream.

And from the far corner, half concealed by the shadows between the candles that illuminated the sheet of parchment before him, half concealed by the cowl over his head, Brother Oborion's large eyes shifted, a fiercely penetrating, large-pupiled stare melting into something soft and dissembling.

Like a force that, intense and focused and directed outward, was suddenly withdrawn.

A smile slipped across his wrinkled lips, then vanished.

THREE

Outside, beyond the windows high in the keep of Bordeaux castle, the winds howled promises of a night of chilling rains that would strip the remaining leaves from the trees. Entering the solar, Lord Huon sank into a well-cushioned chair and stretched his feet out before him. He sighed relief for the end of a strenuous day, shifted his shoulders and relaxed further, smiling at the maidservant who proffered a cup of mulled wine. Accepting it, he sipped, and smiled more broadly at his mother's acknowledging, upward glance.

Here, in her solar, amid rich, colorful tapestries, fur rugs, and finely carved furnishings, the family had collected of an evening ever since he could remember. Huon drank slowly, savoring the way the hot wine curled and settled in his stomach. He watched his mother's rapid and facile use of the needle as she worked on yet another piece of the exquisite embroidery that seemed to be her favorite leisure pastime, and glanced down at the beautifully intricate patterns of scarlet and blue that edged the sleeves of his own overtunic. The dowager Duchess had adorned them all, he acknowledged with appreciation. With care, as well as craftsmanship . . .

He shifted uneasily, startled to notice the amount of silver that twinkled in the dark mass of her braided hair. She had always seemed young . . . but watching her now, he saw, as he had never done before, fine-lined skin and the etched thinness of her features. The strain of years of resolute and solitary duty made a harsh imprinting over a unique and regal beauty.

Perhaps he wouldn't have noticed, he thought, save, that of late, she had bequeathed most of the rule of Bordeaux to him. That, and he was sobered by what lay before him. Soon, it would fall entire on his shoulders, and such added duties as the King would require. Boyhood, Lord Huon thought ruefully, was gone. A happy and peaceable time it had been under his mother's sure and absolute rule, he acknowledged. His gaze slid to the pair seated on the rug before the hearth fire, silently engrossed in a game of chess.

Children, he had always thought them, his younger brother and sister. Now, watching them together, he suddenly saw that it was no longer so. Olivia's gown revealed the contours of budding womanhood. And Girard, as lean and broad-shouldered as himself, loomed over the chessboard with a quiet preoccupation that Huon himself could never confine to such apparent peacefulness.

Beloved puppy, he thought affectionately, secure in his knowledge of his brother's adoration. Sipping from the wine, he continued to watch them. Tawny heads bent together . . . Olivia's hair was divided into the braids of a woman and laced with blue ribbon. Girard's, glinting with the same gold and brown lights, tumbled in a loose, waving mass to his shoulders. Girard shifted and moved his rook, and brother and sister looked up at each other. He, with a grin, and she, with a much sterner expression.

How alike they were, Huon noticed then. The same hair, sea-blue eyes . . . profiles. Olivia being merely the feminine version of her brother. Twin creatures . . . Huon stiffened.

And he was so different. More sternly cast of feature to resemble his long-deceased father, the Duke Servinus, he was dark-haired, brown-eyed. With a slow sense of shock, Huon frowned as he recalled something they were all prone to ignore.

In truth, Olivia was half sibling to Girard and himself, being sired by the Duchess' second lord—and named for him as well.

Oliver De Montglave . . . Lord Huon's frown deepened as, with the name, an image from his early childhood slipped across his mind. Nay, he had not entirely forgot looking up at deep blue eyes that smiled at him, nor the gently toned voice that tutored his first attempts to ride a horse.

Twin creatures . . . The same. He shifted uncomfortably and, discovering his mother's alertly watchful stare, retreated to preoccupy himself with refilling his wine cup from the flagon that stood on a table near his chair.

"It is time to retire, younglings," the Duchess announced quietly to the pair by the fire. With unthinking obedience, Girard and Olivia rose to their feet and moved to embrace her by turns before departing the solar for their own chambers. Huon glanced up to see the old maidservant leave as well, then, again, sought refuge in his wine cup, unwilling to deal with his mother's steady gaze, or the appalling thought that had crept like some virulently insidious devil into his mind.

"Thou art troubled, Huon," the Duchess said quietly. Huon shifted, inhaled, then met her look.

"Aye," he said flatly, unable to dispel the monstrous idea. She continued to look at him with unwavering resolve and set aside her embroidery. "I thought it uncanny, Mother, how thoroughly Girard resembles Olivia," he got out finally.

She folded her hands neatly in her lap.

"It has become increasingly apparent of late," she commented tonelessly.

Huon straightened abruptly in his chair and leaned toward her. "I do not remember my father," he pursued harshly, "though I understand I have the look of him. But Girard? He is so like Olivia . . . Nor have I forgot the face of the late Lord Oliver who taught me my first horsemanship . . ." It was hard enough to express at all, let alone directly, this . . . accusation of vile and dishonorable past occurrences.

"I have been awaiting this moment," his mother said with hard calm, surprising him. Then, "Girard is Lord Oliver's child. Not got of thy father."

Huon inhaled violently. To hear it . . . And he had never even thought to suppose—until now. She continued to watch him with frigid regality. He looked down at his own powerful hands, now clenched about the silver wine cup. Calculated.

His brother . . . His heir. Until he got sons of his own.

"Thou were wed to Lord Oliver long after Girard's birth," he gritted, looking up again.

She did not even blink. "Girard was conceived soon after Servinus' death, Huon."

"Then, he is . . . a bastard!"

"It was contrived to appear differently," she said sternly. "I have upheld the honor of the House of De Guienne in all things— even this."

"How can thou say so?" he rasped outrage. "Honor, Mother? Surely what I have only just seen must be evident as truth to others this long while past . . ."

She cut him off. "It is what is *not* known, Huon," she countered forcefully, "that has protected that honor, and thy brother!" He opened his mouth, but she continued, "It is that true honor and repute that surrounds, even today, the name of my dead lord, Oliver De Montglave, that protects both Girard and the name of De Guienne. There are none," she added more gently, "who, having known Lord Oliver, did not love him!"

Huon jerked to his feet, set his wine cup down, and began to pace the length of the solar. The Duchess sat very still, watching him.

"Does he know . . . Girard?" he demanded suddenly.

"Nay." Her answer was immediate. "Nor does he question his birth as thy full brother." She stressed it.

Huon glared. "He is a bastard!" he growled. "Not even got within the sacrament of marriage! Pah! He was bred before my father's corpse had even chilled!"

"I will find no shame of any kind," she shot back with steel resolve, "in that rare and great love I shared so briefly with Lord Oliver to the begetting of thy brother! Aye. He is the younger son, and so it shall remain. I have seen, as thou cannot know, what havoc the birthright of bastardy may wreak upon the soul. It is a bitter and perpetual cup to drink from . . ." Huon stopped and stared at her. Felt something inside fracture into an exquisite and unaccustomed pain.

"What of my father?" he demanded unevenly.

"Being dead, he knew naught of this! Let him rest in peace!" She looked away for the first time, her pose as rigid as his own. "I was a child when I was given to Servinus. Save for this one thing, my life has been given to duty, and to the name of De Guienne . . ." He said nothing. He knew it was the truth, yet . . . "Even my lord Oliver had a care for thee," she went on in a curiously hollow, painful voice. "We arranged it. Girard succeeds to my dower estates, and as the younger son, he is well content. And thee? Thou art the De Guienne entire. Nay . . . Girard worships thee, Huon. Do not take it from him . . ." she half whispered it. "I have a care for all my children . . ."

"It is evident!" Huon got out after a moment, breaking what had become a terrible silence. He brushed past her, unable to bear more, and left the solar. The door closed behind him with a violent thud.

Alone, the Duchess Alice drooped slowly in her chair and bowed her head to stare at her own empty hands that had somehow become tightly meshed together in the folds of her rust-colored gown.

She felt exhausted. And old. It was beyond her control now . . . The children. What she had done for the children . . . Girard and Olivia, got of love.

And Huon. Huon, who had grown into a young man of great pride and violent convictions. Just like Servinus. Aye, Huon would hold Bordeaux easily enough. He was strong. But this . . . ? She glanced at her embroidery, but did not pick it up again.

Now it lay in Huon's hands, and she did not know what he would do.

The opaque night and the hard, driving cold rain matched his mood as Huon strode out onto the battlements high above the keep, then stopped by the parapet to lean against a crenellation in the wall. The cold wind drove the rain against his flank, blew across his face, and howled around a corner to race outward, across the darkness that enveloped Bordeaux.

The voice of outrage . . .

All his life, he had trusted—aye, in the purity and honor of the name of De Guienne. It was the root and core of his pride. But now? To know his mother capable . . .

Even Olivia, who, being but a girl, was got within a marriage blessed by Holy Church and the King. But this other . . . His brother. His bastard brother got by frightful and damning sin. Bitterness crossed Huon's face as he stared into the night.

Worst of all was the secrecy that surrounded the same. A conspiracy, aye, that had endured ever since it had begun. Others, who must surely know as well. Deceitful silence. Powerful silence. This dead man's repute that transcended his own father's honor.

And, if Lord Oliver De Montglave had not died at Ronces valles . . . ? What, he wondered, would have happened then?

Far away, to the north and east, the monk, Oborion, stood in nocturnal solitude upon the highest battlements of the keep in Aix. A light breeze ruffled strands of unkempt hair that, for once, was not concealed by the cowl of his robe, and pressed the folds of that battered garment against his body. He stood erect, alert and taut in a manner that defied the gnarled appearance of his age.

His eyes, large and very dark, probed the night with inhuman keenness. His nostrils flared as he drank in the scents upon the air. And his hands, upheld with fingers spread, felt . . . felt for textures invisible even to his uncanny sight.

He understood the movements of the air that flowed in a liquid-seeming blend of currents across the land. He knew the presence of the night creatures that roamed the forests and meadows beyond the great castle of Aix. Deer that fed with wary attention to the sounds around them. Serfs who slept in wattle and thatch cottages while the night hunters searched for field mice and voles. And the owls that saw as he . . . lofted upon the night winds to make flight with utter silence. His children.

As he had done a thousand times before, he searched for something more, something far beyond the proximity of the land that cradled Aix. Another kind of textured presence that could only be perceived by one of the same ilk. He blinked. Frustration shifted the creases and folds that overlay his face. This time too there was only silence, a void where he should have found the knowledge of being.

A particular and impermeable emptiness . . . He understood its reason and cause. The power that inverted to shield the one who harbored it. The, aye, innocence of the same that wove this interminable vortex of silence. It was the first moment of recognition that he sought, its first reverberations of release to tangibility by no more than a simple acknowledgment of its presence.

Then . . . He stiffened abruptly, his eyes widening further.

Feeling . . . aye. He stretched his fingers out toward the south and east, toward the flavors of another kind of virulent information.

So tangible, the moods of men.

And after a few moments, he lowered his hands and drew the cowl back over his head. A slight smile flickered across his lips. It was something very different from that which he sought. But, connected . . . He turned to walk along the parapet. And useful. Aye, very useful.

• • •

Alone in the chapel during the heart of the night, Charlemagne touched fingertips to the places on Roland's effigy where the marble had been desecrated. Only the face . . . Chipped places and crude scorings defiled the delicacy of the carving and destroyed what had been a perfect likeness.

He withdrew his fingers, letting them close into a tight fist at his side, the only manifest expression of the fury and outrage he felt. He knew who had done it—and why. Malice. Resentment.

Charlot . . . Little Charles. He could not even like the name for this particular product of his loins. Pampered and cosseted as he had grown from one illness to the next, Charlemagne had finally unleashed his disgust and sent the boy to the wars against the Saxon along the expanded northern frontier in the ambivalent hope that either death or manhood would claim him.

Besides, Louis remained to insure the succession. The King's eyes moved upward to watch the sconce flame above Roland's tomb. Turbulent orange brilliance in the still, cool air of the chapel.

Aye. The succession. Kings that must beget kings.

Impossible comparisons, for all Christendom was much vaster now. Roland would have been strong enough to hold the future in his hand. Charlemagne's gaze dropped to the mutilated marble face once more.

Secret child. This was the tomb of a dream, he knew. Not a man. He turned away to stride across the circular nave. The succession. It lay before him still, that pronouncement, and he remained reluctant.

Because of Roland . . .

Aye, he thought then. He would send for the Champion. Lord Thierry of Brittany understood all the implications and potentials of past truths as well as he, and therefore could offer sound advice. He passed through the door and closed it behind him. He would do one more thing, he decided. He would dispatch young Geoffrey De Baviere to carry the summons. Thereby, he knew, he would gain an invaluable and honest assessment of that individual's future usefulness. Especially as Lord Geoffrey had become, of late, Charlot's most apparent intimate . . .

More than ever, Charlemagne knew, he disliked his elder son.

"But . . . if, as thou say it, this is so, then Lord Huon is without true heir, and the Duchess' dower lands are illegally and immorally entailed?" Lord Amaury said slowly, assimilating the information Brother Oborion had brought him as he stared back into the monk's clever, ancient face.

"Just so, my lord." The monk inclined his head. "Being of sufficient age to recall something of those times, it came to my mind that young Lord Girard was born after the death of Duke Servinus, and some considerable time before the Lady's marriage to De Montglave. There is sufficient discrepancy to make a sound case for his illegitimacy, my lord, for Duke Servinus died on the battlefield while engaged in subduing a Basque rebellion. Not . . . in his lady's arms!" he reiterated. Lord Amaury frowned, thinking this would be far more useful if it pertained to Huon De Guienne, rather than his younger brother.

"Do I recollect correctly, young Girard was born at a time appropriate to prove him Servinus' get?" he ventured cautiously.

The monk smiled. "Discover for thyself, my lord, the difference between an infant born at full term, and one delivered a pair of months before he is due," he said promptly. Lord Amaury stared into Brother Oborion's large eyes, seeing . . . Seeing . . . ?

Knowledge. He looked away and frowned.

"Then there must be proofs of some kind," he said slowly. "Witnesses . . . Old servants . . ."

"Or, Lord Girard's appearance?" Lord Amaury inhaled abruptly and shot the monk a hard look. "Both Lady Alice and Servinus De Guienne were of the Roman descent. As thyself, my lord," the monk continued softly. "Ancient blood, it breeds true . . ."

And dark . . . Lord Amaury thought. What else did this cunning old man know?

"Presuming such blatant distinction, surely Lord Oliver De Montglave must have known?" Brother Oborion did not respond, and Lord Amaury pursued his own thought. "It is curious how the King has safeguarded Bordeaux all these years, allowing the Lady Alice to remain unwed, and secure as overlord as is unnatural for a woman . . . Aye. There must be some connection between the dead Lord Oliver and this singular and isolated protection of Bordeaux . . ."

The monk cut in. "Mayhap, my lord, it reflects the depth of the King's regard for the late Lord De Montglave?" His voice became drier. "Assuredly, by such adulation and repute, the Gods are conceived!"

Lord Amaury frowned as he understood the implications of

the last comment. And Charlemagne himself was impossible to know, save, perhaps, in the maze of what he did not do.

"It is true enough that since their deaths," he gritted bitterly, "Count Roland and Lord Oliver have attained to near divine status . . . I had not thought that the same could provide the instrument of conspiracy to exploit the King's devotion to these two. It becomes a point of note that neither the young Duke Huon, nor his brother, have been required to Court as with other highborn heirs . . ."

"The same is true of thy own nephew, Lord Baudoin, my lord," the monk pointed out.

Lord Amaury shot him an acid look. "We are a disgraced house and held to little account!" he grated violently. Brother Oborion nodded. Lord Amaury breathed deeply to recover his control over his emotions.

He thought of his map. He had, he perceived, his fingers set upon two profoundly significant things. Firstly, a young and ambitious Prince. And the second, a territory that was sufficient of itself to compose a kingdom.

"My eternal gratitude, Oborion . . ." he breathed very softly after a considerable silence. The monk met his glance with clever eyes.

"Eternal . . . my lord?" he murmured. Lord Amaury smiled.

The Prince's eyes prowled across the map like a wolf seeking prey, Lord Amaury noted watchfully. He had taught the Prince well during their last two very private meetings. Best of all, the Prince himself had baited the trap into which Lord Amaury was intent that he should tumble.

"I am intrigued to note, my lord"—Prince Charlot looked up suddenly, then leaned back in his chair—"that all the greater fiefs of the central and eastern regions of the realm are . . . confined by the much smaller holdings of independent vassals. Yet, to the west, there is a very different case. There are only two overlords for the vast territory encompassing the coast from northern Brittany to the mountains of the Spanish March where Lord Roger of Roncesvalles rules."

Lord Amaury inclined his head. "Just so, Highness. The Count of Brittany holds the northern parts, and the rest is given to the House of De Guienne in the fiefs of Bordeaux."

Prince Charlot stabbed a finger toward the narrower area between the two. "What of these lands, my lord?"

Lord Amaury frowned thoughtfully and bent forward. "Aaah! Aye. Those are the dower fiefs of the Lady Alice of Bordeaux. I believe they are entailed to the younger of her sons, one Lord Girard."

The Prince met his look, then bent over the map once more. "Lord Huon's heir until he begets . . ." he murmured. "They are a mighty house . . . Aye, I see." He stiffened. Lord Amaury waited. The Prince frowned and looked up. "I do not recall ever having even seen Lord Huon."

"Nor I, Highness," Lord Amaury responded. "To my knowledge, he has never been to Court, or I would remember it."

The Prince's eyes grew cold. "Do not dissemble with me, my lord!" he said with such sudden quiet that Lord Amaury was startled. "I know full well that three times thou have sought marriage to the Lady Alice, and that, each time, my father has denied thy suit. Nor am I fool enough, having some experience with thy mind, to credit any pretended ignorance on the same! It was no altruistic affection that drove thee to seek the Lady's hand!" Prince Charlot stood, his expression fierce. One hand flicked out toward the map. "The reason is there, my lord, revealed in the contours inscribed upon that document! The lands of the fief of Maganze are not so far from the eastern borders of Bordeaux. Combine the two, and there is a virtual kingdom!"

Lord Amaury did not reply. He had wanted to be read, but he had not expected the Prince to assume so much and sudden control.

"Aye, my lord!" the Prince continued forcefully, his eyes glittering. "For all my lack of years, I am my father's son! I will not be duped by illusory promises, or cozened by suggestions! I am the first Prince of this realm, and I *will* have my birthright!"

De Hauteville bowed deeply and deliberately. The Prince remained watchful as he straightened.

"I will not share my inheritance," Charlot said very quietly then. "I need to loose my father's hold upon this realm. I need my own power." Then, "I have Geoffrey De Baviere . . ."

"And myself, Highness," Lord Amaury said very deliberately.

The Prince inclined his head in acceptance, then reseated himself. Touched the map. "The Count of Brittany is beyond reach, but . . ." he murmured. "Tell me, my lord, what is in thy mind."

"How much easier it would be to displace one and find another to replace him, Highness," Lord Amaury said, seating himself carefully. "Most particularly, one who would hold great power and vast domain . . ."

The Prince grinned. "And Bordeaux is far removed from Aix!" Lord Amaury leaned forward. It was a loosing of devils, this, he knew, as he began to speak upon what he had learned.

FOUR

"God's blood!" Thierry De Leon, Count of Brittany, swore as he drew rein at the crest of a hill that dropped precipitously away to the harsh and craggy coast below. "A plague upon these Vikings!" he grated between clenched teeth, his destrier half rearing beneath him. "Now they dare our shores even in winter!" His grip on the reins tightened reflexively as his horse continued to prance restless response to his anger. Lord Thierry barely noticed as he squinted into the sleet that blew against his face, his attention fixed on the single ship heading out to sea, already beginning to fade into the mists that obliterated the horizon. Impossible to mistake that long-bellied form, slung low in the water, the upcurving prow and stern, and the great square sail that billowed out before the wind.

Beyond reach . . . Lord Thierry muttered another invective as he swung his horse about and raised a hand to signal the small troop of knights and men behind him.

"Sir Antoine. Group the men. Let us discover what these accursed marauders have wrought this time!" He pointed briefly toward the south and spurred his horse, sending the beast plummeting down the treacherous hill to meet the trail that followed the shore along the top of the cliffs.

The next bay, he knew, held a fishing village.

Had . . . held a fishing village, Lord Thierry saw moments later as his horse crested a ridge. Ignoring the bitter wind, his face grew stern and unhappy as he slowed the animal to a walk

36

and let it pick its own way down toward the narrow, sheltered bay on the south side of the narrow peninsula.

Despite the sleet and wind, plumes of smoke still rose from one or two places amid the charred remains of numerous small cottages. Fishing boats, now shattered and askew, lay like wooden corpses upon the beach. The sea washed around them with complete indifference. A single crow rose suddenly into the air from the midst of the ruined cottages, its irate cawing rousing the gulls that had begun to pick . . .

"What had these folk to warrant such as this?" Lord Thierry rasped as his seneschal drew rein beside him.

"Nothing, my lord," Sir Antoine muttered, well aware that the Vikings raided for slaves as much as goods. And for the pleasure of it.

"I cannot garrison it all . . ." Lord Thierry gritted in frustration as his horse picked its way between the remains of ruined buildings. He stared at a corpse that lay facedown and bloody, the back split by an axe. He stopped his horse. "Search for survivors. Children. Any that we may succor and remove from here," he ordered quietly. The knight nodded and swung his horse about to issue orders of his own to the men of the troop.

Ignoring them all, Lord Thierry dismounted and drew his cloak tightly about him against the brutally penetrating cold. He left his horse to stand and began walking downhill, through rubble of stone and timbers that remained. He paused once to stare briefly at the splay-legged corpse of an old woman who had been raped, then disemboweled. Near her was a small, bloody bundle of an infant that had been flung against stone to splatter like a piece of gory fruit.

He stopped. It was this that defeated him, he thought grimly, looking toward the sea, thankful for the salt smell and the wind that blew away this other rising stench.

Inland, his fiefs were now peaceful and well ordered. Prosperous. But here, along Brittany's vast and jaggedly meandering coastline . . . Not even the King, for all his resources, could manage this.

It was the sea that protected these heathen, savage Vikings that came down from some frozen wasteland in the far north, where, he had heard, the earth belched forth fire and molten rock. It was the sea . . .

"My lord?" The Count stiffened at the shout, then saw Sir Antoine striding nimbly toward him from the direction of the bay, negotiating ruins and scattered bodies. "My lord. There are none alive save one we found, chained like a dog, yonder." The knight stopped and pointed toward the beach and the stone quay there. Lord Thierry started toward him.

"Only the one?" he asked anyway.

Face grim, Sir Antoine shook his head. "The young women are all gone. And the boys. The rest are dead, save this one man."

"God rest their souls," Lord Thierry murmured as the knight turned to walk beside him, his eyes scanning shattered slate and thatch roofs, the rest on either side of the track that had cut through the center of the village. Not a single beast, either. No dogs . . .

"There, my lord." Beside him, Sir Antoine pointed toward the short jetty that enclosed part of the small harbor. Lord Thierry saw several of his men, weapons drawn, clustered loosely around one of the pylons near the beach. He frowned and strode forward more briskly.

"What goes here?" he demanded in a quiet tone they all knew. To a man, they stepped back to reveal a huddled, ragged thing chained to the pylon, half in and half out of the seawater that lapped about its base. The figure shifted painfully, obviously alive. Lord Thierry scanned the faces of his men. "Why is this creature chained thus?" he asked then.

"For sacrifice to appease . . . ?" Sir Antoine got out and crossed himself. The others flinched. They had heard of such vile, sinfully heathen practices.

Lord Thierry scowled. "Then loose him at once!" he thundered. "We are Christians here!" A man plunged forward to obey, using the axe he held in a single, violent blow to sever the half-rusted links of the heavy chain affixed to the top of the pylon. Then he bent and reached for the ragged creature, gasped, careened backward, and jerked around to face the Count with ashen features.

"It is a leper, my lord!" he called out. Lord Thierry stiffened. The rest, fearless in battle, shrank back to a man in a reflexive terror at the mere mention of the disease.

Leper? There were few enough of them in these parts, Lord Thierry thought, but he remembered seeing them frequently a long time ago. In Spain . . . Shuffling, grey diseased figures, living ghosts that wandered, forever outcast, and stank of putrefaction, their sores and eroded extremities evidence of a fate equatable only with true damnation.

The figure by the pylon moved, raising a head mostly concealed by rags. It drew a hand from somewhere near its middle and reached for the piece of broken chain that still hung from its neck with fingers that looked entire . . .

But lepers were not entire. Lord Thierry's jaw tightened with the realization. He shot a brief, hard glance at his seneschal and stepped across the beach toward the creature, ignoring the icy sea that swept up to wash against his mail-covered ankles. He held out a gauntleted hand.

"Come. It is a sad charity that cannot give thee aid from this bitter cold and wet," he said very clearly. But the creature did not reach out to grasp upon his invitation. Instead, it turned to claw at the wooden pylon, rising up awkwardly to reveal the form of a tall, lean man beneath the worn, sodden clothing that clung to him. Standing upon one leg, propped against the pylon, he clung with his other hand to some rag-bound bundle that had been hidden against his belly. A cripple, Lord Thierry realized as he caught sight of a shortened and grotesquely twisted right leg.

"Come," he said more gently, and looked up to meet the shock of a pair of bright, fierce golden eyes in a bearded face barely visible beneath the hood of what had once been a cloak.

"I need no charity, my lord!" the cripple muttered brutally.

Lord Thierry froze, startled by the sheer forcefulness of the utterance, then frowned, offended by the cripple's ill-mannered behavior. "As thou wilt!" he responded tartly, reaching out to halt Sir Antoine, who, coming up beside him, moved to punish the insult to his lord. "But tell me how it is that thou are alive while all the rest of the folk hereabouts are slaughtered, or taken?"

The cripple averted his face. "I was brought here. I am a slave they have discarded."

Lord Thierry's frown deepened at this peculiar answer. Unwanted slaves were simply killed. Yet he could see part of the bronze slave collar around the cripple's throat to which the shattered chain was still attached.

"It is a strange effort they have exerted, these heathen Vikings, to rid themselves of thee by such means as this!" he commented doubtfully, sensing the truth, and the possibility of information. The cripple hunched a little and shivered violently, but did not reply.

Sir Antoine glanced at his lord, then lunged forward. "Look at my lord when he speaks to thee!" he barked, reaching to pull the cripple about. Then he too jerked back with paling face and horrified eyes. "Mother of God!" he rasped and crossed himself. "What is this creature?" The tattered hood fell away from the cripple's head, revealing long, matted tawny hair, a full beard, and worse—far worse.

Now clearly visible, the skin of the cripple's face showed shredded and peeling like some decaying thing. Lord Thierry gasped involuntary revulsion.

Golden eyes bored into his. Held him.

"That is why, my lord!" the cripple whispered venomously, his free hand moving to jerk the hood back over his head.

Appalled, Lord Thierry stepped back. "God pity thee!" he managed, then swung away, unable to bear either the relentless stare of those golden eyes, or the sheer, revolting horror of the cripple's flesh. "Get my horse!" he roared at his seneschal as he strode back through the wash to the beach. The knight hurried away gladly.

Within moments, Lord Thierry was mounted again, his troop gathered around him. Bitterly, his gaze swept across the blackened ruins of the village. Lost, he thought, for there were none left to rebuild here. And he knew each and every other such coastal village that had succumbed to a like fate. Beyond preventing, the shores of Brittany were becoming abandoned.

Compelled by something he could not define, he turned in his saddle to stare at the crippled man as he struggled grotesquely from the pylon, through the sea, and up the beach. Revulsion, yet . . . He clenched his teeth and spurred his horse the few yards to where the cripple stopped to huddle by the quay. Stopping the animal, he quickly loosed both the wineskin and the provender wallet from the pommel of his saddle and dropped them onto the pebbles in front of the other.

"Take this!" he gritted. "There are no other provisions hereabouts." The cripple looked up, golden eyes bright—wide, startled in that atrocious face. Shocked, he stared back. Felt his nerves fray before a violent sense of having seen before . . . somewhere . . . some time.

Lord Thierry growled incoherently and spun his horse about, spurring the animal away to bolt up the precipitous slopes through the ruined village to the trail at the top of the hill. There, his men behind him, he drew rein again and glared toward the craggy peninsula that defined the southern part of the bay. His seneschal drew rein beside him and looked askance.

"My lord?" Sir Antoine ventured. Lord Thierry arched his brows. "Whyfore . . . ?" The knight's eyes slid briefly toward the beach to finish his question.

The Count inhaled deeply. "There are enough dead in this place. What would one more serve?" he managed. "Even that pitiable thing!" He nudged his horse into a trot and led the way to the fork in the trail that led inland.

Falling into place behind his lord, Sir Antoine watched the Count's back as he rode. It was such as he had just witnessed, he thought, that made Lord Thierry a great man.

Shivering violently from the cold that he knew could not kill him, the cripple huddled against the barnacle-covered quay in a vain effort to elude the brutal onslaught of the sleet-laden winds and stared after the vanished lord.

Perverse fate. Brittany . . .

And instantly recognized—Thierry of Leon. Features unchanged save, perhaps, for the strengthening effect of the lines that time had wrought beside the mouth, in the corners of the eyes, and across the brow.

Brittany . . . The cripple rasped painfully. How well he knew the arms upon that lord's surcoat, on the shield slung from his saddle.

He slammed a door on his own thoughts as the last clattering of horses' hooves died away. Around him, the wind howled accompaniment to the slow, thunderous pulse of the frigid grey seas. A gull cried out once from somewhere above him. He did not look up.

Instead, he dropped down to balance awkwardly on one hand and his sound knee, and reached for that which the Lord had left him. Charity . . . He had forgotten its existence. He touched the fine leather wallet, bulging with provisions. And the wineskin. Food . . . ? He could not remember when he had last been given something to eat, he realized with surprise. But, like other things he had learned about himself, starvation had become almost irrelevant. He did not die of it . . .

Carefully, he disposed both wallet and wineskin about his person, then, still clutching the rag-bound bundle to him, he began to crawl awkwardly up the beach toward the decimated village, jerking forward on one sound knee, with one arm, able to make a nominal use of the mutilated leg he tried never to look upon. Then, shivering and brittle with cold, he reached a low, crude wall that extended from the first of the cottages and lurched upright to stand on one foot.

Slowly, he hopped and clawed his way forward until he managed to reach the portal. Then he let himself fall through it into the comparative shelter within. Colliding with the dank floor of stone and sand, he pulled himself into the farthest corner where part of the roof still remained. Sleet came through the ragged gap made by Viking torches and axes on the other side to collect in large, moist clumps on the rumpled corpse that lay there, staring.

Soon to bloat and rot. The cripple looked away. Before long, he knew, the wolves could come, scenting death, to make use of the cold, fresh human meat. The thought did not disturb him.

He reached for the wineskin and unstoppered it. Sipped . . . aye, sweet, sweet liquid. He closed his eyes and swallowed, feeling every drop that slid down his throat to the neglected cavern of his stomach.

How long had it been since he had tasted such? He made a painful movement of withdrawal. Best not to think on that.

Existence had become an incalculably brutal passage that could only be endured . . . Because he could not seem to die.

Even the Vikings who had enslaved him many years before had grown to fear that, aye, relentless endurance, and the pestilence of the hideous disease that had begun upon his flesh. It was a perpetual and excruciating sloughing condition whereby his skin seemed to decay and fall away, only to be replenished and repeat the process. To worsen.

Reluctant to give him up to their friend, the sea, the Vikings had brought him here instead, thinking to inflict the curse of him upon their prey, the Franks. He thought fleetingly again of the lord who had freed him from the pylon, and whatever fate the tides had to offer, and sipped from the wineskin.

The wine brought some relief from the stinging cold that pierced the very core of him. Hesitantly, he ate a small portion of the cheese and cured meat he found in the satchel. Food, that in the end would make no difference . . . He gave it up.

Unwilling to remain in the destroyed village, he moved out of the hut, then crawled and jerked his way up the steep hill to where great dark rocks jutted up between sea-hardened vegetation.

He sank down to rest behind the illusory shelter of one such outcropping, and listened to the thunder of the sea, now below him. The salt wind whistled through tall, dormant yellow, sharp-bladed grasses, rustled the limbs of twisted junipers and the like.

Wild sounds . . . He drank again from the wine.

After a time, he raised himself and crawled slowly inland to where the woods began to thicken.

Much later still, he set the pair of thick wooden staves he had found and finished with a sharp stone under his armpits and lurched upright to stand without the support of some permanent, unmovable thing. He inhaled deeply, his mouth a slash across his peeling face. Aye . . .

Free to move again. Free to walk in the only manner he could. He stiffened, eyes glittering warily as he felt very briefly, and deep inside, the shade of that man he had once been so many lifetimes ago.

Nay. Again, he closed his mind, and bent to reach for his bundle, and the provender that had been given him. He slung those items about his person with thongs he had contrived of woven pieces of vine stem. Then, with an agility that bespoke his long familiarity with his condition, he swung nimbly out of the woods, up toward a high place where the trees yielded to crags and windblown grasses.

Uncaring of the sleet and wind, or of the brutal, stinging cold, he stood there for a long time staring outward, the penetrating clarity and precision of his sight catching everything.

White-crested waves melted away toward a blurred horizon to join with heavy, overcast skies. Gulls lofted on the winds and swooped over the destroyed village, now hidden from view by the crags around him. And high above them, a dark sea eagle soared in solitary dominion, its pinions spread majestically. He watched it, seeing every feather . . . and its eyes. Fierce and bright, they watched neither gulls nor the human carrion below, but were fixed upon himself.

It was a stare that recognized . . . What?

He flinched violently and jerked his own gaze away. It was always thus when he saw a raptor.

Eagle wings . . . Now, Brittany.

He grimaced and stared toward the south where another jagged peninsula rose up to make a dark grey mass in defiance of the pounding sea. Finisterre, the people much farther inland called this desolate place, he knew. Yet it was not. Since his capture with other villagers from a very different place ten years past, he had learned a new definition for the edge of the world. Far, far away to the north and west, where the sea built mountains of ice, the Vikings dwelt secure in a land that heaved and belched forth soot and fire and deluges of molten rock that hardened into contorted masses where only lichens dared to grow. Where sea birds came in their millions each brief, nightless summer to roost, providing an incredible abundance. And the seals . . .

A heathen place, where Christian things were unknown. Where the fierce northern Gods were rightly enthroned. Mighty Thor, and Woden, and Freya, their voices heard in the thunder of the earth. He knew them all now.

It mattered not. He had no faith of any kind.

Nay, he knew. He did not object to the bitter cold. It matched the numbness deep inside. He turned on his crutches, then began to swing himself toward the south, inland, to where rough gorges tangled with impenetrable forest.

Much later, huddled under a weathered crevice in one of the multitude of inhospitable gorges along the coast, the cripple lay down to rest for the night.

Unable to sleep for knowing that he was returned to a place he had neither thought, nor wanted to see again, he watched the night settle. Darkness threaded through luminous flurries of falling snowflakes, whispered across the still white that blanketed trees and undergrowth and stone, to become a deepening blue that obscured the distances, creeping forward until, at last, it overwhelmed everything.

Brittany . . . again.

Better to be a slave subject to meaningless degradations. Better to be chained to the unthinkable endurance of things that had no connection with . . . Better, aye, to bear the manifest pains of brutal cold and the like than . . .

Shield to hold at bay what had become an internal wasteland.

His fingers moved over the rags that bound the object he still clung to with inexplicable perversity, tracing the form of the lyre beneath.

And he had thought once to be a jongleur?

Long silenced, this instrument. And his voice.

Remembered spells woven in sounds. Tapestries of magic made by music.

Better too, that sort of silence.

Unable to prevent himself, the cripple lay listening to the feathered rustlings of the branches above and beyond him. The other, more sporadic and half-furtive sounds of night creatures come out of hiding to forage. In the distance, he heard the faint, melancholy echoes of howling wolves.

Then, out of the shrouding darkness, he heard another, softly uttered, deep-toned call.

"Whooo . . . ooo," it came again. He froze, his features twisting, then jerked to sit upright as it came a third time. The call of an owl, such as he had not heard in many years—such as he most vehemently had never wished to hear again. His hands clenched into fists. Witchling creatures . . .

Here . . . ? Nay, he thought. Nay! Thou shall not find me! Thou shall not steal away such bitter frozen peace as I have managed to find! Sorcerer! Get thee away from me—and thy familiars!

The monk stiffened abruptly, his nostrils flaring as he turned toward the night that lay beyond the small, shuttered window above the pallet on the floor of his narrow cubicle. He reached quickly to snuff the single candle with his fingertips and rose to his feet to thrust open the shutters and stare out into the night with eyes gone enormous and round, and fierce with intent.

He poised. Inhaled deeply . . . and felt a glimmer of that which he sought to know. Then he reached through the window space to touch the cold, dark air with splayed, delicately shifting fingertips. To touch something more than air.

So . . . he thought. At last. At last . . .

And, after some moments thus, his face gone strangely thoughtful, he opened his mouth and loosed a muted, singularly inhuman cry. A summons, deep-pitched and muted, yet infinite in its reach.

He waited, his arm outheld. After a time, flying silently, a great bird came out of the darkness to alight upon his arm. He caressed the feathers of its head with the fingertips of his other hand and met its stare. Great eyes so like his own.

He spoke to it without words or any audible sound. Night raptor. My friend. Go thou, and watch for me . . .

The bird spread its wings once more and lofted away to vanish into the darkness. Brother Oborion did not watch it go. Instead, he drew back from the window and closed the shutters, his lips curving into a particular and delicate smile.

At last . . .

FIVE

Winter. 792–793 A.D.

"Father!" Dismounting from his horse, Lord Thierry looked up, his face erupting into a smile as his daughter, skirts in her hands, came flying down the steps of the keep toward him. He gave his reins to a groomsman and held out his arms.

"Gharis!" he murmured with feeling, glad to embrace this favorite of his three children. At twelve, she was an exquisite blend of child and woman, a source, as ever, of wonder and delight to him. Drawing a fold of his cloak about them both, he glanced up at the keep and thought with rueful tolerance of his two young sons—waiting, doubtless, to greet him with a more sober and masculine dignity. He walked forward, feeling her slight form against him, up the steps, to the shelter and warmth of home.

"I waited these four days past for thy return, Father," Gharis said. He glanced down into her green eyes.

"The weather turned foul and delayed me," he told her gently, watching a snowflake melt upon her nose.

"A great lord has come from the King to see thee," she announced then. Lord Thierry paused in surprise.

"Is there so?" he murmured. "Who?"

"Lord Geoffrey De Baviere," she said, savoring the words. He caught her tone at once, and forced back an urge to stiffen against the interest he detected.

"Well, then . . ." he said carefully, smiling as he released

47

her to pass into the keep. "I shall see him after I have changed and refreshed myself."

"I have already ordered hot water and such as thou may require, Father," she said with a great deal of dignity.

Lord Thierry grinned, pleased. "My little chatelaine!" he murmured, stooping briefly to kiss her brow. Then, "Where are the boys?"

"With Lord Geoffrey, Father," she told him.

He grimaced ruefully and shook his head. "So I should have guessed when thou first spoke of him. We get few enough visitors of high estate here," he commented, then turned and strode away toward the comforts that awaited him in his chambers. Not, he thought, that he intended it to be otherwise. He had come to savor his relative isolation after so many years spent entangled in the affairs of the Court. Even widowerhood was comfortable, and he was well content with his children.

He thrust through an oak door high in the keep, into a large, fire-warmed chamber. He unclasped his cloak and dropped it, nodding toward the body servant waiting by a large wooden tub filled with steaming water. He removed his helm, pushed back his coif, and unbuckled his sword belt. Geoffrey De Baviere—Duke Naimes' heir. A curious choice to serve as royal messenger? He frowned as the body servant unbuckled his hauberk and drew it from him, then set about disrobing him completely. Charlemagne, he knew from long experience, did nothing without well-considered intent. His frown deepened as he felt a surge of that alertly cautious tension he had lived with for so many years, and had thought to have finally put behind him.

What, he wondered, did the King want of him to send such?

Written by Charlemagne's own hand, it was no more than a simple summons to Aix. Carefully controlling his expression, Lord Thierry refolded the document he had declined to open until the conclusion of the evening meal, and leaned back in his chair to sip at wine and nibble at the sweetmeats before him.

He had caught the flicker of ill-disguised curiosity in Lord Geoffrey's eyes as he had relinquished the missive, and had delayed opening it accordingly. Why send De Baviere with so simple a command when a much lesser man would have served as well? Clearly, the King had something of a complex nature on his mind.

Nay, Lord Thierry thought forcefully as he watched Lord

Geoffrey's blatant wooing of his daughter farther along the table, he was not enchanted by that young man's facile, good-humored charm. Nor by the baser attraction of his striking good looks and lush, dark auburn hair. His Gharis, on the other hand, responded with truly innocent admiration as Lord Geoffrey regaled her with anecdotal tales of the Court, and of his exploits against the heathen Saxons. Gharis, who had neither the years nor the experience to know that men are never heroes when met in close proximity . . .

He felt a surge of dislike for Lord Geoffrey with his ready smiles and flawless, Court-trained manners. It was a different breed of men that were fostered at Court these days, he thought. Not the same. Not the same at all . . .

The Count leaned forward and caught his daughter's eye. She gave a slight nod of understanding and rose to her feet.

"We will depart for Aix in five days, my lord Geoffrey," Lord Thierry said clearly.

De Baviere turned quickly in his chair, his look searching, fleetingly surprised. "I had understood the King's summons to be urgent, my lord?"

Lord Thierry smiled as he held out an arm to his daughter. He leaned to kiss her gently on the cheek as she moved into his embrace. "Good night, sweeting," he murmured, knowing now the document had been examined. "Blessed dreaming . . ." He sat back and watched her as she turned obediently and slipped gracefully from the great hall, well aware of Lord Geoffrey's continued scrutiny. "The winter season precludes haste, my lord," he answered mildly, allowing his gaze to lock with that of the younger man. "I would fail in my duty equally, were I to abandon what must needs be done here to prepare for my absence." Lord Geoffrey looked away and delicately selected another sweetmeat from the platter before him. Brittany, he'd been given to understand, was a wild and sparsely populated part of the realm. Still . . .

The Count's next, sternly toned utterance took him by surprise. "Have a care in thy wooing, my lord! My daughter is not for thee!"

Lord Geoffrey looked up and felt heat rise along his neck. He found a smile. "The Lady Gharis is a most beautiful and accomplished maiden," he tried.

Lord Thierry inclined his head in agreement. "I repeat, my

lord," he said with absolute gentleness. "My daughter is not for thee!"

Lord Geoffrey looked away and found his wine cup. "Aaah. She is betrothed then, the Lady Gharis . . . ?" he murmured.

Lord Thierry did not answer, but, picking up the royal missive, stood. "I bid thee good night, my lord," he said with formal courtesy. "On the morrow, we shall enjoy some hawking?"

Lord Geoffrey rose as well, and bowed. "That would delight me, my lord," he said with honest appreciation.

Lord Thierry nodded and strode away, past the hearth fire in the center of the fairly compact great hall, and soon disappeared from view.

Lord Geoffrey sank slowly back into his chair, aware of the servants hovering in a corner, and frowned.

He had not expected the Count's absence upon his arrival. Nor, his obvious vigor. Slim and fit and hard, the Champion bore few of the signs of age that should have accompanied his retirement from Court these several years past. There were few traces of silver in the Count's rich brown hair. No indication of any infirmity . . . Lord Geoffrey thought resentfully of his own father who tottered toward his deathbed with interminable lethargy. He stood, reached for his wine cup and a full flagon, then, those items in hand, strode from the great hall to seek the chamber that had been assigned to him in the upper levels of the keep.

He had, he knew angrily, been unfavorably assessed. Like Prince Charlot, his own fate waited on the whims of old men . . .

Lord Thierry paused as he reached the corridor beyond the great hall. Feeling restive despite his tiredness, he shifted his shoulders, then drew his cloak about him and left the keep to walk through several inches of snow toward the falcon house against the great stone walls of the bailey. He had promised hawking . . .

He took a torch from the forge nearby and lit it in the embers of the fire there, and, more slowly, walked the last steps toward the well-constructed, wooden building where his birds were kept.

Why am I doing this? he wondered silently, entering carefully, then setting the torch into an iron sconce. He moved forward into the deep straw bedding under the perches to stand in the midst of birds that shifted restlessly, sensing his presence.

A pair of goshawks. His peregrine . . . and the young black

eagle he had caught this summer past. Aye, he thought, reaching to caress the feathers of the older goshawk. He'd let De Baviere use this one. An experienced bird, it would tolerate another's hand.

He moved to touch the other. Then his cherished peregrine. The bird opened her beak and cocked her hooded head as he stroked the feathers of her back. She was a wonder of courage . . .

Hawking had become a favorite pastime over the years. And most of what he knew came from years long past when he had squired Lord Oliver De Montglave. His face tightened at the memories. How different it had all been then . . . His fingers left the falcon and reached for the jesses of the young male eagle. Not fully tamed yet. Few men used eagles . . . He loosed the jesses and set the bird on his arm, ignoring the talons that impaled his flesh through his sleeve. He removed the hood to let the bird see as he proffered a scrap of meat from a nearby pot. It blinked and stared at him out of one fierce, golden eye. Golden . . . eye?

Eyes . . . ?

Lord Thierry froze. Felt something congeal inside. Aye. Golden eyes, such as he had seen but a few days past.

"Mother of God!" he whispered as he touched the bird. "It cannot be . . . ?"

Cripple. He had been the last to see. To recognize . . . so many years ago now. Aye. That same brutally contorted right leg. The same height and frame. And, most of all, those eyes.

Who, having ever seen the man at all, could ever forget that ferocious, intensely direct, golden, aye, eagle stare?

"How could I have not known at once?" he rasped harshly, hooding the bird on his arm, then returning it to its perch. "How?" He seized the torch and, thrusting from the small building, strode across the bailey to clutch the sentry posted by the entrance to the keep.

"Fetch Sir Antoine to my chambers at once!" he ordered brutally. He did not see the startled look the man shot him before hurrying to obey, but strode up the steps, into and through the keep, up several flights of stairs in a corner tower, to the privacy of his own chambers.

Pushing forcefully through the door, he dismissed the servant waiting to attend him and began to pace back and forth.

He could never have expected . . . Nor imagined, to recognize. That frightful countenance . . .

"My lord?" Lord Thierry spun around as Sir Antoine entered the chamber looking tousled and anxious.

"Shut the door," the Count said quietly. The knight obeyed and moved toward him. "I have a task for thee, Sir Antoine." His tone became deliberate. "I depart for Court in a few days to answer the King's summons. As my seneschal, it falls to thee to keep order and security during my absence . . ." Sir Antoine nodded gravely. "There is, however, something else I require of thee."

"Anything, my lord!" Under another circumstance, Lord Thierry thought as he searched the younger man's eyes, he would have smiled. But now the enthusiasm jarred.

"So, I charge thee. Pick five men who are trustworthy for their discretion, and search for that cripple we found these few days past upon the beaches of Finisterre," he pronounced with great clarity. "I will have him brought here. Likewise, he is to be treated with *every* courtesy and respect!"

The young knight's eyes went very round. His face paled slowly. "My lord!" he rasped in shock. "I do not understand? That pitiful thing . . . It is ridden with pestilence . . ."

"It does not matter!" Lord Thierry cut sternly across the protest. "I will have him found and brought here to every comfort of my house. I would do it myself, save that I am commanded to attend the King." Sir Antoine did not reply, but stared at the resolute determination on the Count's face, his own reflecting the horror the cripple had instilled in him.

Lord Thierry waited. He needed an unflinching commitment. He also understood the knight's fear. The fear others would have. Unimportant compared to the identity of the man he sought.

The young knight stiffened slowly, his strong, clean-shaven jaw thrust out a little. "As thou will, my lord," he said with determination, his choice made. "Still, I do not understand . . . ?"

Lord Thierry felt himself loosen somewhat. "That ruined cripple," he said very softly, "was once the greatest knight in Christendom!"

Sir Antoine stared "But, that is not possible, my lord!" It erupted from him. "Thou . . . ."

Lord Thierry shook his head. "Nay, Sir Antoine," he said with gentle sincerity. "I am not Roland!"

The young knight froze, his eyes enormous. "Impossible!" he whispered unevenly. "But Count Roland is long dead . . ."

Again, Lord Thierry shook his head. "Nay, Sir Antoine," he

said clearly. "For all he appears to be entombed at Aix!" He watched confusion chase across the other man's features. "I know for truth, what no other man may," he added sternly, then waited. The knight searched his face and, after a few moments, braced himself.

"So be it, my lord. I will undertake to find this individual," he said with awkward resolve and bowed.

"Sir Antoine?"

"My lord?"

"No word of this to any other soul," Lord Thierry ordered firmly. Again, the seneschal bowed.

"As thou will, my lord," he said and, turning, left the Count to stand alone with his thoughts and the night.

So . . . Sir Antoine thought as he made his way slowly back along narrow, darkened corridors toward his own quarters. Now he was bound to search for a dead man who was not dead after all. A pestilence-laden thing that bore no resemblance whatever to the image in his mind of the glorious and valiant Roland, aye, astride the mighty stallion Veillantif, his unmatched sword Durandal slicing through infidel foe more easily than he, Sir Antoine, could strip an over-boiled capon . . .

Impossible. Impossible . . .

"Sir seneschal?" Thoroughly startled, Sir Antoine looked up to see Lord Geoffrey De Baviere lounging against the door to the chamber given to his use, a flagon in one hand.

"My lord?"

Lord Geoffrey smiled wryly and waved the flagon. "I have found refreshment, sir knight, but none to share its use," he said with regret. Sir Antoine hesitated, honored by the invitation from one so high, yet troubled by other things. Lord Geoffrey arched a brow and straightened. "I do not recollect thy name?" he asked.

"Antoine—of Anjou, my lord. Being the youngest of four brothers, I therefore serve my lord of Brittany."

Lord Geoffrey nodded. "Aye . . . I recollect my father telling me of the Lord of Anjou who was among the company of Peers," he offered and inclined his head. "A noble house indeed!"

Pleased, and curious, Sir Antoine allowed himself to be drawn into the other's chamber. Conscious only of the honor this great, and obviously wealthy young lord bestowed by seeking his companionship, he did not catch the quick, hard, assessing look that

De Baviere directed toward him as he closed the door, before reaching for another wine cup. He filled it, and proffered it with a smile.

At last, Lord Geoffrey thought, he had found a troubled soul. A curious, possibly useful dissonance in this . . . most harmoniously managed place.

Nay. I should not leave here now, Lord Thierry thought as he settled himself into the high-cantled saddle of his war stallion several days later. He sought his children on the steps of the keep. The two boys flanking their tutor. Gharis, unsafe for both her femininity and her innocence . . . And, behind them, Sir Antoine stood like the guardian he was now entrusted to be.

Lord Thierry smiled at his children, covering the consternation that filled him. Soon, he knew, Sir Antoine himself would depart to fulfill that privately given duty. The knight had acquired a new and wary reserve, very different from the forthright, if youthful, honesty that was usual to him. And what, he longed to know, had transpired between his seneschal and De Baviere to make such a fast and easy camaraderie between them? De Baviere, he was convinced, did nothing without an ulterior motive. How well, Lord Thierry thought grimly, he understood the stink of conspiracy . . .

He gathered up his horse's reins, spurred the animal, and turned it to trot toward the gates in the bailey wall. Behind him, his small retinue of three men and a servant followed. His castle remained fully garrisoned . . .

Lord Geoffrey rode up to flank him. "Good fortune rides with us, my lord," De Baviere said pleasantly as their horses clattered under the portcullis, across the drawbridge. "The weather is vastly improved!" Lord Thierry inclined his head in agreement and looked outward to where the winter sun flashed brilliantly across patches of snow, shrinking in the warmer air of the mid-season thaw, glinted on drops of water that fell from frost-laden trees in the surrounding woods.

Impatiently, he spurred his stallion into a hard gallop, recklessly indifferent to the animal's difficulties as it slithered across icy places. Aix—the sooner the better.

SIX

"I am convinced," Prince Charlot said slowly, his eyes glinting in the light of the single candle that illuminated the room, "that my father is entirely familiar with this deception concerning the birth of Girard De Guienne. Why else would he permit the fiefs of Bordeaux to continue in such autonomous isolation all these years? Why else has he not required the Duke Huon and his brother to Court as is expected of every other highborn heir and lord of such rank?"

Lord Amaury's fingers traced a flaw in the cup on the table between them.

"Nor has my nephew, Baudoin," he pointed out quietly.

"That is a different case, my lord," the Prince said brutally. "And thou are kept here!"

Lord Amaury breathed deeply, letting it pass. "Highness. If Lord Huon was bastard got, it would be simple enough to dispossess him. But the consequence of a younger son is so much lesser, and useful only in that he is Lord Huon's heir . . . If this information may be used to expose a heinous and irrefutable wrong, then Bordeaux may be brought into thy hands." Lord Amaury leaned forward. "If it is beyond question that young Girard is not Duke Servinus' get, then . . . there is but one man to dispose—his brother!" Prince Charlot waited. Lord Amaury continued, "And . . . if the King, with full knowledge of these things, has sought to protect the same, even he must be compelled by the requirements of his own justice to resolve it to thy benefit.'' The Prince nodded understanding. Lord Amaury inhaled and went on. ''It *must* be proved that Girard De Guienne is illegitimate, and, therefore, entitled by deception—which is a grievous offense . . .''

Prince Charlot slowly inclined his head.

''Then . . . they must be summoned to Court,'' he said quietly after a few moments. ''By my father.'' He stood abruptly, and Lord Amaury hurriedly followed suit. ''We shall converse again in a few days, my lord,'' the Prince added in the same tone, his voice laden with satisfaction.

De Hauteville bowed. ''Highness . . .'' But the Prince had already turned away and, an instant later, had disappeared through the door.

Straightening, Lord Amaury frowned at the candle, its flame dancing precariously around the wick it consumed. Fate had given him into the Prince's hands, but Charlot showed much the same unreadable obscurity of mind as his sire. Very difficult to control . . .

Nor, Lord Amaury knew, did he ever forget that bastards had been elevated before by Charlemagne's will. Aye, to a status that defied both the rancor and the purity of the noblest in the realm.

''We welcome thee back to our presence, my lord,'' Charlemagne pronounced clearly as the Champion knelt before him in obeisance. He moved one well-jeweled hand in a gesture for the Count to rise, and Lord Thierry did so. Their gazes locked in understanding.

Lord Geoffrey caught the look as he watched from the crowds gathered to greet the Champion's return in the great hall of Aix. He had not forgot even the least part of that information he had prised from the Count's inebriated and troubled seneschal before his departure from Brittany. Aye . . . he thought. He had an axe that, regardless of the direction in which it was swung, could only yield useful result.

He shifted and looked at Prince Charlot, who stood somewhat to the left of the King, at the foot of the dais. He waited until Charlot shifted his gaze from the Champion, then out across the gathered company. Then, just as Prince Charlot's eyes met his and paused, he smiled fractionally and arched one brow.

The Prince did not even blink, but, instead, looked away. A few moments later, he bowed to his father and turned to stroll away through the throng with an affect of bored indifference.

Lord Geoffrey smiled at the nobleman next to him, uttered a remark that conveyed his sense of privilege at having been sent to bring so great a man as the Champion back to Court, then moved on, working his way gradually through the crowd until he too escaped.

Select gathering, the members of the High Council . . . And, his power absolute, Charlemagne helped himself to the morsels of knowledge, conviction, values, and sentiment served up in the discources presented before him, then chose his own way. Prince Charlot had made use of his advice, Lord Geoffrey saw from his place behind his father's chair, and now attended all Councils, listening intently. His own presence was founded in keeping a watchful eye on his father's increasingly senile pronouncements.

He waited as the concerns of this particular assembly were disposed of one by one, then, as the King arched his brows in final invitation and scanned the company with his frigid stare, he stepped forward and bowed.

"My lord Geoffrey?" Charlemagne inquired remotely. De Baviere straightened, glanced hesitantly toward the Champion, seated near the head of the table before the King's great chair.

"Majesty. I wish to petition thee on a matter that has great importance to me."

"Speak, my lord." Charlemagne inclined his silver head a little.

"It is my most earnest wish, my liege, to request of Lord Thierry of Brittany, his daughter, the Lady Gharis, for my wife . . .

"I am fully cognizant of the honor my lord will do me to consider my suit," Lord Geoffrey continued. "I recognize as well a greater benefit to the realm through the alliance of these great eastern and western fiefs . . ."

So . . . Lord Thierry thought as the King's austere gaze shifted to him, this is what that dissembling young monster is about! He smiled a little, rose from his chair, stepped forward, and bowed.

"Majesty. I am in no haste to arrange the marriage of my daughter, who is barely come to the first flush of womanhood. It had been my intention in another year to propose an entirely different alliance."

Charlemagne leaned forward, his expression unchanged. "My lord?"

"Majesty. I propose to bring greater unity along the western shores of the realm through an alliance between the fiefs of Brittany and Bordeaux. I wish to marry my daughter to the house of De Guienne." The King sat back again.

"To the young Duke Huon?" he asked.

The Champion shook his head. "Nay, Majesty," he said more gently. "It wound content me well to wed my daughter to his brother, Lord Girard."

Lord Geoffrey pretended a look of complete surprise and started a little as, behind him, he heard his father murmur.

"Aaah, Bordeaux! Aye. Servinus is a good lord . . ."

Lord Geoffrey shifted and looked up at the King, allowing himself to flare. "But, Majesty. Is not Lord Girard but a younger son with a nominal inheritance?" He added a frown. "I am troubled that my lord of Brittany would decline my suit to favor this lesser alliance. And to a youth untested!" He glanced at the Count's stern face. "Surely, there is a greater benefit in my proposal?"

"Bordeaux?" Duke Naimes said loudly, jerking to his feet to lean upon the staff that age and infirmity required. "Who is this Duke Huon? I know none of that name?" Unexpected aid from a senile old man.

Lord Geoffrey pounced. "Aye, Majesty. As my sire says. Who are those two—Duke Huon and his brother, who have never been seen at Court, and are unknown to us all, save as names? I cannot think my lord's wish to wed his daughter to an untried boy of so much lesser state a comparable suit!" he added harshly.

Charlemagne's expression did not change. Nor did his eyes leave the Champion's face. Lord Geoffrey remained watchful, keeping earnestness upon his own countenance. It was a question of power, he understood. He offered a great, but diffused, alliance that made a caliper of unified interest around much of the rest of the realm. But Lord Thierry's proposal was clever. Through the alliance of blood, he sought the unity of a single, vast region. Nay, Lord Huon would be obligated by blood ties without direct marriage. The brother was sufficient. Lord Geoffrey bowed his head as Charlemagne's gaze swept out across the gathering.

"Majesty . . . ?" he ventured with studious, reasonable quiet. "Perhaps this matter of alliances would be better resolved for the presence of all parties concerned? Duke Huon and his brother are unknown at Court. Their dispositions and capabilities are not understood to the greater interest of the realm, as they should be . . ."

Cunning young jackal! Lord Thierry thought, keeping his eyes on the King's face. Something of a complex and subversive nature was brewing there. The King's eyes met his, and Lord Thierry arched a brow to indicate . . .

"So be it," Charlemagne said. "We will dispatch two members of the Council to carry our summons to Bordeaux, requiring Huon De Guienne and his brother to attend us. Our Champion will be one . . ." Charlemagne's gaze shifted to the back of the gathering to where Lord Amaury De Hauteville sat with bowed head and apparently indifferent demeanor, his function on the Council confined strictly to matters of scholarship. "And Lord Amaury De Hauteville!" the King pronounced.

Lord Geoffrey did not move. He had expected it to be himself, as planned. Lord Thierry, he saw, turned in surprise.

Thoroughly startled, Lord Amaury rose to his feet, then gave a flustered bow.

"I am honored, Majesty," he said. The King nodded, his features remaining expressionless as he waved a hand in dismissal. Lord Thierry turned back to stare at the King, as, amid rippled murmurs, the rest of the company rose and bowed, then turned to depart the Council hall.

Something glinted in Charlemagne's eyes, and Lord Thierry recognized the command. He bowed and walked slowly behind the rest, delaying until the hall was emptied. Then, with only the two sentries on the other side of the great doors, he turned back and bowed again.

"Majesty?" he asked quietly. Charlemagne sat back in his chair, his eyes traveling up the Count's form, from his booted feet, across his tunic and surcoat of simple but excellent quality, to his face.

"The years deal most charitably with thee, my lord," Charlemagne said softly. Then, "We knew another time . . . thou and I."

"Aye, Majesty." Lord Thierry understood.

Charlemagne straightened, his expression hardening again. "To that, we must address the future. The succession. This empire will not endure to succor Christian men unless the right hand holds the bridle."

So, this was the reason for his summons to Court, Lord Thierry realized, then bowed deeply.

"Just so, my liege," he said sincerely. Charlemagne nodded, then stood.

"We are disposed to favor thy suit, my lord," he said very quietly, then strode past him to depart the Council chamber. Private information, Lord Thierry knew as he turned to follow moments later. Charlemagne understood his reasoning and interest in Girard De Guienne very well. An ingredient from a well-known past to be offered up against the uncertainties of the future.

"I do not want thy company, Girard!" Lord Huon growled brutally, keeping his gaze averted as he put his foot into the stirrup and vaulted lightly into the saddle of the half-bred horse the groomsman held. "I prefer to hunt alone!"

Already mounted on his own favorite hunting palfrey, Girard stiffened. "As thou will, Huon," he said quietly.

Mounted now, Huon brought his beast about, then looked up to meet his brother's confusion and disappointment with a fierce, angry stare. "Aye. I will it so!" he gritted, then. "Haaarrgh!" He put spurs to his mount and the animal plunged away to canter toward the drawbridge, the huntsman and a brace of leashed staghounds following in hot pursuit.

Girard checked his own horse's attempt to follow, then, as his brother vanished from view, clattering across the frost-slick timbers of the drawbridge, he let the animal walk forward, needing movement . . . something.

The fading thunder of galloping horses marked where his brother disappeared into the woods and meadows to the south and east of Bordeaux castle. Girard turned his horse in the opposite direction. West, then north, along a track that led around Bordeaux's great outer walls with their high, massive towers that dominated the landscape.

He did not see. Nor did he notice when his horse slithered down a steep bank, lunged across the gully at the bottom, then cantered uphill to amble toward the trees that marked the beginning of the vast forests flanking the Garonne.

Painful confusion . . . He could not understand this change in his brother's manner that had occurred of late. For the past several months, Huon's mood had been unpredictable, aloof. The cheerful, somewhat paternal affection that Girard savored like sunlight was gone, replaced by savage verbal thrusts and angry looks. Aye—anger.

What had he done? Girard wondered, unable to find an answer. Nor, when he had ventured to ask, had Huon replied. It jarred, for Huon's honesty, like his sense of justice and brilliance in all things, rang like a battle axe upon an anvil. Clarion true.

This thing that had to do with himself was secretive and festering, like a wound when the skin closed before the deeper parts were fully healed. Girard exhaled violently and looked up to see his frosted breath disperse into the cold morning air.

Aware of its rider's disinterest, the palfrey slowed, tugged the reins loose, and began to browse upon tall, winter-browned grasses thrusting up through the patches of snow on the ground.

Girard caught sight of a large, mottled and tawny-colored owl perched among the bare limbs of a nearby tree. Unmoving, it watched him with a remarkably resolute gaze. Nor did it take flight as his horse drifted closer.

Glad for some distraction, Girard continued to watch the bird. It blinked once and continued to stare back at him. Strange to see an owl in broad daylight, he thought, tempted to smile at it. Nocturnal creatures, and mysterious, they were thought to be familiars of the spirits that moved through the night. Disconcerting, the ways of wild things . . . and men. Girard shook his head against his own inclination to be fanciful.

Suddenly the owl spread its great wings and took flight, spiraling upward into the air high above the trees. He watched it go, flying more like an eagle, or a hawk, lofting high to become a broad-winged speck as it made for the north.

Unnatural? He shook his head at himself as the bird disappeared from view. Nay, just unusual, he reminded himself sternly, still deeply troubled by this silent, bitter thing that festered between himself and his brother. Huon, who, Girard knew, he loved above all other men . . .

Eyes that were more than the vision of a solitary wild creature marked what they had seen, and lofted high upon the air currents just below the clouds, they headed north along the coast. Looking ever downward, they saw the soft grey, rounded contours of myriad trees, the scattered patches of late winter snowfall, every footprint and trail . . . and every creature that moved.

Like a twinkling ribbon, the Garonne River passed away underneath. And the forests thickened, broken at occasional intervals by upthrusting crags of rock, and more rarely by small hamlets and manors. Far to the left, the sea made a glittering edge against a dark, intricate tracery of coastline, fading away toward an irrelevant horizon.

Owl wings cradled the currents that held them up, performed the labor of transport, leaving the eyes free to roam, to probe among the land-bound creatures below. To search . . . aye, for one of these.

SEVEN

"Pah! This is a futile errand!" Sir Antoine muttered balefully, clutching his cloak more closely about him in defense against the penetrating bite of the wind. "I'd sooner seek a cloak pin in a hayrick!" He glared at the man beside him who had glanced up, then looked around him in disgust.

For two weeks, they had scoured the coast, venturing inland along the northern parts of Finisterre, in a relentless search for the cripple who, despite his incapacity, had proved impossible to find.

Sir Antoine, fully mindful of his lord's instructions, and the observations of Lord Geoffrey concerning the nature and proofs of witchcraft, had brought the search back to the westernmost tip of Brittany, then veered south to probe the desolate, weather-beaten shores, and the densely forested and treacherous landscape of high crags and deep, obscure gorges beyond.

He braced his shoulders—half the day remained. Then he nudged his horse forward and let the animal pick its own way up a difficult path to stop upon a high bluff that overlooked both the sea and some of the terrain to the east. The four wolfhounds, unleashed, and knowing him as they did, followed to settle down around his horse's fetlocks.

Unaware of the gradual shift in the wind, he sat there for some time, staring about him, brooding in frustration over the conflicts between duty and conviction.

Suddenly one of the hounds got to its feet and pointed its

nose toward the south and east. Sir Antoine stiffened as the others joined it. One barked. Another let out a low growl. They looked up at him, eager, yet obedient. Not confident of the result, Sir Antoine grated the word that loosed them, then bellowed for his men to follow. The hounds erupted into a slinking run along the bluffs, then veered south to where gnarled, stunted trees hugged great slashes in the rock. They'd break their necks for a hare, he thought as his horse slithered across a slab of stone in the turf, then plummeted down a steep bank into a thicket of tangling bushes and thorny briers. He heard a shout from one of the men behind him, but the hounds had begun to bay as they bolted on ahead. He spurred his horse forward, raising an arm to shield his face as the animal leaped, bunched— bounded its way through the undergrowth. The others, behind him, were having like difficulties as they tried to keep pace with the dogs. Then as his horse lurched up a steep slope and heaved to an uncertain pause on a bare slab of rock that dropped away into a deepening gorge below, he heard the baying die away.

Then a growl. A snarl. Close by . . . Whatever they had scented before, he knew, they had found. There was a sudden yelp, a howl of pain. Sir Antoine sank spur and forced his horse off the eight-foot drop into the bushes below. The animal almost fell, staggered, and found its feet, then grunted with effort as he lashed it in the direction of the dogs.

Within moments, his horse catapulted him into a narrow clearing flanked on all sides by bushes, sapling trees, and granite. He drew the horse to a halt as he caught sight of the wolfhounds, shaggy, brutal grey shapes in a wary half circle around a tattered figure propped on one crutch, the other brandished before him, backed up against the stone cliff.

Alive . . . The knight's eyes widened in astonishment. The hounds looked to him and whined uncertainly. He barked the word that summoned them, and they abandoned the cripple, slinking back to flank his horse with wagging tails and tongues lolling in gaping jaws.

He would have preferred a corpse, Sir Antoine thought, watching the cripple set the other crutch beneath his armpit. Just then, the other five men erupted into the clearing and drew rein in a group. Sir Antoine nudged his horse toward the figure he had no wish to see again at close range, and tightened his grip on the haft of the short hunting spear he carried. Fierce golden eyes gleamed relentlessly at him from beneath the shrouding rags that covered the cripple's head.

"My lord, the Count of Brittany, has required me to seek thee out and bring thee to him," he declared with loud authority. The cripple's gaze did not waver.

"Did he so . . . ?" he murmured in a peculiar tone.

Sir Antoine frowned. "Aye!" he barked it, then asked the question that haunted him. "What is thy name?"

The cripple's stare continued to bore into him, becoming even fiercer as he swung forward a pace on his crutches, the hideously disintegrating flesh of his face now clearly revealed.

"Like the dead, I too am nameless!" the cripple said with sinister clarity.

Sir Antoine paled, his abruptly tightened fist on the bridle causing his mount to drop its head and back away. The dead? Assuredly, to look upon this creature was to behold the very face of death . . . He heard the rippled, daunted murmurings of the men behind him as they too saw, and summoned his courage.

The cripple advanced again, swinging grotesquely as he made to pass from them. The wolfhounds raised their hackles and growled, but made no move to attack.

"Nonetheless, thou will come with us as my lord wills!" Sir Antoine ordered roughly. Courtesy, the Count had instructed, but there seemed no place for it here. The cripple stopped and looked up at him, eyes glittering.

"Thy lord hath no need of me!" he replied with a cold authority that matched the knight's tone.

Angered, Sir Antoine turned to his men. "Colin! Theo! Take this creature and mount him. As my lord wills, so it shall be done!"

"I tell thee, thy lord hath no need of me!" the cripple growled back, shifting his weight. "Leave me be!" Sir Antoine's mouth became a thin slash as he flung himself from his horse and, ahead of the two he had ordered, strode toward the cripple. Reached out to seize . . .

One of the cripple's staves swooped with lightning suddenness and came down to shatter against the knight's head. Blood spewed at once from his mouth. Sir Antoine poised for a moment, then crumpled slowly to lie in a heap on the sod.

The two advancing behind him stopped in their tracks, their faces going ashen as their eyes flitted from the menace of the monstrous cripple's stare, down to where the knight lay staring toward the sky, his skull shattered beneath his helm.

"Go!" the cripple intoned with malignant venom.

They did so. And an instant later, the small troop sent their horses plunging away through the thickets of the gorge, the wolfhounds following, and pursued by the distracted flight of the frightened, riderless animal that had been Sir Antoine's mount.

The cripple stood very still, propped on the single crutch that remained to him. He listened to the fading array of crashes and thuds that bespoke hasty retreat and waited for the silence to return. And when all had fallen still once more, he slowly lowered his gaze to stare down at the thing he had done.

Young—so young, the knight lay on the sod before him. As he had been once . . . Broken now.

Killed in an instant.

Unthinking reflex—even the certainty of his aim. He stared at unfocused eyes already beginning to dry, the greying face with blood still oozing from mouth and nostrils, then down to the arms of Brittany embroidered on the dead man's woolen surcoat.

He, who had brought no harm or violence to another since . . . Since Roncesvalles. Even when the Vikings had taken him, he had not cared enough to offer the least resistance.

Now this . . . All for knowing that Thierry of Leon had recognized him after all. Sought him.

He did not want to be found. Or remembered.

But feelings long drowned surged up from that anonymous internal place where he had entombed them as his gaze shifted to the pieces of the shattered stave that had been his crutch. His stare went haggard, terrible. He had not known he was that strong. Enduring, aye. Relentlessly enduring, but . . . His eyes moved to where the dead man's sword lay, still sheathed against his flank. Plain steel, with a cross hilt of bound leather and brass, it was a simple thing.

Not like that other, peerless sword.

No witchling blade had wrought this, he knew, staring up, out, to scan the perimeter of the gorge. Only himself. That sheer, directed power he had always attributed to the Dark Sword—and the time so long ago when he had been . . . whole.

Unforgiven. He jerked back. Always unforgiven.

He knew where he had left her. Buried. Hidden away from

the sight and knowledge of men. Aye . . . not so far away. In another, even less conspicuous gorge. Waiting. Like damnation.

He turned from the corpse and, lurching awkwardly on the single crutch that remained to him, began to move laboriously forward, along the floor of the gorge, headed south to confront . . .

That which would have taken a good horse no more than six hours to traverse took the cripple, even with another staff, two days as he trekked slowly through an increasingly brutal landscape. Then, at last, he reached the virtual barricade of nearly impregnable undergrowth and ancient, great trunked trees that blocked the way to a deep and hidden gorge.

Uncaring of tearing thorns and tough, entangling vines, he struggled downward to stop at last and hang upon his crutches, staring grimly at this place he had neither thought, nor intended ever to look upon again.

So well remembered, this secretive cleft in the earth.

Found by accident.

Filled with silence.

High overhead, above the trees and the precipitous granite cliffs, the winds hummed of escape as they fled away. The small brook still trickled across the narrow clearing. And on the other side, the cripple saw before him the same ruined pillars of white marble held together, half concealed by meshed vines and other vegetation.

The remains of an ancient ruined temple to heathen Gods from the times before Christ . . . So Oliver had said.

Oliver . . . He shuddered with pain and hunched over his crutches like an agued thing.

Never forgotten. Always beloved . . . Oliver.

Memories and feelings surged up from his frozen mind and soul like a tempest loosed to scour.

Oliver, who could never grow old. Oliver, whose courage and clarity and gallant honor had defined the very essence of manhood. Wise Oliver, who had brought humanity to the brutal, witch-got, bastard thing he, Roland, was . . . The cripple flinched and gasped at the echo of his own name.

Murdered Oliver . . .

Himself, the murderer. Aye, by those very same, unnatural things that still clung to him like leeches to a drowning man in a bog. His fingers crept to touch the rag-bound lyre still against him.

It had been here that Oliver had taught him to play. It had been here, much later, that he had found the instrument and had made the Song to resolve the treachery of Roncesvalles . . .

And that murder—that single, irrevocable act that lay buried like damnation in a lie . . . The Song had woven the fabric of truth around that lie. Like a shroud.

Two lies. Unforgiven.

He had not died . . . He had not died.

And he had thought to be a jongleur . . . ? A man, after all?

But he had not been able to find words enough to complete another song as he had wandered. Instead, his fingers had meandered like lost souls across the strings of the lyre to find haunting, potent melodies that wafted restless and excruciating into the air. And any who had ventured to listen had soon drawn back, wary. Mistrustful . . .

Even the Vikings who had enslaved him.

What a brutal odyssey the past fourteen years had been. Cold enough to numb . . . almost. Filled with pain enough to smother . . . almost. Manhood . . . ? It eluded the crippled beggar he had become, haunted by things inside. He had endured. For God, what he had endured to learn . . .

Silence.

Entombment of a kind where only feelings turned to stone.

Life would not let him go.

Cold winters, snow and ice such as froze the birds upon the trees, did not do the same to him. Starvation did not bring weakness and death. Thirst shriveled his flesh a little, but did not thicken the blood to stop his heart. Nor, when the Vikings had tried to rid themselves of him by chaining him to rocks below the tides, had he drowned like a natural man. Instead, he had endured the wash of unspeakably cold waters, the agony of raw salt seas in his lungs.

And lived . . .

He looked down at the hands that clung to the shafts of his crutches. Even this disease of sloughing flesh did not consume him as was true for other lepers. He looked up again, across the gorge, then, bitter-faced, swung himself across the clearing and the brook, toward the ancient temple.

He had touched no weapon of any kind since . . .

Grimly, he lurched up detritus-covered steps between the marble pillars, then moved across the overgrown temple court, picking his way awkwardly, one limb at a time. Flesh and wood.

And where the core of the temple rose up in a sheer, vine-covered white wall to join with the granite cliffs, he pushed between young trees and stone on one side to find the concealed, riftlike, narrow entrance to a dark and barren cave.

He paused, his eyes glinting, then lurched forward into the chill, silent darkness beyond to stop inside and hang upon his crutches once more.

There, centered still in the dank, pervasive gloom, her point embedded in stone, stood the Dark Sword, Durandal.

He swallowed as he stared at her, raw, taut, a multitude of things . . .

Aaah, Durandal. Richer hued than obsidian, smooth, pure, incredibly dense, she was, as always, a sword beyond any other.

Her nature was revealed in the wicked, lethal purity of her long, impossibly sharp blade, in the eerie, shifting storm tones and filament lightning streaks that played across her surface. In the eagle-winged cross pieces that were as fastidiously detailed as the pinions of a real bird. Outspread . . . Always ready for flight.

And, above them, unchanged, stood the hilt of the mysteriously perfect, elfin woman form swathed in the dark coils of her own hair.

The only woman he had ever touched . . . The cripple flinched as he remembered that oath. How well he knew the seduction of that hilt that fit the grip of his hand so perfectly as to make the Dark Sword another part of his arm. How well he knew the strange, exotic passion that had filled him every time he had raised her up . . . wielded her in battle.

Peerless, matchless sword.

"Murderer!" he whispered hoarsely, moving forward, then reaching out to clasp . . . Frigid cold that melted at once into potent, witch-warm magic. Invitation, he knew . . . Durandal, who had brought him power and glory and honor. And this . . . Tombs.

"Murderer!" he rasped loudly and drew back. "This is a fit place for thee! Secure from such as I once was!" A different edge crept into his voice. "I do not need thee to kill!" he grated brutally, then swung away to push back out through the portal of the cave.

To see again . . . It brought no absolution, he thought bitterly as he lurched awkwardly across the temple court, down the steps. He was not the same ambition-laden, belligerent boy he had been when he had first touched her. Now, he was other things . . . He struggled on across the clearing, then picked his way up tiny paths that wove through dense undergrowth, around the trees to lead up, out of the hidden gorge.

At the top, he stopped to look up, then toward the east. Now, he was lost, he knew. Lost for feelings that had not died after all. He grimaced painfully. Oliver's face, still so clearly seen in his mind, as though he were yet alive, made the sum of it.

Slowly, the cripple began to move onward, swinging himself toward the east. Away from Brittany, and the Count who knew him.

And in the cavern that had held her in bondage for so many years, the woman hilt of the Dark Sword began to stir. Her hands emerged from the chiton of her hair, and she began to stretch, to grow, merging with the eagle-winged hilt, then engulfing the long blade until her feet came to rest on dank stone. Lavender hues and soft, nocturnal blues played across her form as she turned toward the cave entrance and stared with eyes no longer obsidian and void.

He had come again . . . Roland.

But Roland changed to some unspeakable corporeal pestilence. Become a desecration . . . Tempests swirled through her hair as Durandal trod across the cavern to the overgrown entrance, reached out to touch the air beyond, and found her fingers were stopped as surely as before.

Mere air . . . and he had gone again. She felt nothing, not even the least aura. Her arched brows plummeted thunderously. Lightning flickered violence in the depths of her eyes.

"Nay!" she whispered distant thunder tones and flung herself against the insubstance that held her confined. Howled mistral fury as she was repelled.

But he had gone and left her, bound still.

"It shall rebound on thee, Durandal," the Owl had warned her all those granite-shrouded years before. ". . . he eludes thee . . . What use has a cripple for a sword?"

She poised.

"Turpin?" she hissed like steel across an anvil. "Where art thou? Who are thou become this time?"

But the echoes of her voice diffused into the surrounding stone and vanished. Night raptor and fey, and more elusive than any shadow, the Owl was the only other one who knew the truth.

Not even Roland who was buried beneath decaying meat and unreachable convictions.

"*Aaaarrrgh!*" she cried out, swirling to loose tempest fury and lightning shafts against the relentlessly impervious stone.

"Loose me from this place!"

Nestled against the bole of a gnarled old oak that grew near the northern cliffs of the hidden gorge, its plumage indistinguishable from the wood, a great tawny owl blinked once, ruffled its feathers, then closed its eyes to await the night.

EIGHT

793 A.D.

The snows had gone, and the first greens showed mist soft in the trees and on the ground. Spring had begun, Lord Thierry knew as he drew rein on the crest of the last wooded hill on the eastern side of the broad meadows where Bordeaux castle rose up like a great, pristine monument to dominate the landscape.

"We are virtually arrived, my lord," De Hauteville said quietly as he brought his horse to a halt beside the Count. Lord Thierry nodded response and nudged his horse forward, down a path that led between the last of the trees, toward another track that wound through the meadows beyond to the gates of Bordeaux. He heard Lord Amaury and the others behind him.

A distant kinsman, and disinclined to any conversational excesses, Lord Amaury had proved a quietly pleasant companion during the past weeks of travel, Lord Thierry acknowledged. Not like the brash and arrogant affect of De Baviere . . . He suppressed a frown as his horse walked along the track that led across the meadows before Bordeaux's southeastern walls. Somehow, De Hauteville made him think of the man he might have become, he knew. Always riding a pace or two back. Quiet, in a manner that suited his scholarly reputation, yet proud of carriage. Yet, Lord Thierry decided, it was the quiet of a man who would not be known. Secretive rather than contemplative . . .

Perhaps he would not have decided so, save for the sudden appearance of Lord Amaury's nephew, Baudoin De Maganze, who joined their company some five days before. Dark, and so much like his late sire, Lord Baudoin was an innocently willing youth, who demonstrated a curiously total capitulation to his uncle's every wish or thought.

Aye. Little incongruities, Lord Thierry thought.

He heard a shout and tightened his grip on the reins as his horse began to prance suddenly in response to the appearance of a single man on horseback, galloping recklessly toward them. He halted his mount and smiled briefly at the fluid horsemanship of the young man who rode toward them to bring his horse to a spirited halt. The flamboyance of youth . . .

"Ho!" the young man called out, moving his fine animal to within ten feet. "Who goes there . . . my lords?" Lord Thierry's smile widened at this mixed brashness and sudden discretion.

"We are come from the King to seek one Huon De Guienne, Duke of Bordeaux!" he pronounced clearly. Large, dark eyes in a strong young face flickered curiously as they read the arms upon surcoats and shields, then moved up to meet Lord Thierry's gaze.

"I am Huon De Guienne," the young man said smoothly, nudging his horse closer. "I bid thee welcome to Bordeaux . . ." His eyes continued to search them, Lord Thierry saw, in the manner of one unaccustomed to any save his own vassals.

"I am Thierry, Count of Brittany," he introduced himself, then moved a hand to indicate the others. "My lord, Amaury De Hauteville, and his nephew, Lord Baudoin De Maganze." The names meant nothing, he saw as bows were exchanged. "We are come upon the King's business, my lord."

"Then I greatly welcome thee, my lords," Lord Huon responded with prompt courtesy. "I am glad to offer thee such hospitality as is due the King's true liegemen." He turned his grey stallion about and led the way then, across the remaining stretch of meadow, toward the drawbridge. Across it, and into the great outer bailey of Bordeaux castle. Barked orders brought servants and groomsmen scurrying to attend them. Lord Thierry glanced at young Lord Baudoin as he dismounted and relinquished his horse, catching a look of simply impressed curiosity. Behind the youth, he caught a quickly disguised look of stern assessment as Lord Amaury stared after the powerfully made, richly clad young Duke Huon just before that individual turned to smile at them. He tucked a feeling of caution into his mind and strode toward Lord Huon.

"Chambers are even now being prepared for thy comfort, my lords," Duke Huon said, moving up the steps that led into the great keep. "For the present, I would offer refreshment . . ."

"Such would be most welcome, my lord," Lord Thierry said pleasantly. "The journey from Aix is a long one."

The young Duke's eyes met his curiously. "I understand, my lord. I was at Aix when but a young boy, too briefly to remember. I have not been beyond these fiefs since."

Lord Thierry nodded as he followed the younger man's carefully polite lead through the large oak doors into the keep. "It is to address that . . . isolation that we are, in part, dispatched here by the King," he offered.

Lord Huon stopped, his face suddenly eager. "I welcome any duty the King may require of me!" he said fervently, then held out a hand. "This way, my lords."

Like a blow, the precision of his memory, Lord Thierry thought as an hour later, changed from armor into clean and richer attire, he entered the vast and luxurious great hall of Bordeaux's keep. At the other end, the young Duke stood alertly at the foot of the long dais. In the center, and a little above him, a figure sat in a large chair. Lord Thierry glanced at Lord Amaury as the other joined him, and advanced across the stone floor. The figure on the dais stood up, poised and regal, a slim woman in richly embroidered robes of russet and gold, the fillet of her rank containing the sheer veil that covered her hair. The Duchess Alice . . .

As he reached the foot of the dais, Lord Thierry felt a violent sense of shock. The clarity of his memory showed how much time had stamped that exquisite beauty. Frail now . . . Sheer impulse converted his bow into a smooth drop to one knee as he reached for her small, outheld hand and bent to press his lips to the back of it. He looked up to meet her gaze.

"My lady, for Charlemagne, by Grace of God, King of all western Christendom, greeting." He loosed her hand and rose, his gaze still locked with hers.

"Bordeaux welcomes the King through his liegemen, my lord." Her response was assured and powerful. Then, very softly, her dark eyes searching him. "Thou are much changed I think, Thierry of Leon."

Lord Thierry felt heat rise up his neck. "I endeavor to keep faith with that example of wonderful and puissant honor we were fortunate enough to once know, my lady," he managed honestly. She stiffened, ghosts slipping across her eyes. He stepped back and to one side to make way for Lord Amaury and young Baudoin De Maganze. Watched the absolute regal dignity with which she received the proprieties of the pair, somehow turning them into supplicants, and remembered how Lord Oliver De Montglave had never been disheartened by any form of power. He understood, he thought, how Lord Oliver could have so loved this lady.

He heard a sound behind him and turned to catch sight of a pair of figures just emerged through a door in another corner of the great hall.

They approached, both richly clad, one tall and lithe, the other shorter and in girl's attire. Lord Thierry's eyes widened. His breathing suspended, and he felt as if he'd been kicked in the midsection by a horse.

Impossibly vivid ghosts . . . Nay. Not ghosts, but alive. It was Lord Oliver who trod toward him with supple grace and, aye, that same generous smile. Whose unforgettable sea-blue eyes bore the same look of gentle curiosity.

Another shock in the change that had come over Lord Huon's face as he stepped forward. Cold now. Remote and withdrawn.

"My lord Thierry, Count of Brittany," the young Duke introduced in clipped tones. "My brother, Girard De Guienne, and my sister, the Lady Olivia De Montglave." Lord Thierry managed a bow and tore his eyes away from Oliver, reborn in this youth who stood before him, to look at the girl. He felt another surge of shock, for she was an exact replica for the Lady Aude De Montglave. But this was Oliver's daughter, he reminded himself forcefully, straightening.

"My lord . . ." The girl curtsied and lowered her gaze, as shy as Oliver's sister had been.

"Well met, my lord," Girard spoke then. Even his voice, Lord Thierry thought, inhaling deeply. "We are honored to welcome the King's Champion."

"It is a mutual honor, my lord," Lord Thierry found a reply. "The repute of Bordeaux is without stain or blemish." Young Lord Girard's open smile provided reply as Lord Thierry caught the hard look in his brother's eyes behind him. Half brother, he knew then . . .

"It is time for hospitality and refreshment, my lords." The Duchess took control with clear authority, flicking imperious fingers toward the watchful obscurity of nearby servants. "Bordeaux must welcome the King's liegemen in a suitable fashion. There will be time enough later to attend to the reasons for thy journey!" Lord Thierry turned, his poise recovered, then caught the youthfully hypnotized fascination with which young Baudoin De Maganze stared at the Lady Olivia. He smiled.

"She is glorious . . . !" Baudoin breathed as he adjusted the cloak pin that fastened that garment to his shoulders.

Preoccupied, Lord Amaury frowned. "Who?"

"The Lady Olivia!" Baudoin looked his surprise at his uncle's obtuseness. Attentive then, and aware of his purpose in requiring his nephew's presence, Lord Amaury found an answering smile.

"Aye, Baudoin," he said softly. "She is most fair. And," he added clearly, "well dowered with fiefs near adjoining thy own." Caught between the enchantment of his new infatuation and this sudden, practicable suggestion of an alliance, Baudoin flushed. "It will do no harm for the lady to discover a like passion for thee!" Lord Amaury pointed out with some asperity. His color heightening further, Baudoin looked away. He understood the implicit order very well. Like most of his uncle's instructions, this too was indirectly stated, but intended to be absolute. He bit back questions concerning the difference between bedding a willing serf girl, as he had recently discovered how to do, and the much more ominous task of wooing a lady of such high estate as the Lady Olivia. A lady, moreover, who was well guarded by a pair of powerful brothers. He flinched as he caught his uncle's impatient look, and fled the chamber.

Noting the discreet quiet with which the door closed behind his nephew, Lord Amaury's frown deepened. I have erred, he thought. I have seen him trained and schooled. I have shielded him from the world, and now he is a rabbit!

He continued to frown as he crossed the chamber, then stopped by the casement to stare out through the single window to where the morning sun danced across the lands beyond Bordeaux's outer walls.

I am losing my patience, he admitted to himself.

Beyond the conventions of propriety for host to guest, the Lady Alice had not acknowledged him by so much as the least fraction. He, who had openly wooed her . . . His fingers curled to make taut fists at his sides. Instead, she had given all her interest to the Champion on the pretext of shared remembrances of times long past.

Yet he had learned what he wished to know. The look of shock upon the Champion's face as he first met young Girard De Guienne had answered any doubts or questions that remained concerning that individual's true paternity. Lord Thierry had once served Oliver De Montglave, he knew.

And Lord Amaury had caught the watchful, cold closing of the young Duke's face as he saw the Champion meet his brother. Lord Huon knew the truth. Raged in silence over it . . . Useful? Perhaps.

Nor, beyond his initial shock and understanding, had the Champion given any other indication that he knew the truth of the bastard Girard's origins. Instead, he had adroitly occupied the evening hours with sociable conversations and pleasantries on all manner of subjects. Conspiracy? Girard De Guienne had powerful friends.

With a violent sigh, Lord Amaury composed himself as he turned away from the window, resuming the pleasant manners and discretion proper to a guest as he left the chamber.

His succinct narrative of his own history concluded, Lord Thierry fell silent and stood very still as the Lady Alice moved away from him, turned, and seated herself on a stone bench amid the new budding vegetation of the arbor. She looked up at him.

"I was correct, my lord. Thou are greatly changed," she said quietly. He inclined his head.

"I have been fortunate, my lady," he acknowledged, holding her look with his own, finding mutual understanding. Her eyes probed him then.

"Thou saw," she stated.

"He is his father, born again, thy son," he told her truthfully. "He does not know, I think?"

She looked down to fingers that interlaced over the gold and amber of her girdle. "He does not even imagine."

Lord Thierry inhaled deeply, slowly. "Huon is aware . . . ?" he pursued.

"Aye," she whispered.

And here they were, he thought, watching her. Two aging and duty-laden people with curiously remote, yet entangled histories, becoming intimate on the matter of their children.

"Has he always known?" he asked gently. She looked up and sighed.

"Nay. He discovered it for himself but a few months past."

"There are difficulties, I see."

Tension and unhappiness slipped across the curves of her mouth. "He is torn between his love for his brother, as he has always known Girard to be, and his betrayal by myself. He is Servinus' son . . ." That summed it, Lord Thierry thought, and inclined his head.

"However got, and cognizant of his heritage, the King hath no small consideration for the welfare of young Lord Girard, or for the promise of value inherent in his blood," he offered then, privately imparted information. "Being, after a fashion, parent to the greater child of the realm, the King knows full well the worth of such a shining honor as was embodied in Lord Oliver. He grieves still . . . And hopes . . ." he added. She continued to look at him, searching.

"I have a care for my children," she stated.

Lord Thierry inclined his head. "It is well known, my lady."

"Girard is in every way his father's son."

"In part for that hope, the King requires both Lord Huon and Lord Girard to attend him at Aix La Chapelle, my lady. He intends to confirm Lord Huon in his inheritance . . ."

"And Girard?" she asked, standing once more.

"I do not know, my lady Alicia," he told her gently.

Her face froze suddenly. "I am Alice, my lord!" she said in icy tones. "That other name died with my lord!"

"Forgive me!" Lord Thierry bowed deeply in apology. She looked at him for a moment, austere and powerful, yet acutely frail and solitary. Her expression softened fractionally, then she turned away and left him to stand alone in the chill spring air.

Time enough later, he thought, to broach the matter of the approved alliance he sought for his daughter . . .

"I swear"—Girard grinned at his sister as he entered the family solar at the close of the evening three days later—"he follows thee about with all the moonstruck worship of an orphaned lamb!'' He bowed to his mother and sprawled comfortably in a chair. Olivia stiffened over her needlework but did not look up.

"Who?" she asked with icy disinterest. Girard's grin widened.

"Young Lord Baudoin De Maganze—as thou know well enough!'' he retorted and watched color rise along her throat.

"Pah! He is a boy!''

"He is man enough to woo thee!'' Girard pointed out truthfully. "Nor is he ill-looking! Indeed, he is most amiably disposed, and but needs to be removed from his uncle's rule, as I see it!''

She looked at him then. "He may woo as he will, Girard,'' she said forcefully. "But I will have none of the sons of my father's murderer!''

Girard shifted uncomfortably, needing to establish a fair-minded view. "I understand, Olivia,'' he said more seriously. "But I will not credit the son with the heinous misdeeds of the father . . .''

" 'Tis simple enough for thee, Girard,'' she cut in. "Thou are Servinus' son, and thus know different feelings on the matter!''

From his place by the fire, Huon stiffened visibly.

"True . . .'' Girard began, looking at his sister and leaning forward to pursue the debate.

"Enough!'' The Duchess' voice silenced him. Both turned to look at her. "We are not gathered to bicker over the attributes, or inherited treasons, that belong to the House of Maganze! Know that I will *never* countenance *any* alliance between the House of Guienne, and the blood of De Montglave, and that other!'' She had their undivided attention, the Duchess saw, settling back to fold her hands in her lap. Girard accepting. Olivia relieved. Huon alert, watchful. She moderated her tone.

"More importantly, know this,'' she continued. "These great lords were sent in courtesy for the worth of Bordeaux, to deliver the King's summons requiring both of thee, Huon and Girard, to attend the Court at Aix La Chapelle!''

Huon didn't even blink. Girard's eyes widened in surprise.

"What could the King wish of me?'' he asked. "Huon, well, I understand, but . . . ?''

Again, she cut him off. "That is for the King to know! These lords depart for Aix on the morrow, and will convey word to the King of Bordeaux's obedience. Huon, Girard, thou shall prepare to follow as immediately as may be arranged.'' Huon nodded briefly.

Girard murmured acceptance, ''Of a certainty . . .''

''There is one other matter,'' the Duchess went on, her eyes passing from one son to the other. ''Assured of the King's wishes, my lord Thierry, Count of Brittany, has proposed an alliance between our names and fiefs such that would strengthen and benefit both most profitably. I have accepted.''

Huon moved away from the fire, his stare intent. ''What alliance is that, Mother?'' he asked quietly. She met his look.

''Lord Thierry wishes to wed his daughter, his eldest child, the Lady Gharis, to Girard,'' she stated very clearly. ''I have agreed.''

''Me . . . ?'' Girard rasped astonishment. Huon's eyes widened briefly, then narrowed to something hard and suspicious. ''Why me? What about Huon? He is Duke of Bordeaux, after all . . .''

''Just so, Girard,'' the Duchess responded at once. ''As Duke of such a vast demesne as Bordeaux, and by his rank, which is second only to prince, Huon's marriage is a matter of state and must be decreed by the King. Understanding this, Lord Thierry proposed a different alliance to link Brittany and Bordeaux through both thy inheritance of my dower estates and manors, and the blood of our respective houses.'' Girard was silent. Huon did not move at all.

Olivia giggled. ''Now thou have real reason to fret over the subject of wooing, Girard!'' she retorted. Seeing Huon's poised stillness, the Duchess frowned.

''Enough!'' she commanded. ''Go thou, Olivia, Girard, and banter elsewhere!'' Olivia grinned more broadly at her brother's expression as they both obediently stood and moved to leave the chamber. Girard smiled uncertainly as he reached the door and shot a dry look at his brother.

''Truly, Huon. I had hoped to learn from thy example in this too!'' he said, slipped through the door, and disappeared.

Huon scowled, but still did not move. The Duchess watched him, keenly aware of his new, frigid quiet.

''I am *not* a fool to be duped and toyed with!'' Huon erupted with sudden violence, glaring at her. ''The Count of Brittany is the King's honored Champion and may wed his girl wheresoever he chooses! Nay! It is some other thing that brews here! I saw for myself, the instant he saw Girard, Lord Thierry knew the truth of his getting!''

"As Lord Thierry squired my late Lord Oliver before his own knighthood all those years ago, it is no surprise that he should see the resemblance!'' the Duchess began with asperity. Huon moved to loom over her.

"Do not play games with me, Mother!'' he snarled. "I think something is afoot here that extends even to the King!''

"I am sure that Charlemagne himself has always known the truth of Girard's begetting!'' she countered icily. "And I know the King will always give precedence to the worth of the man over his origins . . .''

Huon's eyes accused her. "Aye! Mark the *bastard* Count Roland!'' he stressed, aware of thoughts that had been provoked by conversation with Lord Amaury on the same. "I have the right of it!'' he affirmed harshly, staring at her face gone ashen and frigid.

"As I have said before, Huon,'' she retorted. "There is no cause for thy distempered, even jealous displays over thy brother's origins!''

"I note this secretive and unnatural near worship of the dead De Montglave!'' he shot back. "It is simple enough, my lady. I have a care for *my* father's name! I'll not see that buried beneath falsehood and deception!''

"Then desist upon this course! Thy father's reputation is unblemished, Huon, and so remains! Mark me well. Do thou continue so, thou will make a foe of thy brother to the damage of thy own interests! Do thou forget that his devotion to thee serves the strength of Bordeaux? *That* is of tantamount importance . . .''

He did not answer that, but strode past her to thrust himself from the solar. The door slammed behind him like a blow.

Alone, minutes later, in the privacy of his own sleeping chamber, Huon crossed the room, stopped by the casement, then pushed open the wooden shutters that held the night at bay.

The outrage of desecrated trust. Broken faith . . . His mother, who found no fault with her sin. And Girard, whose devotion was tempered by wariness of late, still looked at him with simpleton ignorance. A tool, he thought, waiting to be used. Aye, he'd learned much from his conversations with the intriguingly brilliant Lord Amaury over the past several days on the affairs of the Court and the men there. He had come to perceive quagmire difficulties that could well smother his own name—and life.

Now, this alliance between Brittany and his brother? It was a proof that others sought to disinherit him through the person of Girard. To obliterate the last pure De Guienne blood . . .

Lord Amaury had remarked upon the conspicuous differences between the two. Surely to be recognized as well by others when he and Girard stood before the King at Aix.

What then . . . ?

What then?

NINE

Candles flickered on the great oak table that dominated the isolated antechamber, responding to the light breeze that wafted in through the single narrow window on the other side. Prince Charlot seated himself with possessive arrogance in the chair across the table, and behind him, Lord Geoffrey stood watchfully. Lord Amaury met the Prince's mistrustful stare with openfaced steadiness. Critical, this encounter after nine weeks of absence.

"That first strategy we devised must be changed, Highness—my lord," he said with conviction. "I have learned much. It will not serve to dispose of Lord Huon on the eastern frontier *after* he has come to Court." De Baviere shifted his stance. The Prince frowned. Lord Amaury continued with thoughtful care, "Hear me well. I no longer underrate the extent of the King's protective interest as it embraces the House of De Guienne. Destroy Lord Huon and, assuredly, the younger, bastard brother will take his place. I have seen how Lord Girard's appearance proclaims his paternity. I have also seen the absolute silence of the Duke's vassals on the matter . . .

"And . . ." he stressed it, "Lord Girard has a powerful ally. Even now, he is betrothed to the Count of Brittany's daughter." Lord Geoffrey stiffened, his expression hardening. Lord Amaury inhaled. "Nay. Lord Girard must be dispatched for the King to countenance an alliance between Lord Geoffrey and the Count of Brittany—as would be most beneficial to thee, Highness . . ."

He bowed fractionally. "Now. Can Lord Huon be made a traitor proven *before* he reaches Court, then Bordeaux is much more readily taken!" The Prince leaned forward, interested.

"How, my lord?" De Baviere spoke. Lord Amaury met his look.

"With both heirs gone, only the Lady Alice remains. She must be wed then, and Bordeaux given to a new lord."

Cynical recognition crossed Prince Charlot's face. "And who should this lord be, I wonder?" he murmured.

"Myself, Highness!" Lord Amaury responded smoothly and at once.

"Aaah! It gets back to that, then!" the Prince sneered.

Lord Amaury shrugged. "Even so, Highness. As Lord of Bordeaux, I would wed my nephew Baudoin to the Lady Olivia and, thereby, consolidate an alliance between Bordeaux and the fiefs of Hauteville, Maganze, and Montglave. Verily, is that not a kingdom of itself to lay before thee . . . ?" He bowed again, more deeply.

Prince Charlot searched him for some moments with narrowed, thoughtful eyes. "It would serve, my lord!" he said eventually, his young face intent and cunning. "Aye. It would serve!"

Lord Amaury leaned forward, meeting the look with an intensity of his own. "Heed the importance of this detail, Highness. Neither Lord Huon, nor his brother, must be allowed to reach Aix. For the least case, should one survive, then he must be a proven traitor beyond any refutation!"

"Aye. 'Tis sensible!" Lord Geoffrey murmured.

The Prince glanced at him, then returned his gaze to Lord Amaury. "How may all this be accomplished?" he asked then.

Lord Amaury smiled very slowly. "What more terrible treason may there be, my Prince, than an assault upon thy person, and the future embodied therein?" he asked softly. Behind the Prince, Lord Geoffrey's eyes widened. Lord Amaury continued, "Even now, Duke Huon and his brother journey to Aix to answer the King's summons. Girard is a mere boy, untried. Easily killed. Lord Huon is fiercely tempered and rigid in his honor. I think he may be easily coaxed to assault, and thereby induced to treason!"

"He could not be such a fool!" Lord Geoffrey broke in. Lord Amaury's eyes glinted as he met the younger man's stare.

"Easily—if he did not know the true identity of the one he assaults!" he pointed out smoothly.

Prince Charlot lunged to his feet, then he began to smile.

"Aye. Who other than myself!" He gave Lord Amaury an honestly appreciative look. "Simple enough, while . . . hunting, to arrange a disguise that may be later removed and disposed!"

Lord Geoffrey frowned. "Thy person would be put at risk, Highness. Lord Huon is no longer a boy . . ." The Prince stiffened at the implication.

Lord Amaury shrugged. "Highness. As I have witnessed, Lord Huon's training has never got beyond the practice field. Bordeaux is too well managed for that!"

The Prince nodded, soothed. He had learned on the frontiers the vast differences between the training of skills and the actual practice of war. That and, he understood at once, the possibilities that could be garnered from his father by such risk.

"I am content with that!" he said, glanced at Lord Geoffrey, and grinned. "Aye, my lord. In a pair of days, we shall go . . . ahunting!"

"I would be honored to accompany, Highness?" Lord Amaury asked before De Baviere could remark.

The Prince looked at him, brows arching, eyes hard. "Thou, scholar?"

"I am not unskilled, Highness."

"So be it!" the Prince conceded generously, then strode from the chamber and closed the door behind him.

Straightening from an obeisance that had gone unnoticed, De Baviere exhaled loudly and searched De Hauteville's face as the older man stared after the vanished Prince.

"It is hazardous, this scheme . . ." he ventured.

"Is it?" Lord Amaury countered softly, meeting his look.

De Baviere frowned. "The Prince's very life is at stake, resting entirely on thy assessment of the skills of these De Guiennes . . . !" His eyes widened slowly as Lord Amaury continued to stare at him. "Mother of God!" he swore then. "It is a deeper game than I conceived by far . . . my lord!" he rasped. Lord Amaury's dark eyes were filled with malevolent resolve. "Thou would see Prince Charlot killed!" De Baviere breathed it.

Lord Amaury did not respond at once. Then, when he spoke, his tone was appallingly deliberate. Quiet. Reasoned. "What kind of king, my lord, do thou consider Prince Charlot would be? I know him as thou may not! He is no Charlemagne . . .

He is sly and avaricious . . ." Contempt slid like threads of
color through his voice. "Better for us both, my lord, were
Prince Louis to inherit. He is honest and pious and . . . generous!"

Lord Geoffrey stared in frozen fascination at the man before
him. Finally, he exhaled with audible violence.

"How are thou come to this presumption?" he asked.

"Who else could know these princes better than the one who
taught them?" Lord Amaury countered reasonably. "I am not
an ignorant man!"

Lord Geoffrey flushed, suddenly conscious of his own limited
capacity for reading and writing. Then, "Shall we have our wish
then, my lord?" he ventured toward agreement. "I will have
the Lady Gharis and the office of Champion. Thou will have
Bordeaux . . . ?"

Lord Amaury inclined his head. "Who will deny us, my
lord?" he countered softly.

Lord Geoffrey was silent for a time. Then his mouth became
a resolute slash. "No one . . ." he answered.

Lord Amaury bowed with terrible grace. "No one at all!" he
sealed it very softly.

Within three more days, they would reach Aix La Chapelle,
Girard knew, setting his favorite falcon on the pommel of his
saddle, then loosing his cloak to bind it to the pack behind him.
He recovered the bird, winding the jesses through the gauntleted
fingers of his right hand, and inhaled deeply, welcoming the
fresh, sweet warm air that blew against his face and the open
throat of his tunic.

Lush, bright new greens made clouds of burgeoning growth
to cover the branches of the trees. Thick new grasses carpeted
the meadows and gullies like dense, living velvet . . . And blos-
soms nestled here and there amid the rest, offering perfumes and
color in the early summer. Beautiful . . . He had enjoyed the
past weeks of continual travel, Girard knew. Riding across hereto
unseen parts of the realm, enjoying the hospitality of new manors and people, and, in less populous areas, camping under a
brilliant dusting of stars, scattered across a velvet dark sky. He
glanced back to where Huon rode a horse's length behind, at the
head of their small company of men at arms and servants.

The pleasantry he had intended to utter died on his lips.

"I favor some hawking while we ride," he said instead. Huon

nodded but did not remark. Girard turned forward in his saddle and, with a grimace of regret, nudged his horse forward, and removed the hood from his peregrine. He and his brother grew ever more distant, he thought unhappily, loosing the jesses that held the bird, then lofting her. The falcon took flight, lofting rapidly to spiral above him, becoming a dark speck against the brilliant blue of the sky.

Girard nudged his horse again, and grinned as the animal broke into a precisely obedient canter. It had taken most of the some four hundred and fifty odd miles they had journeyed thus far to damp the young stallion's passionate exuberance at the faster paces. His body flowing with the horse's movement as the animal swept down a long hill toward a large meadow, he raised a hand to shield his eyes against the glare of the sun and watched his bird.

The falcon circled once, above the clustered trees that grew on the northern slope of the next rise, then glided toward the meadow on the crest of the hill beyond. It cried out once. Girard answered it, then leaned forward as his horse catapulted across a small wash gorge and bolted across the turf toward the gap in the trees . . .

Huddled for concealment in the undergrowth on the wooded rise, a ragged creature started at the sound of that harsh, keening outcry. With awkward stealth, and unwilling to be discovered by the two mounted men he knew were lurking in the trees on either side of the gap, the cripple shifted to part the tangled branches before him. He stiffened, eyes widening slowly as he watched the approach of an unarmed, richly clad figure on a lanky great horse, galloping across the meadow below toward him. He blinked, then stared transfixed, his eagle-keen vision seeing familiarity in the bareheaded youth with his tawny brown hair and blue eyes. He knew . . .

He heard a movement behind him and froze. Armed knights bent on ambush, not hunting, he realized. There was a sudden crashing as a horse erupted into motion, and then he saw a tall, muscular knight thunder down toward the youth, lance at an angle, lowering smoothly to point at the unarmed man's breast.

Totally astounded, Girard brought his horse to a plunging halt as a fully armed knight on a burly dark warhorse exploded from the trees and charged downhill toward him. He caught a brief glimpse of an unmarked shield, glittering, cold blue eyes on either side of the nasal of the helm. Lowered lance—its point aimed for his breast. Girard opened his mouth to call out, but the knight swept toward him, mere yards away. He slammed his heels into the young horse's sides, sending it forward, making it veer. He saved himself by slinging his weight over onto his mount's off side. Searing pain ripped through his left thigh. He gasped. Jerked himself violently back into the saddle. Unbalanced, the young horse stumbled, floundering badly. Hauling hard on the reins, he kept the animal from falling, then turned it . . .

Cried out . . . Raw agony pierced his middle, stripping the very air from his lungs. Something massive thundered by. There was a cracking sound, and pain redoubled to tear him apart. He saw the broken point of a lance fall away, tried to find his reins . . .

Everything reeled. So many colors . . . and he could not feel anything at all. The sky was brilliant as he fell away from it. Collided with something . . . shattered into darkness.

"Mother of God!" Huon rasped as he reached the crest of the southern hill, saw Girard tumbled away from his horse like a heap of murdered rags. The young stallion bolted in panic, and the knight who had assaulted his defenseless brother slowed his destrier, discarded his broken lance, and drew his sword.

Sheer reflexive outrage . . . Huon reached for the shield on his saddle bow, drew his own sword, and sank spur.

"Who are thou, murderer?" he roared as his stallion careened down the hill toward the knight.

"Thierry of Ardennes!" the other barked back across the space between them. "I right the wrongs thy sire committed against my house, foul Bordeaux!" Meaningless name, and the grudge claim. Huon roared his father's battle cry and lofted his sword. Raised his shield, and swing his blade down as he reached the other knight. The other swept past him as his sword skeetered along the blade that met it. He swung his own horse about. Sent it charging uphill to where the other turned his mount, then made the beast leap down . . . Nay. He knew that stroke. He ducked and used his shield to deflect the blow. Gasped as the thing slammed against his shoulder and split. He shook it off his arm and sent his horse up through the gap between the trees, buying time enough to wrap his cloak around his arm as he heard the other knight's thunderous pursuit.

He galloped around a lone tree in the clearing beyond, reined his mount, and gathered the beast as the other knight shifted to accommodate the change of direction, then charged.

"Butcher!" Huon roared. "Thou'll not have me as well!"

He dropped the bridle, trusting his stallion's training, and, his sword twirling in his right hand, raised the other to fling his cloak up as the stallion bore down upon the other. It flung its weight to jolt the dark horse, and the cloak swept up to tangle with the knight's sword. At the same time, he brought his own blade across and under the other's upraised arm, gambling with all the strength in him. He felt the jar as the weapon slashed through mail, then flesh. Heard a high-pitched astonished howl as his horse swept him past.

He jerked, clinging to the weapon he must not lose, and felt it come free. He tightened his grip, and recovered the reins to bring his horse about again.

The other reeled in the saddle, his shield falling slowly from an arm gone abruptly lax as the knight's horse crested the hill, slowed, then disappeared from view. Instinct sent Huon in pursuit. Sword held firmly, he charged up the rise, then drew his animal to another halt as he saw the murderous knight tumble away from his saddle, then land to lie half concealed by the tall grasses of the clearing. Its rider gone, the dark warhorse stopped in confusion.

Huon flung himself from his saddle and strode to where the body lay. Dead . . . His blow had splintered ribs, driven armor into a lung to make a bloody hash beneath surcoat and hauberk. He did not care as he caught the look of surprise that held the dead man's blue eyes wide open, his mouth, filled with bloody froth, agape.

"This is just!" Huon hissed. "To wreak murder upon an unarmed man!" He shivered then, swallowed awkwardly. "My brother . . ." he whispered slowly as multitude realizations slammed like hammer blows across his consciousness. "Girard did not deserve such a fate . . ."

He turned away and, recovering his horse, walked down the hill, through the gap in the trees, to that other meadow.

Recognition . . . what he saw. Uncaring of the two who fought and swept on up the hill to disappear over the crest of the hill behind him, aware of the third mounted knight who still lurked secretively in the trees on the other side of the gap, the cripple lurched up onto his crutches and jerked recklessly through the undergrowth, then tall grasses, down to where the youth had fallen a few yards distant.

He glanced toward the southern hill and saw the small retinue of the Lord of Bordeaux scramble to recover the loose, panicked horse, then begin to approach. He stopped above the body that lay scarlet bloody in the turf, and froze.

Raw shock . . . Nay. Aye.

Oliver! Murdered again . . . Abandoning his crutches, the cripple dropped down beside the long, bloody form and reached out to touch . . . Oliver. Real, and young . . . Bordeaux. Wits scrambled to remember across feelings gone awry for the ferocity of their passion. Oliver, who was alive after all, in the person of his son . . .

Flesh . . . The cripple's fingertips traced across the face. Not stone. Nor decay. He found the wound that ripped apart the young man's flank. Blood oozed in lethal rivers to soak the fine blue wool of his tunic. His hands clutched at the cloth, pressed against the torn, gaping place to staunch the flow . . . So precious, this blood.

"Thou shall not die!" he whispered hoarsely. "Thou shall not die. Not again! For God, not again!"

There was a low moan, and the eyes before him fluttered open to see, incompletely focused. Even their color . . . Oliver. Precious, puissant Oliver.

"Thou shall not die!" the cripple grated passionately. The eyes found him, widened in a curiously remote surprise, then dulled for pain and closed once more. The cripple gasped, looked down. The blood seeped between his desperately clutching, hideously scaled fingers, began to clump, and thicken. Stop. He thought. Stop . . .

He heard a shout and looked up at the men who rushed toward him. Stopping abruptly to pale and shudder at the sight of his face.

"Leper! Aaah . . . Sweet Jesu! 'Tis a leper!" Tangled, unimportant cries of revulsion. Only one thing mattered . . .

Something pricked against his back.

"Get away from my brother!" Growled menace, and he jerked his head around to see the grim, sweaty face of a dark-haired young man whose well-bloodied sword prodded against him. He looked back at the face he knew so well. Loved . . . Everything focused as he pressed against the wound. Absolute and honed, his will . . .

"Thou shall not die!" he rasped again. Plea. Command . . . He hardly felt the blow that knocked him away, or the hand that clutched at his ragged clothing and flung him asprawl in the grass, or the reflex that caused him to curl protectively around the hidden lyre against his middle.

"Get away from my brother!" Huon roared again, delivering a propelling kick to the hideous apparition. Then, driving his sword point first into the sod, he dropped down beside Girard, saw the terrible wound that ripped his brother's flank apart. Contaminated now, by the ghastly leper's hands.

There was a low, awkward gasp. Girard's eyes opened, flickered a little, then focused. Then, incredibly, Girard smiled a little.

"Ah, Huon . . . Thou are safe . . ." he whispered, then lost consciousness once more. Jolted to the core, Huon raised his head and barked harsh orders for a fire to cauterize, for a litter to be built.

His eyes dropped to his brother's wound again. His brother, aye . . . There was blood everywhere, but no longer flowing. Girard still breathed, if faintly. He could not survive such as this, Huon thought desperately. Belly wounds always killed by inflamation that no physician could prevent . . .

"Thou are avenged already!" he whispered it. Frowned. "By God, the King shall know of this injustice!"

Without his crutches, and hardly aware that he did so, the cripple crawled away to stop and sit against a thicket at the edge of the woods. He stared back toward that atrociously injured and . . . aye, so important youth.

"Thou shall not die . . . Not this time," whispered fiercely. More than prayer, more than litany, it wove circles of meaning through the air of his mind.

And, when at last, they raised the youth and set him on a litter contrived of cloaks and lances and moved away to disappear over the hill to the north and east . . . he bowed his head, huddled down, and looked at his own hands, covered now in blood turned brown and dry.

Oliver's blood.

Nay . . . He had never forgot the nightmares sprung from that small, toddling boy who had rushed so eagerly at him in the bailey of Bordeaux castle all those years ago, crowing, "Fairy. Fairy man!" Who had seen what he could not bear to know . . . The same as this, but grown now, like memory given form because he could not set it free . . .

He was alone, the cripple realized when he raised his head at last. Not quite . . . He watched a falcon plummet, jesses trailing, toward some small prey concealed in the grasses on the southern slopes of the rise across the meadow. It disappeared, and he heard its cry of triumph. Oliver had enjoyed falconry, he thought . . . so too, his son. He shifted and crawled toward his crutches. And as he reached the staves, then hauled himself upright, he heard the bird cry out again. In distress—he turned toward the sound and saw a flurried blur on the far hill. Its jesses had tangled, he knew, and began at once to swing himself toward it.

A fine peregrine, he saw as he reached it. Its jesses were caught about the large hare it had killed. It looked up at him, fierce-eyed and watchful. He crouched down slowly, reached for the bird, then loosed it by unwinding the jesses from about its legs.

Remembered another time, long ago, with Oliver . . .

"Thou shall go free, I think," he whispered awkwardly. But the bird hopped forward to clutch his forearm with its talons. Truly tamed. He flinched, remembering Oliver's special way with raptors . . . and other things.

And the child's name was Girard.

"Go!" he rasped urgently and lofted his arm to release the falcon. It took to the air with a cry, flew in a brief circle, then returned to land on the arm he reluctantly held out, pecking once at the dried blood on his hand. They shared that, he thought grimly.

He continued to sit there for a long time, festering and raw inside, gently stroking the peregrine's fine plumage.

If. Aye, it came to that . . . multiple ifs. Past and present. And future. Some hope to warrant the future. Subtle justice. And, perhaps, a little redemption.

Much later, he jerked himself upright on his crutches, and recovering the carcass of the hare to feed the bird, the falcon perched on his shoulder, he turned toward the west and began plodding methodically back the way he had come. Brittany first, he knew. Then Bordeaux.

It all depended on the life of that one youthful man who could not, must not die . . .

Lord Amaury waited until every last sound had died away. Then, when there was only the rustling of the leaves of the trees in the light breeze, he spurred his horse uphill, erupting into the meadow where he had last heard the sounds of combat.

Bursting through a thicket, he saw at once the Prince's burly destrier grazing with greedy preoccupation. He caught sight of a dark shape in the grass beyond the animal, pushed his mount forward, then flung himself from his horse to take the last two steps toward it.

He stopped, his mouth tightening.

Charlot lay sprawled on his back. Beneath his helm, the flies had already found the eyes and mouth of a grey face frozen into a look of total astonishment.

"Now thou have learned," Lord Amaury said with venomous satisfaction, "no man is secure. Not even a prince! What better expression could thou wear than amazement!" He knelt down carefully to examine the cloak that was wound around the Prince's sword. The blow that had driven clothing, armor, and ribs deep into the Prince's chest to make a mortal hash of it. He stood and quickly turned to the pack bound onto his horse's saddle. Loosed it, then set it on the ground beside the royal corpse and began rifling through its contents.

Within moments, he had replaced the unmarked surcoat with one that bore the Prince's arms. Had set the gold circlet of Charlot's rank on his helm. He stripped away the thin covering that concealed the painted arms on the Prince's shield, added a few details, then gathered up all the evidence of deceit and concealed them under an unlikely thicket at the edge of the woods. He walked back to his horse and took the hunting horn from the pommel, raised it to his lips, and blew upon it. Once . . . then again.

Lord Geoffrey would hear and understand, he knew as he went back to the corpse and knelt down to find an expression of appalled grief. Lord Geoffrey would bring the rest of the hunting party, would carry his own pretext of horror and shock into pure outrage as they got the body back to Aix.

How smoothly it had been accomplished . . .

TEN

Like a crown, and vaster than the enormous castle of Bordeaux, Aix La Chapelle rose up with wonderful and intricate complexity to gleam with a faintly golden hue in the afternoon sun. Lord Huon hardly noticed as he drew rein a quarter of a mile distant from its gates to stare briefly, furiously, at his destination.

Grimly, he looked down at his brother who lay unconscious between the exhausted men who bore his litter. Incredibly, Girard had not yet died during the past two days of travel. Instead, he lay there, breathing still—barely. Ragged, spasmodic efforts . . . Ashen-hued, and deep in a swoon, he was beginning to waste from the fever that consumed him.

"We go direct to the King!" Huon growled at his men, and sent his horse forward, down the hill.

The doors to the Council chamber burst open with a great thudding. And like a fierce wind that would not be stopped, Lord Huon pushed past the guards and strode across the floor, his eyes fixed on the ageless silver King, his men behind him. The sheer force of his determined intensity stopped the business that was being conducted, froze all gathered there to look at him.

He stopped before the dais and, instead of dropping to one knee in proper obeisance, held himself rigidly erect.

"I am come to require the King's justice!" he declared harshly, unheeding of the grating of chairs as Council members

94

rose and prepared to defend their King. Charlemagne arched his brows and stared back. Am I so old as to be amused by this uncouth brashness? he wondered. Jesu. He is Servinus all over again!

"Who art thou to so impertinently demand of us?" he asked in frigid tones. The dark eyes before him did not waver.

"I am Huon De Guienne, Duke of Bordeaux, come with my brother in answer to thy summons, Majesty. For that obedience, we were waylaid and attacked! My brother, who was unarmed, lies wounded unto death! And I, by God's will, am alive to proclaim this murder, and the foul killer slain by my own hand!"

Charlemagne stood. "We do not tolerate such uncouth, ill-tempered displays, Lord Huon!" he pronounced frigidly and stepped down from the dais. "Nor do we brook even implicit slurs upon our justice!" He moved forward to draw aside for himself the cloak that covered the body on the litter. Torn tunic and stained bandages against the flank made evidence . . . His gaze moved up to the ashen quiet face. He had expected resemblance, Charlemagne knew, but not to this exactitude . . . He spun around to face Lord Huon. "We understand the reason for thy hot words and indiscretion, my lord, and will pursue the matter later." He shifted to stare commandingly at his Champion. "For the present, let chirurgeons and leeches be brought to attend to the preservation of thy brother's life!" He shifted again to stare down the uncompromising, dark-haired young lord before him. Lord Huon dropped his gaze at last, and bowed. Charlemagne moved a hand, and Lord Thierry strode forward.

In the privacy of the large, finely appointed chamber that had been accorded them, Huon watched as the chirurgeon and his assistants worked silently over the feather bed on which Girard had been laid. They stripped and cleansed the body. Applied fine cautery to the wound, to those places that still tried to bleed a little.

The chirurgeon, a younger man than he had expected, turned to accept a jar from one of his servants and looked up.

"It is a very miracle that this youth still lives for such a wound, my lord," he said in slightly puzzled tones. Suddenly remembering that ghastly, vehement leper, Huon frowned uneasily. The chirurgeon reached into the jar and withdrew a handful of slimy little wriggling white things. Maggots, Huon knew at once, and swallowed revulsion as the physician turned back to his brother.

"These creatures, given by their design to feed upon putrefaction," the man explained, "will remove the same from this injury. In a day or so, they may be removed and the wound can be sewn. To do thusly now would seal in the humors and fever and assure his death . . ." He pressed his grim handful into Girard's mangled flank, and Huon looked away, totally repelled. A hand touched his shoulder.

"A revolting and unusual procedure, my lord. But it works very well. They do not consume good meat." Calmly spoken. Huon looked at the Count of Brittany. Behind them, the chamber door opened abruptly, and both men turned, bowing reflexively as Charlemagne entered. The King inclined his head and strode past them to stop and stare grimly down at the bed. The chirurgeon and his assistants bowed and melted back.

"Who did this vile thing?" Charlemagne demanded harshly, turning suddenly to lock gazes with Lord Huon.

"A knight without arms upon surcoat or shield to identify. He proclaimed himself to be one Thierry of Ardennes, seeking vengeance for some wrong my father wrought . . ." The King stiffened visibly, and Huon saw Lord Thierry's eyes widen as they sought the King's in some inexplicable exchange. Charlemagne turned to the chirurgeon.

"Attend this man with all care, physician," he ordered. "We have need of him!" He moved then, nodding toward the Count of Brittany, who moved at once to follow the King's departure from the chamber.

"There is no Thierry of Ardennes, my liege. Ardennes is ruled by Bevis De Aisne who wed the sole daughter of that line . . ." Huon stiffened as he caught the Champion's barely audible remark.

"We are aware, my lord . . ." The door closed on Charlemagne's quiet response.

Slowly, Huon's eyes widened. He inhaled awkwardly and moved to stand by his brother's side, ignoring the chirurgeon's attentive fussing. Ashen as stone, unmoving save for the awkward rise and fall of his ribs, Girard, by natural events, should be dead.

Feelings surged up to something potent, ugly and brutal. Brother . . . ? Huon thought. Clear enough, his course on the conviction that his brother would die. But now he felt it like something insidious and overwhelming, this secretive and protective aura that clung about this . . . aye, bastard. His half brother, no more.

That was his foe, this simmering brew of deceit.

Frowning, he flung away from the bed and strode from the chamber to find the great hall and the evening's assemblage of the Court. I am an honest man, he thought furiously as he strode along the corridors beyond, I will *not* dissemble!

Carefully holding the Prince's sword as he had found it, still tangled in the folds of the cloak, Lord Amaury rode grimly at the head of the returning party of hunters as he led the way through the gates of Aix. The clatter of horse's hooves died beneath swelling whispers and cries as people came rushing forward to stare at the Prince's stiffened corpse. Lord Amaury led the way into the inner bailey and drew rein before the main steps of the keep. He dismounted, still holding the principal evidence, and turned to the men behind him.

"Bring His Highness' remains," he ordered and waited as, with absolute silence, the others loosed the bonds that held Prince Charlot's body to the saddle of the stallion that still trembled and skittered beneath its grisly burden. Then, two to the legs, two to the shoulders, they lofted it between them, already blueing and rigid and beginning to swell.

Glancing at De Baviere, Lord Amaury turned and led the way up the steps, through doors that melted aside to admit him, past appalled faces, straight into the great hall, then down the length of it to where Charlemagne had risen. Stood now.

There, before the dais, Lord Amaury stopped and dropped to his knees.

"Prince Charlot is dead, Majesty!" he announced with somber clarity. "Most foully murdered!" A violent hiss swept through the Court as De Baviere dropped to his knees beside him. Behind, the huntsmen and others slowly lowered the Prince's corpse to the ground.

Charlemagne did not move as he stared down at the body, but the lines upon his harshly unreadable face deepened suddenly. Looking up, Lord Amaury saw, then stood. Stepped forward to hold out the Prince's sword. The silence was palpable.

"Here, my liege, in this cloak, is the evidence of the treachery used to kill the Prince!"

"How?" Awful, the tone.

"His Highness broke away from the rest of us as we chased

a stag, intent to pursue a boar he spotted. I caught sight and
gave chase. We were soon lost to the rest, and I soon separated
from His Highness as well. When I came upon him later, it was
to hear the sound of conflict. I saw him tumble from his horse
as I approached. Slain. Murdered, my liege''—he loosed the
cloak and held it out—''by some armored man who fled upon
catching sight of me . . .'' He turned quickly, searching faces,
then caught sight of the young Lord Huon standing near the edge
of the crowd to his right. He pointed. ''There!'' he called out
loudly. ''That is the one I saw!''

Charlemagne's frigid pale blue eyes shifted. Huon, astounded,
went rigid and began to pale as folk gasped, those close by
drawing back and away from him. He lunged forward then,
jerked to a stop beside the corpse, and stared down at the unmistakable face of the man who had assaulted Girard and himself.

''That is the knight who ambushed my brother and sought my
murder as well!'' he roared outraged protest, looking up toward
the King.

''Here is the King's own son, Prince Charlot, whose person
is sacred and accountable only to the will of God!'' Lord Amaury
countered furiously, stepping forward. ''What man could mistake the arms upon his breast? Or on the shield that he carried?
Nay, Majesty! This is foully wrought murder that I''—his tone
hoarsened briefly—''was unable to prevent!''

Huon stared in dawning realization at the scarlet and gold
dragons embroidered upon the Prince's torn and bloody surcoat.
Not there before. He looked up.

''This is a lie, Majesty! A contrivance . . . !'' he rasped it.
''I am Huon De Guienne. The honor of my house is beyond
refutation. My life is gladly given to my liege.''

''False protests!'' Lord Amaury's voice cut like an axe as he
once again held out the cloak. ''I witnessed the end of it when
the Prince sought to defend himself! Deny this!'' Huon stared
at the cloak. Knew it. ''Aaah!'' Lord Amaury hissed, reading
his face.

''These are all lies!'' Huon bellowed then. ''My brother and
I were ambushed by an unmarked knight who claimed to be one
Thierry of Ardennes . . .''

Again, Lord Amaury slashed across him. ''There is none such
of that name! Such a wild claim declares a desperate falsehood!
I say, my lord, thou are found out.''

"Silence!" Charlemagne's voice thundered across them all. Every soul froze at once to stare at him. He pointed to Huon of Bordeaux. "Take that one! Lock him away. We will see him disposed!" he ordered.

"I am unjustly accused . . ." Huon began, going for his sword hilt. But hands seized him, smothered his outcry, and stripped away his sword. Overpowered and bound him, then bore him, thrashing furiously, from the great hall.

Grief now, Lord Amaury thought deliberately as he caught the Count of Brittany's watchful stare, then bowed his head and inhaled deeply. He shivered a little, and dropped the evidence of the cloak as though he could no longer bear to touch it. Then, slowly, he held out the Prince's sword to De Baviere. Lord Geoffrey took it, his eyes searching briefly from a face gone strained and harsh. And as the King stepped down from the dais to stand above the body of his son, Lord Amaury answered the look, shuddered again, and turned toward the corpse.

"Come, my lord. We have another duty to our Prince," he whispered and crossed himself. He did not see the Champion's frown. Only Charlemagne, who strode away from the body and the great hall with impregnable self-containment.

Blue pale and naked, cleaned of grime and blood and the final oozings from bowel and bladder, the Prince's corpse lay still, grimly posed amid the fresh linen on his bed. The last stinking foul air had blown at last through the opened shutters of the window, into the night, and was now replaced by that peculiarly heavy, fetid sweetness that proclaimed the onset of decay.

"The rigor begins to pass, my lord." Brother Oborion looked up from manipulating the corpse's fingers. "He will soften by morning and be ready for proper arrangement."

From his place on the other side of the bed, Lord Amaury nodded. "So be it," he murmured. Behind him, De Baviere, who had watched through the whole process as well, half gagged, repelled by the pure, cold deliberation he heard.

"I must go," he managed awkwardly. "There are other things that require my attention." Lord Amaury turned to look searchingly at him. Their course was indisputably set now, he understood. His mouth tightened as he sketched a bow.

"Fare thee well, my lord," De Hauteville said with atrocious gentleness. De Baviere nodded and strode thankfully from the room.

Inside the chamber, hearing Lord Geoffrey's footsteps fade away, Lord Amaury sighed deeply and met the monk's large, bright eyes.

"I think young men are not hard enough for conspiracy," he murmured slowly. "They are too passionate and impatient!"

"Perhaps, my lord," Brother Oborion responded equably. "But that one was suckled and weaned on intrigue."

Lord Amaury moved his fingers to caress the corpse's cold, smooth skin. "Lord Huon, I do not doubt, will be executed on the morrow, and with Lord Girard dispatched as well, De Baviere will shortly have his way and the Count of Brittany's daughter!" he said.

"Girard De Guienne is not dead, my lord."

"What?" Lord Amaury rasped, stiffening.

"Grievously wounded, my lord—Prince Charlot accomplished that much. But Lord Girard is not yet dead and lies now in another chamber attended by the King's own physicians, and," the monk stressed it, "under the King's protection."

Lord Amaury's brows gathered in a thunderous frown and his mouth compressed into a vicious slash. "A pox . . . !" he began to hiss, then cut it off to glare at the monk. "Mayhap thou could contrive a posset or some such thing, to finish the business?"

Brother Oborion shook his head. "That would be rash at this time, my lord, and could well reveal thee."

Lord Amaury inhaled at the caution. "Aye . . ." he muttered, looking down at the Prince's corpse. The eyes were closed now, lids held down by weighted coins. Again, slowly, he began to stroke that cold, smooth boy's skin, examining the damage made by the mortal wound where the skin was torn and bone and meat showed through. "Aye . . ." he murmured thoughtfully. The monk moved to unfold another linen sheet to spread over the body. "Not yet," Lord Amaury whispered, looking up, his eyes glittering as they met the monk's. "This skin is still fresh enough," he said slowly. The monk poised watchfully, his gaze steady, bright. "Aye, and who will know when the body is spiced and garbed and set upon the bier for burial . . . I will have it!"

Brother Oborion cocked his head a little.

"I *will* have it!" Lord Amaury repeated forcefully.

"Better to let it rot with the rest, my lord," the monk murmured warily. "There are less conspicuous sources of parchment!"

"I have a different . . . and very particular use for it!" Lord Amaury hissed at once. "Or do thou demure for fear of tampering with a royal carcass, Brother Oborion?"

The monk smiled slowly. "There is naught that men may do to frighten me!" he said with melodious conviction.

Lord Amaury did not notice, his mind locked about his plan. "Then bring the hide to me as rapidly as thou may, and I will instruct thee then on its disposition. For my part, I will insure thou are undisturbed." He turned and strode to the door of the chamber, moved through it, and quietly closed it behind him.

Alone, his large eyes glinting canny and deep in the candle glow, the monk continued to stare after the departed De Hauteville. A peculiar smile chased across his wily, gnarled face. Amusement . . .

"Aaah! Little man!" he murmured delicately. "Little man! How precisely thou serve!"

He blinked once and looked down, reached with one hand and pointed to touch the Prince's corpse at the base of the throat. More neatly than if it were cut with a knife, the skin parted, gaped, as his finger traced down across the sternum and belly to the groin.

So easily done.

Fine tapestries adorned every wall with color and designs. Furs, scattered across the floor, covered the cold stone, and finely carved, beautifully inlaid furnishings bore testament to the presence of every convenience in the King's most private apartments.

Desolate luxury . . . Charlemagne sat staring at the hearth fire that burned on the other side of the chamber. No one came to disturb him here. Not his women, or his children. Even the pair of body servants moved like well-trained ghosts to attend to his requirements.

So it had been for the past decade and a half since Roncesvalles. Since he had confronted the son he wanted. Not dead. Worse than dead. Buried in anonymity.

Now, Charlot. Murdered . . . And he felt nothing at all, Charlemagne knew. Grief, like love, had been given to the other. The succession was decided now. It would come to Louis after all, unless he survived this last of his get . . . He stiffened and frowned at the sly creaking of a quietly opening door. Turned in his chair, prepared to curtly dismiss the servant who ventured to enter, and saw the Count of Brittany instead, poised at the entrance.

"It is death, my lord, to enter here without our leave!" he said in repelling tones, rising to his feet.

The Champion's face was resolute.

"Then I must be a dead man, my liege!" he responded, moving deliberately into the chamber, then waiting until the guards had closed the door behind him. "Loyalty, Majesty, compelled me to come with concern to thy interest."

Charlemagne inclined his head. "Speak, my lord."

"I am troubled by things that surround His Highness' violent demise . . ." Lord Thierry inhaled deeply. Charlemagne watched him. "I think there is grievous mischief afoot. Perhaps even some scheme that has gone awry . . . I am uncertain. But there is a contradiction between this accusation and the substantive proofs, and the equally evident injuries wrought to Bordeaux. Majesty. For all his brashness, Lord Huon is neither a fool, nor disloyal. I cannot conceive he would *knowingly* perpetrate such a deed. Indeed, that ignorance is his chiefmost claim to innocence. And Girard De Guienne may yet die of his wounds . . ."

Charlemagne cut frigidly across the Count's speech. "The Prince is dead of unnatural cause. A prince's person is sacrosanct, for therein lies the fate of a realm!" He could give his son this much, he thought. "For that alone, we will dispose even the accused to warn others—and there is evidence sufficient to do it."

Lord Thierry bowed his head to study the floor.

"I understand, my liege," he ventured carefully. "It is the evidence itself that I question." He looked up again to meet Charlemagne's stare. Continued, "Beyond that it is common enough to wear armor while hunting—as I do myself—but the arms of war such as I found on the Prince's horse? And what man could fail to recognize the arms upon that shield to know his Prince? Lord Huon stated most clearly that the knight that assaulted his brother and himself bore no emblem whatever on either breast or shield . . ." Charlemagne stood like granite. Lord Thierry frowned, then inhaled to finish it. "If the fate of a realm is ordained by God through the sanctity of His earthly princes, then too the guilt or innocence of a man before his accusers is assuredly decreed by God in the outcome of a battle between accused and accuser, for God is always just!''

The twin horns of the bull of faith, Charlemagne recognized, remaining silent for a time. Honest, this man . . .

''Old fox!'' he said very softly then. ''Thou, of all our vassals, know best the rightness of that!'' The Count looked down, his features shifting. It was a reference to that time when he had stood up to disclaim his uncle and defend the truth of the Song of Roland. Had won.

''Just so, my liege,'' he replied. Charlemagne turned away from him.

''So be it, my lord,'' the King said at length. ''We are well advised, and will act according.''

Lord Thierry bowed deeply.

''Go!'' Charlemagne said without looking back.

The Champion obeyed.

ELEVEN

There was little dignity left to the tall, dark-haired young Duke of Bordeaux as he was borne the length of the great hall, his wrists and ankles manacled, his clothing soiled and askew. Few missed the way his head turned and his eyes widened as he was hauled past the bier on which lay the peacefully composed, richly robed, and draped remains of Prince Charlot before being forced onto his knees before the King.

Charlemagne sat unmoving on his throne in the center of the dais. Beside him, on his right hand, sat the thin, solemn-faced boy who was now undisputed heir to the realm. The King shifted forward, his gaze dropping to the unkempt figure hunched before him.

"Huon De Guienne, Lord and entitled Duke of all the fiefs of Bordeaux," Charlemagne intoned with illusory quiet. "Thou are accused of the most heinous of crimes, the murder of Prince Charlot, heir to this realm!" Huon stared up into the King's implacable features. Tried to rise, to stand, but was prevented by the hands of guardsmen pressing on his shoulders.

"It is a lie, my liege!" he retorted loudly. "Not for my life, nor for any other thing, would I knowingly commit such treason!"

Charlemagne shifted forward. "Yet thou have confessed already, my lord!" he said harshly.

Again, Huon tried to lunge to his feet and was prevented. Instead, he called out with clear conviction. "I have admitted, and willingly, only to the just slaying of a knight who called himself Thierry of Ardennes, and who bore no arms upon shield or surcoat to identify him. Just, aye, for he had already felled my unarmed brother . . .'' His voice died away as the King sat back and looked up, past him.

"For the sake of the honor that has made the name of the House of De Guienne among the greatest of our realm, we require this man's accuser to stand before us now and affirm his testimony!'' Charlemagne pronounced then. Startled, Lord Amaury looked up from his place, half concealed amid the throng of the court. He had not expected this. His wits alert, he stepped through the crowd, then pointed at Lord Huon.

"I, Amaury De Hauteville, bear witness to the vile treachery that slew the Prince,'' he said with clarion assurance. "His Highness fought bravely, I cannot doubt, to his own defense. I witnessed the mortal blow, wrought by unchivalrous trickery that disarmed him with a cloak, then murdered him!''

"Lies!'' Lord Huon roared out, shivering with outrage and confusion as he glared at De Hauteville. He had not thought this man to be his foe. "I . . .'' he began.

"*Enough!*'' Charlemagne grated over it all. "An end to this wrangling! We will deliver proof of innocence or guilt into God's hands! With the rising of the sun on the morrow, thou, Lord Amaury De Hauteville, will prove the truth of thy accusation by trial of arms. Thou, Lord Huon, will engage to thy defense. God's truth will be provided in the outcome, and,'' he stressed, "the last confession of the man compelled to meet his Maker!'' The King stood as he finished, then stepped down from the dais to walk the length of the great hall, pausing briefly to bestow the kiss of peace on the brow of the dead Prince before abandoning them all.

Relief, or hope . . . Huon's shoulders straightened as he stared at Lord Amaury's cold face, his body acquiescing to the guards who pulled him to his feet. Scholar. Tutor . . . Aye, Huon thought. He would be vindicated on the morrow, his honor restored . . .

"Lock this man away again, and keep him so until I come to see him prepared for his trial!'' Startled, Huon jerked his head around and saw the King's Champion looking sternly at him. He scowled furiously at the Count as he was borne ignominiously backward out of the great hall to be returned to the dank, windowless chamber where he had been chained since the day before.

Lord Thierry grimaced faintly at the expression as he watched young Bordeaux being dragged away. He turned slowly, looking at the monks and others who had come to loft the dead Prince's bier and bear it away to the chapel before the burial mass. He paused then, his eyes narrowing as, beyond, on the far side of the great hall, he caught sight of Amaury De Hauteville and Geoffrey De Baviere together. There was a brief exchange, and the two parted.

Lord Thierry frowned. An unlikely pair. The scholar and that young vulture . . . De Baviere had been Charlot's friend, he recalled, his frown deepening. He was well aware of his own reaction to something on Lord Amaury's face, caught earlier when the king had pronounced trial by combat, causing him to take Lord Huon into his own custody.

He turned again and strode purposefully from the great hall.

"The fever does not abate, my lord, for all the wound is cleansed and sewn as well as may be." The physician shook his head unhappily. "Truly. That he lives still . . . That he hath endured so long. It is a very miracle, my lord. Nothing less." Lord Thierry nodded as he stood looking down at Girard De Guienne.

There was little evidence of miracles in the effort-filled, rasping breaths Girard took. Or in the pallor of his flesh, and the way it had melted into his bones to become an unsavory gauntness.

They could only wait . . . and pray, Lord Thierry thought, reaching to briefly touch that hot brow. He straightened and looked directly across the chamber to where Bordeaux's squire sat helplessly watching.

"How many came with my lord Duke?" Lord Thierry asked. The man stood at once.

"Four. And myself, my lord."

"Where are the rest?"

"With the horses, my lord. I am here, for my lord Duke is . . ."

"Aye. I know!" Lord Thierry cut him off, moving a pace or two closer. "Heed me well, then. Summon the others of Lord Huon's men. See that they are well armed and set them to guard the Lord Girard. No one may enter here, save the physicians, myself, or the King. At the first light of the morrow, thou, and thou alone, will come to me. I have another duty for thee then!''

Uncertainty flickered across the squire's face. ''My lord Duke . . . ?'' he began to question.

''I am no foe to the House of De Guienne!'' Lord Thierry said harshly. ''Do it!''

The servant bowed obedience, and Lord Thierry turned to stride briskly from the chamber. He had his own quiet methods for insuring justice.

Lord Amaury frowned at the evening light that filtered like scraps of sheet gold across the chamber to touch the stone of the floor but a foot in front of the chair in which he sat.

Had sat for more than a couple of hours now . . .

His fingertips traced across the exquisite pages of the newly completed and bound Aristotle. His finest work . . . Yet, for once, his craftsmanship brought no consolation. He closed the book and set it on the table beside him. His mouth tightened bitterly.

Still, he could not rid himself of this hauntingly pervasive sense of unease. Like a blow that shocked to the core . . . It had come unexpectedly at the end of the funeral mass for Prince Charlot when all the Court had assembled to watch his entombment in the chapel.

''Ganelon . . . !'' Duke Naimes had turned from the sarcophagus to welcome him with loud senility. ''How fitting thou art here!''

He had protested hoarsely his own name, but others had stared, stepped back. And he had fled. Aye, fled . . . those associations so obviously in the minds of others. The entrapment that closed still, like a vise around his life.

His nephew Baudoin, who would squire him on the morrow, stared at him with silently unhappy, puzzled preoccupation, until he could no longer bear the sight of the boy, and had grated brutal dismissal.

And Lord Geoffrey had become elusive of a sudden . . .

He did not fear the battle before him, Lord Amaury knew. For all his defeat of Prince Charlot, Lord Huon was still an untried boy, and he had the incalculable advantages of experience and cunning . . .

Lord Amaury stiffened as he heard a deliberate scuffling by the door, and swung around to watch it open.

Brother Oborion slipped through and closed the door quietly behind him. Glided lightly across the chamber to stop before De Hauteville.

"They are both well guarded, the De Guiennes, my lord," he announced. "The Count of Brittany has insured their protection."

Lord Amaury nodded tersely. He had expected as much. He changed the subject. "It is truly wonderful how thou contrived to keep the body from seeping," he murmured.

The monk inclined his head. "Wax!"

"And the other? Is it prepared as I have instructed?"

"I have it still," the monk responded smoothly.

Lord Amaury scowled and stood, his temper frayed. "This is not what I asked . . ." he began harshly.

"I am aware, my lord!" the monk interrupted with melodious authority, his large, dark eyes gleaming differently. "Ingenious as it may be to use the thing to discredit and condemn Prince Louis on the animosity between the two brothers, it is to serve a very different purpose!"

Lord Amaury went rigid, absorbing the blatant, even contemptuous disobedience, his only trust shattering. Fury swelled up.

"Who are thou to defy *me*, little monk!" he snarled. "Thou are my servant! It is not for thee to decide what may be done or not!"

Brother Oborion smiled. Lord Amaury's hand went to the dagger at his hip. Brother Oborion's smile widened.

Goaded beyond endurance, Lord Amaury drew the weapon. "Have done with thee, then! I'll tend the rest myself!" he hissed, lunged forward, and drove the weapon to the hilt into the old man's chest. "I have no need of thee!" he added and let go. Stepped back.

Blood did not appear on the monk's coarsely unkempt grey robe. Nor did he fall. Lord Amaury froze, his innards congealing . . .

Brother Oborion continued to stand there, smiling. The pupils of his eyes dilated until they obliterated the brown irises and made twin pools of mesmerizing, terrible, penetrating darkness. One gnarled hand came slowly up to close about the hilt of the dagger. Then he withdrew it and held it out to De Hauteville, the blade unstained.

Lord Amaury stood, transfixed by impossible terror.

"Who am *I*, little man?" the monk inquired with sinister gentleness. "I am thy master! I am the father of thy perversity! Thy teacher! It is thou who serve me!"

"Satan!" Lord Amaury gasped it.

Brother Oborion shook his head, amused as he moved forward to set the dagger on the table, then picked up the new-made Aristotle.

"Nothing so simple!" he denied softly, fingering the leaves of the book delicately. "Though, among my own, I have sometimes been called the Lord of Mischief!" he added. "Curious— for all thou have learned on the matter of parchment, thou hast never recognized this dead man's skin I wear!" He closed the book. "This is well prepared for my use," he murmured, and the volume disappeared into the loose folds of his robe.

Incoherent, overwhelming terror. Lord Amaury realized dimly that he was trembling. He thrust backward and sank with clumsy incapacity into his chair. Brother Oborion's smile was almost paternal as he stepped back toward the door.

"We must part now, my lord. I think we shall not meet again! I wish thee well in the fulfillment of thy ambitions!" Gently courteous, his tone stung like a scourge.

"Thou!" Lord Amaury rasped incoherently. "Thou have brought me to this, and now abandon me . . . ?"

His hand on the door latch, Brother Oborion shook his head again. "I do not interfere with the destiny of men, my lord. Thy fate is entirely in thy own hands!" he said, and disappeared.

Lord Amaury shuddered violently as though stricken with the ague. Fate . . . ? He stared at the wooden beams and blackened iron work that composed the door, unable to see anything else.

Temper went nowhere in a dungeon. Huon writhed to relieve the cramping tension in his bound arms. Futile. There was no relief. Nor any for the rage that consumed him. Only a virulent, consuming appetite for the battle that lay before him. Vindication—vengeance for his damaged honor.

Muffled thuds punctured the silence beyond the bolted door. There were abrasive scraping sounds, then he flinched as torchlight flared with abominable brightness to dispel the darkness.

"Bring him out!" Huon heard the voice. Blinked and shook his head. Hands clutched his already overstrained arms and jerked him upright. "This way!" It was still night, he realized as he was drawn forward, out of the cell.

"What is this?" he demanded, seeing then four armed men in unspecific livery.

"This way!" one repeated, ignoring him. And then he found himself propelled forward between them, forced to walk with short, scuffling steps for the chains that bound his ankles. Along a corridor, up steps he could not have managed alone. Then, along another complex array of empty halls. And suddenly he was pushed through another door that thudded shut behind them.

Huon blinked, and realized he stood in a well-adorned apartment, brightly lit by a hearth fire and numerous candles.

"What is this?" he grated, dry-mouthed.

"Be still, my lord!" The order came with forceful quiet as the King's Champion appeared. Huon's eyes widened in surprise. "Remove his chains at once!" the Count ordered, moving closer. "Then stand watch outside to see we are not disturbed!"

Huon clenched his teeth against sudden tearing pain as his wrists were freed of the manacles that bound them. Awkwardly, he brought his arms in front of him, feeling the chains that bound his legs being struck away. It was possible to stand again, freely, naturally. Behind him the guardsmen slipped away, the door closing behind them with a muted thud.

"Why am I here, my lord?" Huon demanded as Lord Thierry continued to stand before him, watching with brisk efficiency.

"Of first importance, my lord," the Count ignored his question, "is that thou refresh thyself." He pointed to a table on one side of the chamber, well laden with fine edibles. "Thy squire is here to attend thee."

Huon stiffened mistrustfully. Frowned. "Why am I here?" he repeated.

The Count frowned impatiently. "For thy safety, Lord Huon!" he said crisply. "I know not what plot, or folly, brought about Prince Charlot's death at thy hand, but I see twin lances directed both at the King, and at the House of De Guienne. For my office of King's Champion, I will see justice done!"

"And that is why I was thrown in chains and bound like a condemned peasant before my trial by arms?" Huon flung out, his face white with anger.

"Exactly!" Lord Thierry retorted. "Bound and guarded by my own men to secure thee from further mischief, or," he stressed sharply, "from thyself committing further and irrevocable harm beyond what has already occurred!" Huon could not answer that, and watching him, the Count's expression softened a little. "For the same, I have insured Lord Girard an equal protection," he added.

"Girard . . . ?" Huon got out. His . . . brother, aye, who was betrothed to this man's daughter.

"By some miracle, he still lives." Lord Thierry moved toward the table. "Come. Eat and refresh thyself. I have likewise made sure thy squire, thy arms and warhorse are entire and prepared. The rest falls to thee—and the King's will."

Huon found manners enough to murmur something incoherent about gratitude, and walked stiffly to the table to see the offerings of sweet breads, roasted capon, and fresh cheeses.

He had little appetite, he realized minutes later as he chewed a mouthful of well-spiced meat, then sipped from the cup of mead his squire had poured. Hunger was eroded by uncertainty. He watched the Champion who sat now at his ease, by the hearth fire on the other side of the room. Understanding the significance and usefulness of his own demise, Huon decided that he did not trust the Count of Brittany at all.

The night breezes stilled to presage the coming of dawn. Alone, high on the battlements, secluded by the first easings of darkness, Brother Oborion stood. The gnarled fingers of one hand lightly caressed the feathers of the large bird perched upon his other forearm, and his eyes gleamed with thoughtful satisfaction as he stared out across the night. He raised his arm.

"Aye. Go thou. Be free and natural again," he murmured in tones only the owl could hear. The great bird spread its wings and took silently to the air, disappearing moments later, into the dark grey sky. "It is for me to conjure now. Patiently . . . and it *will* be fulfilled!" the monk added before turning to melt back toward the interior of the keep.

TWELVE

The morning sun was radiant gold as it hung in the east to silhouette the blue-shadowed stone walls and towers of Aix. Sunglow danced across the meadows to the west of the great castle, heightening the fresh, diverse greens of the countryside. And the sky made a brilliant, cloudless blue canopy over the whole.

Baudoin hardly noticed as he assisted his uncle to mount the great liver-colored warhorse. Instead, accustomed to being braced against his uncle's ever-scathing authority, he was troubled by Lord Amaury's silence since he had come at dawn to fulfill his office as squire. He was further perturbed by the look on his uncle's face. Lord Amaury was grim-featured and pale. Haggard. His dark eyes were haunted and elusive, circled by shadows of fatigue. Uneasily, Baudoin held out his uncle's shield. Watched as De Hauteville bent to slip his arm though the thongs. Then he offered the lance. Straightening, Lord Amaury took it without a downward glance. Baudoin stepped back and looked across the field to where the King had just seated himself on the dais erected to one side of the field of combat.

Afraid . . . ? Baudoin stiffened with shock as the idea spread across his mind. Was his uncle afraid? His gaze flitted to the other end of the field where the young Duke of Bordeaux sat a restless great beast of bright chestnut color. Impressive vision . . . Yet Lord Amaury had contemptuously proclaimed the younger man's temper and inexperience. He glanced again at his uncle's face, then stepped back unhappily, his duties complete.

How could his uncle be afraid to defend the justice that he had so forcefully avowed . . . ?

Aye, he was ready, Lord Huon thought, settling the balls of his feet more precisely in the stirrups and accepting his shield from his squire. Restored by food and bathing and clean attire. His hauberk of fine chain mail gleamed clean and bright beneath the blue and yellow surcoat of Bordeaux. His weapons were intact and in order. He had checked them all . . . He took his horse's reins and accepted his lance, hefting it once to adjust his grip, then frowned as he looked to where the Champion now stood. Fully armed, the Count was alertly positioned just below the King's left hand. The Champion had done him well, and justly, Huon was forced to acknowledge. But . . . Aye, like the rest of this, he smelled schemes.

He shifted his gaze to the other end of the field, staring then at his accuser. De Hauteville was his foe, for the moment, resplendent in colors of sienna and black.

There was the grim, loud winding of a horn, and Huon pricked his stallion forward with his spurs as the King stood up from his place on the dais. The crowd around the field of combat stilled at once.

Both horses gnashing the bits and curvetting in hot-tempered anticipation, the two armed men met at mid-field, then turned toward the King to draw rein a few yards from the dais. Charlemagne spoke, his voice carrying across them all.

"A prince of Christendom is dead, slain by a vassal's hand. To determine the guilt or innocence of the slayer in doing most vile murder, or being impelled to this act by unwitting mischance, we require that the accused and the accuser fight to the death! God's truth will be revealed in the outcome! Let it be done!"

The King reseated himself. Lord Huon, bowing from the waist in unison with his foe, was startled by a brief look of surprise on the Champion's face as Lord Thierry stared toward De Hauteville. He glanced toward his foe, but Lord Amaury was already wheeling his horse away. He spurred his own mount toward the other end of the field, brought it about, and held it back, hefting his lance once more to await the winding of the horn that would proclaim the start of the battle.

It came . . . A keening that lofted high upon the morning air. Obliterated in an instant beneath the thunder of charging horses.

Couched lance held sure against his ribs, Lord Huon leaned forward, his point lowering to set direct for the right side of De Hauteville's shield. The glint of sharp steel on the tip of the other's lance bespoke a like intent. Then, suddenly, De Hauteville's lance shifted, the point angling up and inward. Huon jerked to one side to elude the blow that would have mulched his head inside his helm. Felt the twisting jar of his own lance as it skittered across the other man's shield, then deflected into the air. De Hauteville's destrier swept past him . . . Huon let his own horse bolt forward, then drew the animal to a sliding halt, spun it on its haunches, and spurred it to charge again. De Hauteville, he saw at once, managed his mount with equal facility.

He tightened his grip on his lance. Aimed as before . . . Saw De Hauteville's lance point direct for his breast, and shifted his shield up—in. He braced . . .

Shock. And a violent cracking sound as De Hauteville's lance point caught on his shield. Straps broke as he was jerked aside, and the shield ripped away from his arm. His own blow caught on the other's shield, arched the lance to make the weapon erupt against his ribs. It sprang from his grip and shattered.

Clinging with all his strength as his horse swept on, Huon caught a brief glimpse of the other man, torn from his saddle, tumbling. He grunted, recovered his seat, and brought his destrier to another plunging halt. He shook his half-numbed shield arm and saw De Hauteville pick himself up from the sod. Huon drew his sword and smiled a little. The advantage was his, he knew.

But this was a trial. He slipped his feet from the stirrups and vaulted down to release his mount, and heard a low hiss pass through the crowd as the animal spun away. Nay, not for any reason, even his life, he knew, would he have his name stained further by even the least cry of inequality in this battle . . .

He strode forward, sword held before him at the ready. De Hauteville waited, sword raised, shield up. Huon advanced. Swung . . . Caught the edge of Lord Amaury's sword as it came up to deflect his blow. Haggard-faced, the other man, he noted with sudden interest and smiled. Struck again.

And again . . . But De Hauteville proved skillful beyond his expectations, Huon found as his blows were deflected, or caught, by shield or clever counterstroke. He realized with surprise that he was being forced backward, into defense. Then, suddenly,

Lord Amaury snarled furiously and lunged forward to rain a flurried series of blows . . .

Without a shield for protection, Huon set his other hand on the hilt of his sword. Countered and jumped to one side as a sweeping blow came under his own to slash through his surcoat. He brought his sword down. Found naught save air as the other leaped nimbly to one side. He turned his weapon's arc into a lunge, heard a grunt, and felt it slide across a mailed thigh.

There was a stinging jar against his hip. He thrust forward again, furiously trying to get out of the defensive. The face . . . But De Hauteville stepped aside, and Huon barely twisted away from the countering sweep as his sword point impaled on the upward lift of the other's shield. He drew back, half dancing movements. Poised. That shield. De Hauteville made a horizontal stroke instead of the lunge he expected. Huon spun away on the ball of one foot, and brought his sword down with all the force he could summon, straight through the rim of the other's shield. Something slammed into his ribs at the same time. He heard a gasp and jerked his sword free, twisting back to keep from being felled himself. Hard to breathe as he saw De Hauteville stumble to one side, the broken shield sliding away from a bloody left arm . . . Huon growled. Aimed and swung in a risky stroke. And saw his point nick the mail at the base of De Hauteville's throat.

But De Hauteville ducked, then lunged forward. Huon barely avoided the blow that would have spitted his belly. He brought his sword down in a swooping, angled arc. He clenched his teeth as the other stumbled, hauberk rent as his forward thigh gushed blood. Huon jerked back, then committed it all, driving forward, straight for the heart. He hardly felt the numbing pain that swept up his left leg . . . saw only that his sword point drove straight into the other's belly.

Sword and body, he jerked back. Went to one knee and saw De Hauteville stagger back to crumple to the sod, right hand coming up, sword abandoned, to claw at the bloody place above his belt.

Huon jerked himself upright, stepped awkwardly toward the other as he sprawled more loosely on the turf, then knelt again.

"Confess it, my lord!" he rasped out brutally, loudly. "Thou have falsely accused me!" De Hauteville's eyes focused on him from a face gone ashen beneath mail coif and nasaled helm. He gasped, his features twisting in pain. "Confess it!" Huon grated.

But De Hauteville's breath rattled in his throat. His lips parted, and a look of pure venom crossed his eyes before they became vague.

"Murderer . . . !" Lord Amaury whispered through another rattle, then went slack. Still.

Huon stared, then drew back slowly, feeling pain, and looked toward the King. He was breathing hard, he realized as he groped to recover his sword, then used the weapon as a prop to stand once more. And wounded. Innumerable cuts that began to sting . . . Charlemagne's face remained implacable.

"I am innocent of murder!" Huon shouted then. "This man is dead, and justly, for I was falsely accused!"

Myriad eyes watched. Charlemagne stood.

"Thou are acquitted of murder, my lord . . ." Huon inhaled. "Yet," Charlemagne intoned with awful clarity, "by thy own admission, a Christian prince is dead of thy hand. Thy life is spared, Huon De Guienne, but for the rest, all else is forfeit! Thy fiefs and rank . . . Be it known to all that thou are henceforth banished from our realm! Only by the performance of some wondrous task equal in worth to the life of a prince, may thou restore thyself to our sight! *Go! Get thee away from us!*"

Huon's breathing stopped. The blood drained from his face. But Charlemagne turned away, stepping from the dais to move away across the trampled meadow toward the towering monument of Aix. Unable to move, he saw how the Court melted back as well to slip away in clusters of two or three.

He swallowed . . . unspeakable feelings. Victory—vindication. Now, he was disinherit, banished . . . He saw the Champion head toward him, then stop, features troubled.

"I would not have seen it so, my lord," the Count said with regret. Huon could not answer as outrage welled up. Awkwardly, he resheathed his bloodied sword. "Come. I will see thee tended before thy departure . . ." Lord Thierry offered.

Huon scowled and looked at him. "Leave me alone!" he growled, and limped forward, toward where his squire stood, holding his war stallion. The Count did not follow.

"Get food and other necessaries for travel, then mount thyself and come to me here!" Huon grated the order as he took the horse's reins from the squire. The man stared at him. Managed a disjointed "Aye, my lord . . ." But Huon turned away, standing rigidly erect despite the bloody gash in his leg, and reached instead to stroke gauntleted fingers along the sweaty places on his horse's neck.

Totally alone at the western edge of the field of conflict, Baudoin stood peculiarly still, watching as the crowds of highborn and officials melted away, watching as Lord Huon too abandoned the field to stand by his horse in the distance. Watching the abandoned place in the middle, where Lord Amaury's corpse lay in a heap. Untouched . . .

It was his kinsmen's duty to attend to it. To arrange burial, he knew. His only near blood, his uncle, who had ruled every aspect of his life since he could remember, was dead . . . A puzzled look crossed his face as he continued to stand there. He felt no anger, nor surprise. Only a curiously strange shock of sorts. A feeling of relief at the realization that he was totally free of his uncle's rule.

Free . . . It wafted across his mind like a sigh. Slowly, he forced himself forward, walking across the turf until he reached his uncle's corpse. He stopped and looked down at Lord Amaury's blueing lips and eyes that stared like opaque dark stones toward the sky. He had never realized before, he thought, the extent of his uncle's power over him . . .

He started as a shabby figure trod silently past him, then knelt on the other side of the body to reach out with an old, gnarled hand, first closing the dead man's eyes, then making the Sign of the Cross over the body. The monk looked up, and Baudoin recognized the old man's face at once. His uncle's servant . . . He met the fluidly regretful eyes in a face as weathered as the bark of an ancient tree.

"God's will be done," the monk murmured. "Peace be on his soul." Remembering the drawn, haunted look on Lord Amaury's face, Baudoin nodded and made the Sign of the Cross over his own breast. The monk stood up with agued stiffness.

"Thy service to my uncle's scholarship is concluded now," Baudoin managed. "Thou are from the monastery at Tours?"

The monk inclined his head. "I am, my lord Count."

"I release thee then to thy house."

Again, the monk inclined his head. "I am grateful, my lord," he murmured, then, to Baudoin's surprise, moved away across the turf and bent abruptly to retrieve an object lying a few yards distant. He straightened, turned, and held the thing out. A battered shield, Baudoin saw at once, and recognized the damaged arms of Bordeaux.

"There is one last service I may perform, my lord," the monk said, holding the shield and moving closer again. "I would repair this shield and bring it to thee to give to the Lord Girard De Guienne when he recovers from his wounds. Such an offering will enable peace between thy two houses. So my lord Amaury would have willed . . ."

Baudoin stared at the thing, understanding fully the significance of such an act, as, unbidden, another image came into his mind. That of the Lady Olivia De Montglave . . .

"Aye. Do it," he decided. "And bring it to me as soon as may be. Enmity from this day's execution of the King's justice will serve no beneficial purpose." The monk bowed and retreated. Baudoin glanced down, then turned suddenly and walked briskly toward the castle to send other servants for his uncle's body. He had, he realized, no desire at all to ever see it again. Life, for him, had, in the past few moments, just begun.

Despite his intention not to look back, Huon drew rein at the top of a long hill well to the south of Aix and turned his destrier so that he could see. Aye . . . From this distance, the towers and walls of the castle gleamed pure and diminutive above the billowing foliage of countless trees. Bright and innocent. Innocent . . . ? Something ugly crossed his face as he stared. Forbidden to him now. And the land through which he rode.

And Bordeaux . . . His own fiefs. His birthright. His reason. How cleverly and thoroughly he had been dispossessed. More brutally than if he had been slain, he was disgraced, stripped of honor. He glanced toward his squire and caught that young man's uncertain expression, then lowered his gaze to his horse's mane.

The fever had lessened, the physicians had told his servant. Girard would live. It was a miracle . . . Was it? Inside, he was hard and raw, hollow, naked, and bitter. Not for anything, in his present estate, could he have looked upon his brother's face again. And when the squire had informed him his shield had disappeared, he had snarled that it did not matter. The arms upon it were no longer his to bear.

"My lord . . . ?" the squire spoke hesitantly. "Which way?" Huon looked at him, jaw tightening. Even this man who was his.

"Give me the line of the pack horse," he ordered. The squire obeyed. *"Go!"* Huon snarled then. "Serve my brother as thou are bound to do!" The man flinched, eyes widening. *"Go!"* Huon hissed, tightening his fist about the pack horse's rope.

"Aye, my lord." The other half bowed from his saddle and, scrambling to turn his palfrey's head, sent the beast cantering away, back the way they had come.

Huon did not watch him leave, disappearing down the hill and along the deer trail that led through the trees. Instead, his jaw still taut, and feeling every cut that De Hauteville had inflicted, he turned his stallion's head toward the south. Sent it forward at the walk, the pack animal following like a shadow.

Aye. Better to be alone.

Direction . . . ? That question arose much later as the horses plodded on toward the evening, when his body had gone stiff and sore. Banishment from Charlemagne's realm was tantamount to banishment from all Christian things as well. Was that to be taken from him too, Huon thought bitterly, staring at an imperviously clear sky.

Far to the east, aye—vastly distant, and totally separate from western Christendom—was another Christian realm, he knew. Byzantium, as he had heard.

And to the south lay Rome. The Pope, Adrian, was bred of his own line, he recalled. Direction? Aye. South. For the obligations of blood and the True Faith, the Pope could not refuse him audience, at least.

Charlemagne looked up from the vast array of documents that littered the table before him as Lord Thierry bowed. "He is gone?"

The Champion nodded. "Aye, my liege. His squire returned. He is gone, and alone!" Charlemagne ignored the edge to Lord Thierry's voice, reached for a sealed document, and held it out.

"See this dispatched at once, my lord, to our Brother in Christ, Pope Adrian in Rome. Do it with all haste and assurance of its arrival."

Lord Thierry took the document, his face showing surprise. "It will be done, Majesty."

Charlemagne eyed him and sat back in his chair then. "We have no intention of wasting the potential of the hot-headed young Huon De Guienne!" he said crisply, reading the Champion's mood. "Rather, we will temper him to better value than his sire!

Beyond an excess of pride, there are the makings of a great man. He will go to Rome, the Pope being of his own blood . . .''

He watched as the Count's face slowly opened and softened into approval. The Champion bowed very deeply this time.

"To the benefit of all, thy will be done, my liege!" Lord Thierry said fervently, holding the document to his breast. Charlemagne inclined his head in understanding and dismissal.

His undertunic half over his head as he disrobed for the night's rest, Baudoin De Maganze started violently at the sound of his chamber door creaking open. He jerked free of the garment and spun around to see the unkempt figure of the old monk.

"Thou!" he rasped.

"My lord," the monk murmured, closing the door behind him. "I have completed the repairs to the shield of Lord Huon of Bordeaux, and I deliver it to thee, accordingly." He drew a long, triangular object from behind him and held it out.

Baudoin stared through the dim light offered by the single candle on his clothing chest. No trace remained of the damage inflicted by sword and lance. He moved toward it, seeing that it was most perfectly repaired. New seeming . . . The colors of golden yellow on a blue shield were restored to something brighter than before. The single, rising swan with its wings drawn back to begin flight was the emblem for passion and the rising sun, he knew. Elegantly formed.

"It is wonderfully done, Brother . . . Oborion," he said slowly, remembering the unusual name as he took the shield.

"The metal core was intact, my lord. I have replaced the cover with one of finer leather and have refurbished it completely, as thou see." Baudoin traced his fingertips across the smooth, grainless texture of the hide, then turned it over to see how the edges had been rolled back and sewn, the arm straps replaced.

"This is impeccable craftsmanship," he said honestly. "I will be most glad to restore it to Lord Girard."

The old monk bowed stiffly, his eyes gleaming. "From God comes all skill, my lord!" he murmured piously. "My duties are complete. I pray thy leave to depart now, my lord?"

Baudoin nodded as he set the shield with his other belongings. "I have given thee leave."

"May God's peace and blessing be always upon thee, my

son!'' The monk intoned softly, making the Sign of the Cross, before opening the door and slipping away through it.

"So too, I pray," Baudoin whispered to the night as he moved to sit on the furs of his bed. A troubled look settled on his face as he stared across the room, first at the candle, then at the perfect, brightly proud shield of Bordeaux.

He was the Count De Maganze now. And the Lord of Hauteville—fiefs he had never seen, high in the mountainous lands of Auvergne.

And while servants prepared his uncle's body for burial, he had searched his uncle's possessions. Found himself thoroughly startled by what he had discovered. Strictly, unpreteniously reared himself, he had always thought Lord Amaury practised a like and modest constraint. Simple attire, and the like . . . Not so, he had found this afternoon as, before his eyes, Lord Amaury's body servant packed away quills, inkstands, books, and parchments, and wax writing tablets. Things he had expected . . .

Not so, what he had found himself, buried at the bottom of Lord Amaury's clothing chests. Purses filled to bursting with gold coins and monies minted of silver and copper. The bag of gemstones. Fortunes secreted away . . . Baudoin shifted uneasily, thinking of how strictly Lord Amaury had ruled his fiefs of Maganze. His own, sternly managed boyhood. He stared again at the proud swan of Bordeaux.

Pride . . . ? His shoulders drooped a little. Count of Maganze. Lord of Hauteville . . . Burdened names, and blood, he had learned since he had come to Court. Perhaps his uncle had done him a service, he thought unhappily, stripping him so completely of any vestige of pride so long ago . . .

His eyes canny, deep dark pools, the rest of him another shadow amid the rest, Brother Oborion melted silently along dimly lit, night-darkened corridors to the chamber, near Charlemagne's, where Girard De Guienne still lay.

He smiled a little as he approached the door, flanked by four bored, drowsy men at arms who shifted lazily as they saw him, finding no alarm in his worn habit or appearance. So much care for this one, he thought. How much men cherished their memories . . . It was the key, of course.

His pupils spread as he moved closer, staring at each man by turn. Then he walked past them, knowing they would never know the moment, through the heavy door, into the candlelit chamber beyond.

The physician who attended Lord Girard was slumped and asleep in a chair near the bed. On the far side of the room, the man who had been Lord Huon's body squire lay in blissful unconsciousness on a straw-filled pallet.

Brother Oborion glided silently across the chamber and crouched down beside the chests against one wall, used for the disposing of personal belongings. He shifted, and extracted from the loose, untidy folds of his robe an object wrapped in a square of blue velvet cloth. Lord Amaury's meticulously crafted volume of Aristotle . . .

He passed a hand through the air as though feeling, then shifted to carefully raise the lid of one of the chests. Half empty, it contained the personal property Lord Huon had not taken with him into exile. Neatly, he slipped the book down inside the chest, setting it beneath the folded, richly made garments to appear as something else left behind. He lowered the lid of the chest silently and straightened, then moved smoothly across the chamber to pause and peer down at the gaunt and sleeping youth who lay on the large bed on the other side.

He frowned a little as he stared. Beyond the ravages of injury and fever, beyond the likelihoods of filial reproduction in the random form of natural human regeneration, this resemblance was so exact . . .

It was as though, in the flesh at least, Oliver De Montglave himself lay there. He reached forward with the fingertips of one hand, intent to touch that perfectly composed face. But as his fingertips came within an inch of the skin, he started back, suddenly withdrawing them as though scorched. His expression changed.

It was no accident at all, this . . . Even to the hideous wounding that so much resembled that other, unforgiven deed.

He understood . . . He had even, to some extent, foreseen.

And the one who had wrought it . . . ? Aaah. Powers so vastly beyond his own. Powers held captive by sheer ignorance of their presence had yet manifested themselves in this ingeniously remote conjuring.

Aye. He understood.

He stepped back gracefully, turned, and glided away, through the door, closing it silently behind him. Past guards who would not remember what they saw for the mesmerism he had cast upon them. Moving quickly now, he passed along quiet corridors, down flights of steps, then through, at last, portals that exited the vast keep of Aix.

Outside, in the depths of the night, he became a grey shadow that slipped across the inner bailey, then the outer. He slipped under the portcullis and spread his hands, his fingers, setting them against the great, rough-hewn beams of the upraised drawbridge. He scaled it with the facile ease of a spider, slipping through the gap at the top to reverse himself, then drop downward into the murky, still waters of the moat. There, without creating so much as a ripple, his arms outheld, he walked across and emerged on the far side.

Eyes enormous in his gnarled face, his sodden robe clinging to a frame of supple muscularity, he walked away from Aix La Chapelle.

South . . . Across grey dark meadows, then up a long, opaquely shadowed hill concealed beneath lush, nocturnally soft foliage that whispered gently in the light night breeze.

Sometime later, he reached a clearing where he had once stood before. He stopped. Looked back toward the faintly silvered gleam of Aix, then up toward the brilliantly speckled dusting of stars overhead.

The distant sparkle of other worlds, he knew . . .

He lowered his gaze. Looked around him again. Unchanged, this isolated little spot. It was here, he had been peculiarly banished. Forced to retreat into whatever form of obscurity he could devise for himself . . . Roland, who had sought humanity instead.

Oborion unbelted the cord from around his waist and dropped it. Drew the coarse monk's robe over his head to let it fall as well, into the long grasses on which he stood. Then he removed the worn monk's sandals from his feet, and, dropping them as well, straightened to appear a naked, withered figure in the night.

With both hands, he clutched at the loose skin of his abdomen, then pulled it outward, struggling until it began to tear. Tough, this old man's hide he'd worn and nourished for so long, it was unwilling to let go . . .

Fists closed about the first ragged edges, he jerked and tore, splitting it from groin to chin, tearing it away from one smooth, bloodless shoulder, then the other. He grasped the fingertips of one hand with the other, and, in the manner of one loosing a limb from an overtight garment, drew out an arm, a hand. Then the other.

He reached up with both hands and ripped the hide away from his face, his scalp, then bent, tearing it away as he freed his legs, then his feet. A garment such as he had used countless times before . . . he held the pale, ragged thing out and dropped it with the rest. The crows would find it. Or the ants . . .

Freed again to a buoyantly radiant, vigorous youthfulness, he shook back waves of wood-brown hair from a smoothly perfect, ingenious face, and, moving lightly, trod across the clearing, spreading his arms like a dancer toward the night.

Fingers reaching began to spread and shift, becoming feathers. As he moved, his body compacted, plumage emerging from perfect skin to cover him entirely. His feet melted upward, reducing to talons, as arms becoming wings began to beat the air. Only his eyes remained the same, canny, great dark orbs in circles of feathers. And an instant later, a great white owl lofted silently into the night sky. Spiraled upward . . . then disappeared over the black-shadowed tops of the trees thereabouts, to fly with leisurely certainty toward the south . . .

Part 2

THIRTEEN

Summer, Autumn. 793 A.D.

Nightmares . . . terrible pain. And hands that seemed to reach out from the darkness to touch everywhere along him. So delicately . . . as if he were precious. Yet each contact was excruciatingly palpable—alien. And in the distance where he could not see, he sensed a stark and brutal, isolated place filled with echoes of battle and cries of dying. He was lying . . .

Fierce eyes. An eagle . . . ? And a voice that said, "Thou shall not die!"

Girard gasped, his eyes flying open.

A dream. That dream . . . again, he thought, and saw the physician stoop over him. He found an apologetic smile to answer the other's concern. An arm threaded behind his shoulders and raised him up. The rim of a cup was touched to his lips.

"Here is nourishment and fluids, my lord. Drink to dispel these lingering humors." He sipped at honeyed water. Swallowed, and closed his eyes in exhaustion.

In silence he came, Roland, sweeping through the undergrowth that smothered the temple, lurching in a grotesque parody of natural human movement, to seize her out of the dark bondage of the cavern. In hard silence, he bound her in foul rags torn from his own clothing, hiding her from view as he carried her away, slung against his back as before.

Only as a sword, he knew her. As a weapon, he carried her, the edges of his knowledge a tangible description of her form.

Durandal kept still and cool, guarding the secret of her plasticity. Guarding the freedom that remained to her against his implacability.

After weeks of interminably slow recovery, it was still hard to see improvement, Lord Thierry thought as he watched Girard, sitting now in a well-cushioned chair beside a window opened to admit warm, fresh summer air. He had become so thin and frail . . . Unmentioned, it lay between them with each visit he made, the betrothal that would bond them in time as father and son . . .

"Where is my brother? I never seem to see him when I am awake," Girard asked, looking up. The Champion stiffened unhappily. It had come, he knew, the question he had been waiting for. And dreading.

"Lord Huon is no longer at Aix." Girard's eyes widened briefly, then he glanced toward the servant waiting in another corner of the room.

"He has gone home . . ." he began.

"Nay, my lord. He has not!" Lord Thierry's tone roughened as he cut it off. Girard shifted and looked· at him. "Lord Huon killed the King's elder son, Prince Charlot. For his incomplete guilt, his life was spared. But he has been declared disinherit, and is banished from the realm, being forbidden to return." Tersely, honestly said.

Girard's face went gaunt and terrible as he heard. "Nay!" he whispered it. "Not Huon . . ." One hand moved awkwardly, then the fingers closed around the cloth of the fine, long woolen robe he wore. "Not Huon . . ." Lord Thierry inhaled and gave the particulars as he knew them. Girard looked away, and for some time sat there, staring down at the hand clenched in his lap.

"Why was I not told before?" The question came quietly.

Startled by the tone, Lord Thierry spoke the truth. "For fear of thy own life, my lord. Thou have been so grievous hurt. Thou are Lord of Bordeaux now . . ." Girard looked up at him.

"Am I so?" he whispered. "It is a pitiful endowment then, got of Huon's misfortune. I can never be more than his steward!" He looked away.

Oliver De Montglave, Lord Thierry realized uncomfortably, would have responded in exactly the same way. He shifted, but Girard did not seem to notice. Instead, he bowed his head and watched his own fingers shift aimlessly across his thighs. There was nothing to be said, or offered, Lord Thierry knew, and left.

Panting heavily, the cripple stopped to hang on his crutches and rest at the crest of a steep hill. He looked toward the south where grassy slopes fell away to disappear into dense green forest that spread away in every direction as far as the eye could see. High overhead, the sun's rays beat down, hot and heavy, pushing through his clothing to spread along his ragged, sweatless skin. Beneath, deeper, he felt the pain that had become more evident of late move and thread along his body, crawling, like something independently alive. Always . . . there was pain, though sometimes he managed to forget it. Like the crippled leg he tried never to look upon, it hung there, a part of him that he could not avoid or escape.

He looked up. The falcon soared so easily on the updrafts above and beyond him, and he stood, content to watch its smooth, spiraling flight, its gracefully relaxed certainty of the air. Like Oliver's spirit, in a way . . . he thought. It had become both companion and symbol, the peregrine, as he trudged relentlessly onward, determined to fulfill his silent pledge. A ghost of that other friendship . . . Unconstrained, it hunted, offering its kills to him. He fed it. Sometimes he shared and ate as well.

Girard, the son. Oliver alive again . . . He would not die. Not this time. Not this time . . .

It was a direction he did not fully understand, the cripple knew, yet he was driven by the overpowering rightness of it. Aye. He would give the power of the Dark Sword into the hands of the one she had killed. What better protection could he offer than to bequeath that matchless sword to Oliver's own blood . . . ? As she had served him, so she would serve this other to make reparation for the glory that would have been Oliver's if he had lived. That had been stolen by unspeakable murder.

He looked toward the south again. Bordeaux lay in the distance, somewhere beyond the rippling summer haze that defined the horizon. And the Garonne . . . But he remembered where he had forded it once before. Oliver had been riding with him then . . .

He shifted forward, moved his crutches, and headed slowly down the hill.

* * *

He could not welcome this, Girard thought unhappily as he stood alone near the back of the great hall of Aix. A little apart from the others of the Court, and wearing all the arms and accoutrements of his rank and title, he waited to be summoned by the King. For the first time in his life, he acknowledged, the chain mail felt unnatural and burdensome against a body that was still far too thin.

He glanced briefly around him. Aye. It went far beyond the heightened, fanciful sensitivity of the newly convalescent, this . . . silence . . . that surrounded him.

Looks that came from older men, filled with undertones of knowledge that had to do with something about himself that he was not privy to. Never accusing . . . He thought again of the alienation that had sprung up between Huon and himself before this . . .

Unresolved, still.

And Huon was banished. Disgraced. Wrapped in a silence that was absolute and pervasive, his name was never mentioned at all. It was as though Huon had never existed at all.

Wrong . . . Girard stiffened, then nodded briefly as the steward stopped before him. He did not need to hear the words. He walked past the man, past the flanking crowd of the Court, up the center length of the great hall. He looked up, staring at Charlemagne who sat before and above him. Everything a king could be, this remote, ageless silver Prince . . .

He stopped at the foot of the dais, his helm cradled in the crook of his left arm, and knelt slowly. Bowed his head.

"For obedience to my liege lord, Charlemagne, King of all the Franks, and our most Christian Prince, I, Girard, got the second son of the House of De Guienne, do kneel before my King to receive his will of me." He could not have said it differently, he knew, boldly proclaiming his rank . . . as Huon would have done.

He looked up to see the King rise, then step down toward him. Someone else came forward to proffer something, and an instant later, he felt something hard and circular settle over his hair to rest like discreet bondage about his temples. Huon's coronet . . . he thought. Not mine, this unadorned golden emblem.

He met the King's frigid blue stare for a moment, and had the sudden, unsettling feeling that he had been read, and understood. Charlemagne shifted back to reseat himself on his throne.

"Do thou rise, Girard De Guienne, vested this day of our

hands, and before all Christian men, Duke of Bordeaux, lord of all fiefs and vassals pertaining thereto, to thyself, and thy heirs!''

Heirs . . . ? That made it final, Girard knew as he stood. Then as duty required, he drew the sword that hung from his left hip, shifted it to clasp the blade, and proffered it, hilt first, toward the King. Nay, he knew then, even in the giving of his fealty, he would not betray his brother by his acceptance.

''I, Girard De Guienne, endowed and vested this day, by my liege lord, Charlemagne, to the duty of Duke of Bordeaux, do swear my true and full service to my King as he may require of me, in body and goods and spirit to the fulfillment of every honorable charge upon my soul!'' A simple and accurate re-phrasing had made it an incomplete claim . . . He heard a murmur pass through the large company that flanked him, and saw with surprise that approval, rather than censure, flickered across Charlemagne's hard eyes.

The King leaned forward to grasp the hilt of the sword. ''Do thou, my lord of Bordeaux, fulfill that honor that is thy chiefmost inheritance, to the benefit of all men, and we, for God's trust in us, are well content!'' Charlemagne released the sword and sat back.

It was an unorthodox acceptance, Girard knew, resheathing the weapon. He stepped back and bowed . . . puzzled, sensing again, this mystery that had, somehow, to do with himself.

It was done, he knew, and walked the length of the great hall to find himself surrounded by lords of the Court, all intent to offer their civilities on what was supposed to be an occasion of celebration.

So . . . Lord Geoffrey thought, stepping back to watch after proffering his own elegantly couched complaints, Lord Amaury's suppositions had been entirely correct. Dispose the one, and the other had assuredly taken his place. And though not even a whisper of it was uttered, it was obvious enough in Lord Girard's resemblance to the late Oliver De Montglave the extent to which the King's favor rested on the son.

Now, the bastard-got Girard had become one of the most powerful lords of the land. And to the approval of all . . . Lord Geoffrey thanked the instinct that had made him sever all connections with Lord Amaury before De Hauteville's demise. And after his father's confused outburst before Prince Charlot's tomb that had inextricably linked Lord Amaury with every vile association to Lord Ganelon's treachery, he had found it expedient to remove his parent from the Court entirely, using the pretext of the Duke's failing health.

He turned and left the great hall, to preoccupy himself with the problems of his own advancement . . .

The air was clean, high on the battlements . . . blowing across the walls to ruffle his hair. Alone, thankfully, Girard thought, leaning against the stone. Aye, he needed solitude . . .

"My lord?" Uncertainly polite . . . Girard turned and saw with surprise that Lord Baudoin De Maganze stood before him. De Hauteville's nephew. The other shifted, looking young, uneasy. "Do thou remember me? I came with my uncle, Lord Amaury De Hauteville, to Bordeaux these several months past." Girard inclined his head and found a smile. He had not forgot the uncertain youth who seemed a slave to Lord Amaury's least look.

"I have not forgot, Lord Baudoin," he said gently, his smile becoming wry as it chased across his mouth. "My sister, as I recall, received thy undivided attention!" Scarlet replaced the natural swarthy color of Lord Baudoin's face, and he looked away.

"She is brilliant fair, the Lady Olivia!" he half mumbled, then stiffened. "But that is not why I have sought to be private with thee, my lord!"

"I confess to surprise, my lord!" Girard said with dry curiosity. The other shifted again. Stiffened resolutely.

"It was my uncle, Lord Amaury, that brought the charge of murder against thy brother, Lord Huon."

Girard's face went stern. "So I am given to understand, my lord," he said in a harder voice.

"My uncle was killed in the battle of trial with Lord Huon," Baudoin struggled on. Girard inclined his head briefly. "I am concerned, my lord, for the ill will that would arise from that between our two houses . . ."

"That is a reasonable concern!" Girard said very quietly, remembering his sister's vehemence, yet acknowledging that this hesitant youth before him was the only one since the Champion's single relating of the truth who had even volunteered his brother's name.

"My servant recovered this, my lord," Baudoin pursued, withdrawing the shield he carried from beneath the concealing folds of his cloak, and holding it out. "It was badly damaged. I have seen it restored, my lord . . . and would return it to thee, both to honor the valiant defense of Lord Huon, and to make a token of peace between us . . ." His voice died away.

Paling a little, Girard stared at the arms of Bordeaux. Perfectly restored. Unblemished . . . He reached slowly to take his brother's shield.

"I am greatly moved, my lord," he managed.

"I am glad, my lord," Baudoin said. Girard looked at him, and he shifted awkwardly. "I am aware of my father's repute . . . And my uncle became involved in this . . . damage to thy house. I would not be thought the same as the rest of my blood!" He got the last out in a fervent rush.

Girard did not respond at once, but traced his fingertips over the perfect, sunlit swan taking flight upon a field of blue. His brother's honor . . . His own. He looked up.

"Does not each man make his worth through his faith with his honor?" he asked softly then. "I am not thy foe, unless thou force me to it . . ."

Lord Baudoin's face relaxed in relief.

"I am grateful, my lord," he said sincerely. Bowed and left, walking along the parapet to disappear around a corner.

Alone again, Girard studied the shield, then lowered it gently, point down, to rest against his leg. Huon's shield . . . and he would use it. Carry it.

"By this, I will keep faith with thy honor, Huon," he pledged softly, then looked outward, toward the south where the farthest trees made an intricate, dark green contour against the sky.

The swan of passion, how aptly Huon's symbol . . . Olivia had her own arms, got from her deceased sire—the pelican of self-sacrifice that had been De Montglave's own. As a second son, he alone had not been so endowed.

He had thought, he remembered, to combine the swan of his birthright with the lyre of harmony to represent his own integrity. Not now. Not now . . .

Like the awful and pervasive silence that surrounded his name at Court, Huon had disappeared. Vanished. He could not even send aid to his brother through monies and servants. Girard grimaced unhappily. And the worst lay before him still. He had yet to return to Bordeaux and assume control of the governing of those fiefs. He had yet to tell their mother of the fate that had befallen her elder son.

Huon . . . her pride. How he dreaded it.
Yet he was, he knew, recovered sufficient to ride now.
Nor would he put it off.

Exhausted and sodden, the cripple lay against the tall grasses and reeds along the southern banks of the Garonne. It had been a brutal struggle to ford the river, fighting currents he was ill equipped to cope with despite the somewhat depleted flow of the river that came with the height of summer.

The falcon that had flown in tight circles above him to swoop and screech fretfully alighted on his good leg, its talons clinging to his thigh. He shifted to stroke its feathers. Surprised himself by murmuring to it.

"Do not fret for me. I am not easily destroyed!"

Bordeaux . . . It was a rich and populous land with its rolling, forested hills, clear streams, lush meadows, and frequent villages and manors. Well-fed serfs tilled the soil, or herded. Fertile soil and a temperate climate nurtured both wild and domestic beasts alike. Crops were abundant—barley, oats, and wheat. Turnips and other such roots. Sheep, pigs, cattle, and goats were plentiful, like the grapes from which fine wines were made.

Now, for all of that, and to keep from being driven away, the cripple knew he must travel slowly, even furtively, to approach the great castle undetected. Moving at dusk or dawn. Making use of the dense, mature, late summer foliage . . . Then to await the opportunity.

FOURTEEN

"Aha!" Olivia De Montglave crowed triumph as her arrow thudded into the hare she had spotted some fifty feet distant, flushed into moving by the sound of horses. The little animal tumbled in a somersault and fell, and she turned to grin at the huntsman who rode with her.

"Well shot, my lady," he acknowledged with careful servant's respect. Her smile faded. It wasn't the same as hunting with Girard, she admitted. She'd become an excellent archer under her brother's tutelage, and their hunting together was always high-spirited and filled with rivalry. More . . . a special camaraderie. She missed them both, she knew, Girard . . . and Huon.

She lowered her bow and nudged her horse to walk across the meadow toward her prey.

A falcon plummeted suddenly down through the air, straight toward the fallen hare. Astonished, Olivia watched as it fluttered in the grass, screeched once, then took flight again, struggling to loft the dead animal. Amazement changed to indignation as she realized her game was being stolen right out of her grasp. She raised her bow, took an arrow from the quiver at her back, notched it, drew back, and loosed it. An instant later, the falcon floundered in the air, the hare falling from its grasp. The bird screeched loudly, lost altitude, then, clearly injured, struggled to fly farther, its momentum carrying it toward some nearby thickets on the edge of the woods down the hill to the right.

Olivia stopped her horse and frowned as the falcon disappeared from view. Wild birds never tried to carry off game like that, she knew. Yet she had seen no jesses on the creature . . . She stiffened, catching movement in the bushes. She had not killed the bird, she knew, and trotted her horse forward. She could recover it to heal and tame and add to their hunting birds. Girard would be pleased. She stopped her horse, slung her bow over the pommel of her saddle, and vaulted lightly down despite the tangling abundance of skirts about her legs.

Gathering the excess in one hand, she stepped toward the bushes, pushed forward, parting branches, then stopped, frozen in purest shock . . .

A fair of fierce, hawklike golden eyes stared at her from a countenance that might have been human, blinked once, then widened to something grim and terrible and filled with recognition.

"Lady Aude!" the apparition rasped. Olivia flinched, held by those eyes surrounded by grey. Flesh and rags that were nearly indistinguishable . . .

"I am Olivia De Montglave!" she got out harshly, reflexively. "Daughter of the House of De Guienne!"

"De Montglave . . ." the monster whispered terribly. "De Montglave . . . And thou art the same." She poised, unable to flee from eyes that never left hers. Knowledge there.

"The same as who?" she demanded, beginning to see the peeling, shardlike skin that covered a man. Crutches and ragbound articles beside where he crouched, holding the injured falcon. "Who art thou to know me?" But he flinched away.

"I . . . ?" he whispered, ghostlike. "I am nothing, my lady!"

"Mother of God! A leper! My lady, for thy safety, get back!" The forgotten huntsman pushed past her. Olivia spun, but before she could react, he drew his dagger, reversed it, and flung the thing, point first . . . The falcon shrieked and fluttered.

"*Nay!*" Her shout came too late as she saw the weapon lodge to the hilt in the leper's shoulder. She lunged, pushing the huntsman aside, then rounded on him. "That was beyond needful, Jean!" she barked. "What harm could this pitiful man do to hurt me?"

"He is a leper . . ." the huntsman began to protest.

"Aye! And entitled to our charity for his misfortunate lot!" she retorted ferociously. "Go! Get the horses!"

She turned back to the crippled man and saw that he had

slumped down, blood trickling through the scaled fingers that had come up to clutch at his shoulder.

Entire fingers, for all their ghastly skin, she realized. Not the eroded stubs common to lepers . . . The falcon screeched again and moved to perch on the cripple's thigh, and she saw then that her arrow had broken a number of its flight feathers but had not damaged the arm of the wing. She hesitated, torn between fear of touching and all her training from her mother in the tending of wounds and ills.

True charity could not fear, she reminded herself sternly and took a step toward the man.

"I am sorry for this," she tried. He looked up then, his eyes remarkable . . . bright and clear. She saw that his hair and beard, revealed beneath the worn and filthy ragged thing that swathed much of his head, were a dull, thick, matted golden hue. Not old, she realized with shock. He was not old at all.

"It is of no matter, my lady," he whispered softly, politely. It jarred. An incongruity . . . aye, like his knowledge of her blood name, and that other, disturbing mention he had made. Olivia frowned. For all his hideous disease and beggared estate, this was no common man, she knew suddenly. She knelt and reached toward the dagger still lodged in his shoulder.

"This is bad and must be attended . . ." she began. But he shrank back with widened eyes.

"Nay! Do not touch . . . It will do well enough!" he rasped.

Olivia stared, astonished to realize that his fear was greater than hers. "But that is folly!" she countered. "This wound must be tended!" she added decisively, straightening to swing about and shout for the huntsman. He appeared, looking sullen and holding the bridles of the two horses. Briskly Olivia took the reins of her own animal and ordered him to mount the leper on the other for return to the castle a pair of miles away. The huntsman shifted, staring belligerently back at her. Olivia lost her temper.

"Do it!" she snarled. "It is more than thy life is worth to even question my instruction! Thou have already done this injury against my will!"

The huntsman lowered his gaze, filled with antipathy, and moved reluctantly to loft the cripple upright. The falcon screeched and fluttered as it found new purchase on the cripple's uninjured shoulder. Awkwardly, he helped the leper up into the saddle of the horse that had been his mount. Another look at the

Lady Olivia's set face, and he collected the crutches and the two rag-bound articles of property on the ground. Passed them up as the cripple reached for them and clutched them to him. With utter revulsion, he stared at the scaled, dead-looking skin that covered the cripple's right hand, then, as Lady Olivia turned her horse and nudged it on, took the reins and began to lead the other animal, his mind filling with dire and terrible things.

Ahead of him by a horse's length . . . Lady—girl—woman. A member of that breed of humankind he feared as he feared nothing else. Skewed awkwardly in the saddle to accommodate his twisted, shriveled, and frozen right leg, the cripple grimly kept his gaze averted from the figure before him and let his body flow with the horse.

Flow, aye . . . placid and compliant because this would enable him to deliver his gift to Oliver's son.

Oliver's eyes . . . The shock of seeing. He could not have expected such as this, he knew. Even the name, twisted to fit the apparition of a woman. This too was Oliver's get, conceived before Roncesvalles, and replicating that other, deeply buried burden on his soul. Oliver's sister, who had died for . . . He shut it off.

The horse swayed beneath him, its every movement evoking remembrance as it obediently followed the man who led it. The dagger ground deep in his shoulder, but the pain of it was no worse than he had known countless times before. Red blood seeped reassuringly, a reminder that he was still, in part, at least, a man . . .

He looked up as they began to descend a long hill and saw Bordeaux's bright walls and towers emerge above the trees ahead. So clear in the sunlight. Not forgot in the least detail . . .

I am the ghost, he thought. Not these others.

Glancing over her shoulder as they reached the meadows before the great castle, Olivia was surprised to see the cripple was not slouched over. Instead, he sat erect, staring past her at the castle, his eyes gleaming and bright, as if they knew. A puzzled frown crossed her face. The crippled leper sat like a fighting man, and one who had been thoroughly accustomed to riding. He hardly seemed to notice the weapon still lodged in his shoulder, or the blood that made a bright crimson stain on his colorless rags. Unjessed, unhooded, the falcon clung to the other like something tamed as only Girard knew how to do. And he was taller than the common. She turned back to face her horse's head again. Questions he had evoked . . . Unclear. There was a mystery to all of this, aye, uncommon circumstance.

She had not thought fully on how she intended to care for this injured, leprous man, Olivia realized minutes later as the horses thudded across the drawbridge. Dispatched with a word, a sentry ran quickly toward the keep with summons for the Lady Alice.

A pallet somewhere, and a cautery—and bandages, Olivia thought, standing dismounted from her horse, skirts in one hand as she watched the surly-faced huntsman do her bidding. He lowered the cripple awkwardly to the ground, then propped him on his crutches, where he stood, slumped a little, his other properties hanging against him like distortions of the same ragged grey form.

"What is this, Olivia?" The demand came crisply, and she spun to see her mother appear at the top of the steps that led into the keep, a tirewoman a pace behind her.

"The huntsman wounded this . . . unfortunate, Mother," she answered truthfully. "For Christian charity, I could not leave him so—untended."

"This diseased thing!" the Duchess began sternly, moving down the steps, then stopping suddenly, her dark eyes widening, the color draining from her face. "I know that bird!" she rasped suddenly.

Olivia stared in amazement.

"I know that bird . . ." the Duchess repeated in a voice gone hollow and urgent. "How art thou come by it?"

The cripple looked up. "It was lost. Jesses tangled . . . I but recovered it," he answered with melodious reluctance.

The Duchess descended the last of the steps and stopped before the cripple, her face ashen, seemingly transfixed by his golden eyes.

"What do thou know of my son?" she demanded harshly.

"Girard's?" Olivia whispered unheard, looking at the falcon as realization came.

"He is alive!" The answer came reticently.

"And thou . . . ? Thou . . ." the Duchess rasped harshly.

"I too am alive!" Uttered with terrible bitterness . . .

The Duchess turned suddenly. Rooted by dumbfounded astonishment, Olivia flinched before that look. "Go, daughter! See that the chamber in the east tower is readied for this man!'' she ordered, then turned back to stare again. "I will tend thee myself, my lord!''

My lord? Propelled by obedience, Olivia's own eyes widened farther as she hurried away.

"Come, my lord,'' Lady Alice said firmly, meeting that unforgettable pair of eyes again. "I recollect a certain tenacity of spirit that may enable thee to manage the few yards that remain to the comfort I offer!'' The cripple looked down. Blood dripped slowly to make a small stain in the earth by his foot.

"This . . . disease,'' he whispered it. "It is mine alone.'' He looked up again. She nodded a little, the Lady Alice, curiously unconcerned.

"Come,'' she said again, and turned to lead the way. Teeth clenched, and uneasy, the cripple swung his crutches and followed to lurch laboriously, grotesquely up the steps. This woman, he thought, that Oliver had loved so much . . . so incomprehensibly.

Huddled in a corner on the other side of the inner bailey, the huntsman watched the groomsman lead the horses away. The second beast should be killed at once, its carcass burned until naught remained but cinders, he knew. Shivered in growing terror.

Pestilence . . . The Duchess had been rightly outraged to see . . . Pestilence—and witchcraft, clearly. Spells cast from the unnatural leper to bind her to hospitality. God help them all!

He crossed himself, then jerked to hold his hands before him. Felt terror crawl like worms along his spine, every thread of the garments he wore begin to itch against his skin. Creeping . . .

What were the first signs of this dread disease that had surely been passed to him? He, who had condemned himself to a fate worse than execution for disobedience to keep the Lady Olivia from harm.

But she too had been bewitched. Had been cozened by sorcery to bring the monstrous creature here. He shuddered violently and turned away to find lye to scrub himself with.

Ghosts . . . Who, or what? He, or the chamber that surrounded him? He had been housed in this very place once, many years before, when he had been the King's new-made Champion.

Crutches abandoned, he sat upon the furs that covered a soft-mattressed bed such as he had lain upon before . . . then. And wounded worse than this—in the same place. He clenched his teeth and, staring at the tapestry that adorned the far wall, reached for the hilt of the dagger in his shoulder. He pulled it out and dropped it, hearing it clatter on the stone floor.

Not for him, he knew, could this be a mortal wound. Not even by inflammation. Eluding the presence of the Lady Alice, he looked down at his shoulder. Fresh scarlet trickled reluctantly from the hole. Not the thick, rich gushing he expected, but a thin, sanguinous flow reminiscent of the oozing from a dead man. He looked away to where the falcon perched now upon a carven chest.

Dead man . . . ? A dead man did not endure this pain.

He stiffened as the Lady Alice knelt before him, surprised at himself for only swallowing uncomfortably as she touched, cutting away the rags of his tunic from his injured shoulder.

Oliver's lady . . . He felt keenly aware of the distance in their friendship got from his own incomprehending revulsion for such a passion. Concession now, to close the space . . . ?

He forced himself to look at her. Still slender, even wraith-like, silver threads were plentifully revealed in the dark hair half hid by her wimple. Fine lines etched the skin of her face where there had only been smoothness before. They had both been young then, he realized. And she too had endured since Roncesvalles. It was apparent.

She looked up. "Time for conversation later, my lord. I have fresh raiment for thee." She stated her intention of affording the courtesy that was only optionally bestowed upon the highest ranking of guests. He did not reply. Or move—save to flinch a little as she stripped away the ruined hood that covered most of his head. She continued to disrobe him, even to removing the tattered chausses that covered his legs, and the crude wrappings that covered his feet. Foot—he could not call that other deformed appendage the same, he thought, looking away to avoid it. He saw, instead, Lady Alice fling the bundle of his rags into the hearth fire. Flames leaped gladly upward . . .

She turned toward him, her expression something grim and resolute, as her eyes scanned him, then moved to collect a bucket of water and cleansing rags.

"I can do no less than my lord Oliver," she said sternly, reaching to begin washing his wound, and the rest, feeling him stiffen. Roland looked away. Swallowed again. By her very words and tone, she rendered less, he knew painfully, and yielded to it.

She bathed him then, from the top of his head to every part of the rest, scrubbing, scouring, pausing only to wind bandages over the hole in his shoulder. Trying to cleanse the uncleanable, and succeeding only in removing the crusted layers of grey dirt and grit that had, over the years, become buried in the fabric of his skin.

"This is not leprosy!" she rasped as she finished, drawing back to stare with fierce intensity at his body. "This is some other thing!"

Roland flinched, then followed her gaze to look down at the ragged, grey, pallid skin that covered something resembling a man's body. Scars . . . So many. A twisted, pitted, and pouting seam still bisected his belly from groin to breast. Others, and the brutally contorted thing that was left of his right leg. He cringed violently and groped for the toweling blanket she had set beside him, seeking to cover, and looked up to see her eyes were enormous.

"For God's pity! How is it that thou art alive, Lord Roland?" she whispered. Held by her stare, he flinched back under the toweling cloth, feeling every horror her question contained.

"I did not die . . . my lady!" he got out at last. Apology? In part.

"I knew thee! I knew thee, who were beloved of my lord," she whispered intently. "How is it that thou are not entombed at Aix as all the world knows?"

Roland flinched again. Accusation—of a sort. "I know not who occupies my grave, my lady," he managed slowly. "Only that I have longed for it!"

She did not respond.

"Why are thou come here now, my lord? After all these years?" she asked harshly, warily.

He stiffened a little. "I have a gift for the son of Oliver," he said with quiet resolve. "A bequest from that Lord Roland who was, in truth, killed at Roncesvalles!"

"Thou knew of that?" she remembered young men, and a child.

"Always," he murmured, hunching down beneath the blanket. "It is Roland who is dead, my lady. Oliver lives on!" he added forcefully.

She could not refute it, she thought, staring at him, unable to reply. Dead . . . ? In truth, his appearance was mostly corpselike, denied only by the bright ferocity of his eyes, the brilliant, amber-gold sheen of uncut, now clean hair that hung in rich waves to his waist. Without, she realized, a single trace of the silver of natural age. She remembered the rumors that he was witch got. Rumors that Lord Oliver had scorned as nonsensical fancy, or jealous spite . . .

"What is this gift thou hast for my son, my lord?" she demanded, moving to set new, neatly folded garments beside him, then retreating.

"The sword of Roland, bequeathed to the one most worthy to wield it!" he told her with a curious remoteness, as though he was no more than a messenger.

She did not reply, but met his look, then left him.

"He knew my blood name, Mother," Olivia broke the silence that pervaded the solar. "And he seemed shocked when he first saw me. He called me Lady Aude . . ." It died away as the Duchess looked up from her embroidery, face pale and thin and strained.

"I see," she said coldly.

Olivia was totally puzzled. "I know my father had a sister of that name . . ." she blundered on. "Do I resemble her so much then, this Lady Aude?"

"Thou have much the look of her," the Duchess said with disinterest. Olivia frowned as she watched her parent.

"It is important . . ." she ventured after a moment. "Am I not entitled to know why?"

The Duchess did not answer at once. The response when it came was strangely remote. "The Lady Aude was a girl, betrothed to Roland, who was Count of Brittany and thy father's dearest friend. She died shortly after that terrible battle in which both Roland and Oliver were slain."

Olivia's frown deepened with bewilderment. "Still, I do not understand?"

"Nay. Thou could not!" the Duchess said crisply, bitterly. "The Lady Aude pined away for a love that was crassly reviled! I watched her die, slowly, wasting away for a futile grief after Roncesvalles!" The Duchess looked down, stabbed her needle through her embroidery. Olivia watched her alertly, still trying to find a connection.

"This . . . unfortunate and crippled man? Some lord . . . ? Thou know him, Mother?" she demanded this time.

The Duchess set another stitch. "I know him," she said tonelessly, withdrawn with her feelings to some privately held place.

"Who is he, Mother?" Olivia pressed it. Then again, "Who is he?"

The Duchess looked up.

"He is Roland!" she said harshly.

Olivia stared in frozen astonishment. "But Lord Roland is dead . . . like my father!" she got out. "As they sing of it . . ."

"By some mischance, another is buried in his place!" the Duchess cut in, her tone absolute. "Roland lives, and this leper is that man!" Hard warning darkened her eyes as she met her daughter's amazed stare. "Leave him be, Olivia! It is between us two. *None* other!"

Silenced, Olivia stood very still. Then the Duchess nodded dismissal. "The hour is late," she said more gently. Obediently, Olivia moved to kiss her mother's cheek, then left the solar to seek her own chamber.

Feelings chased her down the corridor . . .

Anger, she recognized slowly. Her mother's bitterness for that long-dead girl . . . and, because it was Roland who had survived after so much time, and not Lord Oliver.

Roland . . . that peerless knight and Champion whose very name meant courage and honor. Whose appearance and deeds had been given an enchanted life through the lyrics and music of a song.

Alive . . . she thought, absorbing the word deeply, knowing what she had seen. How hideously tragic.

Like her own father, Roland could not have become such a legend without sufficient truth to make it possible. "I am nothing . . ." he had said. Pride that had made such heroic prowess before had been butchered by the thing he had become.

Nay, she knew, for what she understood, she could not leave it be . . .

The door closed with a light thud. She was alone . . . Lady Alice set her needlework aside and stared at the hearth fire, breathing deeply and carefully to control the pain deep in her belly. It was with her constantly now, the pain . . . Growing. Like the hard canker deep where her womb was. Like a demon child, that too grew slowly, steadily, eating her flesh away from her bones, felt as a hot, stonelike thing under the skin . . . She kept it hid, and the thinness beneath added shifts and loose girdles.

It was why she had not feared to touch the leprous ruin of Lord Roland. Leper, or some other dread disease she had never seen before? In any event, her days were numbered.

She had known it for some while now, that she would die. She knew too much of signs and ills not to recognize this as one of the many consuming illnesses that drained the body of all vitality unto death. Only one thing was important . . . that she endure until Huon's return. Then she could give it all into his hands and find her peace at last.

She had no regret for that, she knew.

Now Roland had come, like some devil-ghost to resurrect the past, destroying her solace in knowing that soon she would join it . . .

FIFTEEN

Autumn. 793 A.D.

Well aware that she went against her mother's wishes, Olivia furtively opened the door to the circular chamber high in the east tower. She peered cautiously through it, then slipped inside to pause and stare. A single candle still burned on the table, next to a flagon of mead, a goblet, and a wooden tray loaded with foodstuffs. A soft, warm glow permeated the room from the slowly dying hearth fire. She saw crutches, and the other articles, on the floor beside the wood-framed bed on the far side.

He seemed to be asleep, Lord Roland . . . Facing away, lying mostly on his right side, the furs and blankets drawn up over his hips. Too familiar with her brothers to be troubled by his nudity, Olivia's eyes widened at the gleaming mass of bright amber hair that fell along his neck, tumbled over shoulders that were broad—seemed smoothly muscular. She blinked, caught by impressions made by distance and dim light that totally refuted his crippled, leprous condition. And his age . . . Of course, he was cleaned now. Rags and filth had combined of themselves to make him a horror . . . but?

She ventured closer, curiously peering down to see how the shadows and fireglow combined to reveal the perfect symmetry of his features. Under that dreadful skin, and the beard, lay what had once been an extraordinary beauty . . .

He stirred. She swallowed and froze as he shifted over his injured, bandaged shoulder, winced, and opened his eyes to see

146

her standing there. His eyes went stark wide, and he shrank back violently toward the wall, clawing for the covers.

"What do thou here?" he rasped. She stared, caught. Amazed.

"I . . . my lord Roland . . ." she half stammered, then saw the stain in the bandages over his right shoulder. "I had thought . . . to see how thou fare," she bludgeoned on. "I found thee, after all. And it was because of me thou are injured . . ."

"How do thou know my name?" he cut in roughly, staring at her, all fierce-eyed and taut. He feared her, Olivia realized with amazement. She collected herself.

"From my lady mother," she said truthfully. He grimaced. She inhaled. "Lord Roland . . . I never knew my father, for my birth occurred even as he died . . . My lord, thou were his chiefmost friend . . . ?" The rest of her request died away as he continued to stare at her, his expression changing into something raw and brutal and painful. He looked away.

"Aye," he whispered very softly. "I was Lord Oliver's friend!" Olivia swallowed, her fingers making knots in the folds of her gown. This man had loved her father, she knew. Still did. He looked at her then, eyes deep. "Thou hast no need to ask me to know thy father, my lady," he said roughly. "Do thou look at thy brother, for he is the same in every aspect as that Lord Oliver I was once blessed to know!"

"My brother . . . ?" Olivia whispered in confusion, feeling the blood drain slowly from her face as it became impossible not to understand. "Which one?" she asked, meeting his look, beyond being repulsed by his hideous complexion.

He frowned. "Who else but the Lord Girard who so much resembles thee?" he countered roughly. She stepped back.

"Nay? It cannot be so! I alone am got De Montglave's child by my mother's second marriage . . ." But the truth was there, in his eyes. Girard, who was not got as all the world thought him to be . . . "I—I . . ." she groped, shocked to the core, then gave it up to flee in a quiet whirl of skirts and a muted closing of the chamber door.

Roland . . . The name that summed all he had once been had returned to claim him more completely than he had imagined, he knew as he continued to sit there for a long time, staring about him at every detail of the comfortably equipped chamber to which he had, aye, let himself be brought.

". . . birth occurred even as he died." Roland shifted uneasily to hear it echo through his mind. They were two—Girard, falsely called De Guienne, and this other, this girl he had not known about, born as well, near the demise of Oliver's sister.

He shivered and huddled down into soft blankets and furs.

She . . . this Olivia, who looked so much like. Nay, he had not forgot the inscription he had read on her tomb at Aix. "Aude the Fair, Blessed in Death for a most Faithful Love."

His for that . . . How faithful?

How . . . dead?

Only much later did he find refuge from his thoughts in sleep.

The hearth fire burned away the fuel that remained in the grate to become faintly glowing embers. The candle, exhausting both wick and wax, guttered and died. And the night moved on to reveal different shades of darkness.

And beneath the filth-stiffened rags that bound her, the Dark Sword, Durandal, listened to the whispers in the silence. Considered that which had transpired.

Lord Oliver . . . Aye, that mortal, human creature, an upstanding, earth-got beast that she had slain to strip away the last of Roland's infancy. Regenerated . . .

This girl who had come like a ghost from the past to claim him. And that other he had mentioned.

It had recoiled. Doubly so.

Roland . . . who belonged to her. For whom she had been forged of tempests and thunder. For whom she waited . . . still.

By whom she was possessed, compelled through passions as honed and singularly linear, as frigid and sharp-edged as the very blade she was made to be.

She dared not move, or assume her other form. To act . . . Durandal knew angrily. The falcon that he had found—found?— even now watched the night from its perch on the chest across the chamber, its eyes too keen by far to miss the least implication of movement.

Raptor, that had recognized its lord. Hated bird, for the fealty given so completely, yet, somehow, sprung from the same Lord Oliver he still clung to with such tenacious perversity . . .

And, far, far away . . . in a very different place, where melded clouds obliterated the stars and loosed a gently persistent rainfall, a white owl perched high against the trunk of an old, gnarled tree. Its keen dark eyes watched with interest through the withering autumnal foliage the pair of men and two horses encamped in the dubious shelter below.

A curious pair of travelers, these two, huddled in their cloaks against the damp and chill. One, dark-haired and fiercely sober of countenance, was in the prime of his youth. A fighting man . . . the armor he wore beneath cloak and surcoat glinted faintly. A troubled man. The other was entirely different, Aged, weathered. White-haired and tawny-skinned, his attire combined a blend of wanderer and monk. In his latent youth, he had been a fighting man, then, for a time, a slave in heathen lands. He had become at last a peculiar sort of hermit who served the Pope by carrying messages between eastern and western Christendom.

The white owl knew them both, come from Rome, a city now buried in the night some twenty miles to the south and west. Once a curiously pristine and populous testament to the dominion of an empire, Rome crumbled gently, slowly now, its former glory eroding into a past long vanished. White stone gone grey. Roads through which wild grasses had found root and grew . . . Only the Church still occupied those cleaner, more spacious places that remained.

In a private audience with the Pope, Huon De Guienne had learned how he could restore himself. Charlemagne intended to put an end to the two-year-old war between Harum Al Rashid, Caliph of Baghdad, and the East Roman Empire, ruled by the boy King Constantine, and his mother, the Empress Irene. To that end, he wished to form an alliance with the Caliph, thereby restraining Byzantium to establish the full credibility of Rome as the seat of the True Faith.

It was for Huon De Guienne to accomplish that alliance, with the only aid of the near-heathen monk Sherasmin.

Or die . . . and be forgotten. As God, and Fate decreed.

Raindrops rolled like jewels from the plumage of the white owl as it watched and listened and waited with the incalculable patience of one to whom time and the elements were no more than momentary cycles. It blinked once and lightly ruffled its feathers, then moved its head to stare serenely toward the east . . . a most perfect predator.

Under any other circumstance, Girard thought as he saw the distant gleam of Bordeaux's towers above the orange and red of autumn-hued trees, he would have grinned delight and spurred his horse to race the last few miles for home. Not now.

Not this time. Instead, he shifted Huon's shield, suspended on his left arm, and touched it briefly with the fingers of his right hand. This was a homecoming he could never have wished for, bearing such horrible tidings. To see his mother's face . . .

The rest behind him by more than a horse's length, he let his young stallion pick its way down a hill, through a grove, and along a deer trail that skirted the nearest village to the castle, across the meadows to his right.

A swineherd, guarding his beasts as they foraged among new-fallen acorns, looked up as Girard sent his horse from the woods, across the strips of tilled land, barren now, their plantings harvested. He nodded acknowledgment as the serf made obeisance, then to others who gathered near their clustered, wattle-and-daub cottages some sixty yards to his right. Well-fed folk. Healthy . . .

His serfs now, although they could not know it yet, he thought and looked away, springing his horse into a canter. It did not matter to them, so long as they were justly ruled.

So Huon had said once, likening their devotion to that of dogs. Girard had been less certain.

My brother's keeper, he thought uneasily. But I am not my brother . . .

He thanked the instinct that had caused him to conceal Huon's shield beneath the folds of his cloak; later, when engulfed once more by Bordeaux's walls, he found himself surrounded by welcoming shouts and stares. Castle folk that seemed to appear out of every crevice, their faces showing curiosity as they saw he rode alone. Keeping the shield hid, he drew rein in the inner bailey and dismounted.

"Girard!" Called out, his name resounded like a bell. Relinquishing his horse, he turned at once to see his mother and sister appear at the top of the steps that led into the keep. Olivia's face was alight with gladness. He strode toward them both, finding a smile for his sister, then, as he reached her, a kiss of fraternal greeting for her brow. He turned and bowed deeply to the Duchess.

"Mother!" he half whispered it as he straightened, shocked to see how thin and strained she looked. "I am home," he offered, then bent to kiss her cheek.

"Thou are changed, Girard," she said, searching him with familiar, knowing eyes. "Thou hast the look of one who has been grievously ill . . . ?"

He shifted awkwardly toward the doors of the keep, glancing briefly at Olivia. "Aye. Well . . ." He smiled in apology. "We shall talk later. It has been a long journeying, and I would disarm myself first." He promptly walked inside to stride across the great hall, toward the stairs that led to his own apartments.

A lifetime had passed since he had left, he thought grimly.

Home . . . Familiar comforts and possessions surrounded him once more. Carefully, Girard set Huon's shield on the finely carved, walnut table that flanked one of the walls in his bedchamber, then drew off his helm and set that down as well. He pushed back his coif, and as he reached up to unclasp his cloak, he heard the door open. He turned instead to see Olivia enter.

"Welcome home, Girard!" she said, and flew into his embrace. He hugged her tightly, his half sister, who had always been more a part of him than the rest, but she drew back and looked at him with widened eyes.

"How is this, Girard?" she asked. "Thou are thin to frailness?"

"I took a wound in an ambush." He shrugged it away. "It has taken a long time to heal, that is all." She read him better than that, but said nothing as she helped him remove his cloak, then took the garment and set it aside. He looked exhausted. And there was a new sobriety that marked him, she saw, and did not press him. Girard would tell her in his own time . . .

"Here," she said instead, taking the belt that carried the scabbarded sword and dagger he wore. "Let me give thee comfort." She too felt a new solemnity as she helped him further, removing the chain mail he wore, all got from what she had learned. Blood completely shared . . . he was her full brother, her father's reflection as Lord Roland had said. It made a profound difference to know this thing Lord Roland had revealed.

"I missed thee," she ventured after a time. He met her look and nodded with new reticence. "It is not the same, I think?"

"We are no longer children, Olivia," he said quietly, yet with an edge of regret that revealed his own awareness. "That is the difference." He smiled fleetingly. "Go now. Tell Mother I will shortly attend her."

Olivia nodded and swung away to obey.

• • •

"I am relieved to see thee safe returned, Girard," the Duchess said as she accepted his filial gesture of affection from her favorite chair in the family solar. "Particularly as it is clear thou have been unwell?" Girard straightened and drew back, recognizing the cool determination in her voice. He could never have steeled himself enough to face this, he realized, shifting uncomfortably and glancing to where his sister stood watching him as well, but with a peculiarly alert, new searching quality.

"On the last part of our journey to Aix, we were waylaid. I recollect little of it, being felled at the outset. It has taken me some time to recover from my wounds."

The Duchess stood, her gaze sharpened and fixed on his face. "And Huon?" she demanded.

"He was unharmed."

"He has not returned with thee?"

"Nay." Girard's stance went rigid, his voice tight. "By some mischance, and during that ambush, it seems that Huon killed the Prince Charlot. For that, he was tried by battle. He won, which proved he killed the Prince unknowingly . . . He was condemned to perpetual exile from this realm, and was disinherited of all property and title . . ." He fell silent as the Duchess sank back into her chair, her face going ashen, haggard, and terrible.

"Nay!" she whispered. "Huon? He is incapable of such treason . . ."

"Huon killed his chief accuser, Mother," Girard cut in. "Lord Amaury De Hauteville . . ." Her fingers tightened to white-knuckled fists as she stared.

"Who else?" she rasped. "I should have sensed it!" Then, "And thou . . . Girard?" Question, or accusation? He looked down.

"I am Duke of Bordeaux now, Mother," he said tonelessly. "Vested by the King."

Silence hung like devils whispering. The Duchess stood up slowly, her eyes never leaving his face.

"I see!" she said at last, coldly, awfully uttering it, then turning away to depart the solar in a swirl of skirts.

Girard swallowed as he stared after her, strangled by feelings he could not deal with. Olivia inhaled sharply and he jerked a little, saw her staring at him with rounded eyes.

He struggled. "Does she think I had some part in this?" he

rasped awkwardly. "God help me. I do *not* want this elevation to my brother's estate. I have only grief for his misfortune . . ."

Even now, half smothered by this terrible news, she could not escape the force of what Lord Roland had told her. Olivia stared at her brother, seeing every detail of him . . . knowing. Ghosts . . . She blinked.

"I do not know, Girard," she whispered slowly. "I do not know . . ."

"The wound heals well, my lord." Lady Alice heard her own matter-of-fact tone as though from some other place. Watched herself as she wrapped fresh bandages around Roland's right shoulder. "I am glad to see it." Perverse civility. It was remarkable to her how that part of her remained as controlled and deliberate as ever. Far away now, as it had been ever since Girard's return a few hours before. The rest screamed outrage at Huon's disgrace . . .

She completed her task and stepped back, watching as the . . . thing, called Roland, raised undertunic and robe to cover his shoulders once more, replaced the throats of the garments to close them again.

Witch creature. Apparition . . . She moved to the table where she had set the silver flagon of wine she had brought with her, poured some of it into a cup, then moved toward him again, to offer it.

"Refreshment, my lord," she said softly, watching as he took it—sipped—then drank slowly to drain the whole. Such a little sin to kill this monster who had conjured upon her son . . .

He looked up as he gave her back the cup. Satan's eyes . . .

"This poison will not kill me, my lady," he said quietly.

She froze. "Poison, my lord?"

"Aye! Even I could not mistake that bitter aftertaste! Yet, I tell thee, it will not destroy me!"

"Witch!" she hissed utter revulsion, stepping back. "I knew it!"

Still his eyes bored into hers. "Witch got—by repute such as has haunted my life, Lady Alice. And bastard as well!" He spoke in a tone curiously devoid of feeling. "For whatever truth there is in it, I have sought no part . . ."

"Witch!" she rasped again, gone haggard as she stepped farther from him.

"And if I am such—a witch?" he cut in sternly, frowning as

he reached for his crutches and jerked up to hang on them. "Then I have only one single thing from that heritage—being condemned to endure that which would kill a natural man!

"Where is the profit in what I have endured?" he asked her then with softly terrible bitterness. "Or in this condition that I am reduced to?" He bent a little. Gasped. "And this poison . . ." He grimaced, forced himself to straighten. "Aye, I feel it! To the least drop. Yet it will not kill me."

"What have thou wrought upon my sons?" she grated then, her eyes glittering with both fury and terror.

"Naught, my lady . . ." Pain twisted across his face. "Save that I witnessed a treacherous ambush that near killed the lord Girard. If there be any witch power in me from that blood thou so revile, then it has been given in incessant prayer for his life!" His eyes widened slowly. "Sooo! He is returned, the Lord Girard?" he whispered, reading it on her face.

"He is made Duke, while my other son, Huon, is banished and disgraced for a treason I know he could not commit! This is thy doing, Lord Roland!"

He shook his head. "Nay!"

"Aye!" she countered fiercely. "I have not forgot that unnatural weapon with which thou stole from Lord Oliver the office of King's Champion! Nor have I forgot how thou seduced him to love thee beyond the natural even for a brother! Now, thou have contrived with spells to elevate my second son over the honor of the rightful lord of these fiefs, and seek to seduce him further to his damnation by the pretext of a gift accursed . . ." Her eyes narrowed. Her hands were fists against her skirts. "Girard, who is got Oliver's son as we both know, has no need of any such devil's aid to defend his honor, or to bring him glory!"

The truth skewed like a misdirected arrow. Roland straightened and stared at her, then realized . . . "He does not know, this son of Oliver . . ." he breathed softly, recalling the shock on the girl's face when he had spoke of it. The Duchess did not answer, but stared back at him with utter hatred. "I see it. He does not know!" He leaned forward a little. "How is it that thou have denied him the knowledge of the truth of his birth? Nay, my lady. I am not the one to be accused! I think that this thing that has happened to nearly destroy Lord Girard and dispose his brother is the consequence of thy own determined secrecy, for surely I am not the only one to recollect the child he was when Oliver still lived?" He bent, and with remarkable agility scooped up the bundle he had made of the Dark Sword, quickly stripping away the rags that covered her to expose the brilliant dark purity and blue-toned lightning hues of her blade. His voice went raw, hoarse as he continued.

"It was once said of us, a Roland for an Oliver . . . For that to be fulfilled, and for my soul's peace, I *will* give my gift to defend the life of his son! It was by this blade—in my hand— that Oliver died at Roncesvalles!"

She crumbled then. Fist to mouth. Shuddering. Eyes gone round in a face that was no more than ashen skin over bone.

"Nay!" she whispered.

"Aye!" he rasped hideously. "And for the witch in me, what better to protect the blood of Oliver than the powers of this, aye, unnatural sword!" He set the weapon between arm and body, and swung on his crutches toward her. Past her. She could not move.

The falcon cried out once as he passed through the door, then into the short corridor beyond, an undefined creature garbed in a long fine robe, the folds swinging with him, hair like golden fire about his shoulders. Only his hands and face were exposed to reveal his pestilential condition . . .

Like some shattered, disconnected thing, the Duchess turned slowly and followed him, then stopped as he disappeared from view, lurching down the steps that led to the great hall and the rest below.

It was too late.

It had always been too late . . . she realized slowly. Oliver had damned himself and his blood to perpetuity, by that very love and loyalty he had given to the ghastly witch-thing that called itself Roland.

"Holy Mary, Mother of God!" she whispered. "Satan is come among us!" She crossed herself with a hand that jerked. "Preserve my soul . . ." she murmured helplessly, and turned to take a different route along the corridor that led by another passage to her own chambers in another part of the keep.

Roland paused at the entrance to the great hall, his teeth clenched as he fought down the swirling pain of the poison in his middle. He watched the pair of servants about the business of furnishing the hearth fire in the middle, and remembered his way about the great castle from those times before. The solar, he thought . . . He made the Dark Sword more inconspicuous against him using the folds of his robe, then reached up with one hand to draw the cowl of the garment over his head, partial concealment at least for his vile countenance.

Then he swung himself across the hall, past the servants who stared but did not know what to do, toward a stairwell he remembered on the other side. Laborious ascent . . . And finally he swung along a shadowed corridor, aware of his own perverted feeling of stealth as he sought the chamber he remembered.

He stopped silently beside the closed door. Listened, and heard the crackling of a hearth fire on the other side. Then, very carefully, he opened it and stared across the large, luxuriously furnished room, his gaze fixing on a figure that sat drooped in a large chair on the other side.

Oliver . . . young, alive again. But thinner than he should be, this son. Exhaustion and other things showed upon his face. Roland inhaled painfully as he swung himself silently through the portal into the solar. Had he been so simpleton, he thought, to believe this would be an easy thing?

"My lord?" he said, his voice deep, clear.

Thoroughly startled from his reverie, Girard lunged to his feet and twisted around. His eyes widened as he saw a tall, crippled man whose face was concealed under a hood, garbed in a long robe, and supported by a pair of crutches.

"Who art thou to come into this private place?" Girard demanded, stepping forward.

"My lord. I bear a gift for thee." Hanging on his crutches, Roland kept his head bowed a little as he drew forth the Dark Sword and held her out. Chill now in his grip—and rightly so, for her warmth and shimmering power and songs belonged to this other before him.

Already surprised by the crippled man, Girard stared in astonishment at this other thing, so clearly proffered. A sword . . . But such a sword as he had never seen before. Dark—almost sinister. Darker than steel could ever be, it had a blade of impossible length. Even the hilt, which appeared to be made of a pair of flawlessly carved, outspread wings. The whole was far beyond any craftsmanship he knew about.

"This . . . ?" he asked, stepping closer. "How is it that thou bring this wondrous thing to me?"

"I have ordered the evening meat to be brought here presently, Girard . . . Aaah!" Olivia's voice was a chaotic dissonance as she swept into the chamber in a flurry of green skirts. Jerked to a halt. "Lord Roland!" she gasped loudly.

Girard stared at his sister. "Thou know this man?" he asked at once. She shot him an uncharacteristically wary look that said she did, and, moving around the tall cripple, came toward him. "Lord Roland?" Girard repeated unevenly, staring at the crippled man and the extraordinary sword. "There is only one who ever bore that name, and he is long dead . . ."

"He is the same!" Olivia's voice was brittle, certain.

"Who I am is of no importance, my lord," the crippled man cut in fiercely. "Only this sword, called Durandal, which is gifted to thee!"

Like something from a recurring delirium, the stranger's tone sounded eerie and familiar. Frowning, Girard stepped forward to peer intently at the face below the shadowing cowl. Golden eyes—as he had seen before in those mad, terrible dreams.

"I know thee!" he whispered and lunged with one hand to sweep back the cripple's hood. He paled and gasped as he saw the entirety of the man's hideousness, the brilliant contrast of hair and beard. "God's pity!" he breathed.

"Take the sword, my lord! It is my gift to thee!" the cripple said commandingly, the Dark Sword still held out before him. Durandal, Girard recalled words from the Song, was the name of the sword of Roland. He tried to collect himself. Roland . . . ?

"I think thou seek to gift the wrong man. I am but a second son. It is my brother, Lord Huon, who is the true heir . . ."

"Not so, my lord Girard!" the crippled man cut in with harsh command. "It is for thee. None other! For the blood that is thine entire, and for what I once was, I make, as is my right, this gift to thee alone! *Take* it!"

Girard glanced at his sister who stood very still, her face paled, yet knowing something he did not. Hesitantly, he reached and let his fingers close around the suggestively complex hilt of this unique weapon. Silken textures, undefined—yet it molded perfectly to fit his grasp. And he felt at once the strange chill that seeped from the sword to penetrate his skin. It shifted, melted into something warm and potent. Nay. No common weapon this, he knew as he stared at it.

He looked up again to meet those intense golden eyes. Saw ferocity and other deep, pain-filled, and passionate things. And the ruin of what had been the most puissant and valiant of knights.

"Is it so important then, my lord, that I accept?" he asked softly.

"Aye!" The reply was instant and rasped with odd, harsh passion. Questions . . . Girard did not ask them, but turned and looked at his sister. Olivia stood poised and tense. Roland and Oliver . . . Aye. He thought perhaps he understood as his fingers shifted over the seductively perfect grip of the sword Durandal.

"Thou do me great honor, Lord Roland," he said carefully, "to entrust to me this sword whereby I may guard my sister's blood and name. For the truth of who thou art, and by respect for the chivalrous love that made the twin names of Roland and Oliver both legend and example, I accept for the Lady Olivia, who is De Montglave's daughter . . ."

"Girard!" she hissed loudly. He turned to stare at her. "That is not why! Can thou not see it . . . the truth?" she demanded roughly. He frowned, puzzled. Her gaze shifted toward the cripple. "Lord Roland gives his sword to Oliver's *son*!" she pronounced very clearly.

"What?" Girard whispered. The cripple bowed his head. His hands made fists around the hafts of his crutches.

In the hearth, the fire cracked violently.

"That is the truth as thou have told me," Olivia said tautly, "is it not, my lord Roland? Girard is got my full brother. He is Lord Oliver's son, and so like, as thou said it, to be a perfect replication of my father!" Girard froze with shock. But she went on, looking at him now. "It is true, Girard. I have had time enough to realize. Huon is thy half brother—and I think he knew it, for we have grown of late to be much of a likeness, thou and I . . ."

"It is true, Lord Girard, as I know from Lord Oliver's own lips," the cripple said quietly. "Nor is there a prouder birthright!"

Like something from the grave, Girard felt the assurance of certain knowledge, and that devotion that had become a renowned and legendary thing . . . given now, to himself.

Shocked to immobility, he felt the spreading of realizations. Aye . . . little puzzles that were suddenly now explained.

"It is given, my bequest," the cripple said then. "I will go now." He made a swinging turn.

"Nay!" Girard lunged forward in sheer reflex. Stopped and swallowed awkwardly as he met the other's golden eyes. "For the brotherhood between Roland and Oliver—and for this," he jerked out, shifting the sword he held, "thou hast a place here, my lord. Do thou stay. Let us give thee such as is thy right for that?"

Roland shifted, and looked toward the girl. Both of them . . . Aye, she too . . . he bowed his head and knew brutally that he had no wish to leave. There was nothing else left beyond Bordeaux's walls. Yet . . .

"That Roland is dead, my lord!" he said harshly. "This is but a leper's shell that remains!"

"Nay, my lord!" Girard countered with a curious, groping gentleness. "For . . . my father's . . . sake, it could never be so!"

Startled, raw, Roland looked up to meet blue eyes known as nothing else. Yielded.

"So be it, my lord," he whispered slowly.

SIXTEEN

Exhaustion crawled along his limbs. The wound in his flank ached where it was supposed to be healed, and his eyes stung from half a night spent sitting in a chair, holding the Dark Sword, Durandal, and staring at the embers of the fire on the other side of the chamber.

Vigil . . . ? Not exactly. Girard knew he was slowly pulling himself together through a badly pummeled consciousness to accept a truth he had never even imagined. He was Lord Oliver De Montglave's son. Not a De Guienne at all . . .

Olivia had told him much. How Lord Roland had been discovered and brought into the castle . . . And the tragic thing that had been the glorious Lord Roland himself had finalized it. Softly, awkwardly uttered, the crippled leper had succinctly revealed the ambush he had witnessed, his own recognition, and the other knowledge he had from long before.

The presence of the falcon made proof enough . . . Returning the cripple to the chamber in the east tower, Girard had known the bird at once. And the dreams that had haunted his delirium? He understood now, how he had roused enough to see the same leprous Lord Roland bent over him, praying for his life . . .

Nay, for Lord Oliver's sake—and his own now, he could not let the crippled man resume his abandoned, beggared, and aimless wandering. That living death of lepers . . .

Now, as well, he understood Huon's remoteness. Huon had known the truth—for a time, at least. Yet knowing his brother's

160

even excessive forthrightness, Girard could not understand why Huon had kept silent . . .

He probed deeper, back to what he knew of the time of his birth. Lord Servinus' death . . . and his mother's second marriage that had occurred so much later. Nothing even mentioned . . .

Girard jerked to his feet. She knew. She knew . . .

Very carefully, he moved to set the Dark Sword on the table by his brother's shield, then, uncaring of the darkness, or the hour, he left his room to seek his mother's apartments.

The resistance of the aging tirewoman was quelled with a glance as Girard thrust past her into the chamber. He saw his mother at once, illuminated by candle glow, lying huddled and fully clothed amid the furs on the large bed. He stopped abruptly by the side of it, shocked by that, and by the new, ugly haggardness of her. Saw her thin hands twisting restlessly around the beads of a rosary.

"Mother?" She stopped moving. "Mother . . . How is it that I am Lord Oliver De Montglave's son?" He tried to keep his tone gentle. "I must know the truth. I have a right to know." She twisted and looked at him. Dark eyes, like Huon's. Silver shimmering through her hair. "Why have I never been told of this?" He reached toward her . . .

"Do not touch me!" she hissed. "I am defiled enough!" Girard jerked back. Froze. But she looked away, her head rocking a little. "My sins, and I am damned for nurturing them!" she intoned. Girard felt his skin crawl. "It is too late to undo . . . The name and honor of De Guienne are betrayed! Bastard seed! And now he is come to claim thee even as he seduced thy sire . . ."

Not like this, Girard thought desperately, wanting only sense and truth. "Who?" he gasped harshly.

"The witch, Roland!" she snarled, black-eyed and staring.

"For God . . . !" Girard whispered, paling.

"God," she murmured desperately, looking away again. "There it is . . . Without the embrace of the sacrament, Satan lurks to feed on every sin. And I am damned as well, for my own weakness. *Go!* Get away from me! Let me seek God's consolation before I die!"

"This is madness!" Girard whispered, jerking back convulsively, his nostrils flaring as they caught a strange, rotten sweetness in the air. Bile rose in his throat. He saw the candles lit under the crucifix on the far side of the room where his mother habitually prayed. No incense . . . And the eyes of the tire-woman staring at him.

He fled.

The door to his chamber shut like a trap. Girard crossed the room and sank down onto the furs that covered his bed, sickened, drained of vigor. His hands shook, he saw in the dim glow that came from the hearth.

Not like this, he thought again. Not this skewed and hideous, half-mad revelation . . . Secrets kept so well he had never even imagined. He looked up and saw the pale gleam of the swan on Huon's shield from the table on the other side. Now, he understood the discord that had arisen between himself and his brother. Huon's rigid sense of honor had been defiled by this deception. Outraged entirely, knowing his bastard brother was his heir. Now Duke in his place . . .

". . . fulfill that honor which is thy chiefmost inheritance . . ." the King had said. Girard shuddered. Even Charlemagne knew the truth. How many others?

"I am a bastard," Girard said aloud, slowly, carefully—hearing it, and knowing full well the significance of unsanctified birth. Totally sapped, his wits clouding to incoherence, he sank down to lie in the darkness. And the name of Oliver De Montglave reached out like a palpable force from beyond the grave to touch and affect everything. Change everything. Now, this gift from the ghostlike ruin of Lord Roland—this sword unlike any other, given for a love that also transcended, had texture and power.

Honor? Duty? Under swimming senses that sank toward unconsciousness, Girard knew that clarity had vanished behind clouds of confusion.

In the dormant silence of deepest night, the woman hilt of Durandal clarified from the reflective, concealing garment of dark ambiguity she had woven, to watch and listen. She turned her diminutive head to stare with virulent obsidian eyes at the sleeping form of the young man on the far side of the room. Temper wove streaks of muted blue shimmering along her blade. Fury—for the giving that Roland had done.

This too was bondage. And still he remained unaware of the forces he utilized. Unmistakable, the formula that made this human so obviously Oliver reborn. Face. Hair . . . every detail. Even the flank wound was a practical reiteration, with the crucial difference that he had survived it, to make an undoing. And Roland, still clinging to his disastrous humanity, did not know what he had wrought.

Temper softened into something provocative and thoughtful as she watched the sleeping man. She found a space in the entrapment that surrounded her. Aye, something seductive. The means by which to reverse it and bring, through service, this human creature to serve.

She shifted fluidly, wings and blade remaining still, her eyes growing dense as one hand emerged from the filament wealth of her hair to point toward the sleeping mortal.

"Dream of me . . ." she whispered, her voice like the trailing path of a night breeze. "Aye. Do thou dream of me, my lord."

He shifted then, the young human Girard. And in the manner of one profoundly, naturally asleep, drew his legs up and curled as his arms reached to embrace the pillow on which his head was cradled.

The resounding slam of the door in response to the tug of her hand as she fled cut off the ghastly tirade that filled the room beyond it. Shaking in every limb, Olivia gasped and leaned back against the wall beside it. Blinked back shocked tears as she suddenly saw her mother's chief tirewoman huddled on the other side of the corridor, wide, frightened eyes fixed on her. She fought for control.

"Why are thou not within, Aliena? Attending to thy Lady's needs?" she demanded harshly. The woman flinched visibly.

"The Lady Alice bade me attend the leper in the east tower," she whispered unevenly, crossing herself.

"Then do it!" Olivia said at once.

"But, my lady?" The woman whispered hoarsely, her eyes flitting toward the door. "Do thou not see what has become of Lady Alice from . . ."

"Fool!" Olivia burst out. "The Lady Alice suffers a fevered raving got of grief for Lord Huon! *Never* from the giving of God's own charity!" But the woman shrank back. Already shaken badly, Olivia's temper flared. *"Go!"* she ordered. "Care for thy lady! I will see to this other myself!"

The tirewoman scurried crablike across the hall and vanished in an instant, through the Duchess' door.

Still glowering, still shocked hollow, Olivia clutched at her skirts and hurried away. Fled . . . ? Aye. Girard, she thought. But Girard had risen shortly after daybreak, and was in some other part of the castle, taking control and attending to the business that had come to him as lord.

Feet shod in soft doeskin moved with light-footed silence. Only her skirts made a sound, rustling a little as she stopped abruptly before the door that marked Huon's chambers.

Pity Huon. Pity Huon, who had been betrayed. Who was now disinherit and exiled. Olivia shuddered. Never—never could she have imagined to see her mother so, become in an instant a haggard wraith, a dark-eyed harpy from whom issued an unspeakably hideous diatribe that still rang in her ears.

And the venom of it . . . "Go," the duchess had hissed. "I do not wish to look on thee again. I am dying, and I will finish it alone!" Pity Huon, who alone of them, had been bred pure and undefiled. Oliver's blood, carried in herself and Girard, tainted—bewitched to curse them all . . . And Lord Roland, who was a witch.

"Mad!" Olivia whispered hollowly, needing sense and reason. She thrust through the door into the bedchamber beyond.

Empty. Dim for the shutters that blocked out the day. Chill for the lack of a hearth fire. It seemed desolate—the air a little dank, musty on the nostrils.

Huon's absence was excruciatingly apparent.

She looked around at his personal properties. The baggage chest that had been brought back from Aix. Rich furnishings and tapestries. The arms he had favored most. A gold flagon of unique design. A crucifix, given to him one Easter by their mother. A reliquary passed on to him and got by Duke Servinus during one of the southern campaigns that had preoccupied that lord. Carpets got as well from the Infidels to the south . . .

And in one corner, her gaze fixed on a spiderweb that was spread between stone walls and roof beams. Dust weighted one end. The rest was a delicate, perfect net across that neglected space. She saw then as well the insect poised in the center. Round-bodied and large, its legs spread like rays—waiting, as spiders were wont to do, for some other creature to come along and, unsuspecting, become entangled in the doom it had woven.

How apt . . . Olivia swallowed against the nightmares her mother had made. Took a determined grip on herself.

"I will *not* forget that God made thee as well!" she told the creature forcefully, and left to find her way to the east tower.

As she entered the chamber with the food and ale she had remembered to collect, Olivia saw that he stood propped between left leg and crutch, staring out of the single, narrow window in the outer wall of the tower chamber. Beyond stiffening, he did not respond to her entrance. Gold and amber played through his hair, and he had drastically shortened his beard, revealing the line of the strong jaw beneath. Linen undertunic and chausses covered his tall, lean frame, his shriveled right leg ending in a knotting of cloth below the skirts of his tunic.

"I have brought food and drink, my lord," she said, setting the supplies on the table. "I have come in my mother's place to attend to thy injury."

He jerked around at that, eyes wary, like a wild thing. "There is no need, my lady. It heals!" he said roughly. Her eyes moved to the light brown seepage that stained the right shoulder of his tunic.

"Nonetheless"—she stiffened with determination—"it is only good sense that I change the dressings." He glared even more fiercely. "Mastiffs bare their teeth and growl when they are afraid as well!" she challenged then, remembering earlier impressions. She struck true, she saw, for he froze. She drove it home. "I am easily capable of distinguishing the man from his misfortunes!" she told him truthfully, realizing as she said it that she was no longer repelled by him at all.

He yielded suddenly, lurching with remarkable agility to seat himself on the edge of the bed on the other side of the room.

So Oliver would have said—word and tone, Roland thought painfully, lowering his head, then raising his hand to unlace the throat of his tunic, drawing it away from the bandaged place.

He *is* afraid of me, Olivia thought, gathering up clean linen strips and unguents, then moving to kneel before him. All taut and intense, he looked away to stare at the stone wall as she set to work, removing the soiled bandages, seeing closely his ghastly skin. Fierce eyes, set mouth. Underneath, pain—a great deal of pain—held in check by sheer will. She felt a surge of pity as she cleaned his wound, a narrow gaping, the edges puckered back like the layers of a desiccated onion. Dead-looking flesh, save for the thin serous fluid that oozed slowly forth . . .

In herself, a lifetime of confidence and pride and knowledge fought back against the battering her mother had inflicted. She knew very well how to tread the firm soil of clear, sound good sense.

"Art thou a witch?" she asked very softly. He jerked to face her, his eyes going wide . . . haunted and terrible.

"Witch got!" he rasped baldly. "For God, I pray, never a witch!"

She nodded, seeing terror. He twisted to look away, more fiercely withdrawn than ever. She continued cleaning his wound, then began winding clean bandages around it, and recalled a different kind of intensity from the past spring, when young Baudoin De Maganze had offered posies of primrose and crocus, and honestly given flatteries.

Nay, she knew then, remembering that other, terrible thing her mother had revealed. Lord Roland could never have carried his feelings on his sleeve for all the world to see. Nor could he ever have been a facile courtier to woo. He was too rough, his terrors, deep terrors, held tightly behind a shield of ferocity. Aye, his roughness was fear got.

Finished, she drew back and rose, taking the soiled bandages, then dropping them into the hearth fire to burn. Still, he sat there, his withdrawal palpably intense, staring away as he moved one hand to replace his garment. She frowned a little.

"Do I resemble so much the Lady Aude who was betrothed to thee that thou cannot bear to look at me?" she asked then.

He twisted, his face harsh, his head ducking down as he groped for his crutches, his hands making fists around the hafts. She had struck again, she saw.

"There is no good to be got of my presence here!" he rasped it out. "I must leave . . ."

"Do thou fear to stay, Lord Roland?" Again, Olivia challenged him. His head came up, his eyes met hers.

"I must go!" he growled, defying her.

"I have a need for thee to stay, my lord," she said then. "I wish to understand that friendship that bound thee to my father to make such a love that is, even today, renowned and praised and sung about . . ."

He flinched. "That Roland died long ago . . . with Oliver," he whispered hoarsely.

Olivia shook her head. "Nay. Not so," she said with conviction, and saw him shiver concession to the truth. "Aaah, my lord. Thou art a very battlefield of intensity!" she murmured an acknowledgment of her own. Something raw crossed his eyes, then, strangely, he slumped, defeated.

"I will stay," he whispered.

She did not answer, but, having won something unclear, left very quietly.

Ghosts . . . Roland looked up after the door had closed. Stared at it. That other thing that Oliver had said to him, come again from the daughter's mouth to tear, and haunt. To bring to life . . . To catch him more surely than a lance in the ribs.

How could he leave now . . . ?

The night air made a cold draft as it wafted in through the open window where Girard stood, had been standing for some time.

"Have thou seen Mother, Olivia?" Girard asked quietly, continuing to stare out. Keeping warm in her chair near the hearth fire, Olivia looked at him. His profile showed tiredness, strain.

"I have. She is very ill."

He nodded without looking at her.

"She wishes to die. God help me, Girard," Olivia crossed herself, "but I think she will . . . This tragedy with Huon, I think it has broken her. He was her pride . . ."

"Aye," he whispered. Then, "I could not have come home to worse circumstances," he said in distraught tones. "Huon . . . Now this . . ."

Olivia thought she understood. "Ah. She cursed thee too." He turned then and stared at her, all braced.

"I *am* Oliver De Montglave's son," he told her. "But there is more. I am his bastard!"

Olivia's eyes widened. "Never say . . . !" she breathed. "Mother? I cannot conceive she would . . . And Lord Oliver?"

"A simple counting is sufficient to verify it!" he cut in sharply. "And as I have also discovered today, I was born before term!" Olivia stared. His face strained and unhappy, Girard met her look, then lowered his gaze and turned away to stare once more out of the window. "It is true . . . And now, for the different circumstance of my birth, I must discern my proper and exact duty . . ."

Olivia inhaled deeply. "I think that is clear enough, Girard," she said carefully. "Thou are vested Duke by the King's hand.

This does not change that. Lord Roland knows the truth, assuredly, yet he has blessed thee in the gift of his own sword . . .''

"He is a witch . . ." Girard began.

"That is mother's guilt for past sins speaking!" Olivia said briskly, frowning. "And her grief for Huon. I know not by what circumstances Lord Roland survived the battle of Roncesvalles to have another mistakenly entombed in his place, but he has clear enough been crippled since. He is a diseased and misfortunate man. No more . . .

"Mother's pride is as great as Huon's, and that is her undoing now! Nay. I'll not see devils where there are sensible explanations, Girard! Nor is it like thee to think so!"

"And when the vassals of these fiefs learn the truth, as they must do . . . ? And see this . . . leper harbored among us? Who will see devils then, Olivia?"

She did not answer at once, but stared at him, her hands clenching slowly in her lap.

"Then they will honor and give fealty to their true lord as the King has made to care for them!" she said slowly, with forceful determination. "And they will respect the Lord who was crippled in battle and lives as a guest with us, for the rest is easily disguised!"

"God's will be done," he said, still staring out of the window.

"Beyond doubt!" she affirmed. He did not respond, or move.

"The snows come soon, I think . . ." he said much later.

SEVENTEEN

794 A.D.

White cold specks tumbled from thick grey skies to alight on bare stark trees and empty meadows, on the thatched roofs of manor cottages, and on the high stone towers of Bordeaux castle. And with the snows came a muted, chill silence that poised to embrace the individual resonances of each slightest sound.

Even that final, soft exhaling of air that accompanies the soul's departure from the flesh.

The Duchess Alice De Guienne De Montglave died with the first flurries to brush soft white quiet into all the crevices of the land, but five weeks after the return of Lord Girard.

There was no warmth at all in the gently weaving light cast by the candles on the chapel altar, or positioned at the head and foot of the bier before it. Winter chill had pervaded every stone of that small place and seeped forth like something hard against the senses, demanding the will, a reminder of the disciplines of faith.

Sensors burned slowly, their perfumed smoke spiraling upward in delicate threads to diffuse and blend with the thick, sweet rancidity of the air.

In a shadowed corner, the tirewoman, Aliena, knelt with uncompromising determination through all the hours of the pre-burial vigil, on knees gone numb and brittle. For her soul's sake, and for loyalties that stretched back a lifetime, she would not leave until the Duchess had been disposed into the tomb that awaited her beside that of Duke Servinus.

Uncounted, the years that had passed since Aliena had come as a young girl given to serve the youthful virgin bride Lady Alice had been then. She had attended her lady through nuptials and consummation, through the months of breeding, then the birth of Lord Huon. She remembered still Duke Servinus' pride in his new son. And, later, when he was but fresh laid in his tomb, that furtive affair at Court. The second marriage that had sprung from it. She had midwifed that second birth. And the third. Sin—sprung forth without natural travail.

Now, she knew what she knew.

She had not left the Duchess in all those days and nights of slow, torturous dying. Save for that business of the leper witch in the east tower, her faithfulness had been absolute. The Lady Olivia had brought the monster among them . . . a demon who used a dead man's corpse and name.

By charity, the Lady Alice had been struck down, returning from that tower to seek her bed, never to rise from it again. Instead, she had lain there, refusing to eat, barely moistening her lips, shriveling away, and occupied with desperate prayer. The rest, like a clipped wildflower, had died . . .

Aye. Aliena knew what she knew.

Learned when those bright children of De Montglave had come to see their mother. And, from times long ago, when she too had heard the rumors of Lord Roland's getting, seen the friendship that had been born between him and Lord Oliver. She had watched when Lord Girard had come a second time, his features distraught, seeking peace—as he had claimed it. The Duchess had asked only if he had accepted the gift. His reply had been, aye. Then, ashen-faced, he had left.

She had watched as well, these two twin creatures, Lord Girard, now Duke, and his sister, come during the daylight hours to kneel and pray and grieve before the bier . . .

False children, Aliena knew now. Nurtured in a wrongful secrecy. Seduced by truly cunning witchcraft. The signs were clear enough . . . The Lady Olivia attended to the demon in the east tower now, and was unharmed, unmarked for it. Aliena's chilblained fingers made knots in the fold of her gown as she stared across the winter darkness that hid much of the surrounding chapel.

Pity Lord Huon, the rightful Duke, who was dispossessed by sorcery . . .

Hollow, muted clickings and a light thud came from the entrance to the chapel. Aliena froze, her eyes widening with fear for her own safety even in this sanctuary. She turned her head to stare at the dark-shrouded figure that stood there. Saw, as it emerged into the dimly revealing candle glow, glimpses of a single leg, and crutches, of height, and glinting eyes, and facelessness. The creature swung itself with an eerie quiet ease along the aisle toward the bier. There it stopped. The greater illumination revealed a man's form and gloved hands upon the staves that propped him up. A single, normal leg . . . the other, bent seeming, misfitting, like a beast's . . .

She could not have risen to flee, even though she wished . . .

He did not kneel, but continued to simply stand there. Then, after a time, he reached out slowly, to touch the corpse. The tirewoman's innards made a somersault of terror as she heard his sigh waft across the chapel, and saw one of the Lady Alice's frozen hands shift to fall away from the crucifix upon her breast, the fingers splayed, held upward, as though for defense.

"Is this how thou have abandoned them, my lady . . . Oliver's children?" Aliena heard him ask in a deep, melodiously powerful tone. She shuddered, her own heartbeat sounding like thunder in her ears.

"So be it, then . . ." he said, accepting in the same unnatural tones, as if he heard. He turned away from the bier, and Aliena gasped convulsively as she caught the gleam of fire in a pair of fierce, brilliant eyes beneath the hood that concealed his face. He started at the sound and swung like some great swooping thing toward her. Aliena quailed back with a pitiful, incoherent squeak. But he stopped, stared for a moment, then turned again, and passed away, down the aisle, vanishing once more into the cold night.

Unable to rise for the ague that rooted her knees to the stone floor, Aliena shuddered violently and stared again at the body of Lady Alice on the bier.

The misplaced hand with its desperately splayed fingers, slackened very slowly, as though with helplessness, as it went lax upon the rest. One of the gold coins set upon the eyes to keep them closed slipped, then tumbled down to roll away across the floor, chinking dismally on the flagging. And as the last sound of it died away, the eyelid parted, opening to let the dead eye stare once more.

Shivering, her knuckles pressed to her mouth in terror, Aliena stared in uncontrollable terror.

Satan had come to claim them, the Lord Girard and the Lady Olivia. She knew what she had seen. Hellfire disguised as eyes, one goat's leg concealed beneath his garments . . .

"We are all doomed now . . ." she whispered helplessly.

Death was incapable of elegance, Roland thought as he finished his return through the night-darkened keep of Bordeaux and closed the door to his tower chamber behind him. All rigor and rot in the end, its perfume a manifest offense.

He swung himself across the chamber to stop on the other side, pushing open the shutters of the window at once. Then he inhaled deeply of the sharp, cold air. Clean air . . .

That grotesque corpse was barely recognizable as the Lady Alice. Lying there in richly embroidered robes, it was some kind of grimly accusing parody instead. He had felt it at once—and keenly. Even now.

"Whatever is witch in me had no part in this dying!" Roland muttered defiant self-defense.

There was no answer. Only snowflakes that emerged out of the night to waft impartially through the window, alighting upon the rich garments he now wore.

He looked down at his own gloved hand upon the sill. At the fine, dark kidskin that covered the other thing beneath to give him back a man's hand. A large snowflake wafted down to settle on the knuckle, then began to melt slowly away.

Outside, there were drifts enough to bury anything.

But not himself . . . this time.

And he, who was witch got . . . ? Roland swallowed against new, pervasive uncertainties and remembered the nightmare crone who had mothered his infancy and early childhood. Even that singular condition of his bastardy had been distorted and confused by a twofold claim of paternity . . . Charlemagne's incest-got bastard? Or the Owl's unnatural child? Both were fraught with frightful and damning implications. Together, they made a complex, unresolved vortex that swept around and clung to him.

And magic . . . ? It was not so simple as dour pronouncements, ill-tempered curses, and malice-laden looks. Nay, he understood that now. Air, water, earth, and fire, such were the elements that composed all things. Of these alone, air penetrated all else with an absolute and thorough cunning. Invisible. Intangible. It flowed in currents like moods. Or bent—as when he breathed. Surrounded, aye, to capture in the end.

So too magic . . . ?

The accusation hung still, in the silence, reaching through that brutal truth he had confessed to demand some other reparation for that terrible wrong. An undoing of what could not be undone.

He had taken up the gauntlet in the only way he had understood to be possible. Oliver's children who were, strangely, his to care for now.

It was the Lady Olivia who made the difference. He had recognized, even as he had made his gift to Oliver's son, the final act of severance from all that had gone before, even as it opened before him. It was this girl, this other child he had not known about, who had stayed him.

Aude's face and form and voice. Yet she came briefly each day to bring him necessaries. To haunt him with Oliver's words and intonations. To confront his withdrawn silences with Oliver's own wily, fearless, and perceptive tolerance. Oliver . . . Olivia? He flinched.

She had brought him the fine clothing he now wore. Had said, "There, my lord. Let the leper be put away, and be thou a man again!"

A man? Roland stared frowning into the night. It was all he had ever tried to be. That was the crux of it. Aye, for beneath the fine linen and wool he now wore lay that implacable, unnatural endurance. And something new, for the dagger wound did not heal as it should. Instead, dry now, it continued to erode, gradually becoming an increasingly painful, ragged pit in his shoulder. Another exacerbation of his condition. Part of the pain that increasingly welled up like a sea tide, through his deformed leg like something screaming for release, before subsiding back, merely to wait.

A man? he thought bitterly.

"What am I?" he whispered, turning slowly on his crutches to stare at the chamber that housed him now. Fine tapestries and furnishings, and the falcon that watched him from its perch held an answer he did not understand in its eyes.

His hand made a fist upon the sill. Grasping nothing . . .

He had yielded up Durandal.

What use was a sword against the very air . . . ?

"I am afraid!" he rasped it slowly, words he'd never before uttered.

Delicate, even brittle, the mood of the people of the fiefs of Bordeaux as they gave their oaths of fealty to Girard, now, though well known, who was most unexpectedly their Duke. Expressions of loyalty and duty that were given like a habit covered questions and troubled wonderings as people thought of the banished Lord Huon, and the suddenly dead lady whose rule they had known for so long.

For Girard, it was a time of new and relentless testing as he took control and spent his days seeing to every aspect of the welfare of his fiefs, determined above all else that nothing more should go awry.

And for the hours he spent alone, he felt keenly the changes brought by his altered identity. Burdensome and troubling, it affected everything he had ever understood and believed, to leave a wake of uncertainty. Sometimes he sat quietly, holding the sword Durandal, feeling that curiously impossible smoothness of texture, the ever-shifting weight and heft of a sword that seemed to be more life and movement than object or instrument. Durandal, who represented a kind of honor and valor he had thought, once, he understood very well.

He found a peculiar solution after one of his rare and brief conversations with the strangely reticent Lord Roland. The older man described how he had used the sword, and how he had worn it in a baldric upon his back, the blade being far too long to carry in the customary manner against the left hip. Then, he rode out across his lands, finding sense of a sort, in carrying both such a noble and famous weapon and his brother's shield. Huon's honor and his own, combined.

The one a fact. The other yet to be made.

And delicate as well were the subtle, persistent dreams that came to haunt his sleeping, to touch and heighten his senses, enticing him into longing for the wonder for the dark-eyed Eve-woman who smiled at him from some point just beyond his reach. Aye, whose form was a mystery and a seduction, revealed in fleeting, moonlit shadows. Whose hair made flowing dark clouds of silk that danced about her. Whose fingertips came out to trace exquisite sensate miracles across his skin.

Dreams that dissipated each time to leave him unfulfilled and longing . . . Dreams, Girard told himself during the daylight hours, that reflected his uncertainties and hopes for his forthcoming marriage to the Lady Gharis of Brittany.

The interment of the Dowager Duchess of Bordeaux brought an abrupt end to Olivia's girlhood apprenticeship to all the duties of chatelaine. The winter months that followed became a time of sober actualization as the full burden of those many responsibilities fell onto her shoulders. Every detail of husbandry became her care. From the youngest scullion to turn the spits in the kitchens, to the clutch of tirewomen who did the weaving and sewing and other household tasks. From the condition and distribution of the winter stores, to the supplies of fodder for the fine horses stabled within the castle walls. From the meals that were served in the great hall each evening, to the dispensing of charity to the needful.

And while Girard spent so much of his time beyond the castle walls, Olivia gave her spare moments to the fascination of Lord Roland. Sensitive to what she had learned of him, and ever conscious of his intensity and isolating fears and pain, she used a mixture of shrewdly applied tact and sharp-wittedness to coax him from the tower chamber into the mainstream of the daily life of the castle.

Concealed beneath the attire she had provided, he began to join the formal evening feasts in the great hall, quietly accepting a place at the high table as befitted his rank. He swung himself about, remaining reticent, yet watching everything. Even eventually venturing out of the keep into the bailey beyond to study and touch the fine horses that were a part of Bordeaux's pride. Tall, elegant stallions and powerful mares, from which were raised the best of warhorses and the fleetest of palfreys.

He knew a great deal about horses, Olivia discovered. He knew all those things a fighting man could know. Yet it was evident in his watchful reticence and rather abruptly offered comments, how thoroughly he had removed himself from those things.

It was intriguing to see him gradually emerge as she listened to the conversations that sprang up increasingly between Lord Roland and her brother during the course of the evening meat. Strictly impersonal, they revolved around such matters as the methods of construction for chain mail, or which resin best bonded a longbow. Or the type of spur most suited to training a young stallion.

Like a spring flower cautiously thrusting its way up through a late snowfall, she thought once, then laughed aloud at the comparison. Lord Roland's look when she revealed her thought set off more laughter, and goaded, she corrected herself, likening him rather to a new thorny gorse bush.

His offerings were fragile, she noted. Knowledge only. Never feelings . . . Discreetly, like one nurturing a seedling in leeched soil, she began to partake of these masculine conversations, using questions to learn about and probe such matters as the techniques of battle, the arming, supplying, and movement of a company of men, strategy, and the analysis of the strengths and weaknesses of fortresses such as Bordeaux castle itself.

It brought her brother and Lord Roland flank to flank as they answered her, she saw. Yet for all his responsiveness, she caught a baleful wariness in Lord Roland's fierce golden eyes, as if he suspicioned what she was about.

Save in the tower chamber, Lord Roland's name was never spoken, as he had brutally requested. Known only as "my lord," Olivia began to catch uneasy or averted gazes that followed him from household members and servants. They were obedient enough, but . . .

Remembering, she questioned the tirewoman Aliena who had attended her mother before the Duchess' death. She got naught but discomfirture and humbly offered expressions of duty and loyalty.

But they were words that sat askew for the tone that underlay them. And slowly, quietly, like a flavor, that peculiar new texture of tense unease began to spread. .

Far, far away, where deep, uninhabited forests of enormous pines rose up like spires above densely tangled larch and oak, poplar, ash, and others, toward the frigid clear skies overhead, where the winter silence as absolute, and a single shout could send snow hurtling down the harsh mountainsides to entomb whatever was below . . . the white owl perched with ruffled feathers amid snow-burdened, evergreen branches to seem no more than another clump of frozen white.

Below, it watched the exhausted struggles of a pair of fur-swathed men as they dragged two thin horses up a steep and treacherous incline to stop in the small clearing just beyond. The owl blinked delicately. A battered-looking pair indeed, they were—these two. The hardships of a winter of continuous eastward travel through Carthinia, across the high, mountainous, and heavily forested lands of Croatia and Serbia to reach at last that rugged, ill-defined border that led to the lowlands of Macedonia, and thence to Constantinople, had left an irrefutable stamp upon the pair.

Reaching the middle of the small clearing, the taller of the two men paused to look around him. Steam from his nostrils made small, quickly dissipated clouds before his face.

"We shall rest here, Sherasmin," he told the other, then took the two unhappy horses and tethered them on one side of the clearing to huddle against the cold and forage for whatever vegetation they could find to chew upon.

"The wolves will find us, my lord," the other said, expressing his reluctance to linger. Hard-faced beneath coif and helm and furred hood, Lord Huon turned from unburdening the pair of horses to look at him.

"Then we shall have some easy meat!" he retorted, pulling saddle and pack from the nag his once-fine, hot-tempered war stallion had been reduced to. "Nor," he added vengefully, "will I lose what is left of these horses to trudge like a beggar into Constantinople! Let them come! I'll be glad to kill them!"

The wizened hermit did not reply, but glanced around cautiously, then began gathering firewood from fallen twigs and the like. He had learned through the course of this brutal journey the futility of attempting any dispute with Lord Huon.

"Still. I mislike these forests, my lord," he muttered later as he used flint and tinder to set fire to the kindling he had gleaned.

"So thou have said before!" Lord Huon's reply was clipped as he crouched down on his haunches and rummaged through the contents of his pack to draw out the half-frozen rabbit he had shot earlier that day. He gave the carcass a look of disgust. "I must hunt again today if we are not to starve further!" he muttered, passing the carcass to the other man. "Here. Roast this scrap!" He caught the wary, furtive glances Sherasmin cast toward the surrounding trees and glared.

"I will not credit thy suspicion of these forests as some unnatural realm, save as another ploy to discredit my choice of the more direct route to the east!" he said harshly. "Think again on how much farther we would have had to go if we had followed the coast as thou would have had us do!" Sherasmin did not reply, but hunkered down into the folds of his cloak and added larger sticks to the small fire. "Nay. Even forth this," Lord Huon pursued, modifying his tone somewhat, "it would have been sheer folly to sail through winter storms. Better to trust to our own wits and strength than to depend on the frailties of others!"

The old man looked at him and shrugged.

"For the many times I have made this journey, my lord, I have always avoided these forests. The Infidel believe . . ."

Lord Huon scowled. "We are Christian men who give our trust to God!" he said sharply. "I will not give credence to the superstitions of heathen savages!"

The old man shook his head. "It is folly to underrate the Infidel, my lord—as I have said before. For my years as a slave, I have seen much that we would do well to learn from them! And I tell thee, there *is* a reason they claim these forests to be inhabited by Djinn! Mark me, my lord. We are watched. I have sensed it this some while past!"

"Pah!" Huon spat his disbelief, then stood, grasping his bow and slinging his quiver across his back. "We need food! I go now to get it!"

Settled by the growing warmth of his carefully nurtured fire, Sherasmin watched the young lord stride away across the clearing, trudging through the deep snow to disappear beneath the dark canopy of the great trees on the other side. He sighed. Lord Huon had courage enough for ten, he acknowledged. But his anger and pride were, unfortunately, of a matching proportion, and gave him a corresponding lack of discretion.

He looked up to scan the trees, feeling again that which he had sensed before. Silence pervaded the clearing, coming from the great trees themselves. Trees that held the air and smothered the light that tried to penetrate this ancient stretch of forest, leaving the floor dark and barren of undergrowth. There were few deer about, or ibex, and other such. Poor hunting. Even the wild creatures were wise enough to stay away. A light rustling sound came from behind him, and he twisted, squinted, and saw a large, pure white owl spread its wings and take flight from a large tree to his right.

No natural bird was that pure of hue, he knew at once, transfixed as it looked down with an eerie, almost amused stare, before fluttering upward to disappear into the forest beyond.

Sherasmin shivered and crossed himself. The Infidel tales were correct. This was a sorcerous place . . .

Broad wings and snow bright, soft plumage made soundless flight as the white owl soared above the trees, watching the careful, struggling passage of the man who hunted along the ground below.

Earth-bound and clumsy for the tracks he left in his wake that revealed the debilitated condition hardship and stubbornness had wrought. Aye. It was time now, the owl knew, to take control.

Perceiving the man's direction as he sought prey, the white owl floated on a little farther, then descended through the trees to alight on the snow in a craggy, diminutive clearing. It ruffled its feathers once, then spread its wings to the air. Began to shift . . . to grow. Form became ambiguous, stretching upward, shifting through myriad illusions of color made by a fractured beam of sunlight that touched the process. Feathers melted inward like some introspective hallucination, then vanished altogether as the form of a young man emerged.

Large brown eyes glinted in a canny, handsome face. Mischief danced across perfect lips as he made a spinning movement with one finger in the air. Summoning . . . Conjuring a scrap of mist, then condensing it into a lightly flowing material of brightly pallid, weaving rainbow hues.

He wrapped this around himself, covering his loins, then letting the rest flow across one bare, smoothly muscular shoulder to hang as a rarely buoyant cloak behind him. He smiled a little, and with feet that left no impressions in the snow, he began to walk in a leisurely manner toward the uncertain sounds of the man a hundred yards away from him.

His skill at hunting was of little use, Huon knew. There were no tracks or sign. He'd count himself fortunate to find a burrow with some small animal hibernating in it. Not even birds that would make a welcome mouthful broke the silence of the surrounding trees.

It had become a brutal odyssey, this, he admitted as his stomach cramped for want of food, and the biting cold seeped through armor and clothing to creep through his flesh. He stopped, his mouth becoming a slash as the silence began to close around him. I will not be persuaded by canting superstitions, he thought grimly. I have done no wrong to warrant . . .

"Who are thou, mortal, to *dare* to invade my kingdom?" Gently asked—Huon spun around to stare in purest amazement at the gleaming, half-naked young man who stood before him under the branches of a nearby pine tree. Canny brown eyes locked with his. Huon swallowed. Mortal . . . ? He scowled, shifted his bow to his left hand and reached for his sword.

The young man smiled. "Nay. Thou cannot fight me! It is discourteous in thee even to consider it. A better strategy by far is to answer my question!" He stepped forward, moving with liquid suppleness, and yet, Huon saw at once, leaving no trace of a footprint on the snow.

"I am Huon De Guienne, born Duke of Bordeaux," he got out warily.

The young man stopped, his garment floating around him like suggestions of rainbows. "And I am called Oborion." He inclined his head, replying with exquisite civility. "To those who know me, I am Lord of Fairie! I have seen thy distress and am come to befriend thee, for I have a great love for thy kind!"

An illusion? "Nay!" Huon rasped, realizing that this was some real and unnatural heathen creature. He dropped the bow, drawing his sword with a hiss from its scabbard.

The young man smiled again. "Aye!" he affirmed gently, stepping closer still. Huon lunged, but the young man glided to one side, caught the tip of the blade in one hand and twisted the weapon out of Huon's grasp and tossed it aside in one impossibly synchronous movement.

"This is a poor reply indeed for one who offers friendship and aid!" he said with stern regret. Huon lunged to scoop up his bow, but the other moved like lightning to clutch at the front of his surcoat with one bare, fine-fingered hand. "Nay! Thou shall not insult me further, little mortal man!" he said gently.

"I am a Christian man . . ." Huon began, and tried to jerk himself away. But the creature clung, the fingers of his other hand coming up to thrust through mail coif and grasp his throat. Huon's defiance died in a gasp and he began to claw. Incredible strength. He could not move as blood began to pound against his ears, and air was trapped against the pull of his lungs. Before him there was a mesmerizing certainty in the wily, brown-eyed stare.

"Apologize, and I will forgive!" Oborion said mildly. "The Lord of Fairie is not given to intemperate spite!"

"Never!" Huon managed to gasp. "For my soul . . ." The

stranglehold on his throat increased, and there was nothing else except those clever, deep brown eyes that knew, most thoroughly, what they were about.

"Soul . . . ?" Oborion murmured above the rising thunder in Huon's skull. "There is no such thing for mortal creatures! Pity . . ." Hideous, the regret in the last, and then the thunder swept across Huon's senses, bringing with it a scarlet agony as Huon thrashed and fought.

Then darkness. Like a sunset . . .

Is this how I die? Huon felt himself wonder as everything faded away.

Orborion loosed his hold on the body and watched it crumple into the snow. He shook his head, sincere regret giving a peculiar vulnerability to his face.

"How much I mislike to kill these frail creatures," he murmured to himself. "But it is essential sometimes—and for this! So much pride, and no wisdom to temper it! Still, there are other ways to make a hero . . ." He knelt down beside the body and began quickly and efficiently stripping it of all clothing and armor.

And when, within a few minutes, Lord Huon De Guienne lay pale and naked and cooling in the snow, he reached carefully to point with a forefinger along the dead man's belly, neatly and precisely parting the skin . . .

The silence had become more potently oppressive than ever, joining with the blue dusk as evening settled across the clearing to make the darkness under the trees something solid and growing. The fire crackled and popped loudly as the flames attacked the moisture in the logs the old man had gathered to feed it. Sherasmin had eaten his portion of the meager rabbit while he awaited Lord Huon's return, then, uneasily, had occupied himself with collecting firewood, and hunting through the snow for dried shrubs and grasses, saplings, anything to feed Lord Huon's starving horses. Now, as darkness settled, he huddled by the fire for warmth, husbanding his strength as he grew increasingly troubled by the amount of time Lord Huon had been gone.

One of the horses raised its head suddenly and pricked its ears. Whickered. Sherasmin started violently and, using his staff, jerked himself to his feet to see a figure emerge from the trees.

Familiar. He exhaled relief. "I had begun to wonder, my

lord,'' he said as Lord Huon trudged wearily toward him, nodded, then dropped to his knees before the fire. He looked pale—drained, Sherasmin observed, hunkering down again as the younger man set bow and quiver aside, shivered, and reached out to spread gauntleted hands to the flames. He had no game.

"I kept half the rabbit for thee, my lord," Sherasmin said. Lord Huon looked up, his expression troubled and exhausted. He moved then, reaching into the folds of his cloak to withdraw two objects that had been concealed against his person.

The first was no more than a flaccidly empty provender wallet of the kind commonly used by pilgrims. But the second was a cup of wondrously wrought, intricately interwoven designs of gold and silver, which gave off bright rainbows of color from the jewels imbedded in its surface.

"What treasure is this?" Sherasmin breathed, his eyes widening as Lord Huon grimly held the cup out to him.

"As thou give credence to heathen things, take it and drink!" Lord Huon ordered harshly. Shocked, puzzled, Sherasmin took the cup, opened his mouth as he saw it was empty, then, obedient to Lord Huon's fierce expression, raised it to his lips and tasted the sweet, clear wine that suddenly filled the thing. He sipped, then, beyond help for it, drank deeply, feeling at once the warmth that sank into him from it.

"My lord?" he whispered.

"I was told that if an honest man puts it to his lips, he will taste only the fairest of wines. Any who are false will find their mouths scoured by gall . . . And this"—Huon held out the wallet—"was given as well to provide."

The old man carefully set the cup in the snow, took the wallet, and undid the flap to peer inside and see nothing at all.

"It is empty," he said. Frowning, Lord Huon took it back, then reached inside to withdraw a rounded loaf of wheaten bread. Sherasmin's starved stomach cramped violently at the sight, and with unsteady fingers, he reached for the loaf and began to eat fiercely. "Mother of God!" he managed around a mouthful. "This is a very miracle!"

Lord Huon stared at the fire and huddled down farther. "Nay. It is something else!" he said roughly. Then, interspersed with awkward little pauses, he told of what had befallen him. Of how he had encountered in the forest a manlike creature of radiant youth, lightly garbed in filament material of rainbow hues, such as could not have been humanly made. "The Djinn . . ." the old man murmured once, but Huon did not seem to hear as he continued to tell of how this creature called himself Oborion, Lord of Fairie, and had offered friendship. How he, Huon, fearing Satan and some damning contrivance, had resisted and been smote down for it. How too, later, he had recovered consciousness to find himself still before this same Lord Oborion, who had given him these gifts to mark his favor.

"I have done thee a grievous injustice by my misbelief in thee, Sherasmin," Lord Huon added clumsily at the end. "This place. Truly. It is not natural . . ." Replete with bread and wine, the old man said nothing as he recognized the enormity of this concession from one as proud and determined as young Lord Huon. Aye, he thought, with a surge of magnanimity, before him now sat the makings of a great man.

"By God's will, perhaps, there is a wonderful benefit come to us here, my lord," he offered instead. Lord Huon looked at him finally.

"Aye," he murmured after a moment. "Only as honor will fulfill it."

Later, when the old man lay sound asleep in his cloak, when the fire crackled and spewed up flames to defy the bitter cold and the opaque, quiescent darkness, Lord Huon stood up slowly from his own place beside the fire. With leisurely movements, he removed his gauntlets and examined his hands. Then he thrust back the furred hood of his cloak, unclasped his helm to drop it by his feet, and thrust back the chain mail coif of the hauberk he wore beneath. Indifferent to the cold, he shook his dark hair, then poised for a moment to listen to the silence before reaching gracefully to scoop up the leather provender wallet. Turning from the fire, he walked lightly through the snow toward the two horses that stood in disconsolate discomfort, their tethering ropes slack, under a nearby tree.

The ruined stallion pricked its ears and watched him as he reached out to touch its thin neck. Lord Huon's face sobered to consternation as his fingers traced hide over bone, and sweat-matted, harness-galled, neglected winter coats. Then he reached into the wallet and drew forth sweet, fresh green hay in a succession of handfuls to set before the starving beasts.

"Aye. Eat well of this, for I have much need of thee," he murmured with melodious softness as the two horses began to feed eagerly. "There will be grain as well, later."

When he had finished setting a large mound of fodder before them, he turned and walked back to the fire, there to gracefully reseat himself beside it. He looked eastward to where a gap in the trees showed the brilliant twinkling of stars overhead, where, he knew, the path led on to the last treacherous mountain ridge before the land dropped gently down toward Byzantium. He smiled in anticipation.

EIGHTEEN

"Let me pass, fools!" Lord Thierry roared as he spurred his muddy, sweat-sodden, and heaving horse across the drawbridge, past the pair of guardsmen that stepped out, pikestaffs at the ready, to challenge him. The Count of Brittany swooped in his saddle to thrust with the point of his shield, and the two leaped aside to avoid the blow and barely escaped being trampled by the muddy, grim-faced company of mounted fighting men that thundered behind him. Still at the gallop, Lord Thierry swung his horse through to the inner bailey and drew rein vigorously before the steps that led up into Bordeaux's great keep, dismounting before the animal had completely stopped.

"Here! Take this beast, Etienne!" he barked to the squire behind him, flung around, and ascended the steps two at a time, toward the servants that had appeared through the doors. "I must see the Lord Duke and the Duchess Alice!" he said crisply, pausing. Wide-eyed, they hesitated. *"Now!"* he thundered. They fled as Lord Thierry strode past them, then marched briskly forward into the great hall.

Warm and dry . . . He felt it at once, stopped a few yards away from the hearth fire that blazed in the center. He breathed deeply against his own tension, drew off his gauntlets and tucked them into his belt, then reached up to wipe briefly at the mud and sweat and rainwater that soaked his face.

"My lord of Brittany?" He heard a woman's voice and spun on his heel to see the young Lady Olivia moving toward him with brisk grace from some door on the far side of the great hall. He collected himself. Bowed.

"Just so, my lady," he responded, finding a civility that felt incongruous for all he carried within him. "I must see Lord Girard and the Lady Alice as soon as may be . . ." She stopped in front of him.

"The Lady Alice De Guienne is dead, my lord," she told him quietly.

Lord Thierry froze. "What . . . ?" he rasped, shocked to the core.

She continued to watch him. "Aye, my lord. Succumbed to illness this winter past."

"God's mercy!" he whispered. "I did not know of this . . ."

"My brother, the Lord Duke, is gone to attend to some business at a manor to the east, my lord," she told him then. "I expect his return by nightfall. For the present, I may offer such hospitality as may give thee useful comfort and refreshment?"

Lord Thierry grappled to collect his wits. Such a possibility had not even occurred to him. He had depended on the Lady Alice, on her response to that which he conveyed. Now . . . ? "My men . . . They are exhausted," he said.

Lady Olivia inclined her head. "My servants attend to them even now, my lord," she said reassuringly.

He exhaled violently. "I gratefully accept thy hospitality, my lady," he managed. "But I must speak to Lord Girard as soon as may be."

"I understand." She gave him a curious look, then held out a hand and began to guide him across the great hall in the manner proper to a chatelaine for a high-ranking guest.

Later, bathed, changed, and shaved, Lord Thierry reentered the great hall to see that the evening meal had been set forth. Lesser folk of the Bordeaux household already sought their places at the lower tables, his own men among them.

He saw Lord Girard then, striding toward him, looking vigorously healthy, and more like Oliver De Montglave than ever for the new maturity of his countenance. He felt a sense of shock as his eyes went to the Lady Olivia, approaching beside her brother. Strange, that he had not seen it before, how alike they were, these two . . .

"My lord, we are honored by thy presence. Do thou come,

sup with us," Lord Girard said as he bowed deeply to the older man. Lord Thierry inclined his head politely.

"The honor is a questionable one, my lord," he told the other as he allowed himself to be drawn to a place at the high table on the dais at the far end of the hall. "I am come on matters of grievous concern to us all."

Lord Girard looked at him sharply as they seated themselves. "How so?"

Lord Thierry watched a servant pour wine into a cup by his place and breathed deeply as he drew his dagger to address the trencher before him.

"The Vikings, my lord," he said with controlled deliberation. "They are come again, as every spring, to raid my seaward holdings. More. They are come in such numbers as I have never seen before. Not in single ships as before . . . I have received word from Rouen to the north that they had invaded and destroyed those fiefs by the mouth of the Seine. I know as well, having seen it, that they have wrought terrible destruction on those manors that flank the estuary of the Loire on my southern side, and are now firmly encamped there." He frowned and drank from his wine cup. "I have taken every able-bodied man I can away from the planting to build defenses and fight." He shook his head. "Brittany has never been populous. There are none to spare for failures, and trenches and wooden palisades are poor obstacles against these heathen berserkers . . ." He straightened, his face grim. "This is the worst time of year for resistance. Men are most like to starve in spring, when the winter stores are depleted, before any harvesting can be done . . . When I came south to address these incursions into the Loire Valley, I became convinced, my lord, that the Vikings are set on more than theft and pillage this time. I think they intend full invasion." He saw Lord Girard's eyes widen briefly. "And I found another proof as I rode south to thee. Two days past, I saw northmen disembark along the northern peninsula where the Garonne joins the sea. Five ships—I had not sufficient numbers with me to engage."

"I have had no word!" Girard breathed.

"That is not surprising, Girard." Olivia startled them both by speaking. "To the north and west, there is naught between this castle and the sea save the forests, and the river." She continued with a calmly practical tone, "All the manors are to the south. Or inland. And, I think, these barbarians are not likely to leave survivors to carry word!''

Astounded by her grasp of things, Lord Thierry swung to face her, seated on his other side. "Just so, my lady."

She nodded solemnly. "Together with thyself, we hold the greater part of the westernmost fiefs. We should unite with thee against these Vikings. It is for that, thou are come here, my lord?"

Like hearing a ghost become flesh, Lord Thierry thought. Words and tone the same as Oliver. And she, this little more than girl.

He inclined his head. "Aye, my lady." She gave him a shrewdly understanding look, then shifted her gaze past him, to her brother's face.

"Of a certainty, I will unite with thee, my lord," Girard said promptly. "I will gladly put myself, and such resources as I command to the service of the King's Champion."

Lord Thierry inclined his head again, acknowledging the deference accorded his exclusive rank and greater experience.

"Good!" he stated baldly.

"This is, I think, for truth, a war that we embark upon, my lord," he heard Lady Olivia say, and turned to face her, consternation moving over his features as, unbidden, he thought of his own daughter.

"I fear so, my lady," he said as gently as he could. "We must have every care for thy safety." She met his look with confidence, and smiled briefly—not at all like his sweet Gharis.

"I am not unduly perturbed, my lord!" she commented dryly. "Being reared with two older brothers has given me distinct advantages on the matter of my defense, and my usefulness to this undertaking we embark upon!"

Impressed, Lord Thierry smiled and bowed his head to her. Caught the suddenly arrested movement of a gloved hand reaching for a goblet from the seat beyond hers . . .

He had not noticed in his preoccupation this finely robed man who now sat as well at the high table. Gloved hands, and the cowl drawn so far over his head to conceal his face—curious, singular discourtesies.

"I perceive I am not the only guest to enjoy thy hospitality, my lady?" he inquired then and saw the hooded man retreat deeper into his chair. The Count stiffened and leaned forward as the Lady Olivia followed the direction of his gaze.

"Nay, my lord. Thou are not!" she said with smooth resolve. He glanced significantly toward Lord Girard, who chose that moment to spear a small piece of the well-roasted mutton before them with his dagger. The younger man made a rueful moue.

"Agreement has been reached. It is time for refreshment now, my lord," Lord Girard said gently. "We may talk further later. And with the sunrise, I will have addressed such preparations as are needful to thy support and our mutual purpose."

Lord Thierry exercised his own good manners to eat and converse on lighter subjects. Clearly, he recognized, these two were not going to answer his curiosity. Another glance showed the hooded man had shifted to face away, unwilling to introduce himself—as an honest man would have done. Yet he had more important concerns, he knew, and turned to build a sound rapport with young Lord Girard.

Only later, when the meat had been replaced with sweetmeats and honeyed barley cakes, did he glance again to see the hooded man had disappeared to leave an empty chair. He had not heard a sound . . . Quickly he scanned the great hall, then paused, wine cup to lips, as he caught sight of that richly clothed, anonymous man watching him with eyes that glinted beneath his hood, from a place half through a door that led to the eastern regions of the keep. An instant later, the man disappeared.

Lord Thierry frowned over his wine cup as he drank again. Nay, he thought. Could it be that these two concealed the banished Lord Huon? Their brother. It would explain the protectiveness he'd caught.

Overnight, the castle had become a veritable hive of intense activity, Lord Thierry saw as he mounted his cleaned and rested destrier early in the following grey, overcast morning, prior to riding out with Lord Girard to order defenses for the villages nearest to the great castle. He glanced toward the four from his own battle-hardened company, already mounted and waiting to accompany, and wondered what all these other busy folk really knew of war. Not like his own people . . . Bordeaux had known only peace for a generation.

"My lord!" He turned in his saddle to see Lord Girard striding briskly down the steps that led from the main entrance to the keep. In full armor with cloak and helm, he took his horse's bridle with practised efficiency from the groomsman that held the animal, and slung his shield across the saddle pommel.

"Couriers have been dispatched inland already to muster men and arms with all possible haste," he informed crisply. "For the rest, so that we may march north tomorrow to repel these Vikings that encroach on the mouth of the Garonne, I have summoned Sir Guillaume De Blaye and those who may be readied from the nearer fiefs."

"Good . . ." Lord Thierry began, then froze to stare as the younger man mounted nimbly and took control of his fine, restless stallion. "That sword!" he rasped harshly. Startled, Lord Girard stared back. The Count pointed. "That sword!" he demanded fiercely. "I know it! How are thou come to have it?"

Disconcerted, Lord Girard's fingers jerked up to grasp the hilt of the Dark Sword as it lay against his back.

"This?" He drew it and set the weapon across his thighs.

"Aye, my lord! That!" Lord Thierry grated, his eyes fixed on the storms that laced through the blade of that unnaturally dark and long weapon. "Having known the man, how could I not recognize at once the sword of Roland? Tell me. How are thou come to have it?"

Lord Girard hesitated. Looked down. "It was gifted to me . . ." he said quietly after a moment. Then, "Bequeathed," he amended awkwardly, and returned the monstrous weapon to its place at his back with movements that had none of the impeccable, instinctive smoothness that Lord Thierry remembered in another man all those years ago. "As to my worthiness to wield such a puissant and famous blade . . . ?" Lord Girard looked up again, and met the Count's intense stare grimly. "Well, my lord. It is yet to be proved!"

That jarred. And this, aye, untried boy could not have had the sword for long. The concealed man . . . ? Not Lord Huon as he had supposed. If he did not know what he knew . . . Abruptly Lord Thierry dismounted.

"He is here, I think—the giver?" he asked softly, and found the answer in the young Duke's face. The Count spun on his heel instantly and strode back up the steps that led to the interior of the keep.

There, a cornered servant, held like a snared rabbit in one powerful, gauntlet-covered fist, gave direction, and within moments, Lord Thierry had found his way into the east tower, ascending the steps.

Without ceremony, he pushed through the oak door to the chamber the servant had indicated and stopped just inside. The man who had been standing—nay, not standing, Lord Thierry realized at once, but hanging on a pair of crutches—swung around to face him.

Uncowled this time. The same amber and gold hair he remembered hung about broad shoulders. Unforgettable, that fierce, golden stare. Lord Thierry's breath hissed inward between his teeth at the sight of the face, truly appalling for the flesh that covered it.

"Thou!" he rasped. "I knew it had to be so, Lord Roland!"

"The Count of Brittany!" Roland responded with savage irony, inclining his head. Lord Thierry did not flinch, but closed the door and advanced farther into the room.

"So I am!" he acknowledged. Then, "Thou cost me a good seneschal!"

"I did not wish to be found!" Roland countered at once.

"That became evident, my lord," Lord Thierry said more quietly, absorbing the difference made by fine attire to confine the shock of his leprosy. Seeing as well, no sign of infirmity, save for the one crippled leg. "I sought but to honor thee . . . Now, thou are here. With these two who are Oliver's children."

Roland looked away. "Aye," he gritted.

"Now, I discover thou hast given Lord Girard that nefarious sword with which thou won so much glory!" Lord Thierry pursued. "He knows, of course. I saw it revealed as an undermined confidence . . ."

"Bastardy is an endurable estate!" Roland muttered balefully.

Lord Thierry frowned. "How well I recollect the form of thy own endurance of the same, my lord!" he countered acidly, goaded by the burden of more cares than he wished to contend with. "Shall he die then, Oliver's son, in an attempt to live up to what has become over the years thy own impossibly glorious reputation . . . ?"

Roland spun around, his face stark beneath the shredded skin.

"Nay!" he snarled. "Durandal is given to guard his life as she will assuredly do!"

"Thou are a witch, then, to conjure guarantees?" Lord Thierry demanded softly. Saw the crippled man flinch back.

"Never!" Roland hissed furiously. "I am a man!"

Like a blow—raw, terrible. Tormented.

Lord Thierry breathed deeply, then moderated his tone. "I had but thought, in seeking thee, Lord Roland, to give thee peace and comfort. A small return to offer for that honor thou once restored to me. I have not forgot what we lived through together, all those years ago in Spain. Or the rest . . . But thou have come here instead, to these two, who know none of it, save as tales to be told . . .

"I cannot think it wise, Lord Roland. I have seen already how, for their father's sake, they are determined to guard and protect thee."

"I will leave here as I meant to do!" Roland whispered roughly, turning away again.

Lord Thierry frowned, seeing the nightmares the years and his condition had wrought. "To vanish, I presume, as thou have done before?" he asked in sudden, hard-edged challenge. "To flee? Is it still so bitter a gall to thee, my lord, that thou did not die with the rest at Roncesvalles? With Lord Oliver?" He had struck, Lord Thierry saw as Roland hunched over his crutches. "For all the years that have passed, this idiotic guilt is incomprehensible! Do thou seek redemption by clinging to his children?"

"Leave me be!" Roland snarled viciously, rounding on him.

Lord Thierry began to smile. "Aaah! I read it rightly!" He inhaled then, as Roland continued to stare at him with murderous ferocity. "Thou have never been alone in thy love for Lord Oliver. I too . . . More. I have a care for these two who are got of him. It is my wish, in fact, that Lord Girard proves himself, and succeeds to my own office of King's Champion as I grow too aged for it!

"We are come to brutal times, as thou well overheard last night. To speak of leaving . . . ?" His tone softened a little. "There is a war before us all, and I know of no man better to fight it than thyself!"

"Nay!" Roland began.

Lord Thierry's eyebrows rose. "For all thou resemble naught so much as one of the Devil's own, Lord Roland, it was no bungling and incapable cripple that killed my seneschal! Nor slipped with such facile stealth from the supper table last night! Nay—I will not credit this affliction of thine as more than superficial! Nor am I concerned for the past, which is unchangeable in any case. Rather, I address the present, and the future. For that, I know very well, which others may not, the full value of who thou are and what thou know! Pah!" he snorted away Roland's baleful stare. "I'll warrant thou may still back a good warhorse and thou wish to do it! Nay, my lord, for thy very presence here, thou are caught in the midst of this. There is much for thee to do. Thou have, I think, a rare knowledge of these Viking northmen who seek to invade our shores, and I intend to make full use of it!'' He watched as Roland shifted restlessly, like a horse goaded by spurs. ''On the morrow,'' he continued quietly, ''I ride north and west with Lord Girard and such forces as we assemble today to engage those Vikings who have already set foot and camp upon the shore but thirty miles from here.''

'' 'Tis but a footstep away for them,'' Roland murmured.

The Count nodded grimly. ''We leave behind the Lady Olivia to command the garrison here and to dispatch to us the mustered forces that will arrive forthwith. Mark me well. The people here-abouts know nothing of real war—such as thou and I were weaned on! It makes a difference. And the Lady Olivia, who must take a man's place . . . ? I would go easier to know thou command here to hold these southern shores.''

Their gazes locked for several moments. It was Roland who broke it by looking down.

''I am a leper,'' he reminded Lord Thierry tersely. ''No man will follow that!''

The Count inhaled violently. ''Then do it through the Lady Olivia!'' he snapped. ''For what I see, she is truly her father's child!''

Roland stared. ''A woman . . . ?''

Unable to prevent it, Lord Thierry grinned at the appalled tone. ''Aye! Verily, a woman! Mother of God, for my own children, I know they are far from an incapable breed!''

Roland did not answer, but hung on his crutches, frowning, thinking hard.

Watching him keenly, Lord Thierry finished it.

''Let me offer this point of faith,'' he said quietly. ''For what-ever the idiosyncrasies of God's will, no man dies before his purpose is accomplished! Not even Lazarus!'' He stopped. Saw that he had struck very deep this time. Haunted, brutal things crossed Roland's face, hung like terrors in his eyes. Then he hunched his shoulders and bowed his head.

Lord Thierry tried to soften it. ''Whatever honor I have, what-ever I have become over these years that have passed, Lord Ro-land, I never forget that it is of thy making. By this, I pray, I have done my duty to that . . .'' Lord Roland looked up, his eyes wide. But Lord Thierry bowed, turned on his heel, and left to return to the horses and men waiting for him, knowing exactly what he had done.

The sounds of heightened activity—thump and shout and whinny—came from within the castle walls to waft through the window like noises from another world. Roland moved his hands along the staves that made it possible for him to be upright, and turned slowly toward the sounds.

"Lazarus!" he muttered balefully. More like a cleverly hooked fish thrashing at the end of a very stout line! The Count of Brittany had played him cunningly.

What he knew . . . Aye. It was still there inside. Not gone from him, but merely put away. War . . . Every detail and nuance of war. The sum of his knowledge, and his clarity. He scowled. He knew very well what the northmen could do—would do.

And now the Count had laid uncounted lives upon his shoulders, by declaring this responsibility. His fingers flexed. Not with Durandal . . . but through the Lady Olivia?

Horses champing on their bits, the chink and creak of harness, of arms and armor, and the particular heavy resonance of marching men and horses combined to make a solemn and compelling heartbeat upon the ear. Household folk watched with the troops left to garrison the castle as well, Olivia saw from her place high on the western battlements above the keep, as her brother and the Count of Brittany rode out at the head of their small army, across the drawbridge, then veering north and west, where, shortly, they would disappear into the forests beyond.

Rainfall muffled much of their departure and made a haze of the distance.

"Let us hope, my lady, that this weather persists, for the Vikings scent like bloodhounds the approach of any battalion!" Coolly uttered. Olivia spun around to see that Lord Roland, hidden beneath the clothing she had provided, had come silently up behind her and stood upon his crutches, staring toward the disappearing forces. "Nor are they given to direct encounter, unless they are certain of success. My lady . . ." He glanced at her briefly, then looked outward once more. "Who is thy chiefest vassal for the coastal lands to the south?"

"Sir Thibault De Labouneyre," she answered at once.

Lord Roland did not look at her. "Send for him, my lady.

With all haste,'' he said in the same deliberate tone. ''And when he is come, do thou greet him in the armor of a knight!''

''My lord . . . ?'' Olivia half whispered in sheer astonishment.

''In armor—and bearing arms!'' he said more harshly. ''Heed me well. While Lord Girard is gone, thou rule here, and for what lies ahead, that rule must be absolute—even to the battlefield.'' His tone shifted, becoming calm and exact. ''The western shores of Christendom compose a vast and complex front to defend. Lord Thierry is needed farther north. Lord Girard must defend those other fiefs and shores between here and Brittany. It falls to thee to guard all here, and the southern coast as well.

''I know these Vikings. They are numerous and persistent— and fearless. They know the wealth of these lands, and, in the past few years, have conquered and settled along the southern part of Brittany. For them, the way here is now short and easy.

''They are like wolves. Mark me. For all it is an eerie sound, there is little to fear when thou hear a wolf howl in the night. But when he hunts with his pack, then he is silent, and invisible. Then he is truly dangerous . . .''

Olivia frowned but said nothing as she digested this. Wolves . . . Lord Roland had been succinct, and vivid. He had also defined a very different role for her than she had thought to be her function.

''So be it, my lord,'' she said quietly, after a time, then looked up to see he watched her. She searched his eyes, but he looked away, the rest of his expression concealed by face cloth and cowl. He knew . . . she thought. He had been the greatest knight in Christendom.

She moved her gaze to catch a last view of her brother's forces as they disappeared into the misty green-grey trees half a mile away.

''I think I know a great reassurance in thy presence, my lord,'' she said quietly, expressing only part of her mind.

''It is what I know that is of value, my lady! Not who I am!'' he grated. She did not reply to that, but, after a moment, turned and departed the battlements to begin what he had set her to do.

NINETEEN

This was no more dank and gloomy than the rest of the place, Lord Baudoin thought, pausing at the foot of the steps that exited the subterranean cellars of his late uncle's uncompromising castle. The flickering torch provided light, not relief as he hesitated, then followed the bare, narrow corridor that branched at right angles from the passage and the stores he had just examined. Moments later, he stopped before the single door at the end of it. Tried the latch and, finding it locked, set his torch in the bracket on the wall, and groped through the keys he carried to test one that, so far, had been untried.

He had been shocked, two days before, riding into the high mountainous fiefs of Hauteville, to discover the poor villages with their lean flocks, ragged serfs, and paucity of children. He had also been shocked by the austerity of his uncle's castle. Stark, poorly furnished chambers and halls . . . little more than a single keep, it rose up like another somber grey crag among the rest thereabouts.

A total contrast to the wealth Lord Amaury had displayed on his person, and at Court, and the riches he had discovered hidden in his uncle's chest. Lord Amaury, Baudoin reminded himself sternly, had had control of the Maganze fortunes as well . . .

The third key turned in the well-oiled lock. He collected the torch and pushed through the door to stop inside what appeared to be a fairly large chamber. He squinted at the gloom, then his eyes widened slowly. Well furnished, this place, with a number of massive tables, several chairs. He moved deeper into the chamber.

Books. Aye. There were many books—in stacks on the various tables, between scrolls and parchment sheets, slate and wax tablets. There were numerous jars that, doubtless, contained inks and other alchemous substances. Writing implements and tools of other kinds. Goose quills, brushes, and knives. Cord and needles . . . He stared. Gold leaf shimmered, and jewels gleamed at him from the covers of these richly bound volumes. Treasures . . . He began to frown as he moved slowly around the room to more minutely examine everything.

His uncle had been known as an avid scholar, he knew. But this? It went beyond both reputation and expectation. He lit several of the large candles set at intervals on the tables, then began fingering the objects before him. Here were books and book-making materials enough to delight even so vast an institution as St. Martin's, he thought. All hidden away, like secrets, in the bowels of the earth.

His frown deepened with unease as he traced his fingertips across one lush volume, then moved them to touch the two sheets of pure, smooth, grainless parchment next to it. Craftsmanship and knowledge were obvious . . . Painstaking labor. His eyes shifted to scan the perimeter of the room, seeing the racks on the farthest wall for the curing of skins. Stopped to fix on one smooth, pallid shape still stretched there . . .

Manlike? He knew of no beast whose hide conformed to that shape, he realized, and began moving toward it. Like some headless, generalized shade . . . White. He reached out to touch it. Smooth. No hair or fur at all . . . His fingers jerked back, and he swallowed as the shape seared like a brand through his senses. Manlike. But smaller. His wits reeled like those of a drunken steward attempting to do the sums of accounting for a harvest. And then he remembered how few children he had seen among the impoverished serfs hereabouts.

"Mother of God! What do I sense?" he rasped, turning away to see a chest he had not noticed before. He strode to it, knelt, and flung back the lid to discover leather bags and wooden boxes containing . . . Gold—coin and nugget. And jewels of every sort. Amethyst and pearls. Sapphires, rubies, emeralds, diamonds, garnet—and more. It made a beggar's portion of what he had found at Aix . . .

"There is a kingdom here!" he whispered, drawing back to drop the lid of the chest with a loud thud.

And he had once thought his uncle modest? Using no more wealth than was suited to his high rank . . . ? Never pretentious. It was a lie. So too the rest of these impoverished fiefs, and the rest of the castle above him. "A lie . . ." he whispered, turning slowly to scan the room again, his gaze becoming fixed once more on that shadelike thing on the far wall. "What have thou stolen from my birthright?" he asked the air, remembering a lifetime of the iron rule of his uncle's stewards, tutor, arms masters, and the like. How his uncle's death had been greeted with silent relief, rather than regret. What he now knew of his own father's unforgiven treachery.

Evils that clung to him. Yet, of which, he had no part. Now? He moved again toward that pale hide. Reached out to touch it, and, with the fingertips of his other hand, felt the skin of his own throat. They were the same . . . human skin.

Half strangled, he jerked back and away. For the making of books? Parchment got from human beings . . . "This is the Devil's work!" he whispered hoarsely, retreating farther, then moving awkwardly to snuff the candles and seize the torch, before thrusting back through the door.

"This is no part of my inheritance!" he shouted raw, appalled desperation as the door slammed shut, then swung away and hurled himself toward the upper regions of the castle.

The following morning, astride his war stallion, Lord Baudoin watched with bitter-faced intensity as his men dug down to uncover rotted bodies from the year before in the nearest peasant burial place. Blasphemy to disturb the dead—it did not matter. He had to know the truth. Brutal questioning of nearby villagers had got him nothing more than the names and ages of those buried here.

Still half frozen from the winter, a stench of rot rose up in the air as they were exposed in the surrounding muck. Scraps of cloth and tissue. Brown skin that seeped into the soil around ruddy-stained bones. And on the one, where a child lay, where skin should still have been visible, he saw only meat. Half fluid, it hung in shreds to a child's more fully rounded skull and bright white teeth. The remains of eyeballs made sodden puddles in the sockets. There was no skin . . .

Worms, he knew, ate skin last of all.

"Cover it!" he rasped, his own face ashen, cold sweat erupting on his skin. A man turned away to retch.

He turned his horse away and looked up to where Lord Amaury's grey castle loomed over them, higher on the mountainside.

"Sir Etienne?" Baudoin spoke suddenly, with a harshness that was unnatural. The knight he had brought with him started, then eyed him warily, his knowledge of everything vile attached to the name of Maganze clear on his face.

"My lord?"

Baudoin pointed toward the castle. Found control. "When this is done, see that everything useful is removed from that place. Then I require thee to burn that castle to the ground! I will see every stone that remains standing razed!" He ignored the knight's amazed stare. "Afterward, I require thee to remove all the people hereabouts—and their beasts. Take them to Maganze where they will henceforth live! This place is fit for naught save wolves and crows!" he added violently. "And they are welcome to it!"

He did not see the questioning approval that crossed the knight's face. Instead, he spurred his horse away, up the hill toward the keep, and thought of what he had discovered hidden deep in the cellars. That part of it, he knew, he must attend to himself. If he had any hope of honor for himself at all, it must remain a secret . . .

Black smoke billowed upward to make dense, ominous clouds above the treetops. Enormous tongues of flame streaked upward from the conflagration, weaving in sinuous shapes of brilliant scarlet and orange. And the heat reached out like a blow to shrivel anything within a quarter-mile radius. Great cracking sounds split the fire's consuming roar, then a slow thunder began as the stone walls of the keep of Hauteville came tumbling down . . .

Holding his restive horse in check, Lord Baudoin stared past the mounted body squire behind him with grim relief. It was done. The people, with their belongings and beasts, were already well away from here. Sir Etienne had done as bid with thoroughness and energy. Even those things he'd taken care of himself, packed away, the rest destroyed, were on their way to Maganze to be put to better and humane use.

Someone of honor would have to rebuild here and hold Hauteville for him. Make it prosper . . . Not now, Lord Baudoin thought, and turned away to let his horse trot forward along a goat trail that led westward through the rugged plateau, beginning his long journey to Bordeaux.

Lord Roland's instructions proved shrewd and clever, Olivia discovered as, in the garb and armor of a man, she issued orders to Sir Thibault De Labouneyre, converting his startled disconcertedness over her appearance into a resolute obedience.

The shores that stretched away to the south and west must be defended. Build and maintain armed watchfires, Lord Roland had instructed. Set them by every village, and at regular intervals along the coast to warn the Vikings coming from the sea that a bloody reception awaited them.

From his place behind her, Lord Roland uttered not a sound as she spoke briskly to her vassal and indicated her own willingness to fight as well. It was completely different from her mother's way, she realized then, watching the knight depart. Lord Roland had, after a fashion, summoned her father . . . Lord Oliver. She glanced around briefly at the great shadowed figure he made behind her.

"I swear, my lord, thou will make a man of me!" she murmured lightly. She did not see the sudden, frightened widening of his eyes as he heard.

Word came of the bloody conflicts that were waged against the Viking encampments on the mouth of the Garonne. The half-anticipated rout of these savage heathen did not occur. Grim and costly fighting continued only to hold them at bay, and reinforcements were needed urgently for victory.

In the armor that promised to soon become a second skin, Lady Olivia set herself astride a war stallion and rode out to form companies of those mustered men that came in from the eastern fiefs. Then, organized and equipped, she dispatched them to supply her brother's diminishing, preliminary forces.

She barked orders with a new and crisply efficient authority as she saw to every detail of the arming and defense of Bordeaux castle and the manors and hamlets that surrounded and supplied it. Ordered, as Lord Roland had also suggested, the building of a repelling barricade of sharp-pointed, out-facing stakes along the outer perimeter of the castle moat.

Intense, preoccupied days, filled with a thousand things to know. From the intensified activities of fletcher and bowmaster, armorer and blacksmith, to the tallying of every store of iron and wood, grain, root, and salted meat. From the plowing and planting, to the condition and numbers of beasts and people, everything had to be kept to account.

At her insistence, Lord Roland accompanied Olivia through each of these fiercely busy days, even to mounting a horse and riding out with her. None so much as thought to question her authority, reinforced by her new manlike demeanor and appearance, and by the curious presence of the tall, richly clad, nameless and crippled lord who followed her wheresoever she chose to go . . . Whose silence seemed ominous, and whose only discernible feature was a pair of penetratingly watchful, fierce eagle eyes.

Unnatural, thought some.

Unnatural, knew the tirewoman Aliena as she watched with hard eyes and pursed lips. Whispered her convictions furtively to other household women. The signs were there—in the wars that had come. In the grey wet weather that made muck of the plowing and planting. In the bastardy of the new Duke, and in the woman's weakness of Lady Olivia, who, like Eve, listened to the serpent who rode her shoulder.

It was he, the Devil, who ruled Bordeaux now . . .

Unnatural, knew the huntsman Jean, whose new furtive sullenness caused others to shy away, while he tried to hide the sores that opened one by one, and festered on his skin. Scratched relentlessly at the elusive, prickled itching that slithered continually across him. Who knew very well what lay under the crippled lord's fine, concealing attire, and understood how that same leprosy had been passed to him in spite, because he knew the truth.

Standing in the great hall to which he had just been shown, only moments after his arrival, Lord Baudoin turned at the sound of approaching footsteps to stare at a slight young man in full armor and a surcoat with the arms of Guienne and Montglave flashing brightly from the chest, walking briskly toward him. Behind, he caught a glimpse of another—a tall, single-legged, richly clothed man, who stopped abruptly to hang on a pair of crutches near the back of the hall.

"My lord of Maganze! I bid thee welcome, for all our hospitality must seem rough. We are engaged against a brutal foe!"

His eyes went wide at the formal woman's voice that came from the young man. He blinked, then realized . . .

"My lady Olivia!" Astonishment burst out. He managed a bow.

She inclined her head and grinned. "So I am, my lord!" she agreed crisply. "Lord Girard is not here to greet thee, for he is engaged with the Count of Brittany against Viking invaders along the northern coasts. I play his part here for the present." She scanned his lean, swarthy, yet open face, the large dark eyes. "Not a woman's role exactly—but no matter!" She shrugged, then pointed toward a table and some chairs in a corner beyond the hearth fire. "This is unexpected, my lord. It is something of a grievous nature that brings thee so far from thy fiefs to Bordeaux?" She began to lead the way.

Totally disconcerted, Baudoin followed awkwardly.

"I am here for reasons of a personal nature," Baudoin got out, grappling for coherency. She stopped to look at him. Beyond, he saw the eyes of the crippled man on him, and sheered away by glancing around him. "I have seen how thy ramparts bristle, my lady. Tell me of these foe. Mayhap, I can be of service against them?"

He was still a boy—shy, she thought watchfully.

"I seek only unity between our houses, my lady," he ventured after a moment, his uncertainty and sincerity clearly apparent.

"That, I cannot know, my lord," Olivia said with slow care. Saw that he too was well aware of what lay between them. His father that had murdered hers. He looked away, down, his face unhappy.

"Then I must prove it!" he said with husky intensity, aware suddenly that no usual courtship lay before him as he had hoped for.

"Perhaps . . ." Olivia said coolly, after a brief silence, "the hospitality of Bordeaux will provide some opportunity, my lord!"

He looked up to accept the challenge, and saw that, beyond her, the crippled man with the covered face had gone. He straightened, squaring his shoulders. Met her look.

"I pray thee, tell me of these foe?" he requested clearly.

Behind the firmly shut door of his tower chamber, Roland pushed back cowl and face cloth to scowl at the air.

This one too—the same. So Lord Ganelon must have looked in his first youth.

If only she had not said it—that he made a man of her. She . . . He did not see the woman anymore. Only a slighter version of Oliver. The same in every way—word, gesture, courage . . . humanity.

And he had been caught to love again. Not, as he expected, by some paternal devotion to the son. But her . . . woman. Olivia . . . whom he could never touch.

Now, this other ghost had come. Heart on sleeve.

It wove most frightfully.

Roland bowed his head and clutched the crutches that propped him up like weapons. Rasped in pain. "Mother of God! Is there no peace in all the world for me?"

Victory . . . ? Out to sea, their longships wallowed like contented seals amid the waves. Sails furled, oars unmoving—confident. It was impossible to pursue them there. Girard blinked against the drizzle that trickled from the rim of his helm into his eyes as he sat his spent warhorse at the top of a sodden bluff overlooking the grey seas to the west.

He ached—from bruises, from hours spent in the saddle, in fighting. From raw and absolute fatigue. His nerves hummed like taut bowstrings from the shock he still felt from the savagery of the past week and more of continual fighting. Only the reinforcements sent from Bordeaux had turned the tide in their favor at last. Numbers . . . So many against so few. He looked away from the Viking ships, down toward the ruin of their camp on the northern shore of the mouth of the Garonne to his left. It smoldered in the persistent damp, unable to burn properly. He saw his men moving through the carnage, searching for Christian corpses to bury properly. Leave the heathen for the crows and buzzards, he had told them savagely. He'd not waste his men on Viking dead.

Heathen . . . His fingers shifted around Durandal's cunning hilt, the weapon still resting across his thighs. His own prowess . . . ? This—thing, that swept through foe as though of its own volition. His own hand did little more than direct the blade. Sometimes . . . He heard the rhythmic thudding of an approaching horse and looked back to see the Count of Brittany trot toward him. Lord Thierry stopped his animal then, his gaze fixed on the ships lurking out to sea.

"Mark me. They will be back after nightfall," the Count said. Lord Girard did not doubt it.

"Here? Or some other bay?"

The Count looked at him then, reading the shock of new experience in an unhardened, young man's face.

"We cannot know until they land," he said, then frowned and pointed to a high place to their right. "We shall set a beacon fire here, I think. Then, retreat into the woods to wait." He scanned a horizon that faded into a uniform grey haze. "It is the distance, and the sea that makes this difficult . . . We must man the shores from here to the Loire, where they are entrenched, then drive them out!"

"Divide forces?" Girard asked.

The Count nodded. "Aye, in a fashion. We must spread our resources. I must watch the western shores of Brittany, and the north. Thou hast the south . . . Thou hast done well here, my lord," he added suddenly, in a different, paternally textured tone. "Pity—there will be no time for bridals this summer!" Girard stiffened, something ugly lurching in his middle. What he knew . . . The truth had to be spoken.

"I am not a De Guienne, my lord," he said roughly. The Count looked at him. "As I have but recently learned, I am De Montglave's bastard! I have neither legitimate claim or title!"

The Count showed no surprise. "I have always known it, my lord," he said quietly. "I knew thy sire!" He paused, searching the younger man's face. "There are many who would be glad to inherit Lord Oliver's blood, however got!" Lord Thierry said more sternly. "He was himself a younger son, and every part of his reputation, aye, even as it survives today, he earned! *That* is thy true inheritance, and there are few to equal it! Now. We have other business to attend if we are to stop these seawolves!" He shortened his reins and his horse jibbed restlessly.

Girard forced the other matter from his thoughts. "My lord. For thy general scheme, I too must concern myself with the shores to the south along my own fiefs. We need a third force to hold the middle."

"Bordeaux is secure!" Lord Thierry responded at once.

Girard nodded toward the ships out to sea. "They may go south as well as north . . ." he began.

Lord Thierry shook his head. "Not to fret, lad!" he said cheerfully. "I have left a better general than either thou or I to hold those lands!" Girard stared. The Count grinned. "Lord

Roland!'' he pronounced very clearly, then, spurring his horse, spun the animal around and galloped away down the hill.

More slowly, Girard turned his own horse, then let the beast pick its own way.

"I am not even my brother's steward!'' he whispered unhappily and lowered his gaze to the sword, Durandal, still resting in his grip, the blade eerily clean and thunderous across his blood- and muck-soiled, mail-covered thighs. That crippled, leprous man? And this—his gift? The same sword by which Lord Roland had won so much glory all those years ago. With a glance of dislike, he thrust the weapon back into its place in the baldric at his back. He felt trapped, as though he was becoming lost in other men's accomplishments. "How can *my* honor or repute be got with another man's sword?'' he asked the air.

His horse pecked on a stone and stumbled. Girard collected himself and recovered the beast, then sent it slithering down a muddly incline.

At his back, beneath the plastic, illusory darkness with which she concealed her woman's form, Durandal's diminutive face became alert. Expectant. Poised upon a moment of recognition that sensed a pending opportunity.

Like clustered vultures, the Viking ships stayed out to sea just beyond the Garonne estuary for the remainder of the day. Watch posts and beacon fires were set upon the bluffs to defy the night, and when the morning came, and the mists rolled back before the sun, it was seen that the Viking ships had vanished as though they had never been.

Following the Champion's plans, Lord Girard dispatched a summons to Bordeaux for more men and supplies, and, keeping the bulk of the troops, marched them northward through the forests that flanked the coast. Lord Thierry took a different route, moving inland, where his office of King's Champion made it possible for him to build his forces by mustering additional men from the smaller holdings along his way. Between them, they would form a pincers to retake the rich valleys near the mouth of the Loire. Unlike the bitter, but random, fighting that had occupied them so far, they knew a bitter battle lay ahead.

Marching north, Girard grew to understand the Champion's hatred of the Vikings. Passing charred fishing hamlets, and other such places, he saw the savagery the northmen vented on folk ill equipped to defend themselves. Wolves . . . aye. Elusive.

Stealthy. Brutal for the pleasure of it. And their ships were sighted often enough. Out to sea. Never predictable. Always beyond reach. Free, like gulls, to go where they would.

In chausses and undertunic, unable to sleep, Baudoin shifted restlessly on the furs that covered the bed in the guest chamber he had been given. He frowned at the night. Perhaps he wouldn't have noticed otherwise, but his sensibilities had been heightened by what he had found at Hauteville, by what he carried within him. Now, after two days since he had arrived, he had begun to feel it. Something uneasy. Elusive. Delicate. It wafted deeper than the natural tensions and anxieties that accompanied so much war preparation.

What . . . ? The sound of footsteps thudding hurriedly along the corridor beyond his chamber caused him to start and sit up. He heard the muffled rapping of knuckles upon a distant door, thrust his feet into his boots, and lunged across the room to grope for the door latch. He opened it a little.

"Fetch the seneschal of arms to the great hall! At once!" He heard the Lady Olivia's crisply given order. Peered out farther to see a man's brief bow make shadows in the sconce-lit hall, before he turned and rushed headlong back the way he had come.

An instant later, the Lady Olivia appeared, a slim, nimble figure in chausses and undertunic, her hair flying about shoulders and hips. She seized a torch from a wall bracket, then strode down the corridor to disappear through another door close by. Before he had time to do more than inhale, she reappeared, a hauberk over one shoulder, helm cradled against one elbow. She turned and strode toward him, saw him standing there, and paused to scan his lightly clad frame.

"Do thou arm thyself, my lord!" she said grimly. "That which we have awaited is come!" Before he could reply, she strode away to veer suddenly, not toward the stairwell that led down to the great hall, but along another, branching corridor that led to the eastern regions of the keep.

Understanding, and about to obey, Baudoin froze at the slow creaking that came from the opposite direction, and spun around to see another furtively opened door, a woman's wide-eyed face peering through it.

"We are doomed!" he caught the whisper. A pale hand made the Sign of the Cross in the gloom. "See. He has summoned his demons to destroy us all. It is as I have foretold . . ." Baudoin lunged across the corridor to catch the door just before it closed again.

"What is this talk of summons and devils?" he demanded, seeing a covey of tirewomen. They cringed back. Only the eldest looked up to meet his stare.

"Get thee away from this place, my lord!" she whispered. "We are cursed. The Devil himself dwells among us!"

Baudoin stiffened and frowned. "What nonsense is this, woman?" he demanded.

Her eyes slid. "See for thyself then, my lord. She goes to him even now!"

"To whom?" he asked roughly, understanding part of it.

"To Satan himself! Succubus!" the woman hissed, and jerked the door from his grasp to slam it shut.

Totally startled, Baudoin flung himself away, and ran lightly in pursuit of the direction Lady Olivia had taken. Down a darkened hallway. Up a flight of steps that flanked the easternmost tower of the keep. He poised as he reached the top to see another short hallway, and a door at the end. Ajar—fireglow flickered from the chamber beyond to make ruddy brightness against the dark. He heard voices and moved closer to listen.

"As I recollect, there is naught save forest and marsh between that manor of Talence, and the bay of Caracans for the twenty-five miles to the south and west of here." A man's voice, rich and deep and deliberate. "I'll warrant these are the same northmen that escaped Lord Girard by the mouth of the Garonne."

"Aye. Well word has come, Talence is even now in flames, my lord." Olivia's voice, sounding brutal. "The populace has fled into the woods—those that are not destroyed already!"

"It is a diversion, my lady!" the man's voice cut in. "Mark me. They know of this stronghold. If they may draw thee out, then they will try to take it! The timing is too clever for the troops dispatched to Lord Girard yesterday. Nay. I have another plan . . ."

"What then?"

Baudoin thought he heard a smile in the man's voice. "We will hunt the wolf with wolfhounds, and in silence!" Almost sinister, it was so sure.

"How so?"

"Lothair De Coutras is here, as I bade thee send for. He is a sound and capable man. Give him Bordeaux castle to hold. For the rest, I will have ten men, strong swimmers all, and marksmen with the longbow. Wolfhounds—and the mastiffs. And fleet horses for all, with hooves bound in leather to muffle their passing. I need a bow with a hard draw, and arrows aplenty . . .''

"I will ride with thee, my lord. I am a sound marksman!" she cut in.

"Nay!"

"Who will follow thee, my lord, when all here fear thee as they do?" she asked with acid reasonableness. "Nay. I must come!"

There was silence. Baudoin shifted carefully closer to the open door.

"So be it!" A brutally reluctant agreement came at length.

"What do we do then, my lord?"

"We destroy their ships! Then we hunt them out!" Almost softly uttered.

Olivia's voice made an oddly practical contrast. "Here is armor and helm then, my lord. Huon's—large enough to fit, I think. We meet in the great hall as soon as may be!"

Baudoin shrank back behind the door as she flung through it, turned, and half ran back the way she had come. She disappeared. He heard scraping noises, and shifted cautiously. He had to know—to see for himself . . .

He stepped silently into the open portal and stared across the chamber beyond. A man was seated on the bed on the other side, one leg before him, the other, a grotesquely shortened, twisted thing. He gasped inadvertent recognition. This was the same, shrouded, crippled man he had seen when he had arrived—not since.

The cripple started and looked up, his hair like gold and fire, and as long as a woman's around a pair of hard, transfixing, golden eyes. His face . . . Baudoin gagged with shock. His face . . .

It was a dead thing, ashen-hued, peeling. He froze, strangled and appalled as, with lightning speed, the crippled man lunged up, then toward him on a pair of staves, reached out with one hideous hand to clutch the front of his tunic.

"Maganze!" the apparition hissed, glaring, aye, like the Devil himself.

"Mother of God!" Baudoin rasped, frozen with horror at the thing looming over him, so close.

"God?" the monster grated. "Nay, boy! God played no part in this! This is thy father's doing!" The hand released him, and

Baudoin stumbled backward to collide with the doorjamb. His father—this?

"Nay!" he rasped in total revulsion. But the apparition closed on him to glare still.

"Aye!" it hissed with terrible clarity. "What I am is got of thy father's treachery! His wrongs are not undone, for all he is dead!"

What he knew already. Now this . . . ? Baudoin shivered. "Who?" he managed to whisper.

"Are thou come here to wreak more of the same, or will thou redeem thy father's sins?" Aye, it was a man, a terrible man, asking softly now.

"I am an *honest* man!" Baudoin managed a violent protest against everything he carried. Those eyes that seemed to search his soul.

"Then, prove it, my lord!" the creature said with sinister gentleness. Baudoin straightened. Found courage under shock.

"Who art thou?" he demanded roughly.

The apparition smiled. "For thee, Baudoin De Maganze? I am consequence!" it said very gently.

Baudoin stared for a moment, in total understanding, then turned and hurled himself away.

TWENTY

On his belly at the edge of a high, ragged bluff, hidden by the tall grasses that rustled in the sea breeze, Lord Girard frowned as he peered at the estuary that stretched in every direction beyond and below him. To his left, the river splayed like a hand through broad areas of marsh as they joined with the sea. Long dark shapes on the twinkling waters were, he knew, the Viking ships anchored there.

Ahead, and to his right, the waters of the Loire sparkled in the sunlight between the lush greens of trees and undergrowth rising up along the bluffs on either side of the broad valley before melting away into the northern distance. A single longship, its sail bellied, glided with silent, leisurely arrogance up the river, headed inland. And the small village that had nestled in the shelter of the bluffs on the far side was no more than a blackened scar in the distance . . .

Somewhere on the other side, hidden like himself, the Count of Brittany had brought his forces down through a wide eastern and northern detour to wait, as agreed, for Girard to make the first move before he struck.

Signals carefully, briefly exchanged, using the flash of sunlight on a piece of polished brass—a trick the Count had acquired from the Moors in Spain many years before. His own men, Girard knew, were concealed in small pockets along the southern shores. Fair weather had not made it easier to hide them. Or the horses.

To the east, he could barely see the delicate grey threads of smoke that wove upward into the clear air from Viking fires. They had conquered inland as far as the holdings of Nantes and Rez, destroying those fiefs and the newly constructed monastary there. Now, they were firmly entrenched in the fork where the Loire and the Sevres joined.

The longship sailed on, shrinking steadily as it progressed upriver. Girard scowled. If only he could get to their ships . . . He crawled backward and, using the concealing underbrush, got to his feet and walked back the way he had come, along a deer trail that led to the trees where he had tethered his horse. Reaching it, he loosed the beast, gathered the reins, and mounted. As he had signaled this time. They had no choice but to march east and engage the Vikings in a direct, pitched battle. And the Vikings had the advantage, with their high oak pallisaded camp, the river—and their ships.

Two days later, his cloak drawn close about him to conceal the glinting of his armor, Girard stared through the trees at the high wooden palisades on the other side of the Loire. Round, dark objects were impaled on staves lofted above those walls. Human heads. Christian heads. Heads by the hundreds . . . Crows fluttered about them, picking scraps from the fresher with a dirty lack of conscience.

"For God, it is a desecration!" he whispered slowly and looked away. To the right, the view through the trees was little better. The Vikings had built another settlement on the high ground above the southern banks of the river, close to where the village of Reze had been. Girard turned in his saddle to look at Sir Guillaume De Blaye who had accompanied. "Signal the Count of Brittany," he told his vassal. "Three flashes for attack. One for the morrow."

The knight nodded toward the Viking camp across the river. "They may well see it, my lord," he pointed out.

"That is a risk we will have to take!" Girard retorted. Then, "This is what we will do . . ." Talking softly, he laid out the plan he had contrived.

Quiet darkness . . . The night-active wild creatures had fled the area. The river flowed with silent indifference. And from behind the oak walls of the two Viking fortresses, great bonfires spewed up a ruddy, incandescent glow against the darkness.

Voices echoed in the distance. Deep-throated laughter. Shouts. Screams . . .

Throughout the night, two armies of men moved stealthily through woods and undergrowth to position themselves for the bloodshed that was the only promise of the coming dawn. Under the command of Sir Guillaume De Blaye, one company forded the river in a careful single file to huddle in the sodden marshes and reeds by the southwest corner of the northern Viking camp. One man on horseback rode with furtive haste, carrying messages to the Count of Brittany, somewhere in the forested hills beyond, ready to attack from the north and east.

Lord Girard spread the rest of his troops into three companies around the landward side of the newer Viking fortress on the southern banks of the Loire. A line of men, hidden in thickets and woods, ready to make a direct assault from all sides. Behind them, the archers with fire arrows.

Soft threads of mist rose up from the river to collect and thicken in the air, then spread upward, outward, to engulf every shadow in the darkness, making a resonant amplification of even the least sound. The blowing of a horse, the chink of armor, a whispered exchange. Everything poised . . . waiting.

When the mists began to glow blue with coming dawn, and holding his stallion at the ready, Lord Girard signaled his men to tighten their approach. Almost time . . . He drew the Dark Sword, Durandal, from its place at his back and felt the strange hilt shift like something molten in his grip. Ambivalence surged. He lofted it, and glanced up to see a gleam of blue lightning slither along the extraordinary blade. Sensed again, that power—eager, restless—all appetite.

"Heathen thing!" he whispered under his breath. Then, as the blue mists brightened to a lighter grey, he swung the sword forward, pointing it at the emerging shadows of the Viking walls before him, bellowed the cry that was the signal for it to begin, and spurred his horse to bolt it forward.

The earth trembled under the thunder of galloping horses, the rumbled thudding of running men as they swarmed out of concealment to race in a single wave toward the Viking encampment. Order vanished as Frankish soldiers made to scale Viking walls and found themselves at once engaged by the foe.

A little to the fore of the rest, Girard led a tight phalanx of mounted men to assault the gates of the fortress, those on the edges of the battalion guarding the four in the middle that carried the ramming beam between them.

Wooden gates shuddered under the first impact. Roaring, a berserker plummeted from the walls to kill and be killed. A horse screamed and went down. The rammers rallied and charged again. The gates shivered and cracked and, like airborne devils, giant Viking warriors plunged from the walls to bring instant death to whomever they landed on. Spears impaled. Axes swung through helms and armor, flesh and horsemeat. Girard bellowed to rally his ramsmen and felt Durandal leap in his grip, sweeping toward the great heathen leeches that dropped and clung. One blow, then another. And another. Durandal cut one in two as if he had been no more solid than water . . .

The ram slammed against the timbers of the gate. This time they gave. Once more to finish . . . Girard saw an arm fly away from a torso as Durandal made another deadly arc.

The gates shattered—space. Shouts, screams, roars, made a cacophony that split the air. And flaming, pitch-covered arrows came sailing through the air to hit wood and men and horses. Terrible, a horse's screaming . . . Girard swung his stallion about and gouged the beast's sides to leap it through the opening above a tangle of beams and men. Roared for others to follow him . . .

His horse slithered and halted in the midst of a wave of horn-helmed, fiery bearded northmen advancing to fight off the Franks that followed him. Durandal carried him then, defining his reflexes, singing eerily as it sliced through a Viking neck, swept up to disembowel another, then curved into a defensive, horizontal arc as his horse leaped and bucked beneath him to ward off the Vikings that swarmed behind in an attempt to hamstring the beast.

Again, he spurred the animal forward, chest barreling against the foe, deeper into the compound. Again, he caught a glimpse of the fire arrows that sailed through the air like flocks of scarlet and orange birds to alight on all and sundry. Flames begun to sprout and grow, or damped to spew forth smoke . . .

He heard his own men behind him. His stallion plunged again, and he bolted it forward between two buildings in the very heart of the compound, then reared it up, forehooves flailing, against another wave of spear-armed Vikings. One threw. The stallion shuddered and screamed, and as the beast began to drop away, Girard loosed his feet from the stirrups and threw himself aside to tumble through the muck. He gasped as something heavy landed against his back to twist his sword arm beneath him, and writhed to grapple with a huge, powerful man. Got his left hand loose to find the dagger at his waist, then heaved with all his strength to drive the thing into the warrior's throat. The heathen slumped. Girard jerked away, twisted to find his feet and stumbled upright. Hands clawed. He dropped the Dark Sword to spin and seize a down-sweeping axe, then used his dagger to spite the one wielding it. Took it. Spun again to fight others.

Axe and dagger now, better weapons for such close and bloody hacking. His mouth set, Girard fought on. And on . . .

Lungs heaved for air. Muscles shrieked for effort. It did not matter. Victory was all that mattered, and these great, brutish heathen were so hard to kill. Unafraid . . .

Gradually, the Franks gained the walls, and, with terrible losses, breached them. Fires grew, feeding on thatch and beam. Smoke strangled . . . Gradually, the foe shrank back to small clusters and isolated individuals that still spewed out triumphant shouts as they fought on, finally to be overwhelmed by sheer numbers.

Then, at last, Girard found himself propped against a half-charred wall, with nothing around him but dead. The earsplitting din of battle had died away behind his own gasping fatigue, he realized slowly. The shouts and screams were gone . . . Silence. He shook his head to clear the sweat from his eyes, and looked down to see that his surcoat hung in tatters, that he had an axe in his right hand, a dagger in his left. Scarlet wet. Himself no better . . . He looked up to see one of his own men staring at him with a like befuddlement.

"It is done, I think, my lord," the other rasped clumsily across the distance that separated them. Girard looked around. The dead lay everywhere. The ground was a muck of gore and dismembered limbs—mostly his own men. Everything else was a smoldering ruin, except for the single building that still stood, part of the walls. And the pens against them on the south side.

"It is done," he told the soldier who continued to stare at him. It seemed to take an extraordinary effort to straighten . . . "I must know the count of our dead. Find the wounded . . . They must be cared for." The man nodded, clearly glad to have direction, and moved away.

Girard slowly walked across the compound, staring at the burnt, smoldering stores of stolen grain and the like. At horses sprawled dead—or standing here and there, unhappy, injured.

He slipped the axe haft through the belt that girded his hips, and put his dagger back in its sheath. He walked on through corpses and broken weapons and groaning wounded, toward the breach his men had made in the eastern wall. He stopped and stared out through it, across the river, and saw the other battle still being waged in and around that other camp. Shouts and crashes made an eerie, distant echoing . . . He caught the flash of the Count of Brittany's colors, and saw the man, still astride his horse amid the shifting mass of his men. He turned away. He did not yet know what he had left to use.

Nor, he knew suddenly as he paused in his walking to stare at a clutch of gaunt, ragged, and terrified serfs lying, bound wrist and ankle, in a small pen, had anything in his life truly prepared him for this.

These too must be loosed and tended, he thought deliberately. But for the moment, they were safe enough. He began issuing orders to those he saw moving among the dead, and headed back across the compound toward the gates. He stopped then to look at the carcass of his destrier. Butchered . . . and he had raised the beast.

The sword . . . he realized slowly. He had lost the sword Durandal. He looked down and searched across the tumbled bodies around the carcass of his horse, then caught sight of it under a northman's corpse, a black, living streak in the bloody mire. With one chain mail-covered foot, he thrust the corpse aside, bent, and scooped up the Dark Sword. Felt again . . .

"Heathen thing!" he muttered with antipathy and looked up to see a large group of his own battle-worn men gathering slowly about him. Quietly, he issued orders to them, then began walking back across the compound. Reaching the pens on the south side, he stopped and stared at the trussed, barely human-looking creatures lying in the filth there. Some twenty souls—or more. And they stared back at him with shocked, half-vacant eyes, uttering no sound. They were, he realized with horror, barely more than children. Young boys. Nubile girls.

Sickened to the core for what he understood, Girard thrust through the gate and, still holding Durandal, drew his dagger with his left hand and knelt to cut away rawhide bonds. His own voice came softly, as though from a great distance, uttering meaningless, soothing words of reassurance. These were all that remained, he knew, of the fiefs and villages hereabouts. He worked his way from one to the next, and the next, glancing at starved, haggard faces, bruises and welts. They moved sluggishly when freed, as though they had forgotten how . . . And as he reached through them toward the back of the pen, a sudden movement in the shadows there caught his eyes. He stiffened. Straightened.

A boy jerked suddenly from sandwiched concealment between two others to glare at him with mixed ferocity and terror. One of the Vikings, this lad, Girard realized, shifting to seize the boy as he made to leap aside. But, before thought or intent, his sword arm came up, swept into movement by the Dark Sword that drove of its own volition, straight through the child's upper belly. Through the one who had been behind . . .

Girard stared. The boy's eyes glazed. He uttered a gurgled sound, then slumped down upon the weapon. And, behind him, Girard saw the half-naked girl, still helplessly bound, now transfixed to the wood behind where Durandal had pierced through eyes and skull.

Appalled, Girard stared. A girl. A child . . . and his hand still clutched the monstrous sword as though bound to it. He had thought to make a prisoner of the other . . . Gall rose in his throat, and around him, terrified whimpering proclaimed the lie of what he had said to them.

Something worse than sickened outrage made him jerk the Dark Sword loose and spin around to roar orders to the nearest of his men to finish what he had begun. Then he strode away, across the compound, over the bodies and timbers that cluttered the breach in the wall, across the sod beyond to stop abruptly above the river's edge.

"I am a Christian man!" he snarled. "I do not murder girls and children! Defiling thing . . . How can thou bring honor to my name!" With all his strength, he reached back and flung the sword Durandal away from him.

Like a frigid, elongated bird, the Dark Sword streaked through the air to tumble down . . . down. He stared as it plummeted into the waters beyond the river's edge, disappearing with barely a ripple.

"I am a *Christian* man!" he whispered.

"My lord Duke!" A rasping, breathless shout caused Girard to spin on one heel to see a sodden knight on a laboring, equally saturated horse spur the beast toward him from the western edge of the river. He recognized Sir Guillaume De Blaye. "My lord. We are victorious!" the knight called out as he approached, then flung himself from his animal's back even as he reined the beast in. "My lord! The Count of Brittany gave me to bring thee word of our success!" he got out between gasps for air. "Caution, as well, however. Lord Thierry says this is no time to rest easy. Viking ships may well return in the night as they have been known to do before. His messengers bring word they are still at anchor just beyond the estuary . . ."

Collecting himself forcibly, Girard nodded. "I am shrewdly advised," he said after a moment. "We too have triumphed, Sir Guillaume, though for terrible losses." The knight glanced up toward the broken palisade, his features grim. "Something more than a third," Girard answered his unspoken question and began striding briskly toward the ruined fort.

"We fared much better, my lord. The added company of thy dispatching . . ." the knight said, leading his drooping horse as he followed.

"God be praised for that, at least!" Girard muttered. "Do thou tell me, Sir Guillaume, what Lord Thierry anticipates."

Clouds gathered and congealed across the sky to disguise the sun. Rain came, pouring down in resolute torrents from the heavens. The dead were gathered into two heaps. One for Christian men. The other composed of Viking dead. Horses that had survived were gathered and attended. Those that had been killed were stripped of harness and butchered to feed hungry troops. Wounded Vikings were throat-slit, and weapons were gathered from the mud and distributed among the forces that remained. Rude shelters of charred beams and turf were made to ward off some of the weather as the wounded Franks were gathered and given whatever care was possible.

Later, as the dusk settled in deepening blue tones, Lord Girard walked with slow exhaustion across the compound to the single building that remained. He pushed through the rude portal and stopped in vague surprise to see a small hearth fire on the relatively dry, packed earth within.

The smell of roasting meat was sickening, and on the other side, Sir Guillaume, who held a piece the size of a ham at sword's point over the flames, looked up.

"My lord, there is a wineskin that I found," he said, nodding toward the object that lay beside where he crouched on his haunches, and reading the young Duke's face with absolute accuracy.

Girard did not reply, but moved forward and bent slowly to sit on the hard earth, suddenly aware of chill, of slimy gore and sweat-soaked garments beneath his armor. The fire's heat was astonishing . . . Slowly, he set his brother's shield before him, recovered from beneath the carcass of his stallion, and examined it. Save for dirt, it was hardly even blemished . . .

Easier to think of duty without the monstrous Durandal, he thought. That lethal gift, filled with ominous, unnatural power—and another man's reputation. He inhaled deeply, reached for the wineskin, and unstoppered it to drink with care. Warmth filled his mouth.

"Do they come tonight, Sir Guillaume," he said as he swallowed. "We are prepared." The knight nodded and fixed his gaze on his cooking. He knew his place. Girard shifted the steel sword he had found to replace the other to a more comfortable angle against his left flank and stared across the gloom to where rain penetrated the roof, falling one large, isolated drop at a time to make a slowly growing puddle on the floor.

Beneath the flowing waters of the Loire, the Dark Sword, Durandal, shifted slowly among the weeds and sand where she lay. Hilt wings furled to vanish as she grew, sinuously engulfing her own blade, to become most purely woman formed. Hair wafted like black filament seaweed in the currents to veil a slowly paling skin . . . Then moving with an elemental silence, she rose up from the shallows by the river's edge, and, with the night mists that had begun to waft across the same, trod lightly up the bank to stand among the reeds and tall grasses there.

Black eyes read the night. Her hair made a midnight swathing as she moved a hand to compose . . . She smiled slowly. He had not the power to discard her who had been irrevocably given, this son of Oliver. But he had given her that opportunity she had sensed before, had conjured to achieve . . . had waited for.

It was a sense of presence that made him jerk to sudden, disconcerted, blinking wakefulness. Girard inhaled, nerves frayed as he realized he had not even been aware of falling asleep, sitting there. Before him, the fire had sunk to glowing embers. His knight had gone, and filth had dried to a caking discomfort against his skin.

He heard it again, an awkward gasping noise, and jerked stiffly to his feet. He peered across the building, and, his hand reflexively on the hilt of his dagger, began to stalk the sound that came, aye, from somewhere in the tangle of charred wood and such around the gaping hole on the other side. Someone . . .

Something gleamed—he lunged forward to catch at cold flesh, then froze. Stared down at the ashen pallor of a woman with great black eyes and rivers of tangled, midnight hair. A full, perfect breast jutted at him from between a rent in her robe. He did not let go.

Instead, he poised, eyes widening slowly. Then he heard his own whispered, "Mother of God! It is thou!"

She started. Shrank back. "Sweet Jesu, thou are a Christian man?" He knew that voice from his dreams. Husky deep and filled with rich-toned melodies.

"Aye," he managed, and drew her forward, awe filling him as he saw more. Saw the rents of struggle in a gown that bespoke more than common birth. "So I am, my lady. Girard De Guienne, Duke of Bordeaux," he got out as he drew her up to stand before him, a slight and perfect creature who came no higher than his collarbones.

"I am Roselyn De Cecyll, my lord," she whispered. "I got free of the pens with the others who survived . . . I hid here." Her voice died away. He felt her shiver, and let go to unclasp his cloak, then set it around her. Better than nothing, despite its grime.

"Thou are safe now, my lady," he told her, staring at the woman of his dreams, feeling . . . feeling. Elation, and drowning at the same time. Knowing as he spoke those words, he offered his life gladly on the altar of that promise. She looked up at him with eyes that seemed to touch as clearly as fingertips.

"For that, I am content to give myself into thy hands, my lord," she murmured. He drew her to the fire then, settled her, and stoked it up with faggots, then knelt before her to offer the wineskin and any other comfort he could.

"I think it is God's will, my lady, that brings us together by this happenstance," he got out later, meaning everything. She looked at him with eyes that opened like an embrace, then lowered her gaze shyly to her hands that clutched his cloak around her.

Little mortal man, Durandal thought, thou cannot begin to know the truth thou have uttered.

• • •

The night continued as rain fell, then muted to a drizzle before ceasing entirely. Mists rose up to fill the air with silence, and the scents of earth and vegetation, of burning, and death . . . smothering all but the most immediate view.

And as the mists began to glow with the first morning light, Vikings swarmed out of every conceivable hiding place, out of the fog itself, to bellow berserker vengeance as they attacked.

Lord Girard rallied his Franks and fought, discovering the longships that had sailed upriver during the night. From the northern banks of the Loire, Lord Thierry brought his forces to flank the same. Sent a battalion across the river to reinforce the beleagured men on the southern hill. He dispatched swimmers with ropes to snare the ships that lurked in midriver, and set his archers to shoot great volleys of pitch-laden fire arrows toward them.

One of the longships caught fire well enough to burn and sink. Others, smoldering, melted back downstream. Corpses floated in the currents, or spun in eddies, or washed against the shore to become tangled in the reeds. The rest was bitter fighting that continued through the better part of the day. Melees of men that eroded into scattered, single combats, then, at last, faded into silence.

Slowly, for those that stood, totally exhausted, their weapons reflexively held, the realization came that a complete victory had been achieved.

The sun had sunk to just above the trees to the west when Lord Thierry spurred his tired warhorse up the hill toward Lord Girard's battleground. Behind him followed battle-worn and grimed mounted men and Sir Guillaume De Blaye, who led a spare horse to replace the one the young Duke had lost.

His sword aloft, the Count bellowed out triumph and praise to all who stood and watched him ride through the ruined fort. Then in response to his gleaming eyes, hard, proud smile, they surged forward to realize what they had done in an answering thunder of voices.

Long inured to the sights of dead men and ruins, Lord Thierry searched for the young Duke of Bordeaux and discovered him at last in a tangle of soldiers and other ragged figures. He dismounted and strode forward, shocked to see, for all his apparent lack of hurt, Lord Girard's haggard pallor and haunted eyes. The others melted back as he approached, save for one slight, tattered figure that huddled in the embrace of the Duke's left arm.

"It is done!" Lord Thierry exhaled violently, stopping before the younger man. "And thy part most excellently managed. We have driven them out—for the present!"

A sickened look crossed the younger man's face. "So great a cost . . ." he murmured. "It will take years to rebuild here."

Lord Thierry frowned. "That is war!" he retorted. "Nor am I insensible of our losses. *But*, they are gone honorably to God, and I give heart and service to the living!" He peered at the ragged creature that stood so close against the young Duke, started as she met his gaze with dark, large eyes for drowning, seeing a beauty of unparalleled exquisiteness. He felt his insides lurch in response. "Who is this?" he demanded roughly.

"Lady Roselyn De Cecyll. My lord, Thierry De Leon, Count of Brittany, and King's Champion . . ." Girard deftly turned identification into introduction. "This lady and those few younglings are all that remain of the folk hereabouts," he added quietly.

"Kept for slaves." Lord Thierry nodded, still staring at the pale girl. "I did not know Sir Gyblerde De Cecyll had a daughter?"

She looked down modestly. "I have been much confined," she answered in a voice that was pure seduction. Aye, she must have been kept very close indeed, Lord Thierry thought, drawing back. He bowed, then turned to give his attention to the aftermath of this bloodshed.

"I see thou no longer carry the sword of Roland," the Count observed aloud many hours later as he broke fast with roasted horsemeat. On the other side of the campfire, Lady Roselyn still huddled against him, Lord Girard stopped eating and looked away.

"Nay," he said oddly. "It was lost in the fighting. No matter. It was a cumbersome thing . . ."

Troubled by the tone, Lord Thierry said nothing and continued to eat. Lord Roland had never seemed to find it so, he remembered. A nasty disquiet had settled under his ribs. Lady Roselyn cleaved to Girard with all the welcome faithfulness of a shadow on a sunny summer day . . . His plans, that promised now, to remain unfulfilled. And they had other battles against the Vikings to fight through the rest of the summer ahead, he knew.

Girard . . . Was it his own folly to have thought he saw Oliver De Montglave born again in this overtender boy. Honed, he realized, on an entirely different kind of anvil . . . but. He could find none of the brilliant clarity he remembered so well in this now clearly ambivalent boy.

Oliver, he understood with bitter, final disappointment, had truly died at Roncesvalles.

TWENTY-ONE

Flames billowed up to weave brilliant scarlet and orange against the night sky some two hundred yards away. Reflections slithered and danced across the quietly lapping waters of the bay. Briefly visible, black spike masts toppled, and one by one, each of five ships listed like a drunken pyre, then sank in a great hissing of steam . . .

On the shore, only a small campfire remained of those Vikings who'd been left to watch for their fellows. Twisted black shapes around it were the bodies, shot down by arrows, then rended by the mastiffs. The returning swimmers were nearly impossible to pick out, a silent, elusive cluster of human shapes emerging onto the spit that reached into the bay some fifty yards distant.

Holding her horse still, Olivia grinned at the nearly invisible form of Lord Roland, mounted on the horse beside hers. "Now we may rout the rest of them out, my lord!" she murmured with intense satisfaction. Golden eyes filled with reflected fire met hers.

"Now we go ahunting, my lady!" he said with that lethal deliberation she had come to know so well of late. She heard the smile beneath. "One must be dispatched to bring up Sir Thibault De Laboureyre to . . . cleanse the thickets in our wake!" he added.

"Aye." Olivia's grin widened as she nodded. Always succinct, yet filled with mutual understanding, the conversations

223

between them were never heard by others. Before her men, Lord Roland's silence was absolute.

Horses leaner, harder than they had been before, their coats dull, matted—the hounds as well, tongues lolling in great gaping jaws as they loped alongside—it was a hard-used company of triumphant, dirty men that clattered across the drawbridge, turned their horses, and drew rein moments later in the inner bailey. Poised by a window in the southern stair tower for the shouts he had heard, Lord Baudoin watched Sir Lothair De Coutras emerge from the keep to greet the Lady Olivia.

Still astride her horse, face aglow, her voice rang out. "Sir Lothair! I see thou have persevered here very well! And we have made a rout of the rest! De Labourneyre follows a day behind on our heels. See these men tended with every comfort, for they have done most brilliantly. And the beasts." Lord Baudoin saw De Coutras, with whom he had achieved a sound camaraderie during the past weeks of sporadic siege and fighting, bow and reply. His eyes were drawn to the ghastly crippled creature who dismounted in an awkward swirl of cloak folds from his place behind the Lady Olivia, recovered his crutches from his horse's pack, and set them under his arms. Faceless beneath plain armor and clothing, hood and face cloth, those golden eyes, even from this distance, were unforgettable. The rest? Skins. It haunted his innards.

Baudoin caught a last glimpse of Lady Olivia as she dismounted after the others, a nimble boy of a knight, who dropped her horse's reins and walked slowly up the steps of the keep. Baudoin jerked himself away from the window and hurried on down the rest of the stairs to give his own greeting.

De Coutras and Lady Olivia were talking as Baudoin entered the great hall moments later and walked toward the dais where they stood. He stopped abruptly as she turned to face him, then bowed deeply.

"My lord, the Count De Maganze has given much to our sound defense, my lady," he heard the older knight say, and stood very still before Olivia De Montglave's appraising stare. Felt heat rise up his neck.

"I was well tutored in strategies, my lady," he said truthfully. In that at least, his uncle's scholarship had done him sound service. "I have sought to give such as a loyal ally might," he added, a little hesitantly.

Lady Olivia smiled at De Coutras. "Tend my men, Sir Lothair," she commanded softly. The knight stepped back, bowed, and turned away to do her bidding. Noticing her pallor then, Baudoin watched her carefully, trying as well to elude the looming shadow of the cripple behind her. But she looked at him again, searching his face. "I make thee welcome as a friend may, my lord Baudoin," she said then, very clearly, and stepped forward, hand proffered from beneath the folds of her cloak in the manner of a man. Heart pounding against his ribs, he took it and bowed again.

"I am blessed, my lady!" he offered breathlessly, and saw her smile a little at his impulsive, fervent gallantry. She withdrew her hand gently, turned, and began walking away. Buckled suddenly and went to her knees.

"Pah! I . . . ." she gasped out, then stopped. Baudoin lunged toward her but the cripple swooped ahead of him, crutches dropping to clatter as he half fell beside her.

"Nay!" His cry was rasping. Hideous. Baudoin froze, but Olivia turned toward both sound and monster.

"It is but a flesh wound, my lord. Naught to fuss about, save that I am unused to such injuries!" Blue eyes locked with gold, then she folded slowly, to lie completely lax upon the flagging.

"Nay!" the cripple whispered, reaching out to touch, then suddenly shrinking back to turn his shrouded head toward Lord Baudoin. It was a look that shocked—stripped. Baudoin felt strangled by the stare of those widened eyes. Feelings so powerful as to strike out. Terror—and passion. Such passion.

"Take her!" the cripple hissed, jerking back to grapple with his crutches, rising up like a twisted scarecrow. "Take her! Tend her!"

Baudoin moved as one compelled. He bent to scoop up the fainted Olivia, then saw as the folds of her cloak fell aside the gash in her upper thigh. Loss of blood more than the actual cut had weakened her, he realized. She had said the truth. Holding her close, he straightened and looked toward the monster who still stared at him in command while retreating on his crutches like some frightened beast. Baudoin inhaled and turned away, then bellowed for steward and tirewomen as, still holding her firmly, he strode toward the stairs that led to the private quarters in the upper parts of the keep.

• • •

No harm must come to her. No harm . . . It was a desperate litany inside him. The only prayer he knew. Watching Baudoin De Maganze disappear with her, Roland shrank back, then turned and made his way unseeing toward his tower chamber. He lurched through the door at last, slamming it. Crossed the chamber and, yielding to the pain that crawled through every part of him, dropped his crutches and sank down onto the bed.

For what he was, he had done as he must. He had given her over to that softly unsure, honest young ghost of his old foe.

And love . . . ? This love had come up like a lily through the still pools of defining memory to surface and flower in the shared experiences and common purposes of the last months. Understanding and camaraderie. Something gallant shared . . . It moved through him now, this feeling, more poignantly intimate than before, excruciating.

Something else had risen too, during the past weeks of continual riding as they hunted out Viking marauders to butcher, or fought little skirmishing ambush battles . . . His disease had decided to progress the worsening destruction of his flesh. Pain swelled and ebbed in continual, relentless tides now. His flesh, concealed, was becoming more hideous than ever.

And he would do anything for her. Anything at all . . .

He turned his head toward the wall and closed his eyes.

"For mercy," he whispered to the indifferent air as the pain swelled again. "It must conclude . . ."

"My lord. How is it that . . . ?" Olivia's question broke as she limped through the door, then died at the sight of him, head bowed, half clothed, seated on the bed, his hands like grey talons holding a ragged bundle. She closed the door and he looked up, golden eyes still recognizable in a face that . . . His disease had worsened, she knew, and fought back the need to gag.

"My lady?" His voice was the same.

"I am well enough," she answered the inflection of his unspoken question, her eyes lowering as his hands stripped away the rags that covered the thing beneath, dropped them on the floor to reveal a lyre. Her eyes widened then. Rare instrument, this. Brilliant weavings of gold and brown composed its arms, threaded in coils through the tortoise shell-like box, and sparkled along the strings.

"Take it, my lady Olivia," he said, proffering it. "I bequeath it to thee."

She stared at him, forcing herself past the deepened hideousness, moved forward and slowly took the instrument to feel its silken texture. Its lightness. There, in his eyes, she saw—knew.

"It is thou who made the Song of Roland that so glorified my father and all the rest that fought at Roncesvalles?" she whispered slowly. He looked down, his lush, fire-laden hair more incongruous than ever.

"Aye!" he grated reluctantly. Then, "Take it, for thou are skilled in music. I was never a true jongleur!" He huddled back, closing himself inward, pain obvious. How did he know that she had been well taught? She had not played since Huon left . . .

"Nay," she answered the last defiant bit of it with quiet certainty. "The Lord Roland that I know could never be a minstrel!"

He shifted again, lying back in evident exhaustion, his eyes meetings hers in that wordless understanding they had come to share. She breathed once, hard. Bequeathed . . . He looked now to be slowly, horribly dying. Holding the lyre, she left him silently.

"I regret thy departing, my lord. I have gained much from our discussions." Olivia sipped wine from her cup, then set it down to meet Lord Baudoin's eyes as they lingered over the evening meal ten days after her return. He nodded. He was keenly aware of the amiable companionship that had sprung up between them over the neutral ground of conversations evolved largely around those cunning tracts of strategy with which Lord Amaury had fed his boyhood wits, their common foe, the Vikings . . . It intrigued him too, rather than repelled, how she slipped from being manlike and resolute in armor, to the quietly proper woman's manner that accompanied the woman's attire now. Chemise and robe, her hair as rich as a summer harvest, confined by a maiden's fillet.

"I must tend to my fiefs, my lady, for all I would gladly stay," he said slowly. "Thence to Court. I have matters to put before the King." He had not told her of his wish to rid himself of his late uncle's holdings. She searched him with that remarkable clarity he had come to admire above all else. "I will be here when the Vikings come next spring—with my own force to aid." Silence hung between them.

She broke it. "Thou are become a true friend, my lord," she said solemnly, setting the past behind them both. Baudoin felt self-conscious heat flare along his neck. She did not mock him. How much he had come to love her sureness . . . He looked down.

"For myself—I seek as a suitor may, my lady!" he got it out, looking up again, his own eyes soft dark as they probed. Shadows slipped across her face.

"I know," she said very quietly.

"May I hope at least?" he half whispered it.

She met his eyes steadily. "I will not marry for a time." He swallowed, remembering what he had seen. This other thing. Even thoughts of that crippled apparition, unseen since her return, appalled him.

"It is the crippled—lord?" he struggled, needing confirmation.

She inclined her head. "Aye, Lord Baudoin. It is." Still incredible to him, how she did not fear the creature . . . Not demon and succubus as the tirewoman had said it, but something deeper, even more intimate between them. He had glimpsed enough to see it. She read him. "I honor him for my father's sake, my lord," she told him clearly. "And for my own. He is a great man . . . And one who suffers profoundly, for it is illness, not the Devil's handiwork, that afflicts him."

It was the strength of her clarity, he realized, that made it impossible for her to see spirits in the shadows. He searched her face, seeing stewardship, not secrets on it. She tested him, he understood.

"I am friend enough to wait, my lady," he said at length, his tone quietly resolute, absolutely honest. A smile crossed her delicate, full lips.

"So be it then, between us, my lord," she answered. He smiled slowly in return. It was everything he could hope for.

The leaves were turning now, soon to tumble from tree branches and bushes. The wind blew stronger, colder. The new chill slipped under the folds of his cloak, through the steel links of his hauberk. Lord Thierry stroked his horse's neck, soothing it and himself, as he held the animal still at the top of a rise. His stare was fixed ahead to watch them go . . . slipping south, like so many ants now, in the distance. Soon, they would disappear, Lord Girard and his forces.

The Lady Roselyn as well. The quiet, black-eyed, unknowable Lady Roselyn. Girard would marry her, he knew, yielding to it for the need to guard his own child's happiness.

The alliance between them was a strictly military one, its future continuity dependent on the need to keep the Vikings out, the certainty of their persistence . . . Other, aye, foolish expectations got from a past that could not be resurrected after all had died through the remaining battles of the summer.

Lord Thierry turned his horse about. Barked orders to his men and set them on the march for home.

Clouds with burnished copper tints and silvered edges scudded across the night sky to obliterate the twinkling stars in the firmament beyond—to drown, fleetingly, the waning moon that hung above. It was a restless autumnal darkness. Dried leaves, still clinging to the trees, rustled in the high, unsettled winds. Whistled softly of mystery.

Uncaring of anything save the modest darkness, and the privacy of the byre, filled with sweet-smelling hay, Girard reached reverently to draw his new bride into his arms for the fulfillment of everything he had hungered for since he first saw her in his dreams.

Leaving behind the battles, and the Count of Brittany's watchful presence, he had made a loosely eastward detour in his southward journey to find a priest, and, with one other and Sir Guillaume to witness, had wed his lady. Had promised as well to restore her dower fiefs, decimated with Nantes and Reze.

· Now, in the cradle of the night, it was time to merely feel as he stared into the promises lurking in her midnight eyes. She— so supple, firm smooth against his fingers come alive for touching. Her skin—so pure, gleamed like a pearl in the moonglow as he gently unfurled her from cloak and robe and chemise. He breathed deeply, closed his eyes to feel . . . so much, as he drew her against his uncumbered self.

"Roselyn! How I love thee," he murmured against hair that flowed like silk against his face, clothed them both. She—scented like a fresh, sweet breeze. Sweet shock, sharp delight as his mouth touched smooth, velvet skin, as her fingers threaded through the open front of his undertunic to touch his chest, the heart pounding underneath. Blood raced to his loins. And fire . . . Hardly aware that he did so, he jerked himself free of the last garment between them and sank down with her in the soft, sweet-smelling hay. "Aaah, Roselyn!" he breathed through lips that tingled as he found her breast. "I will be gentle . . ."

"My lord?" she murmured in the darkness, her fingers trailing impossible pleasure through his hair, across his shoulders—down his flanks. Sensate spurs that brought him to rear up between her thighs, then into the very heart of her . . .

Into seas of molten sensation. She made waves to draw him into drowning, to loft him ever higher toward an impossible crescendo that, when it came, left him drained, root and core . . . Left him to sink gently down from the heights, nuzzling against her, holding her close in the night now sanctified.

"Now we are one," he whispered after a time, savoring the tender way her finger stroked him still. She, who had met him to show herself, passion incarnate.

"So we are, my lord." Her voice was like a breeze that slipped through his soul as he sank down toward the wellspring of truly peaceful sleep.

Half under him, Durandal lay there, her black eyes wide as she stared up to where the night sky showed beyond the edge of the crude, warped roof above them. Within her, she scorched away his defiling seed that sought the womb she did not have. Burned it—as she had burned away the Blood and Host of the sacrament she had consumed.

Contempt glided across her pristine features. Wet, human flesh that dried slowly against her. Began to cool. She drew his cloak across them both and felt his dormant sleeping. Simpleton, these disguises of tenderness . . . She grimaced with distaste. This, mere man, clammy, sodden feeling to one comprised of more resolute materials. Oliver reborn . . . Pah! Now, enslaved. She had reversed it.

She, who had been forged to mate with Gods. Or to kill them.

"Girard . . ." Olivia breathed as she watched her brother dismount among the assembly of his men that filled the bailey to overflowing. Whole, at least, she saw at once, but grimmer—leaner than before. Even from this distance, she could see the changes in his face. He saw her, but did not come as she expected, all prepared, for the messenger had arrived two days before, to celebrate his return. Instead, he turned away to lift down the slight, cloak-shrouded figure from the horse next to his, then, with one arm thrown protectively around the, aye, woman, he trod at last toward her.

Surprise heightened by quick impressions of ivory and darkness, Olivia collected herself and sought her brother's face as he reached her, then bent to lightly kiss her brow with but a ghost of the affection they had always shared.

"Olivia. This is my lady wife. Roselyn De Cecyll," he said. The girl offered a faint, shy smile and shrank still closer to him. What of Gharis De Leon to whom he was betrothed? Olivia thought, then bit it back as she saw the oddly isolated, yet happy look on her brother's face.

"I bid thee welcome, as a sister may, my lady," she managed instead, and turned in a swirl of blue and maroon skirts to lead the way into the keep.

The sense of shock did not dissipate. Instead, it skewed through the readjustments of the days that followed. Became something disconcerted, then troubled.

Girard had changed. Drawn fine, terser, he had become remote. He would not talk at all of the battles he had fought, or show concern for the cares he had left on her shoulders. Save once, when he remarked oddly on Lord Roland's presence as though it answered everything. Olivia felt the confusion left in its wake.

Nor would he discuss the plans that lay before them both, but preferred to loose himself in attending to all kinds of sundry details—harvest inventories, the condition of beasts, or serfs . . . Remote, aye . . . but Olivia could not discard her increasing feeling that he had become somehow frail.

His reaction when she realized that he no longer had the sword Durandal. He frowned, shadows crossing his face, and looked away.

"It was lost in battle," he said curtly.

"Lord Roland should know . . ." she began.

"I will not see him!" Girard said harshly, and left her to stare after him, realizing at last that she could no longer touch him. That their like-minded camaraderie had irrevocably disappeared.

She saw too how he fixed his every emotion and tenderness with an almost moon-calf obsession on the young maid he had found and wed to break his contract with the Count of Brittany. Lady Roselyn, who was her sister now . . .

Another puzzle. Delicate and rare, exotic and totally beautiful, she was retiring to a degree unusual even for a cloistered woman. She clung to, or hid behind Girard, who seemed unthinkingly even to speak for her. Nor did she make the least effort to undertake her duties as chatelaine, but left it all to Olivia.

"She has suffered," Girard explained once, clearly well content in the clinging of his lady, who, like a sodden garment, accompanied him everywhere, even, oddly, to riding out with him every time he backed a horse. Yet, Olivia knew, whenever she searched that pure, delicate face, she saw no indication of suffering of any sort. Only smoothness . . . Suffered what? she wondered, finding only a resilient impenetrability in Lady Roselyn's remarkable dark eyes.

Shy? As winter closed around them all, Olivia learned how her brother spent his nights. Long, arduous bouts of passion with his lady—his lover's lust did not seem to settle, or abate, but left a curious stamp upon his features in the mornings when he emerged looking drained and satisfied.

Possessed? The thought came unwelcomed. The air seemed filled with insidious contradictions.

795 A.D.

Winter ushered out the old year, gave birth to the new. For Olivia, it was another milestone in the growing distance from those happier times and people she had once known. Duty was a cloak of habit around her shoulders. Occupation, in a place that had become alien, populated with close-faced folk.

Except for Lord Roland. That was left to her, Olivia understood as she continued her late evening visits to bring him food and necessaries, to tend him, to simply be with him.

He kept strictly within the tower chamber now. Nor did he let her see his skin again, but kept himself completely shrouded. Only his eyes . . . His voice. His disease progressed slowly, she knew.

Brief conversations, for the most part. The understanding between them had grown to something clearer than words. Welcome. Sane . . .

"How clear it all seemed last summer," she murmured once as he stood on his crutches, facing away from her, staring out of the window through which seeped a pervasive winter cold.

"War is simple," he answered quietly. "Kill—or be killed!"

She caught the edge in the last. "They will come again, the Vikings," he added.

"I know. I prepare as I am able—as thou have taught me."

He turned, his eyes showing through shrouding cloth to look at her. "And Girard?" he asked for the first time.

She met his look. "He occupies himself with matters of husbandry. And with his lady wife!" The bones of fact. Roland continued to look at her, then nodded and turned back to the view. He had thought much of late, of how it would have been if both he and Oliver had survived Roncesvalles to continue their lives as entire men. He, who knew nothing of peaceable affairs. Oliver, who had recounted his hopes so many times when they were together. Now, the son fulfilled those things. Now, the son had gone away from him, as, he understood at last, Oliver too would assuredly have done.

Watching him, Olivia read his acceptance of the deeper things between her words.

"Curious . . ." she remarked. "How well I know thee." She smiled a little. "It is a strange love we share, thou and I . . ."

He spun around. "Is it so?" he whispered balefully.

"Aye. It is!" She met the challenge and smiled. "Curious, as well, Lord Roland, how much resemblance there is between this atrocious disease and the repelling terrors that haunt thee!"

He glared, then dropped his gaze. "Aye!" he whispered after a time, giving her the victory.

Unable to sleep despite her weariness, Olivia picked up the lyre that Roland had given her, and moved across her chamber to seat herself in the cushioned bay of the narrow window in the outer wall. Gently, as though to summon past things, her fingers caressed the instrument as she set it in her lap, then, slowly, delicately, began to pluck the strings.

Soft, rich notes that rose up to meet the sound of the racing winds outside that swept across a sleeping land. Clear notes. Like Roland himself, for all he buried himself . . . Buried. Even that was simple somehow. She understood his wish to finish it.

Her fingers wandered to make an aimless melody, then found, somehow, the echoes of the Song of Roland that she had once heard so long ago, played by a wandering minstrel who had been at Court.

It too was clear. Rich, powerful . . . poignant. An event that in the end could never be anything but a memorial. Roland, in his own peculiar way, had died with her father.

Far, far away, in a different land, a young man poised to listen to the currents of air that wafted into his chamber and billowed against the sheerest of silken draperies, slipped around exquisitely fluted marble columns to touch the sumptuous heathen luxuries that surrounded him. With fluid grace, he stepped between the translucent curtains, onto the balcony beyond. He cocked his head a little, in the manner of a bird. His clever brown eyes began to gleam. Then, slowly, he began to smile, for he recognized the summons.

Like monstrous pests coming out of hibernation to torment, the Vikings appeared along every western Frankish shore as the last frosts left the ground in early spring. And like the true friend he had proclaimed himself to be, Lord Baudoin came as well, with a thousand well-armed mounted men behind him, all ready, even eager to fight for the private promises of advancement that he had given out. The fiefs of Hauteville that needed a vassal knight to rule them for the Lord of Maganze.

Bitter-faced, and with his lady Roselyn beside him, Girard rode north to fight along the coasts between the mouth of the Garonne and the southern edges of Brittany. Left behind, Lord Baudoin and Lady Olivia undertook together the bloody battles and skirmishes against the northmen who attempted the rest of the shores of Bordeaux.

The summer bolted past like a high-strung horse. No longer seen among them, common folk half forgot the sinister cripple that had followed their Lady like a shade the year before, found reassurance in the sound good sense, the humanity, and clever triumphs of the Count De Maganze instead. Hard, consuming effort, sound justice, and hard fighting brought, ultimately, victory . . .

But the news that came from the north was less auspicious. There, assaulting in even greater numbers, the Vikings encamped upon the westernmost shores of Brittany. From there, they began to encroach inland despite the Champion's relentless resistance. Fires marked their wake. And corpses . . . And the Breton Marches were forced to yield bit by bit for lack of numbers to defend them.

Then autumn came again. The Vikings slipped away on the

cold, gusting winds, content to leave behind the scars they had made as pavestones to mark the way in the year to come . . .

Olivia dropped her horse's reins for the groomsman to catch as he would, and glanced about her to see her men dispersing to shelter. Then, clutching her cloak about her against the bite of the wind through chain mail, she strode briskly up the steps, into the keep. Girard had returned, she knew. She had seen his banner above the southern tower to announce it. And Baudoin was here . . .

Olivia strode across the great hall, past servants making ready for the evening feast. She glanced around, then passed the dais, and through the door to the stairs that ascended to the private chambers. A minute or two later, she paused outside her own door to hear voices coming from the end of the corridor. Curious, she changed direction, then stopped again, this time just beyond the half-open door to the family solar. She thrust back the hood of her cloak.

". . . to pay addresses to the Lady Olivia." She heard Baudoin's hesitant voice. "My interest has little to do with the gains of such an alliance, my lord, but is got of . . . an honest care for the lady." Boyish awkwardness revealed his honesty. "I am fully aware of the public significances of an alliance between Maganze and Montglave," Baudoin continued with surprising determination. "I know the disgrace my father brought to my name and blood . . . Yet, my lord, perhaps I am not misfortunate. Every man bears a devil of some kind on his shoulder. Having seen the face of mine, I have the means to free myself from the same." Neatly stated. She liked him for that, Olivia thought. She liked him for other things too, discovered through the summer past. His boy's unease that hid a considerable intelligence, surprising courage, and a growing strength and balance of character. Curious, she waited.

Girard's reply came slowly. "I have the right to contract my sister as I will, my lord. I would rather consent to a marriage that considers her well-being than give her for any other necessity. For my part, I leave it to her, whether she will have thee, or nay . . ."

"She knows my feelings, my lord." Baudoin's hesitancy returned. "I do not press her. Rather, I cherish the friendship that grows between us as a sound promise for the future." Enough, Olivia thought.

"Welcome home, Girard!" she said loudly, striding through the door to see the two men, then the Lady Roselyn seated in her mother's chair, her white fingers making delicate pleats in the folds of her rich green skirts. Baudoin stiffened, then began to flush a little knowing she must have heard some of it. He bowed to cover it. Girard spun around, and stared with widening eyes at the sight of her. Olivia stopped before them both, eyes flashing, and swept them both a graceful bow.

"The obeisance of my sex does not seem appropriate!" she murmured and caught Baudoin's responsive smile.

"Olivia!" Her brother looked his shock. Meeting his stare, she pushed aside her cloak to more fully reveal hauberk and surcoat, spurred heels, mail coif, and steel helm.

"For my duty, Girard, this is but simple good sense!" she told him crisply. "I would rather die as a man may, if it comes to that, than suffer a woman's demise!" He knew better than to refute it. Discomfiture crossed his face. "In any case, and more importantly," Olivia continued in the same tone, "I am just returned from De Labourneyre and De Coutras. The stone towers are well begun. They should be completed by spring." She met Baudoin's nod, then saw her brother's confusion, and explained, "To pursue Lord Baudoin's plan, Girard, I have ordered the construction of watch keeps along our shores, each within beacon distance of the next. Stone of course . . ."

"I see," Girard cut in, turning to look at the Count De Maganze, whose complexion darkened noticeably.

"The ancient Romans used such a strategy to good effect in guarding their frontiers, my lord," he got out awkwardly. "I have seen this summer past how it may be effectively used here." His glance slid to Olivia. "I . . . depart on the morrow to ride north to the Count of Brittany. And from thence to Aix, and the King . . ." Girard said nothing. Olivia offered a slight smile, then saw behind Baudoin, the Lady Roselyn had raised her head and was staring at her with wide, black hard, unspeakably cold eyes. An instant later, the look had vanished as the Lady lowered her eyes once more. Shocked by the venom of it, Olivia struggled to collect herself. Found a brief smile for the two men.

"I will rid myself of my dirt before we sup, my lords . . . my lady!" She inclined her head, swung on her heel, and left.

Never, she thought, had she seen such virulent poison on a human face.

• • •

Moonglow came through the shutters in a single, brilliant cold sliver to slice across the chamber. Durandal loosed herself from the sleeping Girard's dependent clutching and slipped from the bed to clothe herself in a night rail. He stirred and curled, unaware. Her eyes flashed contempt, seeing perfectly, despite the darkness. Fury swirled in her . . . And she had kept him safe, this squeamish son of Oliver—as she was bound to do. Rode with him through the wars that appalled him, and wrought discreetly to preserve him from harm. Had brought him through his own lust to loving and obsessed obedience. Her will, that she had only begun to exercise on him . . . So exact, this son?

But when she had seen that other, slighter figure, also of De Montglave's getting, in a man's armor and the rest, with a man's manner to match it . . . she had recognized the truth.

She had been deceived . . . Cozened. Tricked. That which she sought to use was unusable. A substitute . . .

And he had done it—Roland. He had done it, through the woman child, not the son. She, Durandal, who, all those years ago, had mothered his infancy and early boyhood in the guise of a crone, using carefully applied viciousness to hone him, to harden him—and to know as well a deep hate and fear of women that would keep him chaste. Faithful for . . .

She slipped a cloak of mortal weaving around her, then glided soundlessly from the chamber. Lightly, she sped down corridors, along flights of darkened, spiraled steps, until she reached the east tower where he remained concealed. There, she paused for a moment to collect all the mortal-seeming aspects of her appearance more closely about her, then trod toward the door that so terrified all the servants. Terrified every human creature hereabouts—save the cursed Lady Olivia.

She opened it. Stepped through to see him lying, eyes closed, huddled in the furs on the bed on the other side. Roland, who had bound himself into an apparition of purely grotesque decay.

How could he bear to continue it? This . . . Surely, he understood by now?

He shifted, his eyes opening. Then he saw her and jerked back to hide himself farther under the covers.

"Who art thou to come here?" he grated roughly. His eyes that saw . . . aye, only her discretion.

"I am Lady Roselyn De Cecyll, now De Guienne," she answered half shyly. Nay. He did not recognize. "I had to see— for myself—the demon that is said to haunt the east tower." She let the words stumble out, mixed them with fear tones. He stared at her.

"No demon, lady," he growled. "Just a leper, who, for charity, is given comfort to bear the erosion of his disease! Thou are best to keep to thy lord and stay away from me! Lord Girard will not be pleased to find his wife roaming the night like a faithless creature intent to cuckold him!" She felt it then, his thoughts that spun the illusion she had woven through the very air around her, then tightened like a fist to make a sheathing of her form. A binding . . . She stepped back, gasped for the sheer force of it, the power he still did not know he had.

"What goes here?" Lady Olivia's voice made a jarring, dissonant demand as she thrust through the half-open door to set a tray of food and a flagon on the table on one side of the chamber. "My lady!" She swung about to face her sister by law. "What do thou here? This is no place for thee!"

"So I have said!" Roland grated harshly from beneath his coverings.

"I have heard so much. I had to see the truth . . ." her human voice spoke, as Durandal looked from one to the other.

"Aye, well, thou have done so, Lady Roselyn! Get thee back to bed and thy duty of getting an heir for my brother!" Olivia said baldly. "This *man* is in my care. He can bring harm to no one!" Black eyes met blue to widen for what they saw to understand.

He had known about her. He had used Olivia De Montglave's own perception of her disguise to make the form that sheathed her now.

"Do thou not fear . . . ?" She hid it in whispered shyness. Oliver's guileless clarity reborn met her stare.

"Fear what? I trust to God. Do thou not, sister, then look to thy prayers!"

Durandal yielded, retreating from the chamber with something much like furtive haste.

"What possessed her to come here?" Olivia murmured, half to herself as she closed the door. She turned to look at Roland's huddled form. "Sweet Jesu! There is too much talk of witches and demons about this place already!" He sighed, and recognizing the sound, she stepped closer to look at him with consternation. He did not respond to any mention of the pain she knew now that he endured.

"I have brought sweet bread, and soup. Or wine?" she offered.

"I have no appetite, my lady," he whispered and closed his eyes. Sheer helplessness. There seemed naught to do but watch this ghastly disease consume him. She looked around the chamber, moved to refurnish the fire, and noticed . . .

"The falcon?" she exclaimed. "It is gone!"

"I set her free," Roland answered quietly. Olivia swallowed. She understood. She could not reply. Instead, she left him as he seemed to wish.

Durandal stopped in a darkened stairwell. She summoned the lethal tempest of her own power to thrust against her form. Tried to free her hilt wings, her blade . . . flung her rage at the conception that bound her. Anything to cause a change . . .

But the form of Lady Roselyn would not give or yield—even in part. And she remained standing like a mortal creature, unmoving upon the steps. That which she had made for illusion and seduction had become absolute . . .

TWENTY-TWO

796 A.D.

Recently returned to Aix La Chapelle from the eastern frontiers and a series of triumphant campaigns against the now conquered Avars, Lord Geoffrey, now upon his father's exhausted demise Duke De Baviere, found himself honored by being given his father's high place in the Council. Past, unfruitful conspiracies had become shades in the memory. But the guile and ambition that had fed them remained.

With growing interest and alert attention, he listened to the young Count De Maganze, likewise newly returned to Court, as he spoke before the King and Council on the wars along the western shores of Brittany and Bordeaux against the seafaring Vikings. He had not forgot, Lord Geoffrey realized, the Count of Brittany's rebuttal of his suit in favor of the bastard Girard De Guienne. It was, he discovered as he set about ferreting out information, an alliance that had never been fulfilled, for the new Duke had wed some other, dowerless girl.

Lord Amaury's predictions had come true, for the most part. Charlemagne seemed disinclined to even blink in displeasure at the breach of contract. More. Lord Baudoin himself proved a surprise. The swarthy, hesitant boy had changed to become something very different from his expectations. And, incomprehensibly, Charlemagne seemed to favor him. Aye . . . even, astonishingly, to consenting to the Count's proclaimed wish to marry the heiress Olivia De Montglave—the bastard Duke's sister. And, he found out, Lord Baudoin had spent a great deal of

240

time in Bordeaux of late . . . Was, he remembered, connected to the Champion by blood.

What brewed there, he wondered, and dispatched servants to find out.

"By God's own precious blood, this is a sight to wonder at!" Geoffrey De Baviere murmured softly as he pushed to the fore of the crowd gathering along the flanks of the great hall of Aix in response to that which had been heralded from the ramparts. Like the rest, he too stared at the exotic company of heathens that entered, then proceeded toward Charlemagne, enthroned on the dais at the other end.

Black faces made a startling contrast to full, flowing white robes as the Infidels progressed. Each was burdened with some bundle or pack swathed in brightly colored silk or gauze. Nubians, Lord Geoffrey realized, such as he had only heard tell of. To the fore of the group, incongruously walked a battered-looking, weathered old monk. As they reached the dais, the Nubians dropped to their knees in flawless unison, each setting his burden on the stone floor before him, then sinking farther in total infidel obeisance. The monk knelt as well. But to the rear, one of the heathens, swathed completely in garments of blue and silver, remained standing with princely equality.

To the surprise of all, the monk spoke first. "Majesty. I am Sherasmin, servant to His Holiness, the Pope. Before Charlemagne, who is God's anointed King of all Christian men, I bring the embassy of the great Caliph of Baghdad, also called Lord of the Faithful, Harun Al Raschid . . . in the person of his son by marriage, the Emir of Samarra!"

Charlemagne stood and inclined his head. The Emir bowed in the Christian manner, and to the surprise of all, his clear, deep-toned voice spoke the Frankish tongue perfectly.

"Majesty, I am come for the great Caliph, Harun Al Raschid, to bring gifts and offers of peaceful treaty between the greatest of eastern and western princes to the benefit of all men." Charlemagne's cold eyes gleamed. This was what he had sought these three years past. Again, he inclined his head. Again, the Emir bowed. Concealed fingers clicked, and again, with that curious synchrony, the Nubians raised themselves to unwrap the objects they had set before them. Gold caskets of wondrous filigree work emerged, each set with jewels of improbable size and brilliance. Charlemagne's eyes dropped, and every soul in the Court

watched with transfixed fascination as they were opened one by
one, the contents spread before the King.

Speaking quietly, the Emir of Samarra named each object.
"Tissues and silks from distant Cathay. Here are frankincense
and myrrh, so highly prized by Christian men. And amber
from . . ." It seemed endless, impossible, the unfolding of each
rare and exotic gift. "And for the last," the Emir continued,
stepping forward to within half a man's length of the King, one
white hand holding a small, lacquered box, emerging from the
folds of his robes to proffer it. "My lord, the Caliph, Harun Al
Raschid, makes two gifts of worth. Herein, Great Charlemagne,
lies the hair and teeth of that great foe of Christendom, the Emir
Gaudys of Babylon, tokens to prove his death and seal the treaty
he offers. Likewise, for brotherhood between princes, my lord,
Harun Al Raschid, gives to the great King of the Franks, his
Christian son, whom he has honored and raised to be the Emir
of Samarra, and to whom he has bound himself for peace between all faiths, through the baptizing and giving of his daughter
in Christian marriage, the Princess Esclarimonde!"

A muffled gasping passed across the Court. Then silence as
that unexpectedly white hand emerged again, and began to draw
aside the veiling garments to reveal the armor of a Christian
lord. Hauberk and mail leggings. Spurred heels, blue surcoat
. . . and the last to appear, dark, wavy brown hair, and the stern
features of young Huon De Guienne.

Aware of the amazed silence that surrounded him, Lord Geoffrey began to smile slowly in sincere appreciation as Huon De
Guienne knelt down upon one knee, bowed his head, and waited.
Not even Charlemagne himself could have contrived a more mag-
nificent return than this, he thought. Unruffled, Charlemagne
reseated himself, something like a smile flickering quickly across
his mouth.

"Not even Servinus could have managed to be so bold!" he
murmured. Huon looked up, but Charlemagne continued, "For
courtesy to that most honorable of infidel princes, Harun Al
Raschid, Caliph of Baghdad," he pronounced clearly, "we welcome the Emir of Samarra! And to the fulfillment of our judgment on Huon De Guienne, once Duke of Bordeaux, we
acknowledge his accomplishments and welcome him back into
the company of true Christian men!"

Huon rose, then bowed deeply. "My liege!" he murmured fiercely.

"Thou will attend us later," Charlemagne said crisply as Lord Huon straightened. Sensing opportunity, Lord Geoffrey thrust himself through the crowd and walked toward the dais. Saw white-rimmed eyes follow him from black faces. They missed nothing, these silent Nubians, he thought as he bowed to the King, then turned to look at Lord Huon.

"My lord, for the King's grace, I welcome thee to Aix. Do thou follow me, and I will contrive hospitable and fitting accommodation." Dark, canny brown eyes met his—just as fierce as before.

Lord Huon's smile was hard. "I remember thee, my lord De Baviere."

Lord Geoffrey made a regretful moue. "Misfortunate circumstance!" he murmured.

"Aye!" De Guienne nodded slightly, and moved his hand in a graceful weaving gesture. Like shades, the Nubians rose up and melted back across the great hall to where two slighter, heavily veiled figures stood in the shadows by the entrance. Bowing again to the King, Lord Huon turned and followed them. "My lady," he murmured to De Baviere, who found himself following where he had thought to lead.

And then there were brief impressions of slightness wrapped in multitude layers of impossibly rich and delicate materials, of gold ornaments and enormous, dark-shadowed, shy-doe eyes. The infidel Princess?

"This way, my lord. Highness," De Baviere managed politely as he bowed, then turned to lead this time.

Sly man, Huon thought as he followed, the cloud of materials following obediently behind him as a heathen woman would.

"What is this?" Lord Geoffrey half whispered. The servant flinched a little.

"As I have said, my lord. The Count De Maganze is departed from Court this hour past. I watched as thou bade me. He took his squire and others, and I followed to learn that he rides straight south and west." Lord Geoffrey nodded, and, extracting gold coins from the purse at his waist, held them out.

"Thou have done well," he said softly. "Go now!"

He waited until the door had closed, then reached to pour

wine into an ornate silver cup. Raised it and sipped to savor all
the nuances of flavor in the fine sweet wine.

"To Bordeaux. I'd wager Prince Louis' coronet on it!" he
murmured. Why else would Baudoin De Maganze depart so
hastily, in less than a day of Lord Huon's truly wonderful return?
He knew as well that Lord Huon's later private and lengthy audience with Charlemagne had not resulted in the restoration of
his estates and rank. Just forgiveness. Nothing else.

Lord Geoffrey had no interest in Charlemagne's preoccupation
with effecting the downfall of the eastern Christian empire to bring
the heart of Christendom into the western Papacy, or this treaty
that was part of it. He had other, more personal ambitions . . .

Setting his cup down, Lord Geoffrey stood, then strode from
his chamber to find the apartments that had been given to Huon
De Guienne.

"It is concern for justice, my lord, that brings me to seek thee
out at so late an hour," he told Lord Huon minutes later, after
one of the white-robed Nubians admitted him to De Guienne's
antechamber. He sighed a little. "In truth, I am most glad to
see thee returned, my lord," he added in a burdened tone. Lord
Huon stared back at him with peculiarly ageless eyes, and raised
a hand to point to a chair.

Lord Geoffrey seated himself, then glanced significantly at the
two tall Nubians that stood in the chamber.

"They have no tongues!" Lord Huon said quietly, startling
him, then clicked his fingers. The Nubians literally melted from
view. Huon smiled fractionally. "They are slaves, my lord. I am
their life!" he explained. "The Children of Allah see the world
very differently from those of us blessed to know the True
Faith!"

Disconcerted, Lord Geoffrey collected himself with an effort.
"My lord," he plunged into it. "Like others of the High Council, I have reflected much on the misfortunate circumstances that
banished thee from our midst—even greater, for knowing what
thou hast subsequently wrought. It is clear the King will not
recant his judgment that gave thy fiefs and title to thy brother . . ."

Acid bitterness crossed Lord Huon's stern face.

"Why else would I, being made as I am by the great Harun
Al Raschid, Emir of Samarra, and his own son by marriage . . .
why else would I return, but to see my honor restored?"

"Then, my lord, I may serve thee and our realm together!"

Lord Geoffrey said crisply, and began to expound on what he knew. The broken marriage contract. The wars with the Vikings that did not conclude. The rumors of demons and witchcraft that he had ferreted out in Bordeaux. The conspiracy he saw forming between Girard De Guienne De Montglave and the traitor's get, Baudoin De Maganze, through the sister . . .

The impact of his words showed plain enough as Huon stood, then began to pace with restless ferocity.

"This is beyond countenance!" he growled some time after the Duke had finished his monologue.

"I concur, my lord," Lord Geoffrey agreed soberly. "And the King does nothing, being enchanted still, as I understand it from my late father, with De Montglave's blood! More. For what I learned of Lord Amaury De Hauteville's foiled schemes, I think his nephew plans to fulfill them." Lord Huon's hissing intake of breath answered him. "I do not forget that the Count of Brittany is blood kinsman to Lord Baudoin. Strong bonds . . ."

"I must go home! At once!" Lord Huon hissed.

Lord Geoffrey stood. Smiled grimly. "Heed me, my lord!" he cut in. "Do thou wish to be restored entirely to that which is thine by every honorable right, then it is the King himself we must catch here! Mark what I do with the Council tomorrow!"

Lord Huon searched him, ferocity fading to thoughtfulness. "It is a twofold barb, I think," he said at length.

Lord Geoffrey grinned. "I never underrate the King. What I have uncovered by effort, Charlemagne most assuredly already knows. He must resolve it to favor the stronger man! It is a matter of providing him with the choice! I think he will gladly leave it between thyself and thy brother!"

Lord Huon clearly understood as he found a chair and sank into it.

"Thou are a friend indeed, my lord," he said slowly, after a time. Lord Geoffrey's smile grew warm. This was what he wanted—for now.

He bowed. "To the morrow!" he murmured as if in a toast, then left.

His solitude complete once more, Huon De Guienne relaxed in his chair, his fingers resting gracefully on the arms. He looked around the chamber with eyes that gleamed rich browns and golds around their large black pupils, and his expression softened into a smile of amusement.

Cold stone walls of whitewashed granite, like the snow outside. Covered here and there by tapestries. Wooden shutters that did not entirely block the cold drafts of late winter. The floor, bare, made of crude stone flagging. It was impossible to equate this place with those miracles of constructive ingenuity built by the Persians in the distant east. There, mosaics made wonders of design on every wall and floor. Exquisite arches dipped down from lofted, airy ceilings to merely touch the floor, instead of thrusting upward like some stubborn bulwark against the weight above. There, grey was unknown for so much generous light and color. Here, it was a primary hue, broken only, it seemed, by accident.

And he—Huon De Guienne, called by some among the Infidel, a Djinn—had brought the great Harun Al Raschid to submission by conjuring little tricks from the fairy wallet. True magics, understood by a genuinely sophisticated man.

His smile faded. This other before him now . . . it was an entirely different thing.

"Lord Baudoin!" Olivia exclaimed in welcome as she swept into the great hall of Bordeaux in response to the steward's summons. "I had not thought to see thee again for several more weeks!" Her voice died as she saw he looked haggard and travel-worn. He trod toward her vigorously. Bowed, then reached to take both her hands in his. Things in his eyes . . . He pressed briefly, then relinquished his grip.

"It is always a blessing for me to look on thee!" he murmured. Olivia felt color rise across her cheeks. He swallowed, awkward again. "The King has given consent—if thou will have me!"

"That was boldly done, my lord!" Her color heightened further.

"I will have nothing between us but thy will," he said.

She looked down. "Not yet . . ." she said. Looked up again to meet his eyes. "Soon, I think. He is very ill . . ." Baudoin nodded.

"Is it for this, thou are come pell-mell from Court, my lord?" she asked lightly. To her surprise, his face became grim.

"I must see Lord Girard," he said abruptly.

"He is in the north, rebuilding Lady Roselyn's dower fiefs, and setting up defenses for our mother's lands." Lord Baudoin frowned, and she felt confused. "Has thy time at Court been so great a trial, then?" she asked.

He breathed deeply and looked away. "I hate it," he admitted. "There is so much connivance and secretive prying there . . . I swear, were Charlemagne a lesser king, it would all fall into chaos of avarice and discord!" he exhaled violently. Met her widened eyes. "But. I am come here for another reason than these invading Vikings. And only briefly, for I must depart at once to muster the fighting men I promised Lord Thierry this spring. Huon De Guienne is returned from banishment. He is even now at Aix!"

Olivia's eyes widened completely. "Huon . . . ?" she whispered. "My brother?"

He nodded. "The same, my lady," he affirmed gently. "Gloriously returned from Persia and restored to the King's favor!"

"Huon!" she breathed very softly, staring up into his eyes. He took her hands and brought them to his lips, kissing each. "Girard will be so very glad!" she whispered, eyes filling. She blinked and swallowed, and slipped into his embrace. "Oh, Baudoin! This is most wonderful news!"

He closed his eyes and held her close, then bent and found her mouth and kissed. Softly, deeply. Drowning, until at last, she drew back to stare up at him.

"Dearest Baudoin . . ." she murmured, her voice rich with feeling. "Thou are the truest of friends." His face, his eyes, held it all, he knew.

"Thou are all the world to me," he told her. Then stepped back to let her go. "I will return as soon as I may."

"I will welcome thee most gladly, my lord," she promised.

TWENTY-THREE

Impossible not to recognize the blue pennon with its sun and swan of Bordeaux, lofted on the tip of a lance, even from this distance. Behind two Christian knights, white-robed men on delicate horses made a collective phalanx around a litter draped in bright materials, borne by six apparently black-skinned servants. It was a brilliant company that advanced down the long hill from the woods to the east. Serfs ran alongside in brown human blurs.

Olivia raked the sides of the horse she had just flung herself on, and sent it forward carelessly before she had even finished gathering the reins. Impossible to care that it skidded across the drawbridge, half floundered in the mud of early spring. She spurred it on. And Lord Baudoin had told her of this only seven days before . . .

As she reached the steadily advancing company, she drew rein to stare at the brother she had not seen for three years, had not thought to ever see again . . . Huon—beyond mistaking. As dark as ever—and as fierce-faced. She grinned as he stared back, not recognizing, then drew off her helm, thrust back her coif, and loosed her hair.

"Huon!"

The man on the magnificently powerful chestnut stallion drew rein at once, his dark eyes widening slowly as he stared hard enough to bore right through her.

"Mother of God!" he swore. "Olivia?"

Her grin widened. "Aye, so!" She spurred her horse closer,

ignoring the curiosity of the knight that rode beside him. "Aaah, Huon! Welcome home!"

He smiled a little, then looked past her to the gleaming towers of the castle. At the stakes still set like giant thorns along the outer banks of the moat.

"It has been too long!" he whispered passionately. She understood. He pointed suddenly. "What is this?"

"They were set for defense against the Vikings," she told him. "These have been hard years, Huon, since . . ."

"So! I have heard aright!" he gritted and turned his hard gaze back to let it travel up her form. He frowned. "And by what mad witlessness does my . . . brother give thee leave to go about in this hoyden manner to disgrace both thy name and sex?" he demanded softly. Olivia's smile froze—faded.

She stiffened. "It has taken both of us, Girard and I, to rule here for the wars that try us, Huon! I know my duty, and will undertake any part of it!" she retorted sharply, suddenly aware of the amused grin and assessing look of the startlingly handsome knight that rode with him.

"I am returned!" Huon said with finality. "Thou will assume thy proper place!" Olivia stared at him, but he was watching the castle folk who poured out of the castle in a shouting, waving stream to flank the trail.

"Curious . . ." she remarked acidly. "How, for *love* and *grief*, I had forgot my brother's frigid autocracy!"

But Huon did not seem to hear. Instead, he sent his horse forward to make a prancing show as it swept him toward the welcoming crowd ahead. Frowning, Olivia held her own horse back, then found the other, lavishly accoutered knight had brought his horse up to ride beside her.

He smiled ruefully. "Be patient, my lady. Lord Huon has endured enough to embitter even the strongest of souls." She looked at him. He shifted his smile. "I am Geoffrey, Duke De Baviere, my lady," he said politely, and bowed from the waist.

"I am Olivia De Montglave!" she pronounced with simple formality. He continued to stare, and she looked away.

"The proudest of blood is most exquisitely carried!" She heard his smooth voice murmur, and thought that she understood exactly how Lord Baudoin could have conceived such a powerful dislike for the men of Charlemagne's Court.

• • •

They were all tucked away in various chambers for the present. Lord Geoffrey occupied with changing his finery. The infidel slaves, the whispering draperies of his Persian lady . . . Huon walked down the long corridor that branched from their direction, stopped abruptly, his nostrils flaring to scent—aye, the mustiness of disuse. He opened the door before him, then entered fully to peer through the gloom. The air hung here. Furnishings and the like, for all their luxury, were still and dimmed by a light shrouding of dust to make a mood of neglect and abandonment.

He walked slowly about the room, pausing frequently to examine the objects that filled it. Unused things. Things kept as though in the ancient way, to make a tomb for the boy and youth Huon of Bordeaux had once been. Raising his eyes, he saw the cobweb that spread across one corner to make an exquisite tracery from beam to wall. Saw the large spider poised in the center, fastidiously rubbing the first two of its many legs together. He smiled.

"How apt, my small, ensnaring friend!" he murmured, and swung around to see another object, obviously set with care upon the chest by the four-posted bed. He went to it. Reached to trace a finger across the cover of the book, then raised it to touch the supple, fine smooth leaves beneath, each inscribed with the late Amaury De Hauteville's exquisite minuscule. The Aristotle, he knew. He withdrew his hand. Just as he had expected to find it. He searched the room once more with his eyes, then, abruptly, turned and left.

It had been a long time, he thought, pausing in his descent from the upper stories to look across the great hall. Still, he knew his way. He trod then, quietly across the stone floor, past dais and hearthplace, past the supporting columns along the outer parts, and made his way into the small family chapel on the western side.

Built a long time ago, it was an inherently simple place, little more than a high, narrow, vaulted hall adorned with tapestries and the accoutrements of faith. A candle burned upon the modest altar, and above it hung a curiously twisted image of the Christ. A single glazed window bestowed light and color. But tombs dominated. The dead generations of the De Guienne family who had gone before since Roman times. He walked toward the pair that flanked the altar. Duke Servinus lay within the one, he knew. The other? Stopping before it, he traced his fingertips across the simple, stylized effigy of a woman. So . . . They were all gone now—save for two, he thought.

The sound of skirts whispering across the stone behind him caused him to turn quickly and stare at Olivia. She had changed her attire, he saw at once. But her woman's garb did not at all dispel his startled recognition that she was vastly different from that other shade he had expected. He kept his expression fierce.

"Mother died," she said simply. He nodded.

"Where is my brother?" he demanded quietly after a moment.

"I sent word to Girard as soon as I knew. He is in the north, attempting to rebuild out of the destruction the Vikings wrought there . . ."

He cut off the rest of her reply. "How could thou know of my return when I came immediately upon giving my duty to the King?"

She met his stare and stiffened. "News came from a friend—Lord Baudoin De Maganze, in fact, who spared no effort to bring word, presuming us, of course," she added sharply, "to be overjoyed to have thee restored to us!"

"And Girard is in the north, leaving thee here, to manage the rest alone?" She watched his fingertips trace broodingly across their mother's effigy.

"For what I learned through being reared with Girard and thyself, I am far from incapable, Huon!" she retorted. Inhaled deeply. "Girard should be here within a sennight. Or hast thou forgot how much he cares for the welfare of his people—and those, to the north, are *his*!" He did not reply, but watched her. She attempted a softer explanation. "Bordeaux has withstood the raids and pillaging of the Vikings with much greater success than in the north, Huon. There, the devastation has been terrible."

"I am familiar with heathen methods!" he said coldly. "Nor, even for the least instant, do I *ever* forget my honor, or my duty to my name and blood!" he breathed deeply. "But, I am here now!" he added with finality.

Olivia made a last effort. "Know this, Huon. Girard never wanted thy place or title. That has not changed!" She searched him, finding only hardness in his eyes, then gave it up and left him to exit the chapel. So much bitterness, she thought. And now, the small differences that had been between them had grown into something disastrously potent.

Standing very still by the tomb, he watched her go . . . assured and clear. He had not considered this possibility—her.

It made a difference.

Welcome? It was more of an embrace as every man, woman, and child of Bordeaux made clear their joy in Lord Huon's return. No service was too hard, no task too menial to perform . . . and they clung to him, sought him out—individually, or in clusters, as though his smile, or touch, contained some miraculous benefit to be had. And he? Embittered clearly by his loss of rank and estate, and by other, unspoken things that had transpired during his years of exile, seemed to reserve all his smiles and kindliness, all his patience for them.

Control slipped into his hands as though he had never lost it.

Things to think about . . . Olivia knelt down gently beside Roland's bed to stare at him with all the growing unhappiness she felt. This Duke De Baviere, Huon's friend, who pressed his attentions on her. Roland, who no longer rose from his couch, but lay there, clearly in agony, looking like nothing more than a hideously macerated corpse.

Save for his eyes.

"My brother, Huon is returned from exile," she told him quietly that which she had not mentioned before. He blinked, looked toward the ceiling beams, then searched her.

"Lord Huon . . ." he whispered. "I remember how Oliver taught him to ride his first horse. A proud child. Lord Girard will rejoice, I think." Olivia bowed her head, recognizing his associations between her father and the other. "It is not the same for thee?" she heard him whisper and looked up to meet his still keen gaze.

"To my regret, it is not," she told him honestly. He looked away, then closed his eyes.

"Look to thy friend, my lady," he murmured. "This honest son of Maganze." His voice died away. She understood and rose to her feet.

"I do not abandon thee," she whispered. He nodded as if he knew it, and turned his head away.

She slipped silently away. Something more than Roland was slowly dying, she knew.

Instinct sent her along a different route through the night-darkened castle, until she found De Coutras asleep in his quarters in the bailey tower. She roused the knight to startled alarm.

"My lady?" he rasped.

She cut him off. "Sir Lothair, I have an urgent task for thee."

"Gladly, my lady." Confusion slipped behind unthinking loyalty on his face as he came fully awake.

"I care not about the hour. Go at once, upon a fast horse. Seek out Lord Baudoin, the Count De Maganze, and for his friendship, bring him here with all urgency!" She read the question on his lips. "This is to *my* service, not for my brother!" she told him sharply.

He acquiesced at once, and she left him, knowing that within minutes, he would be riding east.

"And what secretive assignation sends my sister prowling through the night when she should be at rest like any other chaste Christian maid?" Menacing softness. Olivia's hand froze upon the latch to her chamber door. She twisted, and saw Huon, his arms folded across his breast, emerge from the shadows of the corridor to stand before her. "Aaah," he said before she could reply, his eyes glittering. "I have heard much of thy . . . fascination with the strange demon, or witch, thou brought here to defile the east tower!"

"No witch, Huon!" she flared in turn. "Just the ruin of a once great man, pitifully stricken by a consuming disease! I but give him charity and comfort while he dies!"

"In the middle of the night?" He countered. "By God's blood, Olivia, I *will* see thee constrained to propriety!" He hissed the last with furious promise.

"Thou have not the right to rule me!" she retorted with equal anger. But he had disappeared.

She was barred from the east tower after that, by Huon's implacable, silent Nubian slaves.

And the audiences began . . . De Baviere beside him, Huon sat in the ducal chair in the great hall for hours, listening patiently to any who wished to approach, sometimes questioning, collecting testimonies of all kinds from the growing numbers that sought him out. The tirewomen, with the aging Aliena, who had watched, then whispered together in private. The huntsman, Jean, who bared his sores and proclaimed the witchcraft that had begun it all. Others then stepped forward to speak of the faceless lord, of the goat's foot they had seen between his crutches, of the wars . . . Lives lost, griefs twisted. Blame for the events that had occurred since Lord Huon himself had been taken from them. Lord Huon, who was himself a victim, and by divine intersession restored to them to put an end to it.

It was like a monster growing, this—something mad and skewed and dangerous, Olivia thought, helpless to prevent it. She too was haunted by a black-skinned slave now.

And Baudoin came in the midst of it, in answer to her summons. Striding across the great hall, his face lit as he saw her, then changed, sobering questions rising in his eyes. She pushed forward forcibly to greet him.

"My lord of Maganze, I bid thee welcome!" she said in a clear, strained voice as he bowed, then turned to look at Huon. "Lord Baudoin has done so much, my brother, to aid and secure Bordeaux against the Vikings. He is uncommon educated on matters of strategy!" she pronounced clearly to inform them both.

Sweet Jesu, what goes here? Baudoin wondered, feeling tension thick enough to slice with a blade. Lord Huon's implacable stare . . .

"So, Olivia! Thou compel us to consort with traitor's spawn? To what end?" Huon demanded. "Have I not been shamed enough already?"

Blood rose up Baudoin's neck. He stiffened. But Olivia spun around, flared. "I judge the man by his worth, not his heritage!"

"I recollect differently!" Lord Huon said coldly. Then, "Thou are unwelcome here, my lord!"

Baudoin looked at Olivia, searching her, trying to understand and give her an unspoken assurance of his loyalty. Saw her tension, and worse . . .

"Welcome, or nay, my lord, I claim that hospitality that is my right of my duty given of the King himself!" he retorted with rare resolve. Two pairs of eyes locked, then to his and Olivia's astonishment, Huon inclined his head.

"So be it! Thou may serve as the King's witness, my lord, as I root out the evil that has accrued here through my absence!" A hand moved. "I accommodate thee as befits thy rank!"

A pair of black-skinned heathens glided toward him. Baudoin spun, and quickly murmured an instruction to his own, wary-faced knight behind him, then, after searching Olivia's face, allowed himself to be escorted away. Half guest, he knew. Half prisoner . . .

What have I done? Olivia wondered, then lunged forward.

"This goes too far, Huon!" she began. "I am betrothed to this man!"

"Not so, my lady!" Geoffrey De Baviere stepped forward. "Thou are betrothed to me!"

"What?" Olivia stared, then, "Never!"

"The documents are already signed, my lady!" He smiled, all smoothness and assurance.

"That is impossible!" Olivia was outraged. Her eyes flitted to scour her brother. "Thou have not the right!" she began again.

"As the *true* Duke of Bordeaux, my lady," De Baviere spoke again, "the right is most assuredly his!"

"He is no longer entitled . . ." she began, then cut it off as she realized. The Nubian who shadowed her stepped forward then, between herself and the two men. She gave it up and turned away.

"How *dare* thou betroth me to Geoffrey De Baviere, Huon! I will not be given to that . . . worm!" Olivia hissed furiously from the center of the prison her bedchamber had become. Her brother watched her with unreadable eyes from his place by the door.

"I have every right, Olivia," he said sternly. "*I* am Bordeaux!"

"Not so!" she countered at once. "Girard is vested Duke by the King's own hand *and* remains so! The King is not like to undo his handiwork!" She inhaled, fighting for reason—for control. For Baudoin.

"The King uses me to undo his mistake!" he said calmly. "Girard cannot be legitimately entitled while I am alive, for his bastardy! And he is proved unfit!"

"For God!" she breathed it. "I had never thought to see thee become so crass!" She moved toward him, attempting to persuade. "I know him! He would give it up to thee, and gladly! Not like this, Huon . . . ?" Closer still. "Surely, it may be gracefully resolved, Huon?" She reached to clasp one of his hands as she searched his eyes, trying to find some trace of the childhood friend her brother had been.

So deep—his eyes. Black pupils distended to obliterate the

soft browns she remembered. Power . . . illusions. And beneath her fingers, the skin of his hand slid a little. Cold—and slightly clammy, like that of a fresh corpse.

She shrank back.

"Do not *ever* touch me again!" he hissed softly, and flung away through the door. Olivia stared, moved. But the Nubian beyond it defied her to follow. She gave it up and slammed the thing.

"He is become a monster!" she whispered horror to the air.

And when Girard came home at last, two days later, his arrival proclaimed by the winding of a solitary horn, Olivia slipped into the great hall behind the Nubian who led the way, to see the throng gathered there to fill it. All folk who had spoken to Lord Huon. Baudoin stood as well, grim-faced and bewildered on the other side, flanked by heathen guards.

Huon stood upon the dais, his feet a little apart, his arms folded across his breast, his stance implacable—cold—dominating the pervasive unease that overhung the rest.

Noises made by the returning men came through the entrance. Olivia saw her younger brother then, all travel-stained. His lady behind him, shrouded by hood and cloak. Girard's face was alight. Her innards plunged. She caught a brief glimpse of huge black eyes, then as Girard strode forward through the crowd, his lady melted back and disappeared.

It was the final shattering of a dream to see Girard's smile, his eagerness, his upraising arms that offered brotherly embrace.

"How overjoyed I am to see thee well and whole and restored to us, Huon!" Girard called out. Olivia flinched. Huon did not move, but glared at his brother, from his place of elevation on the dais. Girard faltered. Came to a stop, and slowly lowered his arms, his welcoming smile fading slowly, painfully, to be replaced by a searching confusion.

"So. We are met again, Girard!" Huon intoned with measured chill.

Girard made another effort. "As I have ever hoped and prayed for, Huon."

Huon's brows rose in fierce surprise. "I cannot think why, my lord," he countered frigidly. "My return cannot benefit thee. As to prayer? I have seen little evidence of that! Indeed, I have heard of naught else save Vikings and witchcraft and demons . . ."

There was a restless murmuring among the crowd. Girard

paled to an ashen hue, shocked by this onslaught, and stared around him in confusion to see the Nubians that flanked Huon, and now himself.

"For God!" Olivia whispered and cringed. But Girard stiffened, then signaled to De Blaye who had followed to stop watchfully farther back. The knight stepped forward and proffered the shield that Girard habitually carried. Girard took it and swung around to face his brother. Held it out.

"Do thou think such ill of me, Huon?" he asked reasonably. "As for my bastardy, which is no contrivance of mine, know that I have *never* sought—or even wanted—thy place. Indeed, I have been but thy steward! Even in my oath to the King, I stated it thus—swore it!

"For my faithfulness to that, I give thee now, thy own shield that I have carried instead of my own, to hold thy name before me!"

Nay, Olivia thought. Nay, Girard. Not this foolish, gallant yielding . . .

The air hung like a poacher from a gallows as Huon took the shield, then began to examine it carefully, tracing his fingertips slowly across it. Then he raised his head to stare down at Girard.

"Is this how thou hope to ensnare me, Girard?" he asked with lethal quiet. Again, confusion flooded Girard's face. "This is not my shield." Huon dropped it to make a grating clatter on the stone before him. "Nor will I bear to touch it, for it is covered with human skin in a manner I have seen only among heathen men!"

Girard's face was but a ghost of the shock she felt, Olivia knew. Human skin? Unnoticed in the corner where he was guarded, Baudoin's face began to pale.

"Nay!" Girard whispered terribly. Huon seemed to tower over him as one of the Nubians glided forward and held out a large, exquisitely furnished book.

"And this, brother?" Huon demanded, pointing. "Discovered like some abandoned boyhood article in my chamber here . . ."

Girard stared. "I brought it back with thy belongings from Aix . . ." he tried truthfully.

"This too is made of human skin, Girard!" Huon hissed. "By what kind of treachery have thou sought to make a demon of me? Have sought to burden me with the evidence of sin so great as to be beyond accounting?" Girard stood frozen. Grey-faced and sickened, Baudoin saw how thoroughly he was trapped by his uncle's unspeakable perfidy.

"For God, and all honest Christian men, I say thou are the traitor here!" Huon proclaimed then. Girard did not even move as the Nubians glided in to seize him, strip away his arms, and bind him. Huon's face twisted, as though with pain. He crossed himself as though in defense. "I say thou are the devil here, thou and that other with whom thou have congress to the harm of all!" he accused. "And thou, succubus!"

This is mad . . . Olivia had the single thought as she was pushed forward to stand with her brother. "Fetch the demon witch!" she heard Huon call out. Heard as well, the threatening, restless murmur from the crowd. Hard to see clearly—she found herself staring into Girard's face. Terrible now.

And, far away, it seemed, Lord Baudoin looked equally appalled.

Then four Nubians swept in front of the dais, dropped something, and melted away to reveal a writhing, desiccated, human-seeming grey thing at one end of which wound lush strands of fire-laden hair.

Roland . . . Olivia realized. Stripped naked. Helpless and in agony. Degraded in this, his dying.

She flung around. "This is no devil, nor a witch!" she called out, finding her own strength. "This is a man. A leprous man."

"Have thou nurtured disease here as well, sister?" Huon asked in the same deadly tone. "Are thou so bewitched as to sacrifice the people of Bordeaux with such a terrible contagion? Who is this creature who thou serve so faithfully?"

Somehow, she had been prepared for this attack, Olivia knew, stiffening further, hearing murmurs behind her.

"He was the beloved friend of Oliver De Montglave, once known to all as Lord Roland, Count of Brittany!" she gave her own challenge.

It was De Baviere who stepped forward. "That is impossible! Lord Roland died these seventeen years past, like the rest at Roncesvalles. He lies even now entombed at Aix!"

"I see it now," Huon cut in, his voice carrying across them all. "How thou, Girard, being Oliver's bastard, born beyond the sanctity of the Church, and thou, Olivia, for thy woman's weakness, have been seduced and bewitched to cause so much harm here. Take this thing . . ." He pointed toward the terrible grey body, lax now, on the floor. "This vile, inhuman thing, and, for God's mercy on us all . . . *Burn it!*"

It was the heathen slaves who swept in to pick up what was left of Roland. Who seized her and Girard, and swept them out through the surging crowd. She was shivering, trembling, Olivia realized. Like a broken thing . . .

TWENTY-FOUR

Curious how complete the pain had become. It engulfed everything else—except, sometimes, when his eyes were open, and he saw glimpses of other things far away on the other side of it.

It had form now, as well. A body of its own that pushed and writhed like something struggling against an excruciating compression. It was alive. It was the only thing of him left alive, Roland thought. He'd done it well—sending her to the other. Maganze's ghost. No, a boy who cared for her as he did, as he might have done under a different circumstance. As he might have learned eventually to do with Aude, except for Roncesvalles.

He hardly noticed when he was picked up. Coverings of every kind stripped away. Nakedness too vanished under the garment of pain. Glimpses of black, heathen faces, white robes. Many people . . .

And somewhere else, looming for an instant over him, he saw another ghost of the past. A dark, fierce face and eyes—eyes . . . The dark lord? But that had been the name the young boy he had once been had given to a foe he had long since disposed of . . .

The dark lord . . . It had been a curiously suggestive name to give the treacherous Ganelon De Maganze. There was power too beyond the sheathing pain, carried like tones from the lyre, in a voice.

". . . *Burn it!*" It? What was left of himself, Roland realized.

Perhaps, he thought, fire could do what deprivation and the sea, and all those other injuries could not. Surely . . . Surely?

He closed his eyes and yielded to the hands that carried him.

Only later, when he felt the pain form, thrust upright against a great wooden stake, felt the chains that were passed around it to hold his body to it, did he open his eyes again to see.

Fresh, sweet-scented air blew across the trees in the distance to stir the shredded skin of his face. There were crowds of people gathered on the spring green sod. Beyond, Bordeaux's walls rose up. Some, much closer, flung faggots on the great mound of wood and tinder around and below him.

Across the turf, he saw the same . . . dark lord, amid the rest—above the rest, upon a great horse of gleaming copper hue. The dark lord? Why did it come again to him, that term, for this . . . different individual? Beside, and mounted between two guardsmen who held her horse, he saw Olivia De Montglave staring at him across the space between them. Drawing at him through the very core of his pain. Nay. Not her. Not such terrible clouds to mar such a perfect clear blue.

Love . . . ? What did he know of love?

Sudden crackling sounded around him. Fire. He glanced down to see torches set to the surrounding faggots. Flames leaped. Avaricious element, it would consume him as well . . . it *must* consume him.

Hot . . . Hot. Roaring as the flames grew. Smoke spewed upward toward the sky in congealing black plumes that sought to fly. Strangling the air . . . His head fell back. He gasped for agony as the flames found his legs, his skin, began to sear through the rotten, sensate meat of it to make a singing agony beyond screaming, beyond any kind of bearing at all.

Pain to resonate against pain . . .

And far away, far above the roaring, swelling conflagration, against a patch of the purest blue sky, he saw a falcon soaring.

Nor, for all the rest that tore him into molten agony, could he understand how he recognized its cry that screeched out a haunting summons for him to soar as well.

He was bound, he knew, as scarlet, impossible brilliance joined everything else to melt into a curiously suspended oblivion.

• • •

Even from thirty yards away, the heat of the fire was palpable as it swelled to engulf the great pyre that had been so quickly put together.

"Watch it!" Huon hissed from just behind her. "For this is how I root out thy incubus!" Then she saw the flames catch at Roland himself. Pale, grey flesh went black, then vanished behind a wall of flame and smoke. Nothing else but fire . . . She shivered. Each split and crack was like a blow. Soon, there would be nothing left save ashes. Roland had died. Roland had died . . . and so much with him.

There was nothing left except to yield to her brother's monstrous power . . . She turned clumsily to see Baudoin watching her. His face was a reflection of the hideousness she felt. Abruptly his mouth tightened. He flailed out at the guards surrounding his horse, spurred the beast into a half-panicked charge to overrun them, then bolted away, down the hill, away from Bordeaux's walls to where his own men camped on the hill beyond.

She could not blame him in the least, Olivia thought distantly, for having sense to seize the opportunity. Someone must survive this. Huon turned in his saddle to watch the other go, did not order pursuit. Instead, he made a signal to the Nubians who still held the book and shield.

"Let it be done thus!" he bellowed out. "Let the evil here be so exorcised!" The slaves ran then in a smooth arc, flinging the two objects into the fire even as it sank down to reveal that its core of stake and man was no more than a charred, blackened heap in the middle.

Like an answering hum, it began then. A cheer of sorts that issued from every throat—and grew. Grew like another kind of monster to become a pulsing, vengeful chant. Huon's horse reared and plunged away. And Olivia saw them then, the crowds that came together, then swept in unison around the pyre, advancing in a wave upon that place where Girard was held, still shamefully bound between four guardsmen.

"*Nay . . . Naayyy!*" Her own scream rose into the air to be lost as the guards melted back before the onslaught of the mob. And Girard, alone, his face ashen blank with shock, disappeared beneath them to be torn, quite literally, limb from bloody limb.

The rest was screams. Screams of horror and pain and refutation. Screams that rent the air. Screams that shattered silence itself . . .

Screams . . . Lord Baudoin hauled his horse to a shuddering halt with a hand that did not feel the bridle, and turned in his saddle to see the mob swarm across the hill behind him to overflow the helpless figure of Lord Girard. Olivia's screams. He shuddered violently.

"My lord! We feared for thee." His knight, and others of his men, he saw rushing toward him from their rough camp to the east of the castle. And Lord Huon sat his restive stallion on the crest of that western hill like a hero. "Mother of God! My lord?" The knight exclaimed at the sight of his face. Baudoin tried—strangled—swallowed.

"Find a place to camp in the woods!" he rasped it out. "No fires. I cannot leave here." Olivia.

"What then, my lord?"

"For God, man, I do not know!" Baudoin rasped with terrible helplessness. "I do not know . . ." he repeated as his men drew him away.

Hidden between strut beam and wall under the outermost parapet of the highest corner watchtower above Bordeaux keep, Durandal watched the fire swell on the hill beyond. Engulf. The populace about it, like so many cattle, led. She felt the loosening that came with Girard's death.

And the fire, with Roland in its midst . . . Like a sigh, she felt the withdrawal of his power that held her—Roland's own binding that had shielded her from being perceived had made it possible for her to elude . . . It slipped back, condensing upon itself into the purest form of quiescent introspection. And Roland, caught in the web of what he did not know, had bound himself into his own conviction of human death.

She heard the screams that threaded through the whistling breeze, and understood. Lightning slithered along her skin under her mortally woven robes. Exultation to feel again . . . free. Free. Restored to her natural tempest self.

She moved her fingers from the folds of the brown cloak that covered her where she perched, and pointed to the air that blew from the west.

Come clouds. Come darkness. Come tempests softly. Blow gentle chaos to confine these mortals. To shroud what I must do . . .

Screaming, shattered woman that remained . . . the single key that could unfurl the truth at last. And the Owl was caught upon a single flaw in his perception. He did not know the substitution Roland had made.

She did not move from where he dropped her on the bed in her chamber, De Montglave's daughter. Instead, she lay there huddled and shivering, face stark, eyes filled with desecrated horror.

Huon stepped back and looked around the room. Saw the lyre that Roland had given her. Time enough to collect it later, he thought, then stepped back again and closed the door on girl and instrument.

She had been broken. All those suggestive, lethal similarities destroyed, he thought, walking along the corridor toward the stairwell that led down to the great hall below. A zealous priest, and De Baviere, would soon mold her into an ordinary woman for breeding. Time would finish it. Now, he had to restore order and reason, confidence to the people who had yielded themselves up. Some things could not be left in disarray.

He paused on the steps to listen to the sounds of distant thunder through a narrow casement in the wall. Storms that brewed . . . Fitting. The rain would make it easier, on the morrow, to scour through the charred pyre to take unto himself that which, finally, he could have.

Dominion.

Olivia sat where he had put her, in the middle of the bed that had been a haven of rest and comfort in another lifetime. Now, there was the shaking that would not stop. The crawling ague of revulsion and horror.

Girard . . . Pity for her gentle brother.

Pity for herself as well. Lost now in what Huon had wrought. Nothing—nothing could have equipped her to deal with such as this.

Huon, who sat in triumph in the great hall below. The rightful lord returned. A hero. Savior . . .

Savior from what . . . ? She still could not understand it. There had been no evil here—only delusions to be disposed of for what they were. Fright-got imaginings.

Imaginings . . .

She heard the thunder rumble closer. Lightning flickered through the shutters. Growing darkness that made no difference . . . The wind gusted to whistle past the walls. And the rain began outside. The heavens wept.

Thunder cracked to shake the very stone. The single candle guttered as a sudden gust blew from the window. Olivia started at the cloaked figure that stepped before her to thrust back the concealing hood with one silvered hand.

Congealing recognition. "Lady Roselyn!" she croaked. Black eyes with lightning in their depths stared fiercely back at her.

"Know me as I am, Olivia De Montglave, who art thy father remade!" the voice hissed like steel across an anvil. "For I am Durandal, called the Dark Sword!"

Sword? Impossible . . .

"Girard is dead," Olivia said slowly. The woman creature scowled, blue tones shifting across the pallor of her face.

"He would have died in any case! It is thy life that is important here! Come!" A hand shot out to clutch about her upper arm. Propelled her forward, off the bed. Olivia stumbled, found her footing, and gasped as a cloak was flung like a shroud about her. She pulled back, but the viselike grip did not lessen. Then she was being pulled.

Across the chamber. Out through the door, then along the corridor. Not in the common direction, but to another stairwell that led to the northern battlements and the narrow part of the bailey there. She panted, struggled to keep up, compelled by that relentless grasp. Down steps—out into rain that came in torrents to make sodden blows as it drove from the sky. She gasped. Lightning flashed across the sky to rent the firmament. She tried to stop, to pull away, but the other figure pulled her onward with relentless strength. Mud—and they ran across it. She could hardly see, and stumbled against the soaked clinging weight of her own skirts.

Then, incredibly, without understanding how the drawbridge came to be lowered in the middle of the night, she found herself being dragged across it, and into the mire beyond.

Suddenly she was released. She fell to her knees, gasping. Looking up, blinking against the rain to see the woman who had called herself Durandal gleaming like some elusive silver and blue ghost in the night.

"Hear me. And hear me well, my lady!" The creature loomed over her, voice fraught with power. "It will be dawn soon, for all I have loosed this tempest to postpone it! Do thou go to

yonder hill. Find the body of Lord Roland and drag it away from
there to some hidden place before he comes!''

Totally bewildered, senses stunned, Olivia stared.

''Lord Roland is dead!'' croaked the last. ''No more than
ashes!'' Blue fire slipped across black eyes. So fierce, that delicate, inhuman face that loomed even closer. This is not real . . .
How had she managed to get to her feet? Olivia wondered. This
could not be real.

''Do it! If thou will rid thyself of the evil here, then thou must
save him from the one who calls himself Huon De Guienne!''

''My brother?'' Not real. That jarred now too.

''Nay, Lady! Not thy brother! But one who has assumed his
form! Go now.'' Urgent hissing words. ''For the love Lord Roland has for thee, find him. Hide him!''

A burned corpse? ''Mother of God!'' Olivia whispered. The
other's eyes flashed contempt.

''Thy God hath no part in this!'' she hissed like a blow.
''Go!''

Olivia fled. Beyond reason, through the darkness and the rain.
Across the uneven sod—staggering through the muck. Lightning
flashed to show the way. Up the long hill that led to the place
where the remains of the pyre still occupied its crest. And how
it was that she obeyed, she did not know.

Roland? He had died. She had seen it.

Then she found that she stood panting amid charred and ashen
fragments. Bordeaux castle appeared in a quick, stark gleam,
illumed to something alien and forbidding by lightning bolts that
skittered across the sky. Durandal—or Lady Roselyn—had vanished.

She stood alone in the rain. Chemise and robe clung heavy
and chill against her. She shivered violently. It was only one
more nightmare upon the rest . . .

Lightning flitted. She saw the remains of the stake where Roland had been bound. The gleam of chains washed clean by the
rain. No bones with them, as she might expect . . . just something blackened and bulky. And the sickening stench of sodden
burning.

''God help me!'' she gagged.

And like something unnatural unveiling, two eyes appeared to
open in the midst of that blackened, formless mass before her.
Golden eyes. Eagle, gleaming eyes that stared at nothing at all.

Impossible . . . Mad. A strangled sound came out of her as

she found herself leaning toward that unmistakable, yet hideously vacant stare. Her own hands reached out, then down to actually touch. She shuddered as she felt. Blackness. Blackness composing a man's form. Impossible . . . Fire burned flesh away . . . Had not burned? His eyes. Roland's eyes.

And Huon, who was not her brother at all, but some other thing? Her hands clawed then. Gripped and pulled. Roland?

Slack heavy, the staring thing she dragged, it yielded like a corpse. She jerked it away from the ruined pyre, then pulled it through long, rain-washed grasses. Lungs heaving for air, nerves stinging and frayed, it was something to fight as she continued, one step at a time, like an overburdened mule.

Down the far hill, away from Bordeaux castle. On and on, she kept pulling until there was nothing left, and she slipped, then fell through scratching bushes into a rain-filled gully. She felt it then, the weight of the corpse tumbling after her to roll and land across her in the mire.

She could not move. She had no strength left for that.

Or feelings to fight with.

There was only the weight of the corpse, and the stench of roasted meat that the rain could not dispel.

The storm rumbled on, fading gradually toward the eastern horizon. Dawn crept up in soft grey tints to show through the hanging clouds. The rain eased to a steady drizzle, trickling down her face, through her hair and garments to join with the mud under and around her. It washed as well, across the black thing that sprawled across her. Roland's corpse . . . incredibly, after that conflagration. Yet no worse than what she had seen when the mob had finished with Girard. One torn-off arm flung into the air, fingers splayed like something desperate for aid. There had been none . . .

Her mother had yielded like this, Olivia thought, feeling the shivering that had gone beyond cold and wet. The eyes in the blackened corpse where none should remain, were whole, unblemished. Dead vacant. It had all gone skewed. Mad . . . Where lay the difference between bewitchment and this? Olivia twisted herself, and felt the blackened thing shift, slack and heavy—firm. She started. The eyes had disappeared into the rest of it. Then, with one hand, she pushed at the head of it, fallen against her thighs—saw a fissure open in the blackened meat through which gleamed . . . ? She jerked her hand away to stare at the palm filled with ashes that the raindrops caught and began to wash away . . .

"Aaah, Jesu!" she heard her own whisper as her eyes returned to the split place. Something pure, almost golden.

She twisted and jerked herself free of it, then reached again to claw and tear, aided by the rain that washed, exposing . . . Impossible—but.

Pure, golden-hued skin. The form of a wide, smooth brow—and cheek, then jaw. Impossible . . . But her hands, like a vulture's talons, went on with their labor, clawing at cracked places, tearing away the ghastly mess that crumbled to wash into the rain-filled gully. A neck was revealed. A broad, smooth, muscular shoulder. A smooth and perfectly muscled arm with a long-fingered, powerful hand.

Torso, chest, and ribs—hips. And a face, beardless now, that was familiar only in its structure, not this . . . beauty.

Roland? The other arm appeared then, and the legs. The left first—normal. Then the right, that freed from the blackened covering began to slowly shift and move like something fluid. Untwisting to become as perfect as the other.

And when it was done at last, she knelt there, her arms clutched tightly about her middle, staring at the creature who lay before her in the mud, revealed in the first grey light of early morning.

Roland? This man creature who was so smoothly, perfectly made. Whose hair made a familiar fire of amber and gold about his shoulders, across his ribs. Whose youth was a gleaming, virgin radiance.

"Oh, God!" Olivia breathed. "Lord Roland?" The form was the same, she realized slowly, as she had always seen before beneath the trappings of his monstrous disease. Disease? Or something else. Was this how he had looked, all those years ago when he rode with her father? Like this? So potently beautiful, purely youthful . . . man?

Witch . . . it echoed from deep inside.

His lashes fluttered, and he sighed deeply, then opened eyes that were alive. Widened to a look of wonder as they fixed on her, then blinked as though rousing from a dream.

"Oliver . . ." he whispered, song soft. "I heard thy call. Where is the pain?" A furrow of puzzlement crossed his brow. "The pain is gone!" Tones of wonder. He blinked again, still staring at her. "Olivia? Am I absolved at last? It is not so bright as I had thought."

She made a strangled, incoherent sound. Absolved? From what? His left hand came toward her then, fingertips reaching to touch the wet, cold skin of her face, and suddenly his eyes cleared to something brilliant and penetrating.

"Olivia . . . ?" Rasped questions in a single word. He saw his own fingers then. Started, and, staring, moved fluidly to raise himself, then look down at the rest that sat now, naked in the mire and weeds.

Slowly, he reached fingertips to touch himself, tracing along arms and chest and belly, then toward his legs to clasp the one that had been grotesquely crippled. "For God's love!" he breathed. "By what miracle am I so . . . healed?" Senses inside that were a wonder, taking flight to feel. Unencumbered after so much binding pain. Free . . .

He looked up toward her then. Blinked and saw clearly, a half-mad and haggard, soiled shade of a girl. Shade as well, of the man he had loved and revered above all others. Had come to love anew . . .

She, who looked to break at the least touch.

"Thou?" He grappled to understand it. Hadn't he died? Bound in flames that had swept up to sear and smother and consume. Far above, a falcon's beckoning cry had come to him even as he had drowned in it. What had happened? He looked at his hands. Raindrops twinkled as they landed on smooth skin, then slipped away. He could feel every one . . .

What had happened? How had it happened—this?

"Olivia?" He looked up at her.

She cringed. "Who art thou, Lord Roland?" she whispered harshly. "What art thou to make a mock of death as only God may do?" He flinched as though hit. Confusion slipped across his face as he looked down at the wonder of his body, then back up to meet her stare.

"A man—I had thought. Nothing more!" he got out with awkward honesty, and knew, even as he said it, that other truth that haunted his life. "A witch!" he whispered. "A witch who sought only to be a man!"

She shuddered visibly. "Then my mother had the right of it!" she grated. "Thou are the curse upon us all! Girard! For God! Girard is *dead*!" She hunkered down, hands coming up to cling to her face. "And I am damned!"

Roland cringed. He reached. Withdrew. He dared not, somehow, touch her . . . He moved again, his new flesh responding with fluid ease to stand upon two feet.

Girard was dead? Girard, who had lost the Dark Sword? He frowned. He had been killed, he knew somehow. Oliver's son. Not Oliver. The distinction had significance. He stiffened.

Thudding hoofbeats proclaimed the advance of a single horseman to the east. Roland spun reflexively to half crouch and stare toward the sound, finding a view through the spaces under the lowest branches of the bushes that crowded against the rim of the gully.

A red stallion appeared on the crest of the hill beyond. He saw the tall, armored man that rode the beast, draw rein, dismount, then stride toward the blackened place where, aye, for truth, he had been chained and burned. The man reached it and bent to scrabble briefly. Then straightened to something alert to stare about him with urgent movements.

The dark lord . . . The dark lord? The old name came back like a blow as Roland stared. Instinctively, he ducked down lower. Something inside that demanded he not be seen. Even from this distance, so clear—the large, black pupiled eyes that scoured the landscape like twin predators. A deep voice that shouted for the foot soldiers appearing on the crest of the hill to search. One hand made a sweeping gesture.

"Huon!" Olivia's voice made a frightened hiss behind him. "She spoke the truth . . . He comes!" On his haunches, Roland twisted around to see her staring past him.

The brother—returned from exile, he realized, absorbing her fear. Memories of a dark-haired boy—become the dark lord now. Other things she'd told him across the pain.

"He is the one who killed the son of Oliver," he whispered the certainty even as it came to him. Her eyes locked with his. Blue sheened truth. "Now, he seeks to destroy thee as well?" She shuddered. Nodded.

A man's rough shout echoed from farther up the hill. Roland responded with reflexive speed, reaching for her hand, then pulling her to her feet, to draw her after him as he bludgeoned his way out of the rain gully, through the thickets beyond to head deeper into the forest.

So easy to run again—deer fleet and nimble. He led her on, ducking past trees and shrubs, lunging up inclines, slithering down rain-slickened banks to race along game trails as he made a wide arc, then veered toward the south.

Her cry and sudden jerk against his pulling brought him to a stop. He turned to see her on her knees, heaving for air and spent. And he hardly needed to draw a deep breath. He crouched down beside her as she sank onto the sod, a near-shattered creature.

He hesitated. Olivia . . . All that was left. He picked her up and, holding her tight against him, walked on, veering to the east then to follow the trails into the rougher land there, searching now for some place to hide, to shelter. Oliver, who had died smiling up at him, whispering blessings . . . She, got of him in every way. There could be no repetition . . .

He stopped at last by a great oak rooted above a rain-swollen brook. Part of the bank, held in its roots and by surrounding undergrowth, made a vertical, almost inverted drop. He slid down into it, then knelt among heaps of soft dead leaves from the previous autumn, and gently set her down. He jerked back to straighten.

"There is safety here. For a time," he stumbled over the words. Olivia shivered a little, her wind recovered, and looked up. He had felt warm and strong and safe while he carried her, she realized, aware of separation. He caught her look, and like a frightened boy looked away to fiercely scan the undergrowth and trees that surrounded him.

Roland. Now compellingly beautiful to look upon. She had never imagined this perfect, lithe, and—aye—mesmerizing golden youth who stood before her now. She collected herself and staggered to her feet. A witch? His fears that clothed him . . . Had clothed him in something else to make a monster? How did she know it to be true? Now, he stood naked and smooth—his manhood. She jerked her cloak away and held it out.

"Here, my lord. Cover thyself!" He started and took it, flinching back as he wound it around his body with an entirely human shyness.

"Huon let my brother be killed," Olivia said then, finding some kind of order in telling the bald truth. "Girard would never have defended himself in any battle between them—even if he had been given the opportunity." Roland nodded understanding. "He tried to kill thee as well. And me? Lady Roselyn . . ." She could not bear to say the other sword name. "Lady Roselyn got me out. Sent me to find thee. Somehow, she knew."

"Girard's lady," Roland murmured, watching her. He looked down. "Not for *anything* would I see thee harmed!" he rasped quietly and turned away to step to the edge of the brook where the waters spread to make a wider, stiller place before rippling on around the corner.

Olivia shivered, all dank and muddy. The understanding that ran between them was still there. As deep as something conjured. And he, so new now . . . She drew her arms around herself.

Feelings. The air made sensate wonders across the skin of his exposed shoulder and arm. Holding the cloak tightly around him, Roland looked down at the smooth surface of the brook as it washed into the corner by his bare feet. Below him, reflected on the surface of the water, he was caught by the face that stared back at him.

Golden eyes—his own. Smooth-skinned beardlessness. And the rest was a composition of features of perfect and youthful symmetry. It was as though all the terrible, intervening years had not touched him at all.

He stiffened slowly as he stared. He had seen that face before, he realized. Not as a reflection from before . . . Roncesvalles. But . . . somewhere else.

He bent closer. The reflection loomed in response to his movement, defining into an even greater clarity. Something inside began to tighten, then to clench. Remember . . . ?

White marble quiescence upon a tomb. His tomb. He inhaled violently, remembering how the sight of it had affected him. How his fingers had touched his face to feel the skin slide over something different from bones . . . He had dismissed it—with effort.

Before that? On another slab, in the heart of that overgrown and ruined temple in the hidden gorge in Brittany. A carven thing also. White marble—the figure of a perfect and sleeping man. A statue, Oliver had so calmly said, of some ancient, heathen God.

Apollo? Holding a lyre . . .

The statue had disappeared. He had found the lyre. Had given it to Olivia. Roland's fingers came up to touch his face. The reflection did the same, and his innards plunged like panicked horses to feel the vibrant resilience of his own flesh.

He jerked back, and the cloak fell away, forgotten as he held both hands out before him, fingers splayed.

The changeling Owl, who had claimed him . . . Names. Apollo—a heathen God. The Djinn of the Dark Sword, the Infidel had called him all those years ago.

Lord of Eagles . . . the dying heathen giant Ferragus had said.

Roland shuddered and spread his arms to feel a prickling sensation slither along his skin. The Owl . . . He could not be Charlemagne's bastard son after all. Either way, beyond any sort of sanctity. The falcon above the fire . . . Eagles?

His eyes went wide as feathers erupted from his fingertips. As he had seen the Owl do once. Golden, these. Not white. Feathers that ruffled soft as they sprouted to order themselves along his arms. Skin that prickled as they slipped forth, seeking, aye, to become pinions.

His wild glance froze on Olivia who stared aghast, her hands pressed brutally against her mouth. She saw what he felt . . .

Lord of Eagles, Ferragus had said. Thou are indeed . . . a God.

"Nay! Nay!" Roland half screamed it, jerking back to flatten against out-thrusting tree roots, then sinking to his knees. Feathers, that vanished then, like a mirage. He shuddered violently, pulled his arms in to clamp them tight against his ribs, and hunkered over.

"For God! What am I?" he rasped, cringing down farther. Olivia's wide, startled, uncomprehending eyes swam somewhere before his own. "What am I?" he begged.

"I do not know, my lord . . ." he heard her honest whisper.

"Haaaargh!" His cry of fear made a keening eagle sound as he doubled over to huddle like a terrorized child. The falcon that had tried to summon him from the flames. That knew him . . . Skin and fingers that itched to spread out—to catch the air. And suddenly he understood what it meant to fly. He could feel it in his arms. Across his breast. Broad muscles that understood . . . dreams?

Olivia stared back, so clearly human before him. Her look searched him like some mesmerized beast of prey incapable of understanding. He closed his eyes, unable to bear her look—his life.

How brutal his life . . . He huddled tighter, shuddering against great sobs that welled up to grieve for the final shattering of everything he'd known, everything he'd believed, fought for—clung to. Left now to leave him behind, feeling like some pillaged thing.

Untouched by such, that soaring, natural falcon . . .

Not so for him . . . Not so for him.

TWENTY-FIVE

Lord Huon frowned down at the blackened sod where the pyre had been. Under him, his stallion fidgited restlessly, sensitive to the moods of temper and frustration that chased themselves across his stern countenance.

No sign at all. No trace of any kind to mark the body that should have been, in some form, among those ashes. Only one sprawling piece of chain gave any clue as to direction.

And the rain had obliterated what tracks there might have been.

He raised his head to scan where his men had fanned out along the flanks of the hill, as he had ordered, searching. Mounted men as well used short lances to prod at thickets and the like, or rode into the edges of the woods to search for any sign of passage.

They could not hope to find, of course, what he could not scent. Or sense.

How? That was the crux of it. How had he been so thoroughly eluded? The explanation lay in part with the girl. Olivia De Montglave? The son was dead. Removed . . . His eyes widened to something extraordinary. And he had thought her broken to become a normal part of the human river. Somehow she had managed to escape . . . It was the daughter—not the son at all.

"Soooo!" he whispered with soft melodiousness. Then he stiffened suddenly, rising in his stirrups to stand, his nostrils flaring as he swung his head sharply to the southeast.

Felt . . . Felt. A brief stretching. A pleading cry. Resonance. It faded away . . . But it was enough to give him the direction that he sought.

He sank back into his saddle and gouged the stallion's sides, sending it in a gallop, down the hill toward the castle, then, as he neared the drawbridge, he veered the beast south to charge toward the stretch of forested hills there.

He did not call for his men. This was a private business.

As he had for hours, Baudoin stood half propped against the bole of a tree at the very edge of the woodlands along the south-eastern rise that stretched away from Bordeaux castle. His horse cropped contentedly at the lush, sweet spring grasses, occasionally tugging at the reins looped over one arm as it sought a particular delicacy. Some distance behind him, and aware of his mood, his men camped in a small clearing in the trees.

Olivia was still behind those indifferent stone walls. Her brother's prisoner. Betrayed by his fear-got abandonment of her. Baudoin had scoured his soul ever since on that . . . Found no answers as he searched himself to figure out how Lord Huon could have known about his uncle's unspeakable practices . . .

He stiffened suddenly, his eyes narrowing as he recognized Lord Huon's tall form and powerful chestnut stallion, appearing through the drawbridge. De Guienne turned his horse and cantered away purposefully, up the long hill to the west where so much hideous-ness had occurred the previous day. That fire-blackened scar was visible even from this distance. He straightened further as fighting men emerged, some mounted, to follow their lord.

De Guienne searched for something, he saw, watching the other dismount, prod around the burned place, then swing him-self up on his horse again. What? The rest fanned out to search the hill, the edge of the woods. Baudoin frowned.

Suddenly he saw Lord Huon bolt forward, sweeping in a pur-poseful charge, down the hill, back toward the castle, then sud-denly, surprisingly, veering to gallop south, straight into the woods.

De Guienne's men did not follow. Sensing opportunity, Bau-doin lunged to mount his own horse, spurring the beast to gallop in pursuit. His sword slapped against his thigh. He jerked his mail coif over his head, found helm and slammed it down, gath-ered his shield from his saddle bow and hung it on his arm. De Guienne, alone . . . He had no fear at all of the confrontation he intended now to bring to resolution . . .

* * *

Another creature, huddled like a dark stone in the concealing forest, rose up suddenly from between a pair of dense, thorn-laden bushes. Black eyes slewed toward the south, lightning shimmering across her form as Durandal felt it . . .

Power, that reached . . . He had awakened.

Lunging like a gusting breeze from the undergrowth, she ran through the trees in pursuit, her form shifting like a shadow to elude the touch of the least twig or leaf, becoming indistinct, illusory. Suggestive of dark wings outspread.

Then, upon a high bank, around which a small brook bab-bled, she ducked behind a large tree to congeal into something grey and craggy and still.

Roland, she saw through the undergrowth. At last, as he should be . . . But huddled like a child. Still vulnerable . . .

The woman, who stood there like a mangled thing, watching. Used up.

She heard it then, horse sounds that approached. And in an instant she ducked down to become a stone-hardened, wizened, opaque creature as she withdrew her own power, coiled it, con-densed it within.

It was unchangeable, he realized bitterly, all that had gone before to bring him to this . . . Still unreconcilable.

Roland slowly let go and raised himself to see Olivia still standing like some rooted thing. Seeing her starkness that made a brutal desecration of those few and precious feelings he had made into a sanctuary inside him. Oliver? There was little left of that revered man in the frail girl who stood there now, hands pressed, white-knuckled, to her mouth. Stark-faced, shabby, haggard . . . Her eyes just stared at him from their sockets. From another plane of comprehension . . .

He opened his mouth to blurt out something.

A sudden crashing sound came from the surrounding under-growth, and Roland spun instead to see a lathered red war stal-lion leap through the bushes and come to a plunging, splashing halt in the middle of the brook.

"Huon!" Olivia rasped a half-mad cry as she saw as well. "For God! Huon . . ." De Guienne's dark eyes glittered as he stared fiercely down at her and brought his horse along the stream bed.

"Little sister! Are thou gone mad to loose thyself here—with this?'' he demanded brutally. "Get thee hence!" He pointed toward the north. But Olivia did not have strength enough left to obey. A few steps only, and she gave it up to sink onto her knees on the muddy bank. Roland poised, nostrils flaring, eyes narrowed as it came again to his mind. The dark lord . . . "For pity!" Lord Huon grated in profound anger. "This has gone too far!" He dismounted with facile grace from the red horse that shied away, and strode toward the narrow stretch of embankment to stop at the edge and glare at Roland. "There must be an end!"

Roland poised, caught by something else behind that stern, dark-eyed stare. Something familiar . . . and canny. Ageless . . .

"Thou?" he whispered hoarsely, and shifted.

"Aye, Roland . . . I!" Lord Huon intoned somberly, removing his gauntlets to drop them on the sod.

"Turpin?" Roland whispered, still searching.

"Just so!" Lord Huon answered, reaching up to remove his helm, thrust back mail coif, and free waving black hair. "Save thou may know me now by my true name, which is Oborion."

"The Owl!" Roland breathed.

"That too, my son!" Huon's hands came up again to his face.

"What is this about?" Olivia summoned wits enough to demand, her gaze flitting between the two of them, her brother and this magical Roland.

"Get thee away from here, my lady, and thou will never need to know!" Huon said brutally. She stumbled back over a tussock. Huon's fingertips hooked into the skin of his face, pulling it, ripping aside. Skin and hair that yielded like another garment to sag around his throat.

She would have screamed, Olivia knew, save she had gone past it. Instead she crumpled helplessly onto her knees.

Hardened long ago by bloodier sights, Roland inhaled, caught by recognition instead. How well he knew that youthful, ingeniously wise face with its crown of wood-burnished hair. The Owl . . .

Huon De Guienne? Girard, who had died. Olivia, who had become a wraith. Accusations welled up inside him.

"What do thou here?" he growled.

Turpin—Oborion's look grew sterner still. "Who else is capable to put to rights that which thou have wrought here?" he demanded in a remembered, agelessly melodious voice. Roland froze. "Thou . . . aye, who have tampered with these mortal children to make them part of thy own obsessive denial . . . It hath gone on too long, and now the consequences reach too far!''

"I . . . ?'' Roland whispered, incapable before this attack.

Oborion inhaled as though summoning patience. "Aye, my son! In part, it is my folly to have left thee to learn as I thought thou would assuredly do! Aye. I have watched thee make of thyself a monster, then thread it further through thy own obsessive guilt to encompass these two . . .'' Roland felt a strangling in his throat. "Hear me now and know. Lord Oliver would have died in any case, being a man, as thou are not!''

What clever lies he spun out of the truth, Durandal knew as she listened from her hiding place. Roland, who had but, in his still-human innocence, to yield himself up . . . She gathered. Poised . . .

Still stunned by his transformation, Roland backed a pace, bombarded by the enormity of these accusations. Olivia, huddled and shivering a few yards distant, was a reflection of all the things that had never touched Oliver. Purity vanished. Intentions skewed to become concealed monsters . . . "Nay!'' he half shouted. Defiance, confusion. "I have no power such as thou claim!''

"Thou do not know, still, even the least texture of the power that is thine, Roland? Mark me. Thy own least thought or wish has its own manifest consequence! Thou, who for grief, wrought again, Oliver's likeness and disposition into these mortal children who are only *half* his blood.'' Oborion moved toward him. "Even to making of the one, an image that would cleave to thee . . .'' He pointed toward Olivia.

"Nay!'' Roland whispered like a tortured child.

"Aye!'' Oborion countered quietly now. "This son of Ganelon De Maganze is another evidence, being grown to a benign and honest young man, for all he bears his father's countenance. That vengeance thou wrought through the Song is long resolved. That is why the son is grown into an honest, *natural* man!'' Oborion advanced again, his right hand coming out. Supple fingers closed lightly to hold Roland's bare shoulder. Jolts of sensation. Roland flinched.

"It is time, my son, for thee to accept what thou are wrought to be!''

"What is that?'' Roland got out.

"Lord of Eagles . . . The infidel giant from Ethiopia knew

thee rightly. Thou, as I, are sprung from the firmament above . . .
And, for the rest, thou have but to look to the tales of men of
every faith that remember the Gods that walked the earth before
men, and from whom men are, in part, sprung!''

Not even the hope of faith was left, Roland knew as he stared
into the certainty of Oborion's relentlessly sure gaze. Everything
was refuted . . . Everything that had composed his life. Even
identity.

Oborion's other hand came up to clasp his other shoulder. ''It
will be set to rights, what thou have wrought here,'' he said in
gentling, paternal tones. His eyes, filled with regret. And knowledge . . . ''Thou have but to learn from me. Let me give thee
thy true heritage. It is a proud one. Come. Accept the kiss of
peace from thy father that we may make a new beginning?''

Needing . . . Roland let himself be drawn forward.

Thunder shuddered through earth and air. Black lightning
streaked down to loose Oborion's grip and hurl him backward,
hardened to bury itself in the middle of his body. He tumbled,
howling, fingers clawing at the thing that spread itself, slithered
up, and grew into a taloned harpy that screamed . . .

''Liar! Deceiver! Lord of Mischief, his power is not for thee!''
Roland caught a brief glimpse of a vulture thing, of a face that
was a hideous parody of bird and human. Then, even as it lunged
down to tear at armor and clothing with its talons, white feathers
erupted from the neck of . . . Oborion. Owl now, struggling to
free itself. White wings beat against black talons, but the harpy
thing raised up to engulf it, tearing, swallowing with predatory
determination. Not even a starved, crazed wolf . . .

Screeches came from the Owl as a wing was torn away, stuffed
into the cavern of the harpy's mouth. A last raw howl loosed,
and Roland saw the woman thing claw at scattered feathers,
consuming them with appalling appetite. Feathers, and scraps of
something else—illusory parts of a human form. Oborion.

Gone.

Crouched still, the creature raised her head as she chewed the
last. Swallowed. Wiped a forearm across a gnarled mouth and
stared with hard black eyes.

The silence was atrocious.

''It was for this—thy safety, my lord, that I was forged,'' the
harpy said. Roland shuddered. Knew then, where he had seen
such a thing before. The sum of every hate he'd ever learned.

"It is thou who mothered me!" he hissed. She stood then, shadows muting, shifting across variations of a woman's form.

"How else to harden thee, my lord, to thy own protection?" Mad reasonableness, asked in a voice like a night breeze.

It was too much. Even his beginnings had been pillaged.

"Thou!" he snarled, hardening, stepping forward. Outrages that had never been forgiven, nor forgot.

"Aye. I—Durandal." Black eyes defied him. "I who am thy own sword!"

"*Silence!*" Roland roared in fury. Saw her freeze to some strange mixture of sword and crone and girl. The power in a thought? He raised a hand, rage driven, and pointed it at her.

"As thou have done to me, so I condemn thee to wander as the hag thou art! A helpless, agued crone, incapable to harm even the least creature! *Go!*"

The air hung still. Through it, raindrops pattered down. The brook babbled as it slid by. A wizened, bent, emaciated old woman stood by the edge of it, only partially concealed by colorless rags. Impotent . . . She glared once, without effect, then turned sullenly and began to hobble slowly away, disappearing at last beyond an outreaching tree.

That monster who had mothered him . . . ? Durandal? Everything else had been shattered. He had gone beyond disbelief, he realized.

Distrust remained. Had grown.

Slowly Roland lowered his hand. Stared at it, and the raindrops that trickled off gold-toned skin.

Lord of Eagles? His skin prickled in response. He heard a low moan and looked up to see Olivia staring at him. A human woman overcome by nightmares. He looked down to see himself. A naked man. A young man, defying the years that had passed.

Rage had vanished with the crone, like an outflung javelin over a cliff. His own bare feet stood in natural grass. Olivia's muddy cloak—the other shambles he did not wish to see where the Owl had been destroyed.

He felt neither gratitude, nor relief. Only isolation.

And love. There was some left. He walked toward Olivia then. She, who could die. He, who could not. He crouched down and reached to touch her cold, moist cheek. Withdrew his fingers at once.

Aye . . . a letting go.

"Be thou peaceful and contented," he whispered the only useful hope he could have for her, straightened, and drew back to look up at the grey sky.

Where falcons and eagles soared . . . away from all this kind of thing. He felt again the prickling slither through his skin. This time, he yielded to it. Silence up there, in the heavens . . . Feathers erupted. His fingers shifted. Sensations everywhere. Flowing, condensing. Arms lengthening, wings unfurling . . . The air made a buoyant caress beneath them. He beat against it, curled the talons his feet had become, and lofted upward toward the clear, clean air above the trees.

A single cry erupted from his throat. A haunting, eagle's screeching, and then he was gone away, lofting upward on an updraft. Away from human things. Away from everything that had ever been of himself, real or otherwise.

Away from all he did not yet know . . .

Disgusted with himself for losing Lord Huon's tracks, Baudoin spurred his lathered horse up a small rise, sat back as the animal slid down a muddy bank on the other side to land in a small brook. He jerked. Saw something a little ahead. A huddled figure . . . a woman.

"Mother of God!" he rasped and hurled himself from the horse to run toward . . . "Olivia? Olivia!" She turned slowly, like someone rousing from unconsciousness. How he had recognized her, he didn't know as he dropped to his knees in the mire before her, totally appalled by the decimated starkness of her.

"Baudoin?" she whispered. He grasped her shoulders gently and pulled her against him to feel her shivering. Beyond, by the edge of the brook, he saw a scattered heap of clothing and armor. De Guienne's colors were discernible. A helm . . . something that looked like shreds of human skin.

"For God, Olivia! What has happened here?" he rasped slowly. Swallowed other things inside.

"Oh, Baudoin!" It was a muffled pleading against his breast. "Do not ask. Do not *ever* ask . . . !" He swallowed again. He had his own nightmare secrets, he knew. He closed his eyes and buried his face against her hair, held her closer as she began to cry. He never would. He never would, he knew.